ARROW'S
FLIGHT

ARROW'S
FLIGHT

Joel Scott

ECW

Published by ECW Press
665 Gerrard Street East
Toronto, Ontario, Canada M4M 1Y2
416-694-3348 / info@ecwpress.com

Cover design: Michel Vrana
Type: Erika Head

This is a work of fiction. Names, characters,
places, and incidents either are the product of
the author's imagination or are used fictitiously,
and any resemblance to actual persons, living or
dead, business establishments, events, or locales is
entirely coincidental.

LIBRARY AND ARCHIVES CANADA
CATALOGUING IN PUBLICATION

Scott, Joel, 1939–, author
Arrow's flight / Joel Scott.

(the offshore novels ; 1)
Issued in print and electronic formats.
ISBN 978-1-77041-426-6 (softcover)
ALSO ISSUED AS: 978-1-77305-198-7 (PDF)
978-1-77305-197-0 (EPUB)

I. TITLE.

PS8637.C68617A77 2018   C813'.6
C2017-906196-8   C2017-906197-6

The publication of *Arrow's Flight* has been generously supported by the Canada Council for the Arts,
which last year invested $153 million to bring the arts to Canadians throughout the country, and by the
Government of Canada through the Canada Book Fund. *Nous remercions le Conseil des arts du Canada
de son soutien. L'an dernier, le Conseil a investi 153 millions de dollars pour mettre de l'art dans la vie des
Canadiennes et des Canadiens de tout le pays. Ce livre est financé en partie par le gouvernement du Canada.*
We also acknowledge the support of the Ontario Arts Council (OAC), an agency of the Government
of Ontario, which last year funded 1,737 individual artists and 1,095 organizations in 223 communities
across Ontario for a total of $52.1 million, and the contribution of the Government of Ontario through
the Ontario Book Publishing Tax Credit and the Ontario Media Development Corporation.

Ontario
Ontario Media Development
Corporation

ONTARIO ARTS COUNCIL
CONSEIL DES ARTS DE L'ONTARIO
an Ontario government agency
un organisme du gouvernement de l'Ontario

Canada Council
for the Arts

Conseil des Arts
du Canada

Canadä

PRINTED AND BOUND IN CANADA   PRINTING: MARQUIS   5   4   3   2   1

RECYCLED
Paper made from
recycled material
FSC
www.fsc.org   FSC® C103567

IN MEMORY OF PETE,
WHO SHOWED ME THE WAY.

CHAPTER 1

The halibut quota filled early, and I was on a plane back to Vancouver by the first week of September. I had shipped on the *Freelund*, a sixty-foot longliner out of Prince Rupert, and we'd had a fair season. It would have been an excellent season had we not been caught with our lines out in a sudden storm on the final trip; with no good choices left, we hauled in a forty-knot gale with seas breaking over the man at the roller, and ended up losing half our gear. We were luckier than some though — a rogue wave took out the wheelhouse windows on the *Covenant* in the same blow, and a shard of glass killed the man on watch, pinning him to the bulkhead by his throat.

It was raining heavily as my flight approached Vancouver International Airport. I looked down at the city's shrouded lights and thought about the coming winter; every autumn for the past six years, I had left the fishing grounds with a large bankroll and a bigger thirst, and every spring gone back out broke, or near enough as made no matter. Sometimes in the off-season I took a job driving a truck or working on construction, but it never made much difference. I could always spend more than I earned.

Drinking, partying, sometimes a few weeks in Mexico or maybe a long, drunken hunting trip into the interior, and at the end of it all another spring and working on the gear before returning to the fishing grounds for another go-round.

I used to think it was fun.

The plane bounced down onto the tarmac, the wheels shrieking as they caught and came to speed. The stewardesses smiled gamely and passed us out the door, saying how special we all were and what a treat it had been to serve us. I walked through the terminal, stepped out into the driving rain, and caught a taxi to Annie's.

I had been staying with her and Danny since my release from prison nine years earlier. Annie was Haida, middle-aged, and stocky, with high cheekbones and a gentle smile. Danny, her youngest, had been born of a brief second marriage to a Scotsman who died of exposure and alcoholism under an East End bridge long before I knew them.

Danny and I met and became friends in prison, his time was up a month before mine, and when I walked out through the big iron gates, he was waiting to take me home with him. I moved into the old house with Annie, her grandfather Joseph, and Danny, and within a month was closer to them all than to the grim remnants of my own family. There was a love and tolerance in that house that wrapped and surrounded you as close and warm as the old Chilkat blankets that hung on the walls.

Annie was sitting at the kitchen table, drinking coffee with Erin and Jaimie, her sons from her first marriage. They were big, powerful men in their thirties, handsome in a fierce way, particularly Jaimie, who had the slow smile and easy confidence of an elder brother. Erin's cheek had been ripped with a hook when he was running his little troller on the west coast a few years earlier, and the jagged scar gave his face a sinister cast as it caught the light.

Annie jumped up and hugged me, and I gave her the ivory hair brooch I had picked up in Kodiak.

"You're looking good, Jared," she said.

I shook hands with the boys and poured myself a coffee and sat down with them for the ritual bitching about shitty seasons, poor prices, and the goddam fish companies. Erin knew the man who had been killed on the *Covenant*, so I brought a heel of duty-free rum out of my duffle bag and poured a shot into our coffee and we drank his remembrance. The brothers recalled others who had gone out and never come back over the years, speaking in soft, murmuring voices of small boats and big storms before finishing up their drinks and heading home to their families.

Annie's grandfather returned from his walk and took the chunk of argillite I had bought in a Kodiak bar off a king crab fisherman down on his luck. He nodded gravely as he accepted it, his soft voice a low murmur of sibilance; although he spoke only in the old Haida dialects, he seemed to understand everything I said. No one knew for sure how old Joseph was — somewhere close to ninety. He was around five foot eight, thin, and a little wasted now, but you could still glimpse the powerful man he once had been. His eyes were sharp and bright, and he always carried himself erect.

He went into the living room and brought back the carving he was presently working on, an old war canoe with the animal clans inside and Raven crouched brooding on the bow. It was a marvel of intricate carving and delicate workmanship; he had likely been doing that kind of thing for three quarters of a century. He never sold anything, just gave the pieces away to family and friends.

"Where's Danny?" I asked.

Annie glanced at the clock. "Still working. He didn't do very well this year, he hooked on with Fly-By-Night again."

Danny could always get a job with the moving companies. The strongest man I know, he could easily manage the big fridges by himself with just a trolley. Stripped down, he reminds me somewhat of a lethargic seal, his body sleek and smooth, no bulging muscles, looking even a bit soft; but then he'd move into something with casual ease, lifting or stacking by himself what might take two other men to handle, and you saw that what seemed soft and flaccid at rest was a sinuous layer of muscle. I had watched him in the prison gym and seen the big-bulked men shake their heads as he worked the weights and pulleys.

We sat companionably in the warm kitchen, the old wood stove in the corner giving off an even heat, the fir snapping, the occasional slow hiss of resin. Every week the boys delivered loads of wood in their pickups, and Joseph split and stacked it inside the lean-to out back. He would work on even the most knotted of stumps, studying them for the longest time, as if searching out their hearts, before he finally raised the axe and struck.

Annie rose and left the room, returning with a stack of mail, which she put down in front of me. "I threw out the flyers and junk mail. There was an overdue bill from the chandlery that I paid off with one of your cheques."

I shuffled through the pile. No personal letters, there never were. Bank statements, some bills, a couple of well-disguised appeals for money, and at the bottom, a bulky special delivery packet from a West End solicitor's office.

"That came a week ago," Annie said.

Inside was a sheet of office stationery and a hand-addressed envelope. The lawyer was brief and to the point.

Dear Mr. Kane,

I have been asked by Mrs. Margaret Calder to act on her behalf with regard to the last will and testament of William Able Calder, deceased.

Please be advised that I have prepared all papers and documents for the transfer of ownership of the sailing vessel *Arrow* from the Calders to you. They have been witnessed and signed by Mrs. Calder and all that remains is your presence at this office to complete the conveyance by signing the Blue Book and associated documents.

I look forward to meeting you at your earliest convenience.

— Robert P. Sproule

I dropped the letter on the table and looked up in disbelief.

"What?" asked Annie.

"It's Bill Calder. He's died. There must be some mistake; the lawyer says he's left me his sailboat."

I opened the envelope. It was a letter from Meg Calder.

Dear Jared,

Bill has died. Although I had been expecting it and thought I was prepared, it still came as a terrible shock.

His mind remained clear and active to the last. Hearing him talk and laugh as always made it hard to realize just how frail he had become. The last couple of months were hard. I had promised to let him remain on the boat to the end; his cancer was inoperable, and he saw no point in undergoing a harrowing course of treatment to delay the inevitable.

His final courage and grace strengthened me, and helped me get through those last few weeks. He was cremated, and his ashes scattered in the Pacific waters he loved so well.

Bill knew I didn't wish to remain on *Arrow* by myself, and neither of us wanted to see her go to a broker; there is little demand for wooden boats of her age, and the thought of her slow deterioration at a dock while her price was dickered down was intolerable to us both.

We felt that *Arrow* might make some difference in your life. Perhaps the two of you will revisit some of her distant anchorages, and she will cross again her old tracks in the South Pacific; I think you both deserve it.

I do not believe we are predestined by events in our early lives to tread a narrow and circumscribed path. We can break free from our personal history and move beyond it, and I hope that *Arrow* will be the catalyst that enables you to do this. You must learn to like yourself, Jared.

Please do not dispute us in this, Bill has left me well provided for; my future is secure. Knowing that *Arrow* will be in the hands of a caring owner gives me great satisfaction.

I plan to return to England. You can write to me care of the lawyer if you wish; he is an old and valued friend.

All my love,

Meg.

I had met Bill and Meg seven years earlier. There was a strike in the halibut fishery that summer, and I had gone out salmon fishing in Georgia Strait with an old Norwegian, just the two of us on his little double-ended troller. The glass dropped sharply the third day out, and we raised the poles and ran for Bella Cove. It had been a good trip, and Carl didn't want to push our luck.

We blew through the pass and tucked in around the headland in early evening. The wind and seas dropped immediately when we turned the corner, and I had my first sight of *Arrow*, an old wooden ketch with gleaming brightwork and a pristine white hull. She was laying into the sunset and seemed to float in a coppery sea of light, her tall amber masts suspended above her. Sometimes that first impression colours everything that follows, and so it was with me and *Arrow*; though I subsequently learned of her sufficient faults, I would forgive her anything.

Meg was in her midfifties then, slender and elegant with close-cropped grey hair arching over high cheekbones and a generous mouth, the kind of woman who would look equally at home working on deck or hosting an elegant dinner party. Her husband was considerably older, tall and balding with a stooped and somewhat frail appearance. He had a strong West Country accent, and his hand trembled slightly as we shook.

Bill was a marine engineer who had patented a new geared winch for North Sea trawlers in the early seventies; the innovation was simple and efficient, its use expanded into other areas, and within five years his royalties exceeded his regular earnings. He and Meg quit their jobs, and their sailing went from a pastime to a way of life. They sold their little coastal cruiser and commissioned a Laurent Giles design from a Bristol yard.

Arrow was forty-six feet eight inches on deck, with a thirty-five-foot waterline and long overhangs. Close-hauled in heavy airs she would pick up another ten feet, and her theoretical hull speed was eight and a half knots. She was narrow in the old fashion, with a beam of eleven foot six, and when loaded for cruising she drew just under six feet, with lead ballast and a cutaway keel.

Her construction was solid mahogany planking, bronze fastened over oak, with natural-grown knees and steel floors. She was heavy by modern standards, at twenty-two tons displacement, but she had a tall set of Sitka spruce spars in her and carried a thousand feet of working sail. Her cabin tops were mahogany, narrow, and close above the caulked teak decks, the cockpit running back to a high, curving transom barely big enough to carry her name in scripted gold letters. She had a low, delicate aspect in the water, but later, when she was hauled, I saw the powerful underbelly that gave her strength.

Depending upon your point of view, she was dated, wet, and cramped, or beautiful, traditional, and everything an ocean-going yacht should be. As we sat in the cockpit and talked that first evening, when I brought them a salmon as a pretext to visit, I could not refrain from running my hands over the coaming and gently clicking the gleaming bronze winches.

The Calders had left England in the early eighties, sailing across the Channel before unstepping their masts on the French coast and motoring down the Seine and through the canals to the Mediterranean Sea. They spent two years in the Med, cruising among the Greek islands and along the coast of Turkey before heading south through the Suez Canal and across the Indian Ocean to Australia.

They were seven years in the South Pacific, anchoring up in New Zealand or Australia for the hurricane seasons and sailing the islands in the winter. In '89 they went back up through the Torres Straits and across the Indian Ocean to South Africa via Chagos and Madagascar. *Arrow* had been dismasted four hundred miles out of Cape Town when a sixty-knot buster blew out of the Southern Ocean and caught them in the Agulhas Current too far outside the hundred-fathom line to run for cover; listening to Meg's quiet, dispassionate voice, you could only guess at how terrifying that must have been.

After refitting in Cape Town, they worked their way through South America and the Caribbean, finally reaching British Columbia via the Panama Canal, Hawaii, and Alaska. They fell in love with the west coast and bought property on Quadra Island, where they built a small cabin for guests and storage, choosing to remain aboard *Arrow* themselves.

Over the next few years, I visited the Calders frequently in the off-season, sometimes spending a week or two sailing with them, Bill at the tiller while Meg and I worked the winches and foredeck. They seldom ran the engine, having no schedules or deadlines in their lives, and our days were spent drifting slowly along with the tides waiting for wind, or storming through a tiny pass with all sails set in a sudden gust, *Arrow* near surfing in the seas. It was peaceful and exhilarating, and over the years we became close friends. They had no children of their own, and I think they grew to regard me as almost a son. I was careful of my drinking around them, and they never saw that side of me.

I had last seen the Calders in the spring, when I'd spent a week with them before the halibut opening. I had flown down from Kodiak between trips in mid-July with the intention of visiting them, but ran into some old crewmates in Vancouver and ended up partying instead. The second night we were in a dingy little fishermen's bar dockside in Langley when a group of sightseers came in, four men in thousand-dollar sport coats and tailored blue jeans with their women. Danny was with me, chatting and charming, and then there was a fight and some broken glass, and I don't really remember the end of it.

I woke up in a West End penthouse with Danny and two of the girls the next morning, and it had gone on from there. They had a

Porsche and unlimited funds, and were thrilled by the primitives they had netted in the bar. By the time I came back down, there wasn't enough time left to visit the Calders. I was saddened now that I had squandered that final opportunity. Bill was a rare friend, and perhaps I would have been able to say goodbye. Now he had made this magnificent gesture. I felt shamed.

I left the house and caught a cab downtown to a little bar and read the letter through again, sitting alone at a corner table with the beer and shooters set out in front of me like glasses of forgetfulness. Sometimes I glimpse a sort of pattern, the dim promise of release, but then, just as it begins to come clear, I fade, to awake the next day with no memory but the sense of some truth just escaped, and another forgiveness lost.

CHAPTER 2

I awoke at daybreak, snapping suddenly out of tangled dreams with my heart pounding and a deep alcohol sweat greasing my body. Pulling on my shorts and runners, I slipped out of the house into the cold dawn and started off at an easy trot, my breath streaming loosely out before me. After the first troubled mile the old cadences reclaimed me, and I picked up the pace until I was sprinting and hung it out as long as I could, and then went back to a slow trot and kept at the intervals for a punishing hour, up and down, fast and slow, until the sweat was streaming and my thighs ached from the acid.

When I returned, Danny was in the kitchen, drinking coffee with Annie and Joseph. He jumped up and came over and grabbed me in a bear hug, raising me gently off the floor.

"Hey, Jared. Good to see you."

"Put me down, for Christ's sake," I wheezed.

"Oh. Have we got a nasty hangover this morning? Not until you say please."

He began to dance me around the room, my toes barely touching the floor. He could keep this up for hours. Annie was smiling.

"Please put me down, you simple son of a bitch," I gasped.

"Okay. Since you asked so nicely."

He set me down, backed off a couple of steps and stood there grinning. He was the handsomest of the boys, with sharper features than his brothers; his Scots ancestry was in his narrow, almost beaked nose and blue eyes, but he had the heavy build, high cheekbones, and jet-black hair of his mother's side of the family. At six-three and two hundred and twenty pounds, he outweighed me by sixty pounds and was six inches taller. He looked almost white, but his father had deserted the family when Danny was still a baby, and his loyalties were fierce and uncompromising. He was more Haida than even his brothers. Once, when we were drinking the ninety proof we bought from the prison kitchen staff, he told me how bitterly he resented his father's side of the family. We had a few things in common.

"How were the last two trips?" he asked. I wondered if Annie had told him about *Arrow*. He would never bring it up.

"Pretty good. Lost some gear in a blow but should clear nine thousand for them both. How about your season?"

"Lousy. One of those years when nothing went right. Every time we made a decision it turned out to be the wrong one." He shrugged. "Back less than two weeks and I'm already working."

I smiled. Danny always found work right after the season, no matter how it had gone for him. He was too restless to sit around for very long.

"Bill Calder died this summer. There was a letter from Meg."

Danny had met them three years earlier, when we'd gone on a ten-day sailing trip up Desolation Sound. He had immediately taken to sailing, and by the end of the second day I had to practically fight him to get to do anything myself. He was so quick that by the time you realized a sheet needed trimming or a sail change was in order, he had already done it. Everything came easy to Danny.

He shook his head. "I knew he didn't have long. How's Meg?"

"She sounds okay. She knew it was coming, of course. They left me the sailboat, Danny. *Arrow*, she's mine! I just have to see the lawyers."

"*Arrow*? She's yours?" He threw back his head and roared. "*Arrow*! Jesus. I don't believe it."

"Danny. How does Mexico sound? We can be there by Christmas. A couple of months to work on *Arrow*, some new gear, and we're gone. She's full of spares and charts, the sails aren't all that bad, maybe pick up a used main."

We sat back and drank more coffee and kicked it around for a while, Joseph watching us with that impassive obsidian gaze, his hands wrapped around his pipe.

"I might be a little short for my end," Danny said.

"Not to worry, I had a pretty good season, I've got a little in the bank, we'll be fine. We can earn some money down there if need be. I worked in that refrigeration shop one winter. We'll pick up a set of gauges, some tubing and gas and spares, we can fix fridges. Shit, you know those gringo cruisers, gotta have their ice cubes and cold cervezas. You're good with diesel engines, pick up the odd job, earn a few bucks. It's cheap down there, we'll catch some fish, beer is around two dollars a bottle and as good as anywhere in the world. What the hell."

Danny studied me thoughtfully. "What the hell," he said at last.

I had thought he would be more enthusiastic, but then he was always touchy about paying his dues. He thought too many of his people didn't. I'd bring him around.

"I've got to get to work. See you later."

He stood abruptly and left the room.

I drained my coffee and headed downtown to see the lawyer.

❁

The office was in one of the grand old buildings on the edge of the financial district in Vancouver's West End; dark red brick with the windows set back and flower boxes sprouting from every sill. The wide entrance doors were carved maple, opening into a small lobby with an old Axminster carpet and a faded receptionist of the same vintage.

She grudgingly directed me into a walnut-panelled office where a thin elderly man in a three-piece suit sat behind a rosewood desk. He stood up and came around it, grasping my hand and shaking it vigorously.

"Mr. Kane. Thank you for coming in. Have a seat. Some coffee please, Miss Jennings."

He sat down and regarded me thoughtfully.

"I suppose you were surprised by my communication."

"Yes. It was a complete shock. I never expected anything like this."

He nodded. "I have known the Calders for over twenty years, ever since they first arrived in British Columbia. I handled their affairs when they went cruising, suggested some real estate investments, that sort of thing. Over the years, my wife and I became friends with Bill and Meg, and we began to see each other socially. In 1996 and '97 they entered *Arrow* in the Swiftsure, and I crewed for them."

He smiled at my surprise. The Swiftsure can be a tough race, out from Victoria into the Straits of Juan de Fuca, around the old lightship, gone now, and then back home again. Near a hundred and sixty miles, often during heavy spring gales.

"I was a keen sailor in my day. Of course, I was younger then. Anyway, as I was saying, we became very good friends over time. My wife died eight years past, and in my subsequent loneliness I found myself spending a lot more time with Bill and Meg."

I had an uneasy feeling about where all of this was going.

"When it became evident that Bill was dying, he and Meg spoke to me of their concern for *Arrow*'s future. I offered to purchase her, and told them I would accept any valuation arrived at by the marine surveyor of their choice. I have a membership at the Vancouver Rowing Club, and she would have been well looked after. They thanked me, but said that after considerable reflection they had decided to bequeath *Arrow* to you, as a no-strings gift."

He paused and took a sip of coffee.

"I must say, I was appalled. I had heard them speaking of you, and, if you will forgive me, nothing they had told me was particularly reassuring: a seasonal fisherman with a prison record who works a few months a year, drinks to excess, and lives with a First Nations family in the East End."

I flushed with anger and started to rise.

"Please," he said. "Hear me out. I want you to understand." He raised his hands in apology and motioned me back into the chair.

"When I found that they had made up their minds and could not be dissuaded, I decided to have you checked out. I have been looking after the Calders' interests for twenty years, and was simply continuing to do so. One of our departments handles divorce cases, and in the course of these we sometimes have occasion to employ a private detective agency. I engaged them to research your background."

He picked up a folder that was lying on his desk and tapped it delicately with his finger.

"Would you like to read it?" he inquired softly.

"No thanks. I've lived it."

He smiled bleakly and opened the file.

"I think it is all here: thirty years old, parents died when you were in grade school, brought up by elderly grandparents. Average grades through high school, no school clubs or affiliations, graduated in June 2007, sentenced to two years in prison a month later for assault."

He looked up. "Seemed rather a stiff sentence under the circumstances?"

I stared out the window. After a moment he continued.

"Served the full two years, released July 2009. Assault charges filed by two customers at Onyx nightclub a year later, settled out of court. Drunk driving charge in 2011, licence suspended for six months. Broke a man's arm in a barroom brawl in Kodiak, Alaska, in 2012, charges dropped when your skipper bought off the plaintiff. Second drunk driving charge shortly thereafter, licence suspended for two years, never renewed."

He looked up. "You no longer drive?"

It was none of his fucking business. After a few moments he shrugged and continued.

"Considered a good hand in fishing industry, changes boats frequently, always gets chances on highliners. Few close friends, no personal assets, small bank account, lives with Native family in East End, etc., etc."

He handed the file across to me, and I ignored it, and he placed it carefully on the desk between us.

"It is the only document, no other copies exist. I was going to show it to Bill and ask him to reconsider his bequest, but by the time I obtained the full report he had passed. I realize if I show it to Meg now, she might never forgive me."

He paused and steepled his hands, reflecting.

I sat and waited for it. He surprised me.

"I will be perfectly frank with you, Mr. Kane. I intend to go to England next month to visit Meg, and I am hoping in time she might consent to become my wife. This may seem very quick and callous to you, but I am sixty-four years of age, and to paraphrase Mr. Einstein, the tracks are rapidly narrowing. I will do everything within my power to ensure Meg's happiness. I am not upset with not acquiring *Arrow*; in fact, I will admit to you that one of my main reasons for wanting the boat was to retain a link with Meg. What does deeply concern me, however, is the likelihood that your possession of *Arrow* will ultimately result in disappointment and grief to Meg. I want you to understand that."

"Oh yes," I said, "I understand that very well. Can we sign the papers now?"

He nodded and picked up a second folder, and pulled out documents with check marks indicating where my signature was required. I signed rapidly, not bothering to read them. My name was already registered in the Blue Book; I endorsed it at the bottom and the lawyer witnessed it. He returned all the papers to the folder and handed it across to me, along with the report from the detective agency.

"Is that everything?" I stood to leave.

"Not quite." He rose and came around the desk and stood beside me. "Please do not think I am opposed to you. I am not without sympathy."

"Yeah."

He smiled thinly and continued. "I did not have to tell you any of this. In fact, by doing so I may have put myself somewhat in your power as regards my prospects with Meg. But what I want you to consider has nothing to do with any of that."

He picked up a sheet of stationery with a cheque attached.

"This is my personal option for first offer to purchase *Arrow* anytime during the next five years, should you choose to sell her. The cheque is for ten thousand dollars, which you may cash whenever you wish. Your acceptance gives me the right . . ."

"I know what an option to purchase is," I snapped.

He inclined his head. "After a period of five years, the option expires. You keep the money in all events. It is ten thousand dollars for you right now, clear and gratis."

He held the cheque out to me.

I turned my back on him and walked towards the door.

"Please consider it, Mr. Kane," he said. "You have nothing to lose by accepting it."

I turned around and faced him. "Okay," I said. I looked at his face for a long ten seconds. He was smiling politely.

"I've considered it," I said. "Fuck you."

❋

It was five miles back to Annie's and I walked it quickly, flushing the anger out of my system. By the time I reached home, I regretted my outburst; in retrospect Sproule had behaved better than me — he had been acting out of concern for Meg, whereas what was I doing but grandstanding? But I didn't want his fucking money.

I went up to my room and poured a long Scotch and stretched out on the bed and began leafing through the ship's documents. I came to the Blue Book and read slowly through the archaic English used to describe and measure *Arrow*, her gross weight and tonnage based on an arcane formula having to do with the number of casks or tuns of wine she could store in her interior volume, her overall length arbitrarily determined as being the distance between her bow and rudder post and so on.

Finally I had read through it all, and then once again, and only the report Sproule had commissioned remained. Reluctantly, I opened the file and began to read. It was a sorry history. I stuck grimly through to the end, then lay back and closed my eyes, and thought how it had all begun.

I hadn't planned any of it.

CHAPTER 3

My father died in a hunting accident when I was nine years old, my mother and kid sister in a grief and alcohol fuelled car crash three months later. There was no money in the estate, and after a few weeks of hesitation, my paternal grandparents took me in. They had disowned my father when he married out of their faith and never contacted him again. It was the first time I had met them, and it was years before I realized their charity was performed not out of love, but Christian duty.

My grandparents were in their early sixties when I arrived, and their lives revolved around their farm and their church. I can't remember being held by either of them. I ran away twice, and was caught and punished for it both times.

Their acreage in the Abbotsford Bible belt had a small dairy quota of six Holsteins; a hired man helped out with the morning and evening milking, and within a year I had replaced him. When Grandfather was not watching, I squirted milk into the mouths of the barn cats that crouched nearby in close attention. In late summer and fall, we gathered the hay and stored it in the huge loft above the barn, where I sometimes played among the close-stacked bales.

I attended the little Presbyterian school, where both teachers were ordained ministers of the church. There had been no formal religion in my parents' house, but I stood my Bible classes like a trooper, belting out the responses with the best of them and getting good enough grades to satisfy my grandfather and avoid the thin malacca rod he kept for my discipline. I sometimes wondered if he had used the same one on my father.

I rose at five in the mornings for the milking, had breakfast at quarter to eight, and left for school right after. It was eight miles distant, and I rode my bicycle; the school bus didn't come out our way. After classes finished I rode home, did the chores and milking, then homework and bed. Many of my country classmates had much the same schedule, and I didn't feel put upon.

Saturdays I worked all day at chores, cleaning the barn and chicken coop, then hauling chop to the feed shed. Sunday mornings we attended church, and sometimes there was a picnic afterwards with big overflowing hampers of food, and games and races for the smaller children.

Usually, though, I had Sunday afternoons to myself, and went down to the river and fished, or rode one of the big dray horses over to the neighbours', a Vietnamese family who worked for the Campbells in return for a ten-acre lease. Their son Loh was my special friend, and the two of us would sit astride Nancy's fat back, urging her into a reluctant gallop as soon as we were out of sight of the house.

It was Loh at first, and then his older brother Ving, who introduced me to the martial arts. Whenever we mock-fought, Loh handled me with ease, even though I outweighed him and was stronger. He showed me some of the basic karate throws and kicks, and when I began to hold my own, Ving gave us some lessons. He held a black belt and ran a weekly class in the community college.

I was attracted to martial arts and practised the asanas religiously, sometimes on the big stiff bales stacked in the barn, and secretly at night in my room. I sensed in the discipline something that would deeply offend my grandfather.

The spring I was sixteen, I completed grade ten, the final year at the Presbyterian school, and that fall I attended Abbotsford High. The school had over three hundred students and seemed huge and cosmo-politan to me, and a bit scary. It was the first time in my life that I heard a girl say *fuck*, and that was before noon on the first day. I went into the library, looked up the old yearbooks, and found my father's graduation photo. It was the first picture I had seen of him at my age. He looked wary and uncomfortable, with short-cropped blond hair above a thin, ascetic face. I wondered if he had ever been happy in those days. There were no clubs or sports listed beside his name. It didn't surprise me. I knew the milk quota had been even larger then.

The school had a quarter-mile track laid out behind it, and I began to run on my lunch hour. There was a girl who came out some days and ran with me. Her name was Jennie Starrett and she was a year ahead of me. Jennie was very popular and came from a wealthy family. My naivety must have amused her, because she asked endless questions about me and my life on the farm. She treated me almost as a kid brother, to the amazement and annoyance of most of her peers. Her boyfriend, Mark, particularly disliked me, although I was never the slightest threat to him.

It was through Jennie that I first discovered sailing, in my senior year. Her father raced a thirteen-metre Beneteau out of the Vancouver Yacht Club, and one weekend she invited me along. On Sunday morning I arose as usual for the milking and pleaded sick afterwards to get out of attending church services. Jennie and Mark picked me up in her convertible at nine thirty, and we were at the club by eleven.

The sailing was a revelation to me. The excitement of the pre-start jockeying and the beauty and grace of the boats on the water acted upon me like a drug. The wind rose just after we crossed the line, and our rail was in the water much of the time. It was all a confusion of sails crossing and sheets snapping, and shouts, curses, and laughter. It seemed a million miles away from the farm and my life. The rough seas didn't affect me, and when one of the grinders slipped and twisted his ankle, I took his place before being asked.

After the race we went into the clubhouse and ate chili and drank beer, and I listened to the stories and envied the flushed faces. I wanted to be a part of it all more than I had ever wanted anything in my life. When I arrived back at the farm, Grandfather stared at my wind-burned face but didn't speak.

The next day at school, Jennie said her father would like me to crew for him for the rest of the season. When I told Grandfather I wouldn't be attending Sunday services for a while, he stared at me for a long time, his eyes a bright, sharp blue above his tightly buttoned collar.

"Like father, like son," he spat out at last, and turned and strode away.

I sailed all that fall and spring, and my happiest hours were spent aboard the boat. I became familiar with the gear and worked through all the positions save helmsman, which was reserved solely for Mr. Starrett. Mark worked the foredeck, handling the big pole and spinnakers with careless, practised ease; it was the prestige position, and he was very good. Jennie came out with us on an irregular basis, filling in for absences from the regular crew, and she was as quick and competitive as any of the men.

In the final race of the season, we were tied with a Peterson for top spot. We approached the last mark five lengths ahead, and had a two-mile spinnaker run to win it all. It was windy and rough, and the bow was shipping water when we rounded the buoy. Mark bent down and clipped on the spinnaker halyard and jumped back, the crew heaved on the line and it shot up empty, fifty feet in an instant, wrapping itself around the forestay before anyone could react: in the wet and confusion, Mark had missed the shackle, and the big red sail still sat in its turtle on the deck in front of him. He stared upwards in disbelief, his mouth sagging open.

Without thinking I sprinted forward and went up the foils hand over hand. In seconds I reached the halyard and wrapped it around my wrist and slid back down to the deck. I clipped on the spinnaker, the crew hauled and the big red sail powered out, and we roared downwind neck and neck with the Peterson. My hands were bleeding through my gloves when I went back to the cockpit.

"That was very well done, my boy," Mr. Starrett said softly. The crew all slapped me on the back and whooped, all except Mark, who didn't speak, not even when we won the race and the Cup by a length, and were back in the clubhouse celebrating.

I left the victory party early, intending to slip out the back door into the parking lot to catch a taxi to the bus station. Mark rose up after me and caught me at the bottom of the stairs. He had been drinking steadily, and his piggy blue eyes were angry.

"Isn't the little hero staying for the party?"

I ignored him and kept on walking.

"I'm fucking talking to you, farm boy."

He grabbed me by the shoulder and spun me around. My silence was making him madder by the second, and maybe that was what I wanted. He was over two hundred pounds, a well-muscled crewcut blond with heavy shoulders and big hands, an all-star linebacker on the senior football team, quick and punishing, with maybe a shot at the Canadian pro league. There'd been some school gossip about Mark and his buddies clearing out hotel bars after some of their away games; I had seen the meanness in his eyes, and believed the stories. I never did understand what Jennie saw in him.

"What do you want, Mark?" I asked him.

"What do I want? What do I want?" He was screaming now.

Of course, I knew exactly what he wanted. He wanted to beat the living crap out of me, and was searching frantically for an excuse. Behind him, people were streaming out of the Yacht Club.

"Nobody calls me that," Mark yelled and slapped me hard across the face. My head snapped sideways with the impact. I pulled my hands out of my jacket and let them hang at my sides. I could feel my lips stretching into a frozen smile. I studied his face. It was very red now, and his eyes seemed a brighter blue. He slapped me again.

"Just like my father," I whispered.

"What?" Mark said.

He leaned forward, as if in inquiry, and I hit him for the first time.

There is a set of exercises in yoga called Pratyahara, or control of the senses. It leads to the withdrawal of self from the physical world, resulting finally in the discovery of the true self. I had been practising it for two years in the privacy of my room at night, trying to escape from a place I hated, but I had never achieved true understanding until now; my mind pulled back, a slow red haze drifted up through my body, and I watched with cold analysis the stranger I had become.

It was a very uneven fight. Mark bounced off the pavement screaming in rage, and I chopped his thick neck twice and drop-kicked him in the stomach. When he struggled up again, his eyes were dazed. I elbow-smashed his face and threw him over my hip. He landed ten feet away. I had never been so exhilarated in my life.

I moved towards him, but something grabbed my elbow. I spun around and side-kicked and went into a low crouch. Everything became very quiet. Jennie had gone to Mark and was holding up his head. There was blood on her hands. Her father was lying on the ground, holding his thigh and staring at me. They were all staring at me. I turned and walked away, and when they were out of sight I started to run, and I ran and ran until I was choking.

When I arrived home the police were waiting.

❁

Mark had a broken nose and cheekbone, a dislocated shoulder, and a severe concussion. It was the latter injury, coupled with the fact that I had left the scene, that led to the aggravated assault charge. My lawyer said if I had stayed around, it would likely have been dismissed as an unfortunate accident. Mark was in hospital for three weeks but eventually recovered fully. At the time of my court hearing, though, he was still bandaged heavily, and that didn't help my cause any.

Jennie's father had been very kind about everything and had obtained a high-profile lawyer for me. They were both confident that I would only receive a lecture and probation; I had never been in trouble before, and my grandfather was known and respected in the community. Mark had been drinking and was clearly the aggressor. Mr. Starrett told the police he had slipped and twisted his leg while breaking up the fight, and nobody had contradicted him.

It was a beautiful June day when my case came up. Summer had arrived early and hot, and the air conditioning was already turned on, its low hum competing with the big bluebottles buzzing up against the closed windows. Mine was the first case called, and we all rose as the judge entered the room. He looked as old as my grandfather. There were about a dozen of us there — some of the race crew, Jennie and her father, and a couple of spectators. As the judge rapped his gavel and called the court to order, I heard the door behind me slam, and turned to look. It was my grandfather. It surprised me: I hadn't thought he'd come.

The Crown summoned the ambulance attendants first. They gave a detailed description of Mark's injuries, which seemed compounded in the retelling. He had even lost three teeth. The report from the hospital said much the same thing and gave a prognosis of full recovery. It included an alcohol reading taken on Mark at the time of admission, and it showed him to be legally impaired. This was all read into the record.

The next witness was the detective who had read me my rights and arrested me at the farm, a big balding red-faced man in his forties, with sleepy brown eyes and a rumpled suit. He summarized the witnesses' statements, and reconstructed the incident. He said it was clear that Mark had followed me out of the clubhouse and provoked the fight. The lawyer questioned him closely about the force required to fracture Mark's nose and cheekbone. My lawyer rose and objected that the detective was not an expert witness in this area, and the judge concurred. He finished his examination by asking the detective how many fights or results of fights he handled in a year. The big detective said probably upwards of a hundred, and yes, this was a nasty one.

My lawyer put some questions trying to downplay the force and expertise of the blows, and the detective nodded laconically and agreed with him for the most part; yes, it was inconclusive, he'd only seen the results, Mark had apparently got up and continued the fight, I hadn't attacked him on the ground, etc. I had told the lawyer about the rumours of Mark's previous fights, but he hadn't bothered to obtain any corroborating testimony; we wouldn't need it, he'd said.

The social worker and psychiatrist were not required to be in attendance, and the judge read out their reports: I was an average student, kept to myself, no close friends, didn't belong to any school organizations or clubs. The psychiatrist found me normal, though withdrawn and reclusive. He said I had no close attachments, not even with my immediate family, but was fully functional. As I sat there listening, my life seemed as bleak and bare as the stark walls that surrounded me.

The judge shuffled the reports, sat quietly for a few moments, then began his summary. He said that he had spent much of his time on the bench in the last few years dealing with violence, and in particular youth violence. He spoke at length about the problem of the Asian youth gangs, and it seemed as if he in some way associated me with them because I had used a form of martial art.

The judge moved on to describe the extent of Mark's injuries, and it sounded as if I had beaten up a helpless drunk. Mark had lost weight, and with his pale complexion and the bandages it was hard to see the confident bully who had confronted me.

When the judge finished his summation, he said it was his considered opinion that the assault charge had been proven, but there were extenuating circumstances, and as it was my first offence, he was giving me a two-year suspended sentence, and releasing me into the custody of my family. He had lifted his gavel to terminate proceedings when my Grandfather stood up and asked permission to address the court.

He was wearing his black Sunday suit, and with his erect carriage and long, flowing grey hair, he was an impressive figure. He often spoke at church services, and his voice was strong and compelling. He never looked at me once the whole time. He told the judge he had no faith in my good conduct, and would no longer have me in his family or his home. He said he had taken me in out of Christian charity and raised me to Christian principles, but I had rejected them. He told the judge it did not surprise him I was in trouble, he had long foreseen it. His cheeks were red and flushed, and his eyes shone with religious fervour.

He began to speak of my father, and bad blood, and I breathed deeply and focused on Pratyahara, and slowly his voice faded. I stared straight ahead at the judge's desk; there was a design incised on the front of it, and I expanded my consciousness and the design became Om, and I heard the mantra in my mind and let it sound and grow until it filled my being and there was no more room for anything else.

After a while the lawyer nudged me, and we rose. The judge's lips moved, but I didn't hear what he was saying. The lawyer nudged me again, and then he spoke, and after another while we all sat down, and then everyone left and they put handcuffs on me and led me to a small room where my lawyer was waiting.

I realized the lawyer was screaming at me. He said it was bad luck my grandfather being such a tight-ass, but if I had spoken up when the judge asked me to, instead of smiling like a fucking zombie, I would probably have been all right; if I hadn't run away from the scene of the fucking fight, I would probably have been all right and what the fuck was the matter with me anyway, and maybe it was right that I had received a two-year sentence. He was a celebrated lawyer and outraged at this small defeat. He lit a cigarette and puffed furiously on it, staring at me angrily.

After a while he said that he probably should have introduced some testimony of Mark's earlier fights, but he really hadn't thought it would be necessary. He would do so at the appeal, and Mr. Starrett would set up a job, and they would find a good family environment for me to live in. There would be no problem in getting the sentence suspended, he positively guaranteed it.

I stood up, and shook his hand, and thanked him for his trouble, and told him there would be no appeal; I said that none of it was his fault and I didn't hold him responsible for any part of it. The actions were mine and I accepted the consequences. I asked him to thank Mr. Starrett for me, and rang for the guards. When they took me away he was staring after me, a frown on his face. I didn't try to explain, and he wouldn't have understood in any event, but I was done with that family, that hypocrisy, and that life. I would find my own way, and if that path started with imprisonment, so be it.

I didn't see Jennie again for a long time. She came out to the prison once, but I didn't meet with her, there was no point. She would only be another reminder of the life I had failed at and was trying to forget. I heard later that she married a lawyer who was a business acquaintance of her father.

I closed Sproule's file. I lay on the bed for a long time, staring at the file, thinking about the past and how it all wove into the present: it had all started on a sailboat, and now a sailboat was giving me a chance to make a fresh beginning, to wipe away the old mistakes and bitterness and move on, and I swore I would not foul up this time no matter what.

I should have known better.

CHAPTER 4

The ferry from Vancouver Island to Quadra was just a motorized barge with a house and bridge built up on her, and space for a few vehicles. I stood at the rail for the brief trip across, and then walked down the gravel road towards the cove with the red government dock where *Arrow* rested. The early-morning overcast had burned off, and the sky was that deep, cold blue that hints the coming approach of winter.

There was no traffic, only the scuffing of my footsteps as I ascended the last small slope and the white-painted tips of *Arrow*'s masts showed, and then the rest of her slowly appeared until I stood at the crest and she lay revealed beneath me. The waters sparkled in the sunlight, and *Arrow* gave small restless tugs at her lines as the inconstant breeze rose and fell. She was exactly as I remembered her. It was only then that the full realization of my good fortune sank in, and I went down and stepped aboard my own boat for the first time. Already it felt like coming home.

The interior was rich with mahogany and brass, the air musty with the scent of polishes and oils and the stale hint of bilges. I opened the port lights and let the fresh air sweep through, then pulled the floorboards and checked the bilges for water. There was only a trace

— *Arrow* didn't take on much when she was tied to the dock; it was when she was working hard under sail, beating upwind with rail down and water streaming across her decks, that she became wet below.

There was a note from Meg on the chart table, taped to an opened bottle of Bundaberg rum.

Dear Jared,

I've just finished cleaning out the boat. Slow and sad work, but I brought a good friend with me, and we finally got through it. So many memories.

I've left everything to do with the boat; tools, sextants, charts, a host of spares. As you can see there are also books and some personal things of Bill's which I thought you might like to have. I have taken everything I could possibly need, feel free to use or dispose of the rest as you see fit.

Bob Sproule and I toasted *Arrow* and her new owner. I wish you all the happiness she brought to us, and ask you to join in a salute to old times and good memories. Write soon.

Love,

Meg.

I opened the bottle and drank a glass to the ghosts of absent friends. The raw liquor burned my throat, and I shuddered momentarily as something cold and prescient walked across my grave.

❀

For two days I worked non-stop on *Arrow* from dawn to dusk, readying her for the trip across the strait to Vancouver. The sails hadn't been used since Bill fell ill, and I took them out of the lockers and ran them up the halyards. One of the light-air genoas was so badly blown out as to be nearly useless, but the jib and heavy-weather headsails were still serviceable. The mainsail needed replacing; the seams had all been resewn and it was covered in patches. It had been recut at least once, and the cloth had no stiffness left in it.

I checked the diesel engine for oil and water, turned the ignition key on, and pressed the starter button. A faint clicking sound rose up from below — if I was lucky, a loose solenoid connection on the starter motor. I removed the companionway stairs and unfastened the forward bulkhead to access it. The engine was an ancient faded-blue Perkins, with the big Lucas starter mounted in as inaccessible a spot as the designer could locate. I smiled at an old memory of Bill working on the engine, his knuckles skinned and oiled, the air and engine both blue.

"All the electrics are Lucas," he'd cursed. "Fucking Lucas, the Prince of Darkness."

I cleaned and greased the connections and pressed the starter again, and the engine turned slowly a few times and almost caught. I suddenly remembered that you had to give it full throttle for a few seconds when it was cold. There was just enough battery left, and then the big alternator kicked in, and she was charging at eighty amps. I left her running and began to take inventory.

The cabin and deck lockers were crammed with equipment and spares: coils of rigging wire, greased and wrapped in brown waterproof paper, spare turnbuckles, a heavy box of shroud fittings, different sizes of copper ferrules and stainless steel thimbles. In the aft locker was a complete Aries wind vane, and under that a hundred-pound Luke storm anchor, broken down to its separate parts and wrapped in an old sail.

Under the quarter berth I found a teak carpenter's chest, beautifully fashioned with mortise-and-tenon joints, the interior lined with green felt and every chisel, spoke shave, plane, and hand drill fitted and locked in its place. I took them out and sprayed them with a light oil, gently rubbing off the tiny rust stains with crocus cloth before replacing them.

Another box, mahogany this time, contained an old Weems &

Plath sextant, heavy and shiny with brass and mirrors, and held in place by the padded and formed interior of the lid. Meg had left me Bill's prized set of old Peetz reels as well, a full ten inches in diameter, mounted on a pair of stubby trolling rods. They hung on the cabin roof in canvas bags, framing the cylindrical containers that held the charts.

I recalled that one of the cardboard tubes had held an over-and-under .410 shotgun and .22-calibre rifle. It stored neatly inside with a few inches to spare, and Bill had rolled and cut up some old charts to stuff the ends of the tube and give it the same appearance as the others. It would escape a casual search, and Bill had carried it since he had left Britain. It was never discovered, and he never had occasion to use it.

After a few false starts, I found the container and pulled out the rifle, a beautiful old Purdey with a carved walnut stock and a hunting scene chased on the barrels. Hoppe's No. 9 and a pull-through were also in the container, and I cleaned and oiled the piece before returning it to its place.

It was getting dark by the time I finished, and I ate supper and went on deck with my coffee. As the light faded, the stars emerged, the constellations faint and indeterminate at first, then slowly illumined: Cassiopeia, Cygnus, Gemini, the Bears, Orion — and at the centre, counterpoise of their revolving, Polaris, the North Star, friend and lodestone of sailors, the Stella Maris of a thousand ancient mariners.

I wondered how many lonely sailors at this precise moment were focusing their sextants on the heavenly bodies, calculating their declension, and locating themselves on the infinite oceans that surrounded them. Not as many as before GPS became commonplace, that was for damn certain. I pulled a blanket around me against the chill and gazed upwards, and thought about warm tropic nights and sultry seas, and the legendary Southern Cross.

Later I turned into my bunk and read, slowly working my way through a Scotch and water. Below the sea berths were long shelves of books, all concerning offshore cruising or one of the associated trades. Bill had the complete set of Pilots and Sailing Directions for all the

Oceans, as well as numerous illustrated travel guides for the South Pacific and a large collection of classic sailing narratives.

I skimmed through a couple of these, but it was my special joy to read from Bill's diaries. Meg had left them all for me; leather-bound and gilt stamped, they stood in a neat row, an even dozen volumes dating from when the boat was first commissioned right up to the time of Bill's death.

He had a very fine, almost copperplate script, and the text was interspersed with numerous illustrations, from the first rough designs of *Arrow* to pictures of harbours, scale drawings of isolated reefs where Bill and Meg had anchored, and portraits of people they had met in their travels. I fell asleep reading the journals, every vivid page affirming in me the resolution to fit *Arrow* out and head south.

In the morning I made lists of what needed doing before making passage and drafted a rough timetable. We would run down the west coast to Cabo San Lucas in November or December, then slowly work our way north to La Paz in the Sea of Cortez. Hurricanes seldom reach the upper end of that sea, and we could leave *Arrow* anchored out in Guaymas and fly back to B.C. in April for the halibut season.

In October we would return to the boat and make ready for a spring crossing to the Marquesas. Then on to the Tuamotus, French Polynesia, the Cook Islands, Tonga, and Fiji; the classic Milk Run. It was an excellent plan, and I drifted off to sleep with exotic ports and harbours drifting through my mind, harbingers of the better times to come.

❀

Saturday morning came in overcast, with a shadowed hint of rain. I was greasing the anchor winch when the slow ka-put ka-put of an Easthope engine sounded across the water, and an old Fraser River gillnetter came into sight around the point, with Danny crouched on the bow and Joseph seated beside a pair of strangers in the cockpit. She pulled alongside, and I caught her lines and made fast to the big steel dock cleats.

The owners were on their way to Campbell River for some steelhead fishing, and Danny had hitched a ride for Joseph and himself. The two men refused all offers of hospitality and headed out, anxious to get in another couple of good hours before the tide turned against them.

"Well, how is she?" Danny asked.

He reached into his pack and opened a couple of beers. Joseph moved slowly and thoughtfully over the foredeck, fingering the stays and shrouds and sighting up their runs where they connected to the mast. It was no surprise to see him: I had learned long since that Joseph and his family never defined or circumscribed his activities by his age; it was implicitly understood that he was welcome to attend every function or outing.

I once made the mistake of mentioning a movie I wanted to see. I was taking a girl who I thought might mean something to me, and was picking her up at eight. At seven thirty Joseph was dressed in his blue suit, freshly scrubbed and sitting by the door, waiting for me. Danny's eyes gleamed as he told me he guessed it was a movie Joseph wanted to see as well.

"She's fine. The bottom needs redoing, but there is nothing major growing on it. Not taking in much water, most of the rigging looks okay. I haven't gone up the mast yet."

There were ratlines to the first set of spreaders and mast steps every eighteen inches from there on.

"The engine is clattering a fair bit, sounds like the valves need adjusting. The running lights are out, I'm not sure if it's the bulbs or the wiring. Nothing too serious, apart from a couple of sails and maybe the upper shrouds. Certainly no problem in getting her to Vancouver and hauled out."

I took a long drink of beer.

"I see no reason why we can't leave for Mexico in a couple of months, Danny. I figure seven or eight thousand to refit, ten thousand max with provisions. We can be there by Christmas."

"Ten thousand, you figure," Danny said.

"Thereabouts. Plus a few thousand to last the winter. We can leave her down there and come back for the halibut in the spring. Then we're gone for a couple of years or so. Until we run out of money."

"Okay, then. I'll get started on the engine."

I had thought he would be keener.

We left at seven the following morning, the sun just rising over the wooded ridge to the east, and the wind coming over the dock. Danny slipped the springs and bow line while I clipped on the jib and ran it up partway. The bow moved away from the dock, as Danny held *Arrow* against the stern line until she swung, and we moved slowly out. I hardened the jib halyard while Danny hauled the main, and we were doing four knots. There were some quick tacks to get around the corner and clear; we were a little rusty and there was current in the pass, and we were both sweating by the time we beat out through it and made the point.

We moved into clear air and put up the mizzen and took off on a long beam reach, the knot meter registering a steady seven. Joseph rigged up the trolling rods and put out a couple of hootchies, Danny made a pot of coffee, and I leaned back and steered in complete felicity. The water hissed beneath the transom, the powerful sails bellied out, and *Arrow* flexed beneath my feet like a living thing. In a few short weeks we would be doing this again, only our destination would be Mexico. It all seemed too good to be true, and I reached down and gently rapped the deck with my knuckles.

We reached Gabriola Island at five thirty and dropped the hook in the lee of the little spit. It was blowing twenty knots outside, but the anchorage was still and quiet, with just the tops of the trees soughing gently. The summer cabins along the shore were deserted and we were alone, save for a pair of fur seals basking on a rock in the last rays of the sun. By the time we finished eating, it was dark and clouded, and the first cold rain began to fall. We moved below, and I turned in early with the diaries while Joseph and Danny played cribbage.

I studied them in the lamplight: Joseph sitting ramrod straight as always, his face impassive as he played his cards; Danny laughing and animated. When Joseph spoke it was in a sibilant whisper, and I fell asleep to the sound of his voice melding with the rain.

By daylight the wind and rain had died, and we motored out of the bay in dripping grey stillness. At ten o'clock the breeze came up again on the nose, and two hours later we were beating into a twenty-five-knot southeaster. *Arrow* was in her element, shoulder down and slicing through the seas at hull speed with a single reef in her mainsail. She was taking on water, and we pumped the bilges every hour. The main cabin stayed dry, the leaks coming from under the anchor winch where the caulking was old and stiff and missing altogether in spots.

We made good time, and at four o'clock we dropped our sails under Lions Gate Bridge and motored through the inner harbour to a berth amid the fishing fleet. We packed our gear and went down the wharf to catch a taxi to Annie's. I turned one last time at the Cannery, and looked back where *Arrow* lay, wet and shining in the reflected light off the water, a swan amid the duckling seiners and trollers that surrounded her.

❀

It took the best part of a week to sort through my gear and decide what to move aboard *Arrow*. During that time I had the boat hauled, and checked the hull with an awl and hammer, tapping each separate plank along its length for softness and fastening. Bill had redone *Arrow* with Monel three years earlier, but I wanted to be sure, and this gave me a chance to know her. The yard shipwright cut out the deck under the winch where it had rotted out, and scarfed in a new piece, matching the patterned teak so perfectly the repair was invisible.

The bottom paint was thick and looked to be holding well, but when I began to sand it prior to recoating, some small chunks fell off, showing bare wood, and there was nothing for it but to remove it all down to the hull. I bought extra butane bottles for the torch, sharpened some scrapers and settled down to work. It was a slow, tedious business, and there was no rushing it.

It was the weekend, and I was surprised Danny wasn't there to help. I had only seen him once since we had brought *Arrow* across. He seemed tense and distracted, and I wondered what was bothering him. He showed the dour Scottish streak of his father sometimes.

I had the Walkman plugged in and was listening to Howlin' Wolf while I worked on the delicate curve of the hull where it rose up to the tiny transom; you had to be careful to turn your wrist as you scraped, or you'd gouge the wood. I was concentrating on the work when a hand tapped me on the shoulder. It was the lawyer, Sproule, dressed in an old pair of paint-stained coveralls. He gave a hesitant smile.

"Can you use a hand?" he asked.

I thought about it for a while. But he was a friend of Meg's, after all.

"Okay," I replied finally. "Scrapers are over there."

He picked one up and began working a few feet down the hull from me. I watched him until I was certain he knew what he was doing. We scraped in silence for a while.

"How did you find me?"

"It wasn't hard. I thought you would likely haul right away, there aren't that many places. This was the third yard I contacted."

I nodded and we scraped some more.

"I would like us to be friends, Jared."

I nodded again and we scraped for another minute. I wasn't going to make it easy for him.

"I have some cold Pacificos in the trunk of the car."

"Mr. Sproule," I said, "you have just taken a giant step in the right direction."

"Call me Bob."

We spent the rest of the day scraping *Arrow*, drinking Mexican beer, and talking about the trip. He had never taken time off to cruise his own boat but had chartered on holidays in the Med and Caribbean, and was keen and knowledgeable. I told him what I thought was needed for our trip, and we discussed water makers, radar, and the desirability of a fridge. He agreed the latter wasn't absolutely necessary but said his idea of hell was a place where the beer was world class, plentiful, and cheap, but you were required to drink it at an ambient temperature of eighty-five degrees. It turned out to be a pleasant day, and by the end of it we were approaching a cautious friendship.

Under his staid exterior was a dry, acerbic wit; he had few illusions about his profession, and a stock of really evil lawyer jokes. When we finished work he produced a pair of thick steaks from the cooler, and we sat in the cockpit watching them sizzle on the barbecue as he told me the latest news of Meg. She had invited him to England for Christmas; he was delighted. I thought they would make a good couple, and silently wished him well.

He told me that the racing season had started at the rowing club and suggested entering *Arrow* into some of the events to test her gear. It wasn't a bad idea; no matter how laid-back you planned to be when someone you felt you should beat threatened, it was impossible not to throw caution to the winds and go flat out. Better for something to fail now, when it could be easily repaired or replaced, than later on, while beating down the Oregon coast. I told him I would consider it, and that I expected him to crew if *Arrow* raced.

We finished the evening with rum and coffee, and Bob took a taxi home. He said it would be bad for his professional image to get picked up on an impaired charge, and he would be back in the morning to help me finish off anyway. As I watched the tail lights fade, I congratulated myself on how quickly it was all coming together.

It all fell apart even more quickly.

CHAPTER 5

It had been a few years, but I recognized the detective straight off: the big slouched shoulders; the bored, impassive face; the wrinkled brown suit that could have been the one he wore to my trial. He was older and heavier, but the sleepy brown eyes looked as shrewd as ever. He took a while meandering through the boatyard, but I never doubted for a second where he'd stop.

"Jared Kane? I'd like to talk to you for a few minutes."

"What about? I'm kind of busy."

He smiled. "I won't take up too much of your time."

I turned my back and went up the ladder on the side of the boat. He followed, nimble as an ape, and settled into the cockpit.

"Nice-looking boat. Well kept."

"You into boats?" I asked.

"No. I restore old cars sometimes. Similar principles, I guess." He gestured vaguely at the large body bulging his suit. "Takes a lot of work to keep anything old in decent working order."

He was perfectly relaxed, slouching against the cockpit coaming, smiling with slitted eyes into the sunshine. A big contented St. Bernard. I could see he wasn't going to leave before he was ready.

"Would you like a beer?"

"Oh yes, please." He winked. "I'm on duty."

I brought out a couple of beers from the bilge and opened them. He took a huge draft.

"Just the right temperature," he sighed, wiping at his lips. "I don't like them icy cold. Kills all the flavour."

I wondered when he was going to get to the point.

"I thought you got a raw deal at your trial."

So he remembered too.

"Funny, I don't recall you saying so at the time."

He shrugged. "No. Nothing I could do, really. You should probably have gotten off. Tough luck getting old Judge Rainer. A kid like that — what was his name?"

"Mark Austen."

"Yeah. A kid like that is worse than most when he's drunk. Family money, big, figures the rules don't apply to him. He'd had other fights before. Course your family didn't do you much good either. The old guy sounding like Jehovah standing up there in his black suit. Jesus, I thought he was going to call lightning down on us all."

To the big detective, my grandfather was just another weirdo. It was a new point of view for me.

"I went back and looked up your record. I guess you met Danny MacLean in prison, huh?"

"Yes. We became friends at the farm. When my time was up, he met me at the gate, took me to his home. His mother lets out rooms. I've stayed there off and on ever since. Up until I moved onto the boat last week."

"Yeah. She told me. Nice boat like this, what's it worth these days?"

I could see where this was going.

"Not as much as you'd think. She's wood, older, not to everybody's liking. Maybe fifty or sixty thousand. It depends. Most people want fibreglass or steel nowadays."

I waited for him to ask me how I afforded it, but he surprised me.

"When did you last see Danny?"

"Four or five days ago, I guess."

He waited patiently.

"Okay, let me think. Monday."

Danny had dropped by after work, and we had talked about the coming weekend, when *Arrow* was due to go back into the water. We were thinking about going sailing for a couple of days, taking some fishing gear and crab pots, maybe check out one of the shallow wrecks off Gabriola Island. He had left after a few minutes, said he had to meet up with some people.

"What's your interest in him, anyway? Danny's clean, has been since we came out."

He watched me closely.

"You haven't heard?"

I felt a cold sickness deep in the pit of my stomach. I shook my head.

"A smash-and-grab. Yesterday on Burrard Street. Three guys involved." His steady gaze never left my face.

I leaned back and closed my eyes and the sick feeling rose up and swept over me.

I had heard it briefly on the late-night news. Another jewel robbery in the West End. There were three men, one in a car and the two who hit the plate glass. They had picked a quiet time, early morning, just after the jewellers loaded the trays. The big guy had swung the hammer and taken out the glass, the other one had swept everything into a sack. The whole thing took under a minute, but it was long enough for the owner to run out and put a bullet into one of them. The wounded man made it back to the car but fell as he tried to get in. The other two drove away. Just another incident in the daily litany of crime in a violent city.

Detective Clarke got up and fetched another couple of beers.

"The stupid son of a bitch," I said numbly. "Are you sure it was Danny?"

There might have been a hint of compassion in the stolid brown eyes.

"Danny is the one in hospital, Jared. They think he might not make it."

I couldn't speak. I closed my eyes and breathed deeply and tried to centre, but all I could see was Danny's face when we'd talked about the weekend. He had been looking forward to it. Why would he do something so unbelievably stupid? He didn't need the money, I had enough for both of us, he knew that. He had been clean since he got out of prison, I was sure of it. If he had been doing jobs during that time, he wouldn't have been able to hide it. There would have been something, a new car for Annie, the house fixed up, something. Oh, Jesus. Danny!

"How did it go down?"

"Pretty much as they said on the news. You heard?"

"Some of it."

"Danny and the second guy got out of the car and went to the windows. They were wearing stocking masks. The third one stayed in the car at the curb, motor running. Danny swung the hammer and took out the plate glass; his partner scooped the trays into a bag. We figure they got between three and four hundred thousand; the insurance assessors haven't finished totalling it yet. They were there under a minute, then turned and ran for the car. The jeweller had been hit before, and he had a gun under the counter. A little .32-calibre. He comes out the door after them, shooting. A miracle he hit anybody — he never even hit the car, we found it later. He puts out two windows across the street and takes out a neon sign as well. But one of the bullets struck Danny in the back, and he fell against the car."

Clarke paused and looked at me for what seemed a long time. "They drove away and left him, and he fell down in the street. He was unconscious by the time we got there. He's still out. They removed a bullet from his spine."

I didn't want to even think what that might mean.

"Can I see him?"

Clarke surprised me again. "He's restricted access, just family allowed in. But I'll take you."

We didn't talk much in the car. Clarke asked me if I knew anything that might help him, and I said no. I didn't say I wouldn't tell him if I did, but he probably knew that already. I was surprised he hadn't assumed I was one of the pair who had got away, but there was still plenty of time for that.

He drove quickly and well, swinging the nondescript sedan through the traffic, pushing into tiny openings, smiling placidly at the angry looks. He cut in front of a small panel truck, jammed on his brakes, and turned into the hospital parking lot. He went directly to the off-limits parking and pulled into the space prominently reserved for the Administrator.

"Fucker's probably golfing anyway," Clarke said as he pulled down the visor with Police Business emblazoned on it in bold yellow letters.

We took the elevator to the seventh floor and walked down the corridor to the end room. It was a single, and a police officer was seated outside the door.

"You figure he's going to spring up and run away?" I asked.

Clarke shrugged his meaty shoulders.

"Procedures," he said.

Annie was standing by the bed, a big greying woman with bowed shoulders. I went over and put my arms around her and we hugged, rocking slowly back and forth.

"How is he?" I asked.

"They don't tell me anything. You know."

I turned to Danny, lying there so quiet in the bed. He had an oxygen mask on, and a blood drip running into his arm. He looked as if he was already dead, and under the white sheets his body seemed shrunk and wasted. Around the mask, his face was stark and grey.

"Has he spoken at all?"

"Not since I've been here. I think he's pretty heavily drugged. They come in every couple of hours and give him shots. He hasn't moved."

"You take off now. Go home and rest. I'll call you if anything changes."

I glanced at Clarke, and he nodded in agreement. When Annie had left, he motioned me out into the corridor.

"I really shouldn't let you stay."

"Procedures?" I said.

"Yeah, well, you know. I'll put you down on the patrolman's list as family, but he'll have to be inside with you the whole time. If Danny regains consciousness and they find out you were in here with him, my ass will be in a sling."

"I appreciate this, Clarke."

"Yeah." The shrewd brown eyes gazed down on me. "You could do Danny a big favour if you think of anything to help us. If he pulls through, it will be a lot easier on him if we get the other two and recover the jewellery."

"He'll pull through," I said.

"If he makes it to trial and doesn't give up the others, it will go very hard with him."

"I understand that," I said.

But we both understood that wasn't how it worked. Danny would never give up his partners, and if he did he wouldn't last long in prison. Even if they were small-timers without connections, nobody liked a talker. They had dumped him, and maybe it was understandable. He was a big man, and he was hit, and bullets were flying. I felt the anger building, deep in my gut: they had left him lying in the gutter like a sack of garbage. But he knew the risks. Big dumb bastard.

I stayed until midnight, when Annie returned with one of her sisters and took over the vigil. They were sitting there in silence when I left, two proud women whose eyes were calm, and whose lives were too often wrapped in tragedy. I wondered how many vigils like this they had sat, how many others of their men they had lost. The average First Nations male in the big city is lucky if he sees fifty.

I caught a taxi back to the docks and fell exhausted into my bunk. My dreams were masked and violent, and I awoke in the middle of the night to the sound of grinding teeth, and my hands clenched into fists. I went on deck and practised some asanas, breathing deeply in the poses until my body was calm. I finished with a long headstand, then went below and slept.

For the next three days, Danny's condition didn't change. I sat at the hospital for hours on end, usually accompanied by someone from the family. I knew some of them; others were strangers. We seldom talked. I sometimes brought a book and read, but the others just sat there quietly, their eyes focused on the screen around the bed as if willing Danny their strength. The only sound was the slight rasp of Danny's breathing and the occasional tread of footsteps in the corridor.

I came to know the different police officers on their watches, and sometimes we talked in low voices about the prospects of the Canucks, or the unseasonably good weather. I couldn't understand why they were still here; Danny certainly wasn't going anywhere. Were they looking for a deathbed confession? Ridiculous; when he woke up was time enough to call the police and get a statement. And why wouldn't the doctors or nurses tell us anything? They just shrugged and said "no change" to all our queries. I asked one of the doctors about the chances of paralysis, and he said the police had told him not to release any details of Danny's condition to anyone, not even the family. It all seemed unnecessary and provocative.

On the third day Clarke showed up and we went out to lunch together.

"Any leads yet?"

"No," Clarke replied, speaking around his double cheeseburger, "absolutely nothing. We've checked all the fences, all the snitches, pulled in everybody we can think of for questioning, and zilch. But it's early days yet. They'll probably lie low for a while, move the stuff later when things settle down."

I studied him. The brown eyes were impassive.

"Why are the police at the hospital? It's been three days now."

Clarke shifted slightly in his seat, his jaws chewing methodically. "Yeah, I guess we'll pull them soon. We thought Danny might come around, wanted somebody on hand when he did. The doctors said he could wake up anytime."

"What do you think he's looking at?"

"Hard to say. Probably eight to ten years hard time. With good behaviour, say he could be out in five. If he makes it, that is."

"Danny will make it." I sounded more positive than I felt. "He's as strong as a horse. No little .32 slug will put him away." I thought for a while. "For argument's sake, what would he be looking at if he were to give up the other two? And the jewellery was recovered."

Clarke smiled. "Well. An optimist. Don't see many of those in my line of work. Let me see. Clean for ten years as far as we know, keeps out of trouble, works steadily, helps support his mother and the old man. If the other two are regular villains, and I'm sure they are, and he's responsible for putting them away, and we recover everything, maybe three to five years. Best case, he's out in eighteen months."

"And his sick time?" I was pressing.

"No. His sentence would start when he entered prison."

"How about the prison hospital?"

"Not unless he's long-term disabled. He's going to do some hard time, Jared." He tilted his bottle of beer and drained it.

"Well, it's all speculation anyway. I know Danny; he'll never give them up."

Clarke stared at me. "I think this one time he just might," he said slowly.

I had the feeling he wanted to say more, but he abruptly pushed away from the table.

"I have to go. Keep in touch."

He walked quickly away. As he vanished out the door, I realized he had stuck me with the bill.

❀

I was back at the hospital, sharing the late edition of the *Sun* with the patrolman on watch, when the nurse came in to change the dressing. She was a tiny thing, young and pretty, and the cop was kidding around with her. She giggled and blushed, then tripped over and around behind the screen. I could faintly see her outline as she bent over Danny. A few minutes later she came out with her stainless tray of soiled dressings and left the room. The policeman followed her out. I could hear them laughing and talking in hushed voices outside the door.

A strange feeling came over me, and I stared at the curtain, and something was very wrong. Suddenly I realized what it was.

Danny weighed around two-twenty, and was lying on his back, and the little nurse had changed his dressings without a sound. But he had been running towards the car when he was shot. The bullet had struck him in the back and hadn't exited — Clarke said they had taken it out on the operating table. She could never have turned him over by herself.

So what dressings had she changed?

I walked over and parted the curtains and stepped behind them. Danny lay unmoving on his back, waxen and still. I bent down and gently lifted the sheet that covered him. There was a foot-long dressing on Danny's stomach, from just below the sternum down almost to the groin. I grasped it at the top edge, and with a quick jerk, pulled it all the way back.

The knife cut was raw and inflamed, the edges a deep curled purple at the bottom where the blade had been shoved in and ripped sideways before it was pulled upwards and out. A killing stroke. When Danny had been shot by the jeweller, the bastards had gutted him like a hog. That was why the policemen were there. To protect him, in case they tried again.

I looked down at the pale face and ravaged body.

"Sorry, pal," I whispered, and I pushed down on the wound with a slow increasing pressure.

He groaned and mumbled and shook his head, and then his eyes gradually opened. His stare was glassy and unfocused, but then he slowly squinted, and then he knew me.

"Hey, Jared," he whispered.

I could feel the idiot grin stretching my cheeks.

"Pretty stupid, huh?" he murmured.

"Yeah," I said. "Pretty stupid."

"What happened?"

I had to lean over the bed to hear him, his voice low and breathless.

"The jeweller shot you by the car."

He nodded and mumbled something, but I couldn't make it out.

"And then your buddies stuck a knife in you, and ripped you open, and left you bleeding like a pig in the gutter," I whispered savagely in his ear.

He looked at me, his eyes half-shut. I don't know if the words registered. This was where the doctor would have told me to leave, I was tiring him.

"Who were they, Danny?"

He closed his eyes and mumbled something. The word sleep might have been in there. I put my hand on the cut, and pressed down hard. His eyes flew open and glared.

"You've got eight to ten years to fucking rest and sleep," I said. "Give me their names."

He mumbled something. Bell? Les Bell? Something like that.

"Say again, Danny."

I shook him, and prodded and cajoled, but he had gone. His face was flaccid, his breath rasping and uneven.

"Danny," I whispered into his ear, "don't talk to anyone. Stay under. Do you hear me? Don't talk."

But he didn't move or react in any way, and finally I went back to my seat. The policeman came back in to the room with a triumphant smile, a piece of paper with a name and number clutched in his hand. It didn't look like a ticket. We chatted for a few minutes, then I got up and left.

The hospital was a pleasant five miles from *Arrow*'s berth, and I decided to walk. It was a glorious fall day with just enough of a breeze to clear away the smog. The great thing about Vancouver is that you can get a beautiful warm spell anytime at all, including the very heart of winter. The down side is that when you don't have these breaks, the weather tends to be sullen, wet, and oppressive. The city is filled with disgruntled prairie pensioners who came out for a brief winter visit, enjoyed a few balmy days, then went back home and sold out. You see them everywhere, little weathered old people with angry, baffled looks, their faces staring resentfully skywards beneath the unfurled umbrellas.

I walked up to Stanley Park, hit the seawall, and started to jog. I began slowly then picked up speed for a couple of sprints, extending my stride and concentrating on form. When I was sweating nicely, I lay back and dropped into my regular seven-minute miles, my mind worrying at the problem.

It could all work out. Clarke had said the thieves probably wouldn't try and move the jewellery for a while. I had perhaps a couple of weeks to find them and make the best deal for Danny. I realized now that he was going to make it, and a huge weight lifted from my shoulders. But there was much to be done.

I poured it on for the last mile, and arrived back at the docks sweaty and exhausted. After a shower and change, I sat in the cockpit, drinking Scotch and thinking it all through. By the third drink, it started to gel, and after a few more it became perfectly clear.

CHAPTER 6

I awoke with a savage headache and a shady recollection of what had seemed so apparent the night before. I washed down some ibuprofen with a glass of stale beer and thought it through again.

If I went to Clarke and gave him the name or whatever part of it I had, he might find the pair and recover the jewellery; it was possible that Danny would get a break, and certain that he would be known to have talked. Clarke seemed straight enough, but Danny wouldn't be his top priority, and a recidivist Haida might well get lost in the shuffle.

If, on the other hand, I could find them myself, I could deal for Danny before giving them up, and we would be in a much stronger position. I knew where Danny hung out and who he usually drank with; that was a starting point. First I would drop in on Annie and see if she knew anything.

Her house was an old two-story with shingle siding and a gabled roof. Danny and I had added on a dormer suite when I'd moved in. There was another suite in the basement, and the money from these plus Joseph's old age pension paid the mortgage with something left over. Annie worked in the canneries during the salmon fishery, and usually made enough to see her through the rest of the year. If she had a bad season, she would waitress or drive a taxi in the winter.

Annie and Joseph were in the big kitchen drinking coffee when I crossed the sagging porch deck and entered. Danny and I had planned on jacking it up and replacing the rotten posts in the spring, put in some concrete footings.

Annie poured me a cup of coffee without being asked, taking the pot off the wood stove, which remained lit twenty-four hours a day. When it became unbearably hot in the summer, she used its twin, which rested outside on the porch. The boys had tried to buy her an electric stove but she had refused.

"I talked to Danny," I said. "I think he's going to be all right."

Two pairs of black eyes studied me intently.

"He woke up for maybe a minute," I continued. "He was making sense."

"That's great."

Annie closed her eyes in quick relief, then smiled bitterly. "Now all he has to do is get well enough to serve his time."

"Yes. Well, we might be able to do something about that."

I told them about Clarke and what he had said about Danny giving up the others.

"I don't think Danny will do that," Annie said.

I couldn't tell her about the stabbing. If she passed it on to the rest of the family, Erin or Jaimie might find the pair and kill them, and then there would be no deals for anybody.

"Why did he do it, Annie? He's always stayed straight."

She looked at me. "Don't you know?" she said softly. There was a sad pity in her eyes. "He needed the money for the trip."

I shook my head. "Oh no, Annie. We didn't need it. We were going to work on the way if we ran out of cash. He had some money put away, he was going to sell the pickup . . ."

My voice trailed off. I remembered it was me who had done most of the talking. Danny had just sat there, smiling amiably.

"Hell, Annie, he didn't need the goddam money. He knew that."

"He wanted to go on equal terms, I guess. You had the boat, you'd brought that. He knew about the rigging, the sails, you'd talked about radar, all the things you'd need for the trip. Danny wanted to buy those, to feel a part of it all. You've got skills, you can work on refrigeration. I thought he wouldn't go, I never dreamed he'd do something like this."

I shook my head stubbornly. "We would have made it. He could have found work. He's a damn good mechanic, he could have learned about refrigeration in a few months, come to that. There's lots of people tired of cruising who want their boats delivered back to the States. We would have been fine."

But it was a lame argument, and I knew it in my heart. I should have guessed; Danny always paid his way. When you went out drinking together you had to practically fight him to spend your share. If you let him, he would pay for every round, throwing the bills on the table with a reckless grin, as if he was splendidly rich and the money infinite.

Well, he had paid his way this time all right, lying in a hospital bed with a bullet in his back and his guts ripped apart. Now it was time for the others to ante up.

"Annie, I've got to find them. Danny wants me to. He gave me a name, or part of one. He was still under the drugs. Len or Les Bell maybe, something like that."

"Doesn't mean anything to me."

She looked across at Joseph. He was cleaning his pipe with a knife that was probably older than he was. It had a six-inch chipped lava rock blade set into an argillite handle, and he wore it in a scabbard on a thong around his neck. He had a habit of staring at me over it as he worked it around the bowl. He shook his head slowly.

"I'll ask around," Annie said, "talk to some of the people. Somebody might know something."

"Was Danny still drinking at the Globe?"

"Except for a week or so when he first got back from fishing. They barred him for a fight he got into, but let him back in after a couple of days. I guess they needed the money."

We both smiled.

I finished my coffee, bussed Annie, and nodded to Joseph. He nodded back. It was our standard method of communication. Annie followed me out and offered to drive me downtown. We climbed into Danny's truck, a fire-red '58 Chevy with oversized tires, a jacked rear end, and a stylized killer whale painted over the entire hood. It was a good thing I wasn't going undercover. Annie turned the key, the dual exhausts fired up in concert with the Waylon Jennings in the tape deck, and we rumbled off.

The Globe is one of the older hotels in downtown Vancouver, and it was frequented by serious patrons even at ten o'clock in the morning. There were already a dozen shaky solitary drinkers trying to get the first couple down without spilling them. As the day wore on the trade would change; at noon the strippers would take over a corner of the huge room, shaking and gyrating to some inner beat that had little to do with their jukebox selections. At the opposite corner was a little dance floor with a few cracked mirrors and a fly-blown strobe light overhead, and a pair of beat-up pool tables bordering it. Another endearing example of the warmth and intimacy of the Canadian drinking scene.

I went to the bar and seated myself on a stool. The bartender slid across a glass of draft.

"Need a shot too?" he asked.

"No thanks."

He shrugged and walked back to the other end of the bar, where a pair of businessmen in rumpled suits were holding up their glasses for refills.

I nursed the beer and checked out the customers as the place gradually filled. The crowd was mainly fishermen and longshoremen, and at eleven a fisherman I knew from the marina came in and started shooting eight ball at one of the tables. He wasn't very good, and when he sat down again I walked over and asked him to join me for a beer.

We talked aimlessly for a while and I ordered another round. He knew I wanted something.

"Tough about Danny," he said finally.

"Yeah. A bad break."

"How's he doing? I heard he might not make it."

"He's still in a coma," I said. "They took the bullet out of his back. I don't know very much."

"The bastards shouldn't have left him on the street, you know." He shook his head. "I mean, even if he was down, they should have taken him. They didn't know how bad it was."

"Any idea who they were?"

He was surprised. "Christ, no. None at all."

"Have you seen Danny in here lately with a couple of guys? Maybe strangers?"

He shook his head. "You know Danny, always in a crowd, always moving around. Never at any one table very long, but I don't recall him being with anybody I hadn't seen before. Just the usual crowd. You know."

I thanked him and left. I went into three other bars and followed the same routine. There was always somebody who knew Danny, but no leads as to who the two men might be. I was starting to feel the beer and went into Chinatown for something to eat, then tackled a few more places. It was midnight when I returned to the boat, sodden and bloated from all the beer. I wrote down the names of everyone I had talked to, and made another list of Danny's friends who I knew. They were all going to have to be talked to, and it would be a slow and probably useless process. I went to bed and tossed for a long time, thinking about how quickly things changed, and how they would never be the same again.

In the morning I woke up feeling tired and depressed. I put on some sweats and went out and ran a hard five miles, alternating wind sprints with slow jogging. When I got back I stank with alcohol sweat. The thought of another round of bar-hopping was unappealing. I showered and changed and walked over to the hospital. Clarke was there, talking to the officer at the door.

"Any change?" I asked.

"No. He's still out."

"What are the doctors saying?"

I went over to the bed and pulled aside the curtain. Clarke came over and stood beside me.

"They say he could come out of it anytime. They've cut back on the painkillers, but they're still worried about infection."

"I wouldn't have thought one little bullet would cause such a problem," I said. "You know, it's not as if it ploughed up his insides or anything."

Clarke regarded me with a long, thoughtful stare. "Yeah, well, you know. I've seen a lot of bullet wounds. Sometimes you're just unlucky."

I squeezed Danny's hand. "Hang in there, big guy."

I might have felt a tiny returned pressure. Maybe I was imagining it.

"Have you come up with anything yet?"

"No." Clarke shook his head wearily. "This one is very quiet. Usually we get something from our snitches, even if we can't make anything stick. But nothing on this one. It's like a goddam tomb out there. Maybe the guys are from out of town and skipped quietly, or maybe everybody is just too scared to talk." He laughed. "I've had Jaeger in three times already. That little prick knows everything that goes on in this town, but he'll never talk about something like this."

His tone was without rancour, almost admiring.

"Jaeger?" I said.

"Yeah. Tough little bastard in his fifties. His real name is something else, but everyone calls him that. He's what in private enterprise would be called a facilitator. Never gets personally involved, never dirties his hands. He just puts people together. If you need a fence for a hundred-dollar TV set or a hundred-thousand-dollar diamond bracelet, he'll tell you where to go. If you want a driver or need something discreetly stolen, he can help you out. All fairly civilized stuff, nothing too heavy. Rumour was, when that kidnapping went bad three years ago and the girl was killed after the ransom was paid, it was Jaeger who gave the guys up."

"An honourable thief," I said.

"No. He's just a dirty little crook, and I'll get him someday. But he'll never talk. I don't have any levers."

"Mmmm. Too bad. Well, I gotta go now. Let me know if anything turns up."

I walked out of the room and down the corridor until I was out of sight, and then I went down the stairs two at a time. By the time I reached the street I was sprinting.

❀

"Jaeger. That's his name. He'll know who the two men are."

We were in the kitchen, gathered around the big oak table with the carved legs. When Annie had brought it home from Saint Vincent de Paul five years earlier, it was covered in chipped layers of old paint. I bought a gallon of stripper and worked on it in the backyard for two days until it was right down to the beautiful quarter-cut veneer that covered the top. I gave it a final rinse of methyl hydrate and left it to dry before laying on the shellac and wax. When I returned to refinish it two days later, Joseph had repainted it in bright yellow enamel. When we sat at it together he would stroke the surface with an occasional smile in my direction.

There were five of us. Joseph and Annie, myself, and the boys, Jaimie and Erin. Annie had told them about Clarke's offer, and there was a lot of discussion. There wasn't a person there who hadn't had trouble with the police at one time or another.

"Even if we believed him, how do we know that Danny really wants to cooperate?" Jaimie was always the slow, thoughtful one. "You only talked to him for a minute, he was drugged, you can't be sure. It's his call," he added.

I could see it wasn't going to work like this.

"There is something else," I said. "I haven't quite told you everything. I want you to promise me something." I went slowly, feeling my way along. "I want you to promise me we will handle it my way. You either stay out altogether, or we do it my way."

"What the hell are you talking about? Stay out?" Erin flushed in anger. "He is our brother, we will do whatever we have to."

"Hear him out," Jaimie said quietly.

"The police statement said that there was one bullet in Danny, a .32 slug in the back. I looked at Danny in the hospital. There was a dressing on his lower chest and stomach, and I took it off. Underneath is a long knife wound running from above his groin up to the chest bone. His partners cut him open after he took the bullet. They didn't intend to leave him alive for the police."

There was a stunned silence.

"How do you want to handle it?" Jaimie asked in a soft voice, his eyes blazing.

Erin stood so abruptly his chair flew over backwards. "We'll find the bastards, that's what we'll do. And then we will do to them what they tried to do to Danny."

His voice was high and reckless, his lips drawn back from his teeth. The scar across his face pulsed with rage.

"And how does that help Danny?" Jaimie asked quietly. "Sit down and hear Jared out."

His big hand went out and pressed Erin gently back into his seat.

We sat around the big table for another couple of hours; they mostly listened while I talked. Annie made fresh coffee and we discussed it some more, and finally we were all agreed. Joseph sat there quietly the whole time, puffing slowly on his pipe.

CHAPTER 7

It was eleven thirty the following evening when I dropped the anchor in five fathoms of water inside Navvy Jack Point. I had slipped *Arrow* out of the berth in darkness with just a small headsail, letting the wind and current do the work. Once I was out into the channel, I dropped the sail and started the engine. There was about twelve knots of wind as I motored up to the point. If I had to go outside it later, there would be more. With luck it wouldn't be necessary.

While I waited I made a few changes in *Arrow*'s rig. I put a reef in the main and angled the boom so the aft end would swing across seven feet above the decks, then hung a two-part block on the end of it and ran a spare mainsail halyard down through so the snap shackle was extending downwards towards the deck. I took the other end at the mast and led it via a pair of blocks to the spinnaker winch and cleated it off. I was ready.

I leaned back against the coamings and waited. They should be coming soon. *Arrow* tugged against the anchor chain, her bow bobbing to the light chop. I had put down the small Danforth and a scant fifty feet of chain. No matter which way it went, we would not be here long. I watched the sky, drank coffee, and wished I still smoked.

It was forty-five minutes before I heard the outboard and another five before they pulled alongside. We had put peel-and-stick over *Arrow*'s lettering so they wouldn't have to blindfold Jaeger.

He was a creature of habit, and they had nabbed him when he came out of the bar on Howe Street at his usual time, eleven o'clock. He had been easy enough to find once we had the name — his business depended upon his being visible.

His headquarters was in the Excelsior, a fashionable bar near the Vancouver Stock Exchange. That made it easier: at night the area was deserted save for bar patrons and the occasional street person rummaging in the Dumpsters. Jaeger's practice was to attend the Excelsior each night around eight, make his contacts, and depart at eleven for the drive back to his home in the British Properties.

Annie had borrowed a nondescript white Plymouth for the evening and spread mud over the licence plates. Jaimie and Erin had gone into the bar at ten while Annie and Joseph waited in the car. When the boys saw Jaeger getting up to leave, Jaimie walked out the door in front of him, while Erin closed in behind.

They had him inside the car before Jaeger knew what had happened. Annie explained that someone wished to talk to him privately, and Jaeger inclined his head in polite acknowledgement. He was relaxed and sat quietly. The boys said the only time he showed any signs of nervousness was when they climbed down the dock ladder into the dinghy.

I reached over the side and helped him aboard *Arrow*. He climbed in through the lifelines gate, a small, dapper man with a three-piece herringbone suit, a grey homburg, and the air of a city banker. He sat down in the cockpit, crossed his legs fastidiously, shot his cuffs and acknowledged me with a nod. He pulled out a silver cigarette case, offered it around, and then lit up with a silver Dunhill. He inhaled deeply, looked down and inspected his gleaming black shoes, then brushed a fleck of dirt off his trousers.

"Now then, gentlemen," he said, "how may I be of service?"

You had to like his style. Jaimie and Erin moved up to the bow, their cigarettes glowing in the darkness.

"We are friends of Danny MacLean," I said.

He reflected for a moment. "Ah. The young man in the hospital. How is he?"

"Not very well," I said.

"I'm very sorry to hear that." He seemed genuinely concerned.

"He will likely require some expensive treatment for a long time, and we thought perhaps his ex-partners might like to contribute."

Jaeger smiled faintly. "I would have thought that Her Majesty's Government would be looking after all of that."

"He may be paralyzed. We might be looking at a lifetime scenario."

He showed the first sign of impatience. "And what does any of this have to do with me?"

"We thought you might be able to put us into contact with the men in question."

He smiled. "Even assuming that I knew the names of the two gentlemen, you must surely understand that the essence of my profession is confidentiality. If I were to reveal names, my business would be at an end. And, conceivably, my existence as well. What you ask is impossible."

I nodded. "There is something you may not know. Danny was knifed by his partners. After he was shot. They gutted him and left him to bleed to death in the street."

Jaeger frowned in distaste. "I hadn't heard that."

I showed him some pictures. Polaroids that Annie had taken when the police officer went upstairs for his cigarette. The bandages were pulled back and the wound shone wetly in the flash.

"Yes, well, it doesn't surprise me, I'm afraid. Regrettable. But unfortunately it doesn't change anything."

"We will pay you for the names. Five thousand dollars."

"It isn't a question of money."

"I can absolutely guarantee our discretion. There will be no come-backs." I stood up and stretched my shoulders. A moment later I heard the soft chink of the chain as the anchor started to come in.

"I really am sorry," Jaeger said. "But it is absolutely out of the question."

"Is that your final word?"

"Yes." He stood as if to leave.

I shoved him back down. "No sense in wasting a nice breeze. Seeing as we are out here anyway, we might as well go for a sail."

The anchor clanked aboard, Jaimie pulled up the ready-hanked jib, and *Arrow* slowly started to make way.

Jaeger tried to stand again. "I don't really think . . ."

Erin's big hands gripped his shoulders. "Relax. We're really very good at this."

"We'd better put on life jackets," Jaimie said. "It's a dark night, and if anyone fell over we would have a hell of a time spotting them in the water."

"You're absolutely right," Erin growled. "Especially if they hap-pened to be wearing a dark-coloured suit."

They stood Jaeger up and fastened his life jacket around him and cinched it up tight, then sat him back down directly under the boom on the port side.

"You had better hook on a safety line as well," I said. "Just in case."

"Good thinking, Captain."

Erin reached up and brought down the halyard I'd reeved through the blocks earlier and clipped it on to the stainless ring sewn on the back of Jaeger's life jacket.

We were running downwind now, doing a slow three knots.

"Hoist the mainsail," I called out.

I swung the tiller slightly, Jaimie hauled and Erin tailed, and the mainsail filled directly above Jaeger. *Arrow* edged up to five knots.

"I really wish you would change your mind," I said.

"No."

He stared defiantly up at me. But he wasn't so relaxed now. He was braced back against the coamings, his hands tightly gripped about his knees.

"Okay. Fuck it, then. Let's go sailing."

I laid the tiller over thirty degrees, Jaimie cranked on the spare halyard, and Erin slipped the mainsheet. Jaeger rose up into the air with a startled yelp, and two seconds later was dangling off the boom, ten feet out from the side of the boat. He hadn't even grazed the lifelines on the way by. *Arrow* was doing six knots now, the motion quiet as we ran downwind.

"How about a beer?"

Erin disappeared below and returned with four cans. He opened them and passed a couple to Jaimie and me.

Jaeger was trying to curl his feet up on the boom, but with the sail up and filled hard, there wasn't much purchase. His hands were locked on the boom end, but his feet kept slipping off. I saw he had lost a shoe.

"Catch," hollered Erin and lobbed the can towards him. Jaeger flinched, and the beer sailed past.

"He doesn't want a beer," Jaimie said.

We drank ours and chatted for a bit. Jaimie stood up and squinted into the darkness.

"I think we're going to have to jibe, Skipper," he said.

"Really? But that will put us out into much rougher water," I replied. "Oh well.

"Don't worry," I called across to Jaeger. "This is a standard sailboat manoeuvre. We do it all the time."

He turned his head slightly and glared at me. If he wasn't such a gentleman, I would have sworn he said fuck you.

He was pale, but he was game.

"Helm's alee," I hollered as I swung the tiller through ninety degrees. Jaimie worked the mainsheet as the wind came across. He went a little slowly, and as the wind caught the main on the weather side, there was a few feet of slack. Jaeger went through the cockpit like a bullet from a gun as the boom slammed across. We all crouched as he went screaming over, and then there was a solid thud as the main came up on the traveller. Erin slacked on his halyard, and Jaeger was parallel with the boom four feet outboard before he dropped back down again and spun crazily. It was a rougher tack, and his feet were touching the water occasionally.

"That was just terrible," I said. "What will our guest think? We'd better have another beer and practise until we get it right."

We did two more jibes. Now that Jaeger knew what to expect, he didn't scream, just closed his eyes tight and tried to curl up as he careened across the decks.

If you have never sailed, it is hard to imagine the difference between the upwind and downwind legs. In a breeze of around fifteen knots, like we had that night, the apparent wind was eight or nine knots as you went with it. The boat was rolling a little, but the motion was easy, there was little spray or noise, and it all seemed very controlled. That was about to change.

"Hang on," I yelled to Jaeger as we brought *Arrow* around into the wind and hardened up on the main and jib sheets. We were still doing around seven knots, but now the apparent wind was twenty-two plus. *Arrow* was heeled sharply and sending spray over the decks as she knifed into the waves, and you had to yell to be heard.

"Tack," I screamed as I swung the helm and ducked. Jaeger blurred by in a sodden mess. The winches clattered and the jib snapped as it moved across and we lay down on the other course.

"Tack," I yelled again, and back we went, Jaeger unable to hang on now, just dangling limply as we sheeted in.

"Tack," I yelled again above the noise, and we began to swing again. "No," Jaeger said. "No."

We lowered him into the cockpit and stripped off his clothes. His face was pale and greasy, and he had thrown up on his suit. We had the Dickinson stove lit in the cabin, and Jaimie and I carried him below while Erin took the tiller. I rubbed him down with towels, keeping at it till some of the colour came back to his face. Jaimie passed him thermal underwear, a heavy flannel shirt, and a pair of wool fisherman pants. He put them on without a word, then took the coffee with the brandy in it and held it in his hands until he had stopped shivering long enough to drink from it without spilling.

"You did well," I said. "You lasted a long time."

"You've done this before?" he stuttered.

"No. But I didn't think you'd last near that long."

He finished his drink and handed me the cup, and I poured him another coffee. We were running in on a close reach, and the motion was easier. He took the brandy bottle and added a good inch to the coffee.

"Their names are Lebel. Henri and Claude, two brothers in their thirties. They came out from Quebec four months ago, and I heard they were dealing in high-grade cocaine. I was surprised to hear they had pulled the jewellery robbery. I have no idea how your friend got mixed up with them."

Neither did I. Danny never did drugs, not even the occasional joint when I offered. One of his uncles had died from an overdose, and he was a puritan on the subject.

"Where do they hang out?"

"I don't know. They were pointed out to me in the Excelsior when they first came to town, but that was a while ago. I haven't seen them since." He shrugged. "If I knew, I'd tell you."

He didn't seem concerned whether we believed him or not. We had enough anyway.

We were running smoothly now, back inside the lee of the point. The engine started up and Erin stuck his head in and nodded.

"Okay. We're back."

I handed Jaeger an envelope with five thousand dollars in it. He took out two thousand and threw the remainder down on the cabin sole.

"For the suit," he said. "You can throw it away."

He climbed out through the companionway and lowered himself into the dinghy, where he sat impassively, waiting for the boys. I thought that he had handled himself pretty well, considering.

Jaimie told me the next day that they had offered him a ride home.

"Fuck you," he'd said, "I would rather walk." And he marched off in his bare feet.

CHAPTER 8

Arthur Chin ran a martial arts school on Victoria Drive, and I some-times visited his dojo on a Saturday morning. I no longer took formal lessons but liked to work on my katas, and occasionally we would do some of the *jiyu kumite*, the free sparring. This morning he had some eight-year-olds on the mat, ten boys and a pair of girls. Their faces were deadly serious as they practised the *junzuki* lunge punch, taking little steps forward then crouching and thrusting out.

I leaned against the wall and watched them. Arthur was five-six, slender, with granny glasses and thin black hair, somewhere around thirty. He was good with the children, smiling and praising as he moved among them, correcting their poses. He looked a lot different than the first time I had seen him, and his lessons were easier.

I was in my first week of prison life when I encountered Arthur in the gym. A large hall had been fitted out with speed and weight bags, a pair of universal machines and some threadbare canvas mats. In one corner was a press bench with rows of stacked weights ranged alongside. The place was busy when I entered that first time, all the equipment in use and benches along the wall where men sat resting or waiting their turn. I wondered why the authorities would want to make the men in this room any more dangerous than they already were. Maybe they thought the workouts cut down on jail sex.

The windows were set high and barred, but apart from that it looked and smelled like all the other gyms I had spent time in over the years. In the far corner, a group of Asians were fooling around on the mat, mock-fighting with a lot of laughter and exaggerated yelling. One of them seemed to be the leader, a skinny kid with shoulder-length jet-black hair and a red bandanna tying it off his face. He was lightning-quick and took on the others in rapid succession, spinning, ducking, and kicking in graceful acrobatic sequence.

There was a heavy canvas weight bag across from them and I went over, did some light stretches, and began to work on the bag. I was prac-tising side kicks, pivoting and thrusting and trying to increase my ver-tical reach, when I became aware of someone watching me. It was the kid with the red bandanna. Arthur used his gang name in those days.

"Not bad," he said.

"Not in your class, though," I acknowledged.

"Oh, I don't know, some practice, maybe a few lessons."

His friends had stayed on the other side of the room. They were looking over at us with little smiles on their faces.

"You'd give me lessons?" I asked warily.

"Sure," he said.

And then he drop-kicked me in the face.

I had been half expecting something, but I was totally unprepared for the speed and viciousness of the attack. It caught me just under the nose and split my lips wide open. The coppery taste of blood filled my mouth. Before I could react, he hit me again, directly on the nose this time, and I heard the cartilage crunch. I tried to chop him and he grabbed my arm, spun, and threw me casually over his hip. I was pushing myself to my feet when he kicked me again. There was an agonizing pain in my ribs. It felt like he had broken one.

I lay there for a moment, listening to the sudden quiet in the gym.

It was difficult to breathe, and I could hear my snuffling in the silence. I started to get to my feet again and Arthur glided in with little dancing steps, his hands extended in front of him.

"I think that's enough practice for today, boys," said one of the weightlifters. It was the big Haida I had ridden down to prison with in the van. Danny smiled pleasantly at Arthur, then turned his back on him and helped me up.

Arthur shrugged. "Whatever."

Two of the guards walked over from the door where they had been watching. They had their billies out and were slapping them gently on their palms.

"Okay, Chin. That's it. Back to the hole. You should get at least two weeks this time."

I wondered how long they would have let it go. Until he killed me, so they could get him for murder? Arthur held his hands out for the cuffs, his face impassive.

"No," I said, enunciating carefully through my smashed lips. "We were just practising. I slipped and the timing missed." I should have stayed away from the S-words.

The big guard looked at me for a moment then shrugged. "Okay. No skin off my ass," he said.

"Or nothe or lipth either," the little one added, and they snickered and walked away.

I went to the prison infirmary and they swabbed and set my nose and put a dozen stitches in my lips. My ribs were sore, but they didn't think they were broken and it didn't warrant a trip to the hospital for an X-ray. They taped my chest up tightly and said if it still hurt in a week to come back.

It was ten days later that I went back to the gym. My ribs were still tender, but it was only bruised muscles. I was taking it easy, just getting the kinks out and a slow sweat starting to build, when I noticed Arthur standing at the edge of the mat, watching. I turned towards him and held up my hands.

"No more lessons," I said. "I just got finished sounding like Daffy Duck."

He smiled and floated up and kicked the bag ten inches above where I had been working.

"You're not pushing hard enough off your back foot," he said. "You have to crouch lower, lift right from the waist."

And we became friends.

Arthur's original sentence had been for two years, but he kept finding ways to extend it, and it was another three years before he was finally released. It had been a good season and I was celebrating with friends in the Harlequin when Arthur drifted in one night and sat in the corner. I took my beer and went over. We shook hands and smiled at each other. His clothes were shabby and he had none of the old dash. He told me he had been out for three months. He said he'd been looking around but hadn't found anything yet.

"Not a lot of jobs for ex-cons," he said, "and I'm getting a little long in the tooth for the gang scene."

His family was well off, but there had been recriminations when he went to prison, and he would never ask them for help. He'd been around to the docks and picked up a few days' work and laboured in construction for a week or so but hadn't found much else.

I knew how it worked. You picked up a day here, a few dollars there, and after a while when you were down enough and desperate enough, somebody came along with a score. And maybe it went down okay, then you did another job and that worked out too, but sooner or later you ended up back inside. I had been lucky: Danny had got me on the fishing boats.

"I've been thinking I might like to open a martial arts school."

"Yeah, well, you know how to do that all right," I said, and we both smiled, remembering.

"I've still got a rep in the old neighbourhood," he said. "I'd get some of that crowd, and I think I could pull in some straights too. All that oriental kung fu shit is becoming fashionable."

"Sounds like a plan."

"I'd only need about six thousand dollars. There's a place on Victoria Drive that would do; rent is seven hundred a month including a little suite in back. A few mats, some posters and signs. Ten grand would keep me going for six months — by then I'd make it or be flat broke." He shrugged. "I can likely get the money, but, you know."

I knew. He'd get it illegally and maybe if he was lucky he wouldn't get caught, but it was always tricky, and some people would know. And when people knew, they had power over you.

"I'll loan you the money," I said suddenly, surprising myself.

"No, I don't think so."

"Listen, I've just come back from the grounds, I have twenty-five grand in the bank, and I don't owe anybody a dime. It's mid-September now and my next trip is in April. If I don't lend you the money I'll be broke by then, I always am. If I loan you the money I'll still be broke by April, but at least someone will owe me. Believe me, it's not a big deal."

I drank some beer while Arthur watched me with an inscrutable look on his face.

"You'd do it for me," I said.

"No, actually, I'm quite sure I wouldn't," he said. I looked into those opaque eyes. I never was one hundred percent sure with Arthur. Then he grinned. "Yes. Thank you."

In a month Arthur had twelve regulars; in three months he was making expenses. He repaid the first three thousand the following March, and it kept me going until the fishing started. When I got back to Vancouver that fall, Arthur paid me off. He had been to a lawyer and drawn up an agreement, and I had ten percent of the business. I didn't want it, but he seemed to need to do it, and I finally accepted. I received a small cheque every quarter, and after a couple of years they weren't so small.

Arthur had married one of his students, a lawyer named Nancy who specialised in labour law, and they had two daughters now. After the first one, his mother had come by, and Arthur had eventually been reconciled with his father and taken back into the family.

I leaned against the wall of the gym, thinking how casual my original gesture had been and how it had all worked out. I tried to tell Arthur later on, to explain that although it might have had large consequences for him, the loan was insignificant on my part, and the ten percent was excessive and out of proportion. He listened carefully as I spoke, then put his arm around my shoulder and squeezed.

"Stay away from the philosophy, Round-Eyes, it's not your strong point."

He had finished with the class now, and they made their formal bows to him. Nancy appeared out of the back with drinks and cookies, and the students rushed over, yelling. Changed back from warriors to little kids in a second.

Arthur and Nancy had bought the building, renovated the upstairs into living quarters, and made his former suite into an office. They had kept the tiny kitchenette, and Nancy made us tea. Arthur and I sat and drank it out of tiny cups; it was sweet and hot.

"I heard about Danny," he said. "Tough."

"Yes. I have the names of his ex-partners. I'm going to find them and bring them in."

Arthur's eyebrows rose a millimetre. This was a big reaction.

"I'm talking with a detective named Clarke. I think we can make a deal, and Danny shouldn't do much over a year. Maybe less," I said, thinking about the drugs. "It's two brothers. The Lebels. They're dealing as well and shouldn't be too hard to find. You still see some of the old faces?"

"Occasionally. I'll make a few phone calls. Are you just going to give them up?"

"More or less," I said. "I haven't completely worked it out yet."

"Well, if it turns out to be more, I would be glad to pay them a visit with you."

He poured out more tea, a slight, scholarly looking fellow who could likely kill you several different ways before you even knew it.

"Thanks, Arthur. I'll keep that in mind."

But I knew I wouldn't take him up on it. He had a wife and family now. We finished our tea and he started making phone calls. I said my goodbyes to Nancy and left. She always looked slightly relieved at my departure, still a little wary of any of Arthur's friends from the old days.

❀

On my way back, I stopped in at the hospital and had a look in at Danny. There was no change. I talked to the officer for a while, and then the little nurse came in. They greeted each other with big smiles and looked at me reproachfully until I got up and left.

I spent the rest of the day working on *Arrow* until it became too dark to see, and then I went inside and listened to the Canucks lose a close one to Toronto. I had just turned off the late news when there was a quick rap on the hull. A thin, weedy Asian guy was standing on the dock.

"Arthur sent me."

"Come aboard."

"No."

He looked nervously around and then walked away. I jumped down and headed after him. We stopped in the shadows by the Dumpsters.

"I get my stuff from these two brothers." His head was constantly swivelling around. "You can't say I sent you." He wiped his nose. "I usually meet them Mondays at the Arctic. Between eight and ten. They go there sometimes for lunch too, but they told me not to come then. You be there at night, and you'll see me. Don't talk to me, don't come up to me while I'm there."

He looked over his shoulder.

"I wouldn't do this except for Arthur. He helped my family when I was inside."

"You haven't done anything," I said. "I won't even be talking to them at the hotel. I promise you." I handed him a couple of twenties.

"Good," he said, and went scuttling off down the docks, nervous as a cat.

❁

I went down to Rent-A-Wreck Monday morning and took the cheapest vehicle they had, a nondescript brown Toyota. I waited until the lunch hour rush was over then left it in the Arctic parking lot, paying for the entire evening. I had time to kill and walked over to Powell Street, where I browsed some chandleries and picked up a few bits and pieces I still needed for *Arrow*. Afterwards I went back through Chinatown and into the Back Door restaurant for a meal. I figured on being at the Arctic for a while, and people who didn't drink would be viewed with suspicion. Best to line my stomach first.

The waiter knew me, and I asked him to bring the special. He returned with a bowl of rice and a plate on which three little fish with accusing eyes lay on a bed of chilis and a muddy green vegetable that looked like what I had scraped off *Arrow*'s hull. The dish was excellent and I asked the waiter the name of it. He pronounced it slowly and carefully and unintelligibly. I'd had a dozen great meals there and would never be able to order any of them again. I paid my bill, left a tip, and walked over to the hotel.

The Arctic was an upscale jock bar decorated with sporting paraphernalia from various Canadian pro teams. On one wall they had three of the numbered Gretzky prints by LeRoy Neiman, under glass and spotlighted along with an old Oilers ninety-nine sweater from the glory years. In the corner, a big-screen TV was showing a Canucks game. I sat facing the screen with my back to the wall. There were about thirty people in the bar, most of them drinking beer and watching the hockey game. I ordered a pint and settled in. It was midway through the second period and the Canucks were up a goal, but Montreal was pressing. Gallagher bounced one off a post on a power play and the crowd sighed in relief.

At eight thirty the little junkie came in and sat at a corner table. The waiter came over and dropped off a shot. He drank it quickly and headed for the washroom. A minute later a stocky man with black oiled hair got up from one of the tables and worked his way across the room, exchanging greetings and catcalls with some of the patrons. He went into the restroom and came out after a couple of minutes, returning to his table, where another man was sitting. Montreal had scored in his absence and they slapped hands. I saw the little addict slip out of the restroom and leave the bar.

I stayed in my seat and drank beer and watched the game. The two brothers were cheering loudly with every Montreal rush now, and the rest of the bar was good-naturedly ragging them. With thirty seconds left in regulation time, Montreal scored again. There was a loud groan from the room, and several people went over to the Lebels and dropped money on the table. The brothers stayed for another hour and then they left. During the time I was there, one or the other of them had gone to the restroom a half dozen times, and twice out into the lobby.

I followed them out. They walked down Davie for two blocks and entered the Starlite Club. I jogged back to the Arctic and picked my rental up from the lot. There was a slot open half a block down, and I jockeyed the Toyota into it and shut off the engine. I found some blues on the radio and hunkered down to wait.

It was two o'clock before the Lebels emerged from the club. They had two women in tow, and everyone was very friendly. There was a lot of giggling and whooping and grabbing as the girls teetered along in their high heels. It looked like the beginning of a long night.

They crowded into a taxi and headed past me along Davie Street. I pulled out and followed a hundred yards behind. After a dozen blocks they turned down Thurlow and stopped in front of one of the classic old apartment blocks that dotted the neighborhood. I parked back a ways, got out of the car, and started walking slowly towards them. They paid off the taxi and entered the building as I came abreast. Through the glass entryway I could see them waiting in front of the elevator. I bent down and tied my laces, and when they got in I went over and checked the bell rings. No names, only suite numbers, one to thirty-four.

The elevator had an old needle dial above the door, and I watched it stutter along until it stopped at eight. I crossed quickly over the road and looked up. No lights on the top floor. I jogged around to the south side and looked up. Still no lights. By the time I reached the other sides, there were lights on in both suites. So, assuming the closest one to the main entrance was number one, they were in thirty-three or thirty-four. I walked back to the car and waited. There was a talk show on the radio now; a lady had fallen in love with her brother-in-law and desperately needed advice. And me with no phone.

At three thirty the door opened and the two women came out of the apartment. They had taken off their high heels and were in stocking feet. One of them had her head down, crying; the other had her arm around her. A cab pulled up and stopped in front of the apartment, and they climbed in and drove away. I waited for fifteen minutes then got out of the Toyota and went to the door. I pressed numbers thirty-three and thirty-four for a few seconds each. Thirty-three lit up and a voice growled, "What the fuck?"

"Your taxi, sir."

"Those fucking hoors left twenty minutes ago, asshole."

The light blinked off. A pronounced French accent.

"Bonsoir, mes braves," I murmured. I turned and walked back to the car. There was a guy on the radio now, he hadn't been able to make love to his wife for a month. He was worried he might be gay. Several chaps called in. Two of them wanted dates.

I drove back to the boat and tried to sleep, but I was too wound up. I did some yoga, the relaxing asanas, and a long headstand, but it was not enough. A secret part of me wanted violence.

I went forward to where the mast support ran down from the over-head, and stepped to *Arrow*'s keel. The massive post had been whipped in white cotton line, each thin coil knotted at two-inch intervals and the whole done over in thick coats of white lead paint. I started with the low, thrusting katas, chopping slowly at the finish, my hands just stopping short. Gradually I stood upright, moving more quickly, wheeling and striking, rising up on the ball and toe of each foot alternately, backhanding and undercutting.

As I picked up speed I let my hands extend and began to strike the column with the half fist and the sides of my palms. I danced and worked, stripped in the golden oiled light until my body glistened with sweat and my hands were flashing knives. Faster and faster until my senses blurred and the post turned ruddy and my arms became leaden and numb.

Afterwards I went outside and the rain lashed down and cleansed me. I stayed there until I began to shiver then went below and towelled dry. I drank a long hot toddy and fell asleep on the saloon settee.

CHAPTER 9

I phoned the police station early the following morning and left an urgent message for Clarke to contact me. He hadn't returned my call by ten, and I was getting nervous. Erin came by to pick me up, and we drank coffee and waited. At ten thirty the phone finally rang.

"Clarke here." He didn't sound happy.

"Danny came to for a couple of minutes," I said. "He was confused, not making much sense, but I managed to get something out of him."

"Where was the guard?"

"He was out of the room. Gone for a smoke, likely. You have to go out on the roof now, you know. Jaimie said there's often more medical staff up there than in all the rest of the wards put together."

I was talking too much.

"When was this?"

"Well, a couple of days ago, actually."

"A couple of days?" Clarke screamed.

"It was mostly nonsense," I said, "just garbled up." I took a deep breath. "He said something about the Bell Brothers. We asked around and came up with a guy who might know them."

"Bell Brothers, Bell Brothers," Clarke muttered.

"I'm meeting the man this morning. He said he's heard something is happening today. He thinks maybe they live in an apartment on Thurlow Street. He's going to give me the address."

"The Bell Brothers," Clarke said again. "Goddammit, I should know that name."

"Look, Clarke, hold off till noon, okay? I'll get the address for you. You can pick them up. I heard the guys were into dealing as well."

There was a long pause. I could hear Clarke's heavy breathing over the phone.

"All right, Jared. Just what the fuck is going on?"

"Just until noon, Clarke. I want you to have a chance at nailing these guys. In a deal, maybe. My contact will have the address for me and maybe something more."

"Look," Clarke said. "If I had a statement from Danny I could maybe get a search warrant and go in. With just your word and no witnesses, it wouldn't fly."

"Damn," I said.

"You come in here and we'll take a sworn statement and see if we can't locate these brothers and get a search warrant and go in. I'll have a man tail you when you meet your contact. These men are dangerous."

"I know. I saw the knife wound."

"I couldn't tell you. So come in now and we'll cover you."

"I don't have time. Besides, the guy is nervous already. One smell of cops and he'll bolt and then we'll have nothing."

"I want you down here, Jared. Now!"

"I'll phone you the minute I have the address."

"Jared! Goddammit! Get your fucking ass —" Clarke was still screaming as I slammed down the phone. Erin raised an eyebrow.

"He loves the plan," I said. "Time to get started."

Erin grabbed the parcels and we jogged down the wharf. I groaned when I saw Danny's red pickup.

"Sarah got called in to work and took the car," Erin said. "We can catch a taxi if you like."

"That's probably worse. The hell with it. Let's go." I glanced at my watch. "We're on a tight schedule, they probably leave for the bars around eleven thirty or so."

The flat box held an old UPS uniform and cap. While Erin drove I changed. The coat was a mile too big for me, but the hat fit fairly well. Glimpsed briefly through a peephole, I should pass.

"It's an old one of Danny's. Annie cleaned and ironed it. We'll dump it later."

"Thirty minutes, Erin. A full half hour. If I'm not out by then, call the cops."

"I still think I should go in with you."

"No. They'd never let us in. Not two guys, especially one who looks like you. No offence, Erin," I added hastily as the big, scarred head swivelled and stared at me.

"Watch the road!" I screamed.

He was doing a hundred klicks and passing everything. I prayed we wouldn't get pulled over. I checked my watch as we turned into the alley across from the apartment building. Eleven fifteen. We should be in time. If they had left, we would have to try again that evening or the next day and hope that Clarke didn't get there first. I had given him the street and the names were close enough. He was nobody's fool.

"Okay, give me the whisky. Thirty minutes. If I'm not out by eleven fifty call it in. I'll meet you in the alley by the pay phone. Try and look inconspicuous."

He rumbled off, smiling.

I picked up the case of Glenfiddich and went up the stairs and set it down by the bell rings and stared at them as if searching for a name. This was the tricky part. I could phone them if I had to, but it would be better if they weren't expecting me. With this many apartments, there was a fair chance someone would be coming or going soon.

I saw the elevator needle move, and after a minute the door opened and a well-dressed elderly couple emerged and walked towards me. As the man opened the lobby door, I said "Thank you, ma'am" into the speaker, picked up my case of whisky, and moved quickly past them. The old gentleman looked at the label on the box and nodded in approval.

I crossed to the elevator and stepped in. I was trembling, and my finger slipped off the eight the first time. I placed the case on the floor and began breathing deeply as I pulled on the soft leather gloves. I concentrated hard and thought of Danny, and brought up a picture of him lying in his bed, his eyes closed, not moving. My breathing slowed and steadied and an icy cold rose up from deep within me. I kept Danny's picture and moved it into the back of my mind as I left the elevator and walked down the hall to number thirty-three.

I reached out and pressed the buzzer, and my finger was as steady as the barrel of a gun. After a short wait, an eye looked out the peephole. I stepped back so he could see the whisky. I think I was smiling. I had planned to talk myself in, but as I watched, the door opened a crack and a head looked out over the chain, and before anyone could speak the man in the UPS uniform holding the case of whisky floated up in the air and his leg arced out like a sledge and the door crashed open and the man inside flew across the room.

I came through the door low, kicking it shut and looking eagerly for the other man. There, at the table, his hands frozen around a cup of coffee.

"No," he said. "Don't kill me. Please. Look, we've got it, it's still here. Please!"

His voice rose up in a scream and I hit him and he flew back and slammed against the table and was silent.

The first man was lying on the floor, moaning softly and holding his shoulder. I went over and lifted his head up by the hair.

"Shut up," I said.

"I'll get it. Please." He was crying. "Don't. Please."

I picked him up and he started to scream and I put my hand over his mouth.

"If you make another fucking sound, I promise I will kill you," I whispered into his ear.

He nodded frantically, his eyes bulging.

"You'll be quiet now," I said, and I removed my hand.

He went over to the living room wall and knelt on the couch. His right shoulder looked two inches lower. He knocked the picture aside and there was a wall safe. He clumsily twirled the knob back and forth with his left hand. There was a click and it opened. He reached in and I leaned past him.

"This what you're looking for?" I asked, and pulled out the revolver.

"No," he said. "The money, it's all there."

I turned my back on him and looked in the safe and listened. *Go for it*, I thought. *Please*. When I heard the whisper of cloth I spun and he had the knife halfway out, his face twisted with rage and pain. I hit him and I felt the bone break under my hand and he fell back unconscious.

Good.

Back to the safe. There was a black leather briefcase at the front. It was stuffed with bundles of money. I pulled a couple out. Hundreds. I ripped them open and scattered them on the kitchen table. Back to the safe. Small plastic packets. I ripped one open. Cocaine. Back to the table, spread it around. The one by the sofa had his head twisted back and his nostrils flared up at me, the septum red and inflamed. I opened a packet and dumped it in and he choked and coughed.

Good.

I checked the time. Eleven thirty. I turned to the safe again. There were some larger plastic packets stacked behind the briefcase. A lot of them. And right at the very back, two canvas bags. Rings, bracelets, necklaces.

I went to the phone and dialled nine eleven. I held a cloth over the mouthpiece.

"Police," I yelled. "Help. They're killing each other."

"Yes sir. Would you please give . . ."

"My God!" I screamed. "I think I heard shots. Quick. Twenty-eight hundred Thurlow. Top floor. Oh my God."

"Give me your name and . . ."

"Eighth floor. Twenty-eight hundred Thurlow. Hurry."

I slammed the phone down and raced back to the safe. I grabbed some packets of money and stuffed them in my coat pockets. I shoved everything else back in the safe and ran over to the side window and looked out. A woman was sitting in a lounge chair reading in a backyard across the street. Nothing directly below. I picked up the case of Scotch and threw it at the window. There was a loud crash as it shattered. I took the gun and fired a shot out the hole. It wasn't silenced, and I heard a scream. I fired a second shot into the couch, flung the gun to the carpet, and sprinted out the door and across to the stairs. Everything was quiet in the apartment block. I jogged down to the basement and went out through the garage. As I turned into the alley, I could hear the first sirens. Erin collected me and we drove sedately away.

✸

I called Clarke at noon from a downtown coffee shop, but he wasn't in. I tried again every ten minutes after that until they finally got sick of me and patched me through.

"Clarke. It's me, Jared."

"Yeah. I'm kind of busy just now."

"I have the address for you. Twenty-eight hundred Thurlow. The Bess apartments. Number thirty-three. And the name is Lebel. The Lebel Brothers, not Bell. It's French. L-E-B- . . ."

"I've got it," Clarke said.

"The guy said there was supposed to be a meet there today. This morning sometime. Christ, I've been calling you since before noon."

"Since before noon."

"Yeah. The guy was a bit late, didn't show up until eleven thirty. And then he was scared. I had to give him more money."

"What was this guy's name?"

"Christ, I don't know, that wasn't part of the deal. But he gave me the names and address. It's like Danny said. It's his tip."

"Yeah, it's his tip," Clarke said. "I'm busy, but I'll be talking to you later. Don't go anywhere in the meantime."

"Be careful. They could be armed and dangerous."

The phone slammed in my ear.

Erin drove back to the boat and we sat there drinking coffee and listening to the radio. Nothing. The six o'clock news carried a brief report of a disturbance in the West End, sounds of shots being fired, police were called in, no official comment.

I opened a bottle of Scotch and we had a few drinks while we waited for something to happen. Nothing did. The eleven o'clock news had dropped the story altogether, and finally Erin left and I went to bed.

❀

A trawler had come in overnight and tied up at the end of the dock while it waited to unload at the cannery. The crew was cleaning the net and throwing the junk over the side, and the seagulls' squabbling woke me up. I knew one of the men and went over for coffee. They'd had a poor trip, and the prices were down. We bitched for a while about American draggers inside the limits and the soft Canadian government, and then it was their turn to unload. I untied their lines and walked back to *Arrow*. The phone was ringing when I stepped aboard. It was Clarke.

"Good morning, Jared." He sounded cheerful. "You going to be around for a while?"

"Actually, I was just leaving for the hospital."

"Good. I'll come down and pick you up." He hung up without waiting for my reply.

I leaned back against the settee and thought about making a pot of coffee. Something pushed against my hips. It was the rolled-up uniform lying where I had thrown it the night before. Shit. I'd meant to dump it.

I picked up the pants and felt the bulk in the pockets. Christ. The money. I had forgotten. I pulled out the neat bundles. Five of them. They contained Canadian hundreds, fifty in each. That would make twenty-five thousand dollars, something to tide Danny over. Not enough, I hoped, for anybody to get too excited about.

Except the last bundle was different. It held American thousand-dollar bills, and there were a hundred of them.

Oh fuck, I thought. But I didn't want to deal with it right now. I put all the money in a zip-lock bag and stowed it in the deepest part of the bilge, jamming it up hard under the oak knees. I took the uniform and rolled it up tight and stuffed it into a garbage bag and emptied the coffee pot grounds over it, then buried it in the big Dumpster on the dock. I was back on *Arrow*, fresh coffee just starting to perk, when Clarke arrived.

"Permission to come aboard?"

"Don't tell me," I said. "You've been reading up on your sailboat etiquette. Do you have your snappy docksider boat shoes on?"

He swung smoothly over the side. "In my business, Jared, you must be a man of many parts."

"Do you have time for coffee? It's fresh."

"Yes."

His eyes fell on the bottle of Glenfiddich.

"Well, well. What a coincidence."

He picked up the bottle and poured a shot into his coffee.

"You have expensive tastes."

"We get it duty-free for halibut season. We fish offshore long enough to qualify. When you take away the tax, the difference between cheap and expensive is only a few dollars spread among six or seven men. At the end of the season, Customs are pretty good about the odd case or two left over. We split it up among the crew."

It was just an unfortunate coincidence. I had asked Erin to pick up a case of decent Scotch to get me into the apartment, and he had happened to buy Glenfiddich.

"Well, anyway, the other case was all full. Busted to ratshit though, of course. Hell of a waste." He shook his head and took an appreciative sip of his coffee.

"What in God's name are you talking about, anyway?"

"Oh, right. You don't know, do you? The Lebel Brothers. That's L-E-B-E-L, Jared." He spelled it out. "We nabbed them. With the goods, so to speak. There was a fight, a bunch of coke lying around. We got a call just before noon, a disturbance, sound of shots. On Thurlow. When I heard the address, I peeled over as well. Hell of a mess. One brother's lying face down on the table, nose broken, head busted open, money and coke all over the place. The other one is lying on the floor by the sofa, doing the chicken. Shoulder is dislocated, jaw broken, lips all smashed. The window is broken; someone threw a case of whisky through it."

He paused in reflection, then said: "Why would anyone want to do that? There were lots of kitchen chairs lying around. Cheap vinyl and chrome, who would've fucking cared?"

He shook his head sadly. "Anyway. Where was I? Oh yes. Gun is lying on the carpet, there's a safe behind the sofa. The brother on the floor he gives us the combination later. The coke and the money, he knows he's all done up. We find a lot of jewellery, looks like the Granville Street job, the insurance boys are checking now. Oh yes, and the coke in the safe. A lot of coke, over half a million dollars' worth, plus another two hundred grand in cash."

"That's great," I said.

"Oh yes."

His coffee was halfway down, and he casually topped it up with the Glenfiddich.

"The chief was so thrilled he nearly wet himself. Lots of PR on this one. He's holding a press conference this afternoon." Clarke smiled cynically. "Got to catch the early news."

"So everybody is happy."

"Well, almost everybody. Of course, there are a few little questions remaining. Like what really happened in the apartment."

He looked at me over the rim of his cup. I waited. He waited. To pass the time, I put some Scotch in my cup. He was still waiting patiently.

"Well, maybe they had an argument," I volunteered at last.

Clarke beamed at me. "We know they were drinking the night before, at a club on Davies. They left with a couple of hookers and partied till four o'clock. The boys were getting a little mean by then, and one of them knocked the girls around a bit. They were glad to help us out. So maybe then they sat around for the rest of the night, drinking and doing coke, and got into an argument."

"Sounds good to me."

Clarke looked at me pityingly.

"And then they get into a fight and practically kill each other, and fire off a couple of shots that don't hit anybody. Then they decide to throw a case of whisky through the window and wait for the cops to come. Oh. And the door chain. It's busted. Did I mention that?"

We each took a long drink.

"What do the Lebels say?" I finally asked.

"One is still in hospital after getting his jaw wired up, the other one is in the slammer. Neither is talking at present. I assume when they get together with their lawyer they will think of something to say."

"What do you think happened?" I asked.

"We questioned all the tenants; nobody seems to have heard anything. One couple were leaving the building around eleven fifteen, they say a messenger was just entering. Not much of a description. Medium height, slim build, pale. He was carrying a case of Glenfiddich."

He stared at me impassively.

"A rip-off?" I asked.

"Yes! That's what we thought."

Thought! I thought. Not think. I wanted another drink of my laced coffee but was afraid my hands would shake. Clarke abandoned any pretence of coffee and filled his cup with straight Scotch. He topped mine up as well, and I thought what the hell and took a big slug.

"The busted door chain might be a few days old, the guys aren't really sure. But say the messenger uses the Scotch to get in, something happens, there's a fight, a lot of noise. He panics and runs out."

"Sounds good to me."

My voice sounded a bit shaky. I wasn't used to this early-morning drinking.

"Yes," Clarke said. "That's what I figured. So I go back to the station and check out the calls. We log them all. This one came in at eleven thirty-eight." He waited expectantly.

"So?"

"We have a tattletale phone system. It shows the calling number and we log that as well." Clarke gave me a shark-like smile.

"And?"

"And the phone call came from inside the Lebel suite."

"Oh," I said. "Well I'll be damned."

We sat in silence for a minute, and then I finished my drink and stood up.

"Time to go to the hospital," I said brightly.

"Sit!" Clarke thundered.

I sat. He poured the last of the bottle into his cup and sat frowning over it.

"Your friend in the hospital might just be lucky," he said at last. "He may just slip right out of this. I told the chief that Danny gave us the names, and his official statement will include the fact that the third suspect in the case remains in a coma in hospital. That will protect Danny, and we get the credit for good police work. The chief will also release the facts about the knifing. There will be a certain amount of sympathy for Danny, and those eastern villains should carry most of the weight. I've talked to Montreal, and they were well known there. A very mean pair, some extortion, some muscle work, likely even a couple of killings, although that can't be proven."

He stared at me and spoke slowly.

"Everyone wants to clear this up, Jared. There were a couple of other calls around the same time from neighbours across the way who saw the glass go and heard the shots. The original call might even get lost, it's not all that important." He drained his drink. "What is important is that we put these guys away, and everybody forgets about all of this and gets on with their lives." He scowled fiercely at me. "Do I make myself clear?"

"Crystal, sir," I replied.

"Good."

He rose to his feet and slapped me on the shoulder.

"Let's go and see your friend, then. I have a feeling this might be a lucky day for him, the day he comes around."

❀

When we arrived in Danny's room, Annie was bent over his bed and they were talking. She turned and wrapped her arms around me, and we hugged in silence. Clarke had a few words with Danny, and the next day he took a full statement of the robbery from him.

By that time the police chief had delivered a full-blown press conference in which the inference was clear that Danny was just a dumb homeboy who had been victimized by the Montreal mafia. The general implication from the media was that he had probably been drunk at the time and not really aware of what he was doing.

I didn't much care what they said or thought, as long as he got off. I slipped out of the room and headed out into the rain and jogged back to *Arrow*.

CHAPTER 10

By morning the rain had stopped and the wind had swung to the northwest, clearing the sky. The sunlight had that extra post-storm brilliance, reflecting on the puddles and sidewalks, refracting in each separate drop of moisture clinging to the trees and bridges of the city. It carried the preternatural clarity of one of the last summery days. The sidewalks were filled with people: joggers, cyclists, pedestrians, everyone smiling and breathing deeply, like prisoners relieved from siege. My mood had lifted with the weather, and I walked the whole way to the hospital, enjoying the bustle and general good spirits that surrounded me.

Danny looked much better. He was propped up in bed and smiled over the heads of his nieces and nephews when he saw me at the door. I walked over to him and we shook hands.

"Thanks," he said.

"You're welcome."

"Jaimie and Erin told me everything."

Not quite everything, I thought. Nobody knew about the money yet.

Danny shooed the kids away from the bed. He gave them a box of chocolates and told them to go out on the roof and bug all the staff who had sneaked up there for a smoke.

"What's new?" I asked when they'd left.

"The Brothers still aren't saying much. They said they were drinking and gambling all night and got into a drunken fight. They have no idea how all that stuff got into the safe. Clarke said they seemed almost happy to be in custody. Very polite, no hassles, just not talking. A detective from Montreal flew in to interview them and talked to Clarke. It seems there is a rumour back there that the boys ripped off one of the big dealers, maybe had to leave town."

"And how are you?" I asked.

He shrugged, then winced at the pain. "I don't really know. I'm chewed up pretty badly inside, they were worried about infection for a while, but it seems that's past now. I can't feel my legs, but they've still got me in a body cast, so I guess that's why. The doctor is pretty vague, says he'll start me on therapy in a few days."

He gave me a tentative smile, but I could see the worry in the back of his eyes. It would be a lot tougher for Danny, I thought — he took his health and strength for granted, one of those fortunate people who naturally excel in sports and contests and never have to sweat and strain for conditioning like the rest of us.

"You'll be all right; it will just take some time. Did Clarke say when the trial will be?"

"They're still threshing out jurisdictions. Montreal has some warrants out on them, and it's a question of who goes first. Clarke figures the charges out here are pretty well airtight and the prosecutor will press for an early trial. They think the Brothers will plead guilty on the jewellery robbery, they'd be fools not to. Maybe make a deal on some of the other stuff. The coke possession is an automatic for dealing, so they should be looking at ten to fifteen years' hard time. If they plead on the robbery I won't even have to testify in court."

We sat there for a while, not speaking, the big unanswered question hanging between us.

"I'm sorry, Jared," he said at last in a low voice.

"What really pisses me off," I exploded, "is that none of this was ever necessary. We didn't need the fucking money. If it was a problem, I could have loaned you some till next season. How could you go along with a pair of animals like that?"

"I don't know, it's strange how things happen. I was at a party and these two guys, we started talking. They had some funny stories about Quebec, I was telling them about fishing, how I'd had a lousy season, needed to make some money for a trip to Mexico. I ran into them again a couple of weeks later, they said they had asked around about me, found out I'd done some time. They were fairly new in town, they needed cash, they'd lined up a little job. That was how they talked about it, just a little job. It was easy, no violence, just run in, smash a couple of windows, and we'd be away. They knew someone who would handle the stuff, give them twenty percent of the ticket, no problem. They needed another guy."

He paused and took a drink of water.

"It all sounded so easy. They had done their homework, nobody would be on the street, a few minutes' work and I'd have twenty or thirty grand. Nobody gets hurt, the insurance company pays up so maybe the premiums increase a couple of points. Big deal." He sighed heavily. "Claude and Henri weren't the kind of guys you want to hang around with, but they seemed to know what they were doing. I thought what the hell. I'd buy radar, a water maker, a fridge for the beer. Then the guy comes out shooting. Bad luck."

"Maybe not so bad after all," I said. "You know those two are suspects in a couple of killings. I wonder if they would have wanted you walking around afterwards. Maybe they planned on getting rid of you anyway. Did you know they had guns?"

"Christ no, there was no mention of guns. I wouldn't have even considered it if I'd known they were carrying. Too easy for someone to get shot. Like me," he added wryly.

"Well, anyway, it's done. Anything you need? I have to be going."

"No. Jaimie is coming back in a while to collect the kids. He's smuggling in some real food Stella cooked up."

We shook hands again. "Take care, Danny."

"Ensenada," he said.

"Puntas Arenas," I replied automatically, but it was a lame effort. We both knew we wouldn't be making Mexico this year. Maybe never, for him. I walked to the door and out, closing it quietly behind me.

❀

For the next few days, I puttered aimlessly around the boat, half-heartedly attempting a few jobs but not really getting much done. I stayed away from the bars and ran every day. Bob Sproule came around once after work and we sat out in the cockpit, bundled up in warm clothing, drinking and talking. He spoke again about putting *Arrow* into some races, and I said I'd think about it, but I had lost the heart for it without Danny laughing and capering on the foredeck.

I told him about Danny and how he'd screwed up, not mentioning my part in any of it. It was part of the past, and I wanted to put it behind me. The Lebels were history. Or at least they were until Wednesday morning.

❀

I was sitting at the chart table, drinking coffee and working on a list of jobs to be done. I couldn't seem to get anything accomplished, so I'd made a numbered list of all the work that had to be done on the boat. I wrote down everything, no matter how insignificant. That way I could always find something to do and cross off the list, thereby feeling a sense of purpose and achievement. I must have read about this in *Reader's Digest*.

I ended up with thirty-seven tasks. I added number thirty-eight — make a list — and crossed it off, but didn't feel any increased sense of self-worth. I was trying to decide between rebuilding the leaking freshwater pump and rewiring a flickering cabin light when the phone rang. It was Clarke.

"Morning, Jared. Got your radio on?"

"No."

"Major fuck-up. They were moving the Lebels from their arraignment back to maximum security. Actually there were four prisoners in the van. They sprang them a couple of miles from the prison. Very slick, a truck in front of them slowed right down, two men jumped out with stocking masks and automatic weapons while another van jammed them from the back. Nobody hurt, two minutes and they were on their way. We've got a description of their van, but they will have changed vehicles by now. So." He sighed. "The bastards are loose again. We put someone back on Danny's room, just in case. I don't think there's anything to worry about, though. They'll be laying low for the next while."

I wondered about that. They had to know the money was missing; the charges would have specified the amount in the safe. Maybe they would figure Danny could help them locate it. A hundred and twenty-five grand was a fair chunk of money, and they had absolutely nothing to lose by killing Danny.

Clarke went on: "The hospital says it's time Danny was out of there anyway. He needs rest and therapy, there's nothing more they can do for him, and they need the bed. We're going to move him upcountry to a place near Hope. He'll be fine there. Can you get hold of the family, tell them so they can visit him before he goes?"

"Yes. What's the name of the place?"

"Oh, I don't know. Restful Acres, Drafty Acres, something like that. You know, everyone in their eighties, lots of blue hair. We've used them before, though, and they're all right."

"Did all four of the prisoners get clear?"

"No. They just took Claude and Henri, left the others." He paused for a moment. "Funny thing though, the guard and the other two all say the Brothers didn't want to leave. Seemed scared."

I thanked Clarke for letting me know. Then I phoned Jaimie and Erin, grabbed a few things, and headed over to Annie's. By seven thirty we were all gathered around the big oak table, drinking coffee and looking down at five neatly wrapped bundles of money.

"I thought I was only taking about twenty-five grand. For Danny when he got out. I figured they owed him something; it would keep him going for a year or so. In case he couldn't work for a while. I didn't intend to take a hundred and twenty-five thousand."

They stared at the money as if it might suddenly leap up and bite them on the ass.

"Well, it's a little late to give it back now," Jaimie offered at last.

"I have a bad feeling about this," I said, "but it's done now. I think the Canadian money is probably okay. You might as well take a stack for each family. I'll check out the American thousands, we can split them up later."

They all resumed staring at the money. Finally Jaimie looked at Annie and nodded, and she spoke for all of them.

"No. You keep the money for yourself and Danny until we see how it all works out. It's too early to tell yet."

"Okay. We can talk about it later. And how about the rest home?"

"I'm with you," Jaimie said. "If the police catch them again, Danny can come back, but he will be a sitting duck out there. I know those places. Everybody goes to bed at seven o'clock, a couple of ninety-year-olds in the lounge drinking Bovril, maybe a night nurse on duty somewhere. Zombie City." He had the Indigenous horror and contempt for the places where white people dumped the old and unwanted in their lives. "Restful Acres, for Christ's sake. Stuck out in the middle of nowhere. Probably no security at all. These people are organized, they knew the police van schedule — how hard would it be to find Danny? The money is just another reason for them to go after him."

He was right. In trying to help Danny, I had only put another nail in his coffin. If I had never seen *Arrow*, Danny would be living a normal life now, not lying paralyzed in a hospital bed with people wanting him dead.

"It's not your fault, Jared," Annie said gently. She could always read my mind. "Danny made his own choices."

True. But I was the one who had laid this particular set of choices out in front of him.

"The main problem I see is getting a day or so of grace, so we can get Danny clear before he's missed," said Jaimie, always the logical one.

"As soon as he disappears they'll send up the rockets, all right," I mused.

I was frowning down at the table when a lean brown hand came slowly over and pinched my forearm. I looked up in surprise. It was the first time I had ever seen Joseph grin. I stared at him in puzzlement. Then Annie started laughing. Jaimie and Erin were shaking their heads.

"Why the hell not?" I said. "You know you people all look the same to us." I picked up one of the bundles of money. "We'll use this for expenses."

Joseph nodded sagely and reached across and peeled off five hundreds, tucking them carefully into his shirt pocket as he rose and left the room.

"That should keep him in chocolate bars and smokes for a day or two at the lodge," I said into the silence that followed his departure. Annie glared at me.

Minutes later, Joseph gave us a brief nod as he passed through the room and out the front door. His hair was slicked down, his shoes were shined and he was wearing a grey homburg and a two-thousand-dollar three-piece herringbone suit that was only a little tight across the shoulders.

"Where is he going?" I inquired.

Erin and Jaimie just shrugged their shoulders, but I knew them well enough to see the effort they were making to keep straight faces. Annie just glared at me.

"You had to tell him he could take the money, didn't you?" she snapped. "You won't all think it's so damn funny when he catches something."

She slammed her coffee mug down and stormed out of the room.

I looked at the boys. "No. Really?" I said.

CHAPTER 11

By seven thirty the following morning, Jaimie and I were on the road to Hope. It was a pleasant drive, most of the traffic heading the other way, into Vancouver for the day's work. We were in Jaimie's Thunderbird, doing the speed limit, not saying much, just enjoying the late-fall scenery. We stopped at Abbotsford for coffee, the first time I had been back since the day I left the farm for my court appearance. It seemed a lifetime ago. I had thought I might feel something, some small stirring of attachment or regret, but it was all as cold and alien to me as the dark side of the moon, and I was glad of it. Jaimie settled the bill and tipped the waitress and we left. I knew now I would never return.

Restful Acres was five miles out of town on the Yale road, resting on a high maple ridge overlooking the river. The lodge was a long one-story building running across the slope of the hill, with two wings extending out the back and down towards the river. There was a patio down one side where a few well-wrapped people in wheelchairs were basking in the thin morning sunlight, behind high Plexiglas panels that sheltered them from the wind. An ambulance with Restful Acres stencilled on the door was parked over the road, a muscular young man with a crewcut polishing it in long, loving strokes.

We pulled up in front of the reception area, and I went inside to the front desk while Jaimie sauntered over towards the ambulance. The director was a pleasant, grey-haired lady in her fifties. When I told her I was looking for a home to place my father in, and Restful Acres had been recommended to me, she was very helpful. We toured the building, chatting to a few residents still capable of speech, and had tea and cookies in the lounge. We remained there talking until I saw Jaimie go back past the front door; I thanked her and stood up to leave. I said she would hear from me in a couple of weeks, and I was sure Dad would just love it.

"How did it go?" I inquired when we were back on the road again.

"Fine. We talked about the ambulance for a while. He's a car buff, put some performance parts under the hood. I asked him if he ever got a chance to take it out for a spin, and he told me all about it. He's picking up a patient at Vancouver General tomorrow at five o'clock. He's done it before, a lot of the residents come here directly out of hospital. He drives into the loading ramp, then goes into the office to clear up the paperwork and sign out the client. The staff bring the trolley down and load the patient in the back and he takes off. Usually they're a little sedated for the trip. It sounds as though he might not even get a good look. He figures he'll get back nine, nine thirty."

"That's almost four hours, even if he spends half an hour at the hospital. The rush hour will have started to slow by then, the trip shouldn't take more than two and a half hours at most. More like two if he likes to drive. So he's stopping for a meal on the way back."

Jaimie nodded. "That's what I figure. So we just have to follow him. Shouldn't be too hard to stick with the ambulance. All we need is a little luck and a dim parking lot."

At four thirty the following day the four of us were sitting in the borrowed van. Erin, Jaimie, and I were squeezed into the front seat, Joseph in the back, sitting cross-legged in the stretcher we had rented from the medical supply service. He was wearing hospital pyjamas under his sweater and sat gazing out the rear window, puffing serenely on his pipe, the calmest person there. Erin was driving and had tuned in to a country and western station. They were doing a Willie Nelson retro, and we listened to his plaintive voice in nervous silence.

Just before five, the ambulance came around the corner and backed into the loading bay. The driver was alone. We waited, and twenty minutes later he came back out past us and swung down Twelfth Street. The high clearance lights on the ambulance made it easy to spot in the traffic.

We let him get a couple of hundred yards ahead and pulled out behind. He drove slowly, staying in the right-hand lane. Erin left a couple of cars between us and followed along. The traffic lights were timed and it was easy. He swung right at Boundary Road and headed towards the 401. We had been hoping he would eat at one of the truck stops along the highway, and it looked promising. We were just starting to relax when his indicators flashed and he swung off on Napier Drive.

"Damn," Jaimie said.

The ambulance rolled along Napier for ten blocks and then turned right into a residential area. We closed up a bit.

"Where the fuck is he going?" Erin said.

"Probably to a restaurant in some busy, well-lit shopping centre," Jaimie said. That would be the worst possible place, full of people doing last minute shopping on their way home.

Just as we were silently cursing our luck, the ambulance flashed on a turn signal and pulled off the road into a small motel. He drove around the back, away from the lights, and pulled up beside a tan station wagon. He switched off the engine and got out. The station wagon door flew open, and a trim brunette jumped out and threw her arms around him.

"Well, well," said Erin.

"Ain't sex wonderful," Jaimie said.

"He doesn't want to be seen, either," I said. "When they leave, we'll tuck in on the other side. It couldn't be better."

The lovers disentangled, and the man took out a little overnight bag and locked the driver's door, and they headed off arm in arm around the corner. I waited for a minute then got out and followed. They were visible through the reception window, and the clerk seemed to know them. All three were laughing as he signed the register and handed the man some bills. The couple emerged again and disappeared into one of the rooms. I gave them a couple of minutes then went back to the van.

"All clear," I said and walked back to the corner of the building to stand watch. Erin went up and tapped on the side of the ambulance. There was an answering rap from inside. Erin and Jaimie reached in and swung Danny out, the stretcher gleaming faintly in the dim light. They ran him around to the rear of the van and slid him in when Joseph opened the door. A short while later they brought the stretcher back, Joseph walking alongside. They put it back into the ambulance, and he climbed in after it and handed out Danny's bag, replacing it with his own. He was going to depress the door lock and crawl into the stretcher. The boys had tried to impress upon him the importance of not smoking, but who knew.

I returned to the van and climbed in the back with Jaimie and Danny. Erin kept the lights off until we were back onto the road, and we drove sedately away. Danny was breathing heavily, his face glistening with sweat under the faint glow of passing street lamps.

"He couldn't reach the latch," Jaimie said. "He had to crawl forward to it."

I switched on the interior light and pulled back the sheet. Fresh blood was leaking out around the bandages.

"Damn it."

"We'll stop at Erin's, and Sarah can rebandage it," Jaimie said. "She's made up a medical kit for you to take."

In twenty minutes we were parked in Erin's drive and Sarah was in back, pouring sulpha powder on the wounds and applying fresh bandages.

"It's not bad. They're mostly healed, just some pulled stitches, and of course the discomfort." She spoke with the blithe disregard of other people's pain that marked the professional nurse. "It shouldn't be a problem if you keep him quiet for the next few days. You're just going a few miles up inside, aren't you?"

"Indian Arm. There's a dozen spots up there to hide out in. I don't think anyone will be looking very hard anyway."

"Check the dressings again when you get up there. Here's the kit, I've listed and described everything. Painkillers, muscle relaxants, even some local anaesthetics. There are tensor bandages as well, you might want them for his back later on."

"Time to get moving." Erin's scarred face peered anxiously over the front seat.

"Take care," Sarah said, hugging Danny and me.

Erin dropped me off at the docks, and I went aboard *Arrow*. I turned on the ignition and pressed the starter button. The engine whined for a few moments, and I throttled right forward and then back, and she coughed once and then settled into a noisy idle. I waited a bit till she smoothed out, then stepped over the rail onto the dock to cast off the lines. To my dismay, I saw my neighbour on the packer coming over.

"Hi Jared. Taking off for a bit?"

I silently cursed my luck. Blackie was a notorious gossip.

"Oh, just heading out for a little fishing and relaxation. Thought I might go up Howe Sound, tuck in behind Gambier Island for a few days."

"Sounds good. Did those guys get a hold of you?"

"Ah, no. Did they leave their names?"

"No, they never. I saw them looking at your boat. They climbed aboard and I went over. Knew you weren't there. Said they'd catch up to you later, not to bother."

"What did they look like?"

"Tough-looking, the two of them. Real big. The third one was ordinary-sized, pleasant. He did all the talking."

Not the Lebels, then.

"He said not to say anything about their visit, they wanted to surprise you. Gave me a hundred dollars American too." He pulled the bill out of his breast pocket and waved it triumphantly.

"Course I took it. But then I got to thinking about Danny, you know? Those bastards who knifed him, I heard it on TV. And those two guys. Mean-looking buggers, they was. I don't know as how I'd want any surprises from them."

"Thanks, Blackie. You're right, they're not friends." I shook his hand warmly to make amends for my previous low judgement of him. "If they come back, tell them I've gone away for a few weeks."

"I will. Climb aboard, I'll tie her loose for you. Oh, by the way," he said as I put *Arrow* into reverse and started edging her stern carefully out into the channel, "they took some pictures too. Of the boat. The guy said he loved old wooden yotts." He laughed and shook his head. "Yotts, he said, real high class he was."

I waved goodbye and headed out into the harbour. Now who the fuck were these guys, I wondered. Of course they couldn't give him a couple of fifties or five twenties. It had to be a goddam American hundred-dollar bill.

The van was parked a mile up the harbour, beside the abandoned cannery where Jaimie moored his troller. There were no live-aboards here; with any luck the place would be deserted at this time of night. The tide was running with me as I came in dead slow then threw her in reverse, and the boys snubbed the lines on the big cleats and warped her in. I got a line on a piling amidships and ran a pair of springs fore and aft to hold her steady.

Erin backed the van up to the edge of the dock, and they slung lines around each end of the stretcher and lowered Danny carefully onto the deck. The companionway was narrow, and it was a bitch to get the stretcher through it and down below. We couldn't keep it level; Danny groaned loudly once when it tilted, and he slipped a few inches. Finally, sweating and cursing, we manhandled it in and set it down in the main salon. We dropped the table to make up a double bed and laid the couch backrests down for a mattress. We slid Danny onto it and wedged him in with pillows. Sarah had given him a shot and said he should stay under until morning.

When we went back up on deck, Erin was screwing a pair of spaced metal strips over the name on *Arrow*'s transom. He dropped a hand-lettered magnetic sign down over them, and from the stern we were *Spindrift*, registered in Seattle, Washington. We took down the Canadian flag and hung the Stars and Stripes on the stern flag-staff, then removed the varnished nameplates fastened across her lower shrouds on port and starboard.

Arrow had been built with touring the canals of France in mind, and both her masts were stepped on deck in tabernacles. We took out a pair of large stainless bolts on the mizzen-mast, disconnected the shrouds, triatic, and backstays, and in half an hour *Arrow* was a sloop. We stored the mast on deck inboard of the bulwarks, and wrapped deck covers around it to break up the outline. Jaimie took off the canvas dodger and stainless bow, and we were done. It wouldn't fool anyone who knew her, but it would pass a casual inspection from lubbers. They would be looking for a sailboat with two masts under Canadian registry.

Jaimie and Erin followed me down into the cabin, moving quietly in the darkened galley. I poured large Scotches all around, and we drank them down in a silence broken only by the low sound of Danny's breathing. He lay peacefully, his features slack and relaxed in the dim light, looking younger, and more vulnerable.

We finished our drinks and the boys went up onto the wharf and untied the lines and I took the helm and motored away. When I glanced back a few minutes later they were still there, standing motionless as statues in the cones of light from the overhead lamps.

The rain had started, a steady, soaking drizzle that wetted me through in no time. Ordinarily I would have set the autopilot and sheltered under the dodger, but now I welcomed the discomfort; it was a small penance for the nagging guilt that now rode me constantly. The lights of Burnaby shone dimly off to starboard, warm and inviting as they outlined the hill against the night. I wondered if any of the people living in those houses had lives as crazy as mine had become.

The big storage tanks came abeam on the port side, and the light for Indian Arm flashed just ahead. I swung *Arrow* ten degrees and started to cross the channel. The moon was showing just enough to pick out the shoreline as we moved along. I doused the running lights and *Arrow* slipped along at a quiet fourteen hundred RPMS. I was probably being paranoid, but better safe than sorry. I had made enough mistakes already.

I motored for another two hours, keeping a close eye on the depth sounder until the blurred shape of Racoon Island finally appeared off the bow, and then ran past it for another thirty minutes before swinging in behind the Twin Islands.

I dropped the hook in five fathoms of water, then went below and brought out my little bag of stash, rolling a fat joint while I considered the situation. Leaning back in the cockpit, I took a healthy drag and stared up at the slowly clearing night sky and thought about Danny, lying drugged and unconscious below, and of the trip we had planned together: the Milk Run, so called by sailors because of the easy, monotonous regularity of its course. So far a tad curdled, I reflected. I smoked and contemplated, but no universal truths unfolded, and I finally went below and turned in.

CHAPTER 12

I awoke at six o'clock in absolute dark and quiet, with none of the usual creaking and sighing of planks and timbers that accompanies even the slightest movement of the sea upon a wooden boat. I lay there, wondering what had awakened me, and then I heard a deep, sighing exhalation, and the soft sound of water folding in upon itself.

I slipped on pants and jacket and went up on deck, casting a glance at Danny as I passed. His breathing was low and regular, and it seemed he had not moved at all during the night.

Just the beginnings of a streak of light showed over the steep wooded slopes that ran down to the shore, turning the water the faintest shade of silver, and in that flat, burnished surface, a ghostly pod of orca was working its way up the inlet. There must have been twenty of them, spaced out across the width of the channel. A big bull, his thrusting six-foot spar fin scarred and torn, was leading them as they moved in slow procession, diving and surfacing at regular intervals. The big mammals were eerily quiet, just the occasional slap of their tails breaking the surface, a low soughing of air and water as they blew. A cow and calf came within ten yards of *Arrow*, the cow rolling over on her side and transfixing me with a mild and curious eye as she swam by, the calf frolicking in her wake.

As the sky lightened, long, pale shrouds of mist moved across the waters, and behind them the orca appeared and reappeared in wet, gleaming flashes of black and white. They finally vanished down the channel, perhaps to head out under the Second Narrows Bridge, and then through Lions Gate before turning into the Straits of Georgia and running north to the prehistoric rubbing rocks of Robson Bight, the primal lodestone of their ancient race. There were so few of them now that you could purchase books of photos delineating each separate one by its individual scars and markings.

I went below to put on the coffee. Danny lay awake, a smile on his face.

"I heard the orcas. I haven't seen them for a couple of years now."

"A big pod. I counted twenty-three of them. One of this year's calves maybe. How are you feeling?"

"Pretty good. It's a treat to breathe real air again. I'm starving. What's for breakfast?"

"Whatever you want. Bacon, eggs, hash browns, toast, and coffee?"

"Sounds wonderful. Can you sit me up?"

I went over and moved the cushions around and braced his back against them. He was as weak as a kitten, and panting when I was done.

"Jesus. I cannot believe how feeble I am."

"What's the pain like now?"

"Not bad if I lie still, but when I move my stomach burns. The doctor said there's a lot of damaged muscle in there. It should come back, but will be painful for a while. He said the therapist would start me on a program of exercises soon. I've been thinking about it. My left arm and shoulder are all right. No pain. I thought we could rig up a block and tackle to the grab rail, and put a sling low down on each leg. I could handle the tackle with my left arm at first, raise and lower them, build up a little muscle strength." He looked up at me like a proud little kid bringing home a good report card. I could see the sweat on his forehead. I turned quickly away.

"Sure, Danny. I'll rig it up right after breakfast."

But after breakfast Danny fell asleep, slumping back against the cushions after only a few mouthfuls of food.

"Guess my eyes are still a little bigger than my stomach," he mumbled. I arranged him back in his nest and went out on deck and dropped the skiff carefully and quietly into the water. I baited the crab trap with the leftover bacon and dumped it off the stern, then rowed over to an old abandoned landing a mile up the inlet.

A track led into the bushes, and two hundred yards in it joined an old logging road that rose up the slope in long transverse cuts against the face. I attacked it like a madman, racing up the uneven ground, hurdling the washouts, forcing every ounce of focus into just that hill, until my mind went numb and the pain in my legs and lungs cancelled out every other thing. I broke into the clear at the crest and fell gasping to my knees with the whole of Indian Arm spread out before me.

When the burning stopped, I could see the suburbs of Burnaby extending to the west, and beyond them the flats of Richmond glistened wetly in the distance. Everything pastoral and quiet from this distance, no hint of the confused lives and turmoil that would be so apparent up close. I rested awhile and then jogged slowly back down to the water.

Danny was awake when I returned to *Arrow*, and I cooked up a chowder with the spider crabs from the trap. He had a good-sized bowl, along with some sourdough bread Sarah had packed.

"That's more like it," I said.

"Yes. Takes a while to get used to something that actually tastes like food again after the hospital diet. What time will you be talking to Jaimie?"

"We set up the first sked for five o'clock."

"You think they'll have found out about Joseph yet?"

"Hard to say. Jaimie said the driver didn't know anything about the patient he was picking up. And he did have other things on his mind. There will be the charts, though, a case history somewhere. They should find out this morning, but there'll be some confusion, I imagine. It might take another day or so before they're sure. Bureaucracy — nobody will want to believe there has been a mistake. God knows, Joseph is the right age to be in one of those places. It all depends."

I switched on the VHF radio and called Jaimie, using the boat names we had agreed on, but it was still too early. There wasn't much radio traffic this time of year; the fleet was tied up apart from a few draggers.

"How about doing the blocks up now?"

"Sure."

I went and rummaged through the lazarette, digging among the lines and spares until I came up with a pair of fiddle blocks and some nylon webbing. I rigged up a couple of purchases with half-inch line and tied them up to the salon grab rails, reeving the ends through and down to Danny. The webbing slings looped around his ankles and fastened to the bitter end of the line, and we were all set. Danny took a deep breath, wrapped the line around his left wrist, and pulled it back a foot. His legs rose three inches.

"I started off with four to one," I said. "We can scale it down whenever you're ready."

"This is fine for now."

After only a few pulls he was already panting. His legs were rising about six inches now.

"Not bad. Another couple of weeks and you can get back to your ballroom dancing."

"Up yours," Danny grunted.

He gave it about five minutes and then lay back, his face drawn and pale. But he was smiling.

"Any feeling in your lower back or legs?"

"No, nothing yet. They said it might be a while before it all comes back."

That was not what they had told me. The doctors spoke of damage to the spinal cord, severed ganglia, and slim prospects of regeneration. They said in cases like Danny's the odds were long against recovering complete mobility. There were no absolutes, they said, but patient attitude and carefully staged therapy were the keys to any recovery.

I prayed that this mess would be resolved soon and we could get Danny back under professional care. Maybe we had made a bad mistake. As soon as they found out about the switch, I would talk to Clarke, see what he thought. He should have heard something about the Brothers by then. They had probably left town by now, gone back east where they were more at home, could hide out among their own people.

I couldn't figure the three men who had been looking for me. It had to have something to do with the Lebels. They couldn't be sure who had been in their apartment, though — neither of them had got a good look at me. I'd worn a hat, everything had happened so fast. Jaeger wouldn't talk, I was sure of that. This hiding out on the boat was fucking crazy; we had enough money now, we could send Danny somewhere safe. There were clinics all over the world. After all, the Lebels were just a pair of two-bit thugs; they weren't about to go chasing off to Switzerland on the off chance of finding Danny at some high-end private clinic. They would be hiding out somewhere, keeping a low profile and staying out of trouble. They'd find out about Joseph today for sure, then I would see if we couldn't get Danny out of the province for a while. Out of the country even, if we could get the official okay. Maybe even if we couldn't.

My thoughts were interrupted by a call from Jaimie on the VHF. I responded and we switched to the channel we had decided on earlier. We chatted about the weather and agreed that everything was calm, no squalls anywhere. I said I was a little surprised by that, I thought there would have been some disturbance by now. Well, Jaimie said, he wasn't surprised in the least, the government was involved in the forecasts, and where bureaucracy was involved, anything was possible. He wouldn't be a damned bit surprised if the weather stayed clear for another full week. I could see he was enjoying this. I wondered if he had stopped in at the pub on his way down to the boat.

"How is the wife making out?" he asked.

"She's fine. A bit seasick at first, but had a good lunch and is feeling a lot better now."

"Give her all my love and lots of little kisses."

He made a smacking sound. Danny raised his index finger.

"She sends the same back to you," I replied.

"Well, gotta go now. Talk to you tomorrow morning. This is the Fraser Three clear."

"Klemtu clear," I said and hung up the handset. I turned to Danny and shrugged. "Nothing yet."

"Joseph will be enjoying it." Danny smiled. "All those little old ladies. I'd love to be there when they finally figure it out."

"It shouldn't be long now. They must have noticed today, a few hours to straighten it out with the hospital, then the police."

"Can you see them trying to interview Joseph?" Danny said. "He knows dialects that haven't been spoken for fifty years."

I smiled at the thought. Clarke and Joseph. That would be something all right.

But it was another two days before they finally discovered the switch. And then only because someone tried to kill Joseph.

CHAPTER 13

When I turned on the radio Thursday morning, Jaimie was already on the air, trying to contact me. He wasn't bothered about anonymity this time.

"Jared. It's hit the fan. Clarke phoned me an hour ago and he's raging. He said if he doesn't hear from you by eight o'clock he's putting out an all-points bulletin on the pair of you. He said he'll charge you with harbouring a felon. He says he is fed up with people messing in police business. He wants Danny back in protective custody right now. He says the chief is screaming at him and the Crown prosecutor is reneging on his promise not to prosecute Danny."

"All this at eight o'clock in the morning?" I said. "I wonder why everyone is so excited."

"I don't know," Jaimie said in a worried voice. "But you'd best call him right away. I thought he was going to have a heart attack right over the fucking phone. You can go up to the landing store, it's only a couple of miles. There's a phone there, I seem to remember."

"I'm on my way."

Danny was listening to the conversation. I had awakened to the sound of creaking blocks and his rasping breath as he worked them. He regarded me thoughtfully.

"Trouble, huh?"

"Seems like it. Clarke's a good head. He'll cool down." I tried to sound positive. "Here's the fruit bowl; breakfast will be delayed, I'm afraid."

I went forward and hauled the anchor, then turned on the ignition key and pressed the starter switch, praying the old Perkins would fire for me. She teased me for long seconds then caught, the cylinders coming on line one after the other. Probably the injectors. I had seen a spare set somewhere but couldn't recall if they were new, or old ones that had already been replaced.

What I really should do was take an oil sample and send it to one of the companies that specialised in engine analysis. They would tell me if it needed a bottom end rebuild or whether we could get away with just a valve job. I focused my mind resolutely on pistons, rods, and cranks, avoiding any thoughts of my pending chat with Clarke.

The little store was shut, but I knocked on the door until the proprietor finally opened it, grumpy and unshaven. I gave him a ten-dollar bill and told him I had to make an urgent local call. He motioned me to the phone in the corner then retreated back to his private quarters, mumbling about the goddam tourists. I got through to Clarke straightaway.

"Good morning, Detective. It's Jared Kane."

There was a long silence. I could hear him breathing heavily.

"Well, you've really done it this time, Jared," he said at last. "Everything is off. No more deals. They want Danny in. Now. They're considering charging you as well. Harbouring a felon, obstruction of justice, something like that, I should imagine — they've got their choice now, don't they? The chief has had me over the coals twice already this morning, and the Crown prosecutor raked me as well." There was a long silence. "Fuck off, you assholes!" he suddenly screamed.

"I beg your pardon?"

"It's those fucking clowns from the detective squad. They keep coming up and putting their faces against the office windows and snickering. Joseph is sitting here. They say Restful Acres hasn't done Danny much good, he's really aged. You know the kind of shit." He muttered another curse, and I heard the sound of papers thrown against glass.

"Has Joseph given you a statement yet?" I asked casually.

There was a long silence. I wondered if Clarke was counting.

"Jared," he said at last, "don't you fuck with me. You know he hasn't given a statement. When I asked him questions at the rest home, he was very co-operative. Of course, nobody could understand a fucking word he was saying. I had a professor out from the university at seven o'clock this morning to translate. Snotty little bastard, madder than hell at us getting him out of bed. Big fucking expert, lectures on west coast First Nations history, dialects, the whole bit. He couldn't understand a goddam word. He says he has never heard anything like this before. He's all excited now, literally begging the old bugger to work with him. Offered him a lot of money. I practically had to kick his ass to get him out of the office. Look at him!" he suddenly screamed once more. "He's smiling."

"What?"

"Joseph! The old bugger! He was smiling at me. Goddammit, I know he understands me. I goddam know it!" He was screaming again. "You old sonofabitch, I'm going to put you behind bars for the rest of your fucking life. That's about three fucking weeks, from the looks of you. How would you like to smile about that?"

I waited. Clarke was panting heavily.

"What was so important that you had to get an expert on First Nation dialects out of bed at seven o'clock in the morning?" I asked finally.

"There was an incident," Clarke muttered.

"An incident?"

"At the rest home. Someone tried to kill Joseph. Or Danny, really, I suppose," he added. "Last night around midnight. The perp came through the sliding doors into the room from outside, it looks like. He went over to the bed, seems like he was screwing a silencer on his gun when the old boy knifed him. Jesus. Have you seen that fucking knife? It looks like something I saw in a museum once when I was a kid. It's got to be a hundred years older than he is. Anyway, we figure Joseph got the guy in the arm or shoulder. The guy stumbled back, missed the door, went through the glass panel alongside instead. Seems like he made it back to the car though, blood all over the parking lot."

"The Lebel Brothers," I said.

"Ah, no, I think not. Anyway, the staff calls the local horseman, he comes in, looks at the files and sees it's a police case and calls the station. They contact me, I call the locals, tell them not to touch anything, and drive down to talk to Danny. I get there and it's Joseph. Jesus, was I fucking surprised." He giggled.

"Of course, Joseph is not saying anything, and they figure maybe some drunk wandered into the lodge and then crashed the glass on the way out. I agree with them, meanwhile wondering how come there is blood by the bed in that case. I thank the locals, say we'll handle it from here, and send them away. Then Joseph pulls the piece out from under the covers. It's got a silencer half screwed on. He signs that the guy came through the door, was creeping alongside the bed when he puts the knife in him. You should have seen the old bugger. Cool as all get out, sitting in bed, puffing away on his pipe, then cleaning it with the goddam sticker. Then he goes into some long pantomime about how just as he swung the knife the guy moved. I think maybe he was apologizing for not finishing him off. Yes! That's it, he's nodding his head."

A long silence. "Ah, Christ, I think I'm losing my fucking mind."

"Did you catch him?"

"No. We figure there was someone else waiting in the car. They had a good two hours' start. It looks like they got clear away."

"How do you know it wasn't the Lebels?"

"Yeah. Well, I was going to tell you about that. We found them. Yesterday morning, in the trunk of a car down by the docks off Powell

Street. They were all wired up, looked like they had been there for a few days. They were worked over with a blowtorch before they were killed. Not a pretty sight."

Good.

"And no leads there either," I said. It wasn't a question.

"No."

"And now they want Danny to come in, do they? For what? Bait?"

"Listen, Jared. He will have round-the-clock police protection. We'll put him —"

"They found out the route and time the Brothers were being transferred. They took out the guard and driver with no problems at all. There had to be at least four people in on that."

"Yeah, I know. But I guarantee we'll protect him. Look, Jared, you don't have a choice in this." He sounded almost apologetic.

I considered it for a while. "Okay, we'll be in at four o'clock."

"Good, just tell me where. I'll meet you with an ambulance and a squad car full of cops."

"At Fulton Pier. Where I usually tie up. We might be a little late, though, because of the press conference."

"The press conference?"

"Yes. Are you taping this?"

"No."

"You might want to switch it on. It will save you having to repeat it to the chief."

"Okay. Jesus. Go ahead, make my day," Clarke said.

"Good morning. This is Jared Kane speaking. It is presently eight fifteen, Thursday morning. At exactly ten o'clock, I am going to phone BCTV News with an exclusive story. I will tell them it is about the Lebel Brothers case. There has been another attempt on the life of Danny MacLean, the so-called third man in the Carter jewel robbery, and he is presently running for his life. That should get them down to the boat. I will have to pick them up somewhere isolated, for the sake of security, of course. Maybe even have to blindfold them at first

— they will wet themselves with excitement over that, I should think. Then I'll phone Bob Sproule, the lawyer, and ask him to come on down and join us."

I thought he likely would.

"Then I'll contact a Native American activist organization. I think probably AIM has the most credibility. They will want to be represented, I'm sure. Annie will be here, naturally, and as the grieving mother she will be doing most of the talking. Danny will be lying on the bunk, obviously a very sick man. I'm sure the news crew will get a statement from Dr. Harkin about the strong possibility he might never walk again. It would be outstanding to have Joseph present of course — he is wonderfully photogenic. Do you think you might be done with him by then?"

"Finish up," Clarke said wearily.

"Okay. Annie will tell the reporters how Joseph, that frail old man" — I ignored Clarke's rude snort — "was worried for his great-grandson's life when the police withdrew their protection. They would not have done so had he been white, of course. The representative from AIM will probably want to say something here. Then Annie will tell how Joseph decided to substitute himself for Danny; how easy it was to dupe the police. Then Joseph, through Annie, will describe the attempt on his life. I don't think the police will be able to explain that away easily. Annie will say that they are going public now because they fear for the lives of both Danny and Joseph."

I paused for breath, but Clarke remained silent.

"Bob Sproule will announce that he has heard from his sources that the Brothers were executed in a gangland-type slaying before the attempt on Joseph's life, and the police have no clues to the identity of their murderers. He may say, in fact, that the Crown prosecutor is reneging on a promise of no prosecution for Danny to force him to be the cheese in the trap. I think the story has everything: a brave, noble old man; the grieving family; the racial element; a police cover-up; the wounded and helpless victim who may never walk again." I paused for effect. "I think it will go national, at the very least."

"Or?" Clarke said.

"Or the police or Crown prosecutor issue a statement saying that — as Danny has given full cooperation to the police, the jewellery from the Carter robbery has all been recovered, the Brothers are dead and Danny may never recover fully — all charges against him are dropped. He has left the country and is being treated abroad for crippling spinal injuries."

"Okay," Clarke said. "Give me your number and I'll call you back as soon as I get an answer."

"Why don't I just call you in a couple of hours instead?"

"Listen, Jared," Clarke snarled, "I only want to save a call to the front desk to get your number from the sergeant."

"Oh, right: 282-3543."

"You always forget about that, Jared," Clarke hissed. "You want to be more careful when you're in this line of work."

He slammed the phone down.

I went outside and sat on the dock and considered my options. I didn't much care for any of them. I was pretty sure they would take the deal; that wasn't the problem. The problem was where to go to ground. We could send Danny abroad for treatment; the money was there. It would have to be away from Canada — out of North America altogether would be even better. But Danny wouldn't like it, might even refuse to go. We couldn't force him. And besides, if anyone decided to look hard enough, they could probably find him.

We couldn't hang around B.C. all winter; it would be miserable — cold, damp, and depressing, raining for weeks on end. We would end up hating each other. Danny needed the sun, warm water, time to lie back and bask and maybe, God willing, heal. He needed Mexico.

CHAPTER 14

Three years earlier, I had gone south with five other fishermen on a sixty-foot seiner. We were heading for the Sea of Cortez to hang out and do some swimming and diving between seasons. We had packed wetsuits and compressors, spear guns, sea kayaks, a small sailboat, and a ton of other gear for a leisurely exploration of the north end. Our first stop was Cabo San Lucas. As it happened, the big luxury liners were anchored in the bay when we arrived, and it seemed a thousand bored women were roaming loose around the town. Our plan collapsed and we never did get any further.

But I remembered the clearance formalities. They were complicated and time-consuming, but only the skipper was involved. He took all the passports and the ship's papers and went ashore, where he spent the better part of a day going between Customs, Immigration, and the port captain's office. Some of them he had to visit twice. But nobody ever came near the boat; not when we entered, and not when we cleared out. It would be easy to get Danny in without an official record.

The big problem would be the weather. Although it had been a good fall so far, it could change anytime now, with the big southeasters roaring in at forty knots plus. We were already well past the best time to leave. *Arrow* could take it all right, but could Danny? When it really started to pound, it would get bad. It could even kill him.

No, I would have to take the boat down to San Diego alone. The family could see about getting Danny down there to meet me. Maybe take him down to Washington State in Jaimie's troller, quietly offload him somewhere into Annie's van. There were lots of small coastal villages where the pre-9/11 casualness still prevailed and little distinction was made between American and Canadian fishing boats.

I'd have to bring out the pilot charts, see just how bad the weather could get off Oregon and northern California in December. It was a bad piece of coast. We'd done a tuna trip south one year in late September. It was the first time I had heard much about El Niño: the warm currents had moved north to Vancouver Island, bringing the fish into Canadian waters for the first time in years. We had chased the big schools all the way back down to Point Conception and got into some heavy gales. I was lying in my bunk one night as we bucked and plunged, then suddenly the rhythm broke and the boat just kept going down, jamming me against the underside of the berth above. We'd dropped so fast the boat had gone out from underneath me. We finally hit, and the boat laid there quivering for what seemed like an eternity, and then slowly she lifted her bow and came back up. I looked up at the white face staring down from the upper berth.

"What in God's name was that?" I asked shakily.

"That," the old Norwegian cook replied, "vas a qveer one."

❀

I was still thinking about the vagaries of the northern coasts when the store proprietor came out on the dock and signalled me.

"Okay," Clarke said, "you've got a deal. Nobody is real happy about it, but it clears the slate, anyway. They decided they wouldn't look too good if they leaned on Danny. And the whole First Nations thing they don't need right now, especially after that patrolman shot the fourteen-year-old Asian gang member last week. The media are hot onto that one. The fact that the little bastard was going after the cop with a four-foot sword at the time doesn't seem to count. So." He paused. "It seems you are lucky again, Jared. But you don't want to get into any trouble in this town now, believe me." He laughed. "Even a parking ticket, you're liable to get five years if it goes to court."

"I think we'll go away for a while. Head south — Mexico, likely. Maybe get Danny in a clinic down there."

"Sounds like a smart idea."

"Clarke," I said hesitantly, "who are these guys, anyway? What do they want?"

"I don't know, Jared. The detective from Montreal, remember he said the Brothers were rumoured to have ripped somebody off down there?"

"I remember."

"Well, I phoned him up again when the boys got crisped. He's got nothing definite, just rumours. But one of the big drug dealers down there has been out to the west coast twice in the last few months."

"When was that?"

"I've got the dates here somewhere."

There was the sound of paper being shuffled and a low curse as something fell off Clarke's desk.

"September twenty-fifth and November eighth flights. Seven days ago. So he was here when everything went down last week."

"He would also have been here around the time of the jewel robbery."

"Yes, but that's not the type of thing he would have been involved in. Besides, if we assume he killed the Lebels for ripping him off in Montreal, why would he have been dealing with them a few weeks earlier? It doesn't make sense. There must be somebody else."

"What does he look like?"

"Why?"

"There were some people around looking for me at the docks three days ago. Two big guys and another one who was in charge. Average size, well dressed. No French accent, though."

"Could be him. Bernard Desjardins, comes from a good family, speaks fluent English. Got into recreational drugs a few years back, was busted a couple of times, the old man cut him off. He used the family connections, started dealing to the smart set, in a few years he was one of the biggest suppliers on the east coast. There was a war out there, and when it was over he was the big man. The drug squad think he might be making a move out here. What could he want with you?"

"I have no idea." A hundred and twenty-five grand, maybe? "They took some pictures of *Arrow*."

"That sounds as if they intend to keep on looking. Do you think you were identified at the apartment?"

"What apartment?"

"Jared. Come on. I'm not taping."

"No," I said. "It all happened too fast. They were groggy, half-drunk, and drugged out. They never had a good look."

"What did you have to throw the Glenfiddich out of the window for, anyway?" Clarke's voice rose plaintively. "It wasn't necessary; a chair would have done just as well."

"For Christ's sake, Clarke."

"Okay, okay. I don't know why they're still after Danny." I could almost see the big shoulders shrugging. "None of this makes a lot of sense to me."

"Well, they won't find us in Mexico."

"Don't be too sure about that, Jared," Clarke replied. "The drug trade runs right down through to South America and beyond. There's contacts and connections all the way."

"All right, then. The Marquesas and Papeete or the Cook Islands, then. There won't be connections three thousand miles out into the Pacific Ocean. We'll just keep going."

Surely the money couldn't be that important to them. They would lose interest once we were out of sight for a while. Unless of course it wasn't just the money. But what else could it be?

"Keep in touch. Drop me a postcard or something."

"I'll do that, Clarke. Thanks for everything."

I hung up, thinking I would miss him. He had the knack of spotting the ridiculous in himself, and the humour in the most mundane or horrifying events. Probably a valuable asset in his line of work.

❦

Danny's face was impassive as I told him the news.

"So now we just have to worry about the bad guys, huh?"

"That's all."

I took out the Bundaberg and added a couple of shots to our coffee.

"To law and order."

"Amen."

We discussed the trip, what I would require to get *Arrow* to San Diego. We'd lay over there for a few days, wait for a good weather window before making the run down to Cabo San Lucas. First stop would be Ensenada, just across the border, a day's sail from San Diego. We'd check into the country there, load up on Pacifico beer and Mexican provisions before we moved on to Magdalena Bay for the fishing and lobsters. After that the run to Cabo and the tourist scene until we tired of that and moved further up the sea into La Paz.

A lot of cruisers just went right up to the top and hung out around Guaymas year-round. Gunkholed while keeping in touch with weather forecasts and running for a hurricane hole if anything big came up. We could do that, but it would pin us down. We would be sitting ducks if anyone found us.

The end of March was the best window for the long run west to the Marquesas; we could leave a little earlier with some risk of bad weather. We talked it around for a while.

"To hell with it," Danny finally said. "Let's go all the way. Mexico, the Marquesas, Papeete, then maybe the Cook Islands, Tonga, and Fiji. Spend the next hurricane season in New Zealand."

"The Milk Run." I raised my cup.

"The Milk Run." Danny touched his cup to mine, and we drank.

Neither of us mentioned that with Danny's back we might not get twenty miles before we had to turn back, but we both knew it. The knowledge cast a pall over the evening, and we didn't talk much after that, just sat there drinking quietly late into the night, each of us lost in his own private thoughts.

CHAPTER 15

I called Jaimie early the following morning, and we decided that *Arrow* would come back and tie up at his dock. We'd keep the single mast and American flag and sneak in after dark. Keep to ourselves, stay out of sight; it should be safe. Jaimie said he'd arrange for one of the family to stay on the troller and keep watch while we were there. Three to five days should be time enough to get the necessary chores done prior to leaving the country. *Arrow* needed a new mainsail and the engine required attention, but we'd wait and sort that out across the border in Port Townsend. The facilities were good there, and at this time of year they wouldn't be rushed with the commercial fleet or overrun with cruising boats. It was a pretty town, quiet and out of the way, and we'd be safe there for the time it took to get *Arrow* ready for offshore.

By nine o'clock we were back at the dock where we had loaded Danny aboard just three nights earlier. It seemed longer. We tied *Arrow* outside of a salmon packer where she was completely hidden save for the single, tapered mast rising incongruously above the fishing boat's squat shape. I left Danny visiting with Erin and Jaimie and went ashore to call Bob Sproule. I had invited him over for drinks aboard *Arrow* before our abrupt departure and wanted to apologize for missing him.

"It's okay, Jared, I understand. Detective Clarke called me."

"Oh. Look, I'm sorry about involving you like that, I was flying by the seat of my pants. Your name just came up. I was trying to impress Clarke."

"No problem. I gather you impressed his superiors, at any rate. I would have enjoyed my little bit. So what are your immediate plans? Clarke said you were heading south."

"Yes. By the end of the week, I hope. A few repairs to see to first, then off to Port Townsend for fitting out. Likely stop off at Friday Harbor for a couple of days on the way, pick our weather for Juan de Fuca Strait. Danny wants to stay on the boat until Townsend, so we'll want it pretty flat for the crossing. We can make it in five hours if we catch the tides right. Spend a week there, get a new mainsail built, install some electronics."

"Can you use a hand? As semi-retired senior partner, I get to take off whenever I want."

"That would be much appreciated."

"My pleasure."

❀

Over the next few days, Jaimie, Erin, Bob, and I worked unremittingly, and the job list steadily shrank. Bob was surprisingly knowledgeable, and if he didn't know, he said so. The two of us concentrated on the electrical system, searching out the frayed wire and bad connections. A lot of the wiring was worn and brittle, and in the end it was easier to replace most of it. It was miserable running the new wires up to the masthead in the steady drizzle, but with a mixture of patience and cursing rage we finally accomplished it.

I bought an eleven-inch GPS to replace the old satnav, and we hard-wired it to the ship's batteries with an external plug-in antenna so we'd have the options of portability or steady use at the nav station.

Erin and Jaimie worked on pumps and through-hull shut-offs, cleaning and greasing them all, replacing the hoses, and installing new seal kits in the big Whale bilge pumps. The list shrank and the remaining jobs grew increasingly difficult or dirty as we worked our way through the list. Erin landed the task of rebuilding the big Wilcox Crittenden in the head, muttering all the while about his people always ending up with the shitty jobs.

Stella and Sarah looked after the provisioning. They repacked all the dry goods in Tupperware boxes or zip-lock bags, which they labelled and stored; they broke down the cases of canned salmon, soups, and fruit and stored the contents in lockers, bilges, and the lazarette; they numbered all the lockers and drew up a detailed plan of where everything was. It seemed like a huge amount of supplies, and the cabin was in constant upset.

Danny was in the midst of everything until Erin unhooked one of the pipe berths from the forward cabin, put Danny in it, and slung him from the handrails. You had to crouch right down to get past him, but it gave us access to all the lockers. Danny was in seemingly great spirits, laughing and joking with the girls as they stowed and labelled, but I watched him when he was unattended, and his face was grim and his manner thoughtful. He was nobody's fool. He knew his prospects.

Joseph was perched on the rear deck aft of the cockpit, carefully going over all of the sails. He sat erect as always, his face impassive, pipe clenched between his teeth, staring straight ahead while running his fingers slowly over the material, stopping now and then to put some stitches in a seam or redo a patch. I watched him working away, seemingly oblivious of his surroundings, but aware of every conversation and hidden nuance, and a wave of affection swept over me.

How different from my own grandfather, I thought. Put their lives side by side, and who would choose Joseph over the other's prestige, estate, or power? But Joseph was the rock of this family, the very core of it; his being and presence gave the rest of them their strength and stability. He was always there, a part of everything they were or dreamed of being. I remembered my grandfather's constant sermons on Christian love and charity with deep revulsion.

This was my family now. I looked at them all: Erin and Jaimie, Danny, Annie, Sarah and Stella and Joseph. I would kill to protect them, and without a second thought. I prayed I wouldn't have to.

It had been a big job, and it was good to be finished. It was three o'clock when the drinking began in earnest, and by five the pattern was set and the party starting to build. Erin and Jaimie had switched to spirits, but I was proceeding on the broad base theory, building up slowly with lower percentages of alcohol, and stuck to the beer. Danny was mixing them shamelessly, and I knew from long experience that he would be the least affected of us all. The boys had brought him out into the cockpit and slung his pipe berth under the boom.

Sarah phoned Arthur, and he and Nancy came over with some lethal jugs of homemade saki. Jaimie disappeared for a while and returned with a twenty-pound salmon; Stella cut it up into steaks and marinated them in soya sauce with sugar, ginger, and garlic. Three of the crew off the packer dropped by to check on her, and stayed on. They had some duty-free over-proof rum stashed away, and they brought it out and passed it around; the party paused, staggered, then kicked up into a different plane, higher and more pure.

By nightfall we had attracted a couple of troller skippers who knew Danny, and a trio of scruffy vagrants who were working the Dumpsters. It struck me that this was rapidly turning into the kind of evening that Clarke might enjoy. There was no answer at his home number, so I called the station and left a message with the desk sergeant.

At eight o'clock we ran out of beer, and Erin phoned up a cabby who brought down another dozen flats and we paid him off in crisp American hundred-dollar bills that I just happened to have handy. What the hell.

Danny was in his old form, a glass of rum in one hand and a beer in the other, talking earnestly to a pretty blond in pigtails and jeans who had come over with a crewman from the packer. Jaimie had the boyfriend deep in conversation and was plying him with over-proof. Danny raised his glass, drank, and winked at me without losing her attention for a second. Annie saw me watching and threw me the big grin that I hadn't seen for far too long.

At nine thirty we lit the barbecue and grilled the salmon steaks. The crew from the dragger contributed a sack of cooked and iced Dungeness crab, and gallon jars of home-pickled herring circulated as well. Arthur had got hold of some fresh cod fillets, squid, and salmon roe from one of the boats and was making what he called round eye sushi, but I could see Nancy rolling her eyes, and only the bravest or drunkest were sampling it.

There must have been fifty people milling around on the two boats by ten o'clock. The packer was pumping music from one of the rock stations out on their deck speakers, and couples were dancing on the foredeck. The noise level had been gradually rising all evening, and it was impossible to carry on a conversation without shouting. It was eleven o'clock when the first drunk fell overboard and his shrieking girlfriend grabbed the flare gun from the bulkhead and fired the rocket up into the night sky. Five minutes later I heard the siren.

The black-and-white raced onto the dock with every light flashing, then slammed on the brakes, leaving a trail of smoke and black rubber in its wake. Before the car had even stopped rocking, the officers were out and over to the boat.

"Who's in charge here?" the big one asked.

He was a good two-fifty, with a big beer belly and a puffy round face and mean eyes. He stood with his legs braced, slapping his nightstick in his palm. Several people pointed helpfully towards me.

"Get up here," he snarled. "What's your name?"

"Kane," I mumbled.

"Kane? Ah Jesus, thank you God. Not Jared Kane?"

His eyes widened in delight and he spun me around and spread-eagled me against the hood of the car. He pulled my arms behind me and snapped on a pair of handcuffs then turned me around and stuck his big shiny face an inch from mine.

"I'll probably make sergeant out of this, Kane," he said. "Get in the fucking car."

His partner opened the rear door, and the big cop grabbed me by my collar jacket and the top of my head and hurled me inside.

"Gotcha," Clarke said with an evil grin as I slammed up against him.

⚙

Clarke had brought two bottles of Johnnie Walker, and I broke out the last of the ship's stores from the bilges. At midnight we ran out of beer again, and Clarke made a phone call. Twenty minutes later the police cruiser showed up again with another dozen flats, and I paid them off in stolen money without the slightest qualm.

The police car's departure was the signal for complete abandon. A high-stakes poker game broke out on the packer's hatch cover, and somebody's wife was doing a slow strip on the cabin top to the sounds of rhythmic clapping and the unsteady focus of a hand-held spotlight.

It must have been three in the morning when I finally ended up on the foredeck with Bob Sproule and Clarke, drinking Scotch and listening bemusedly to the horror stories that are the stock-in-trade of cops and lawyers. Joseph was a silent shadow in the background, the only sign of his presence the outstretched glass as the whisky made its rounds.

Clarke was flying, his eyes a wild streaky red, his voice hoarse and rasping as he made his points. He had won big in the poker game and was in high spirits. He was insisting on accompanying us on the trip. For protection.

"You never know what you might run across in the South Seas," he slurred, pulling out his pistol and waving it wildly in the air. "Desjardins, sharks, naked island women, whatever. I'm ready for them all."

He lurched to the rail to relieve himself, almost falling over the side in the process. He suddenly swung around, penis in one hand, pistol in the other, liberally spraying the decks. Bob and I lunged desperately backwards.

"This is my pecker, this is my gun, I'm ready for anyone," he bellowed loudly. He punctuated the tirade by firing several shots into the air above our heads. I doubt more than half a dozen people even noticed.

"Attaboy, Jared," I mumbled as I blanked it all out and drifted off to sleep. "Keep a low profile."

CHAPTER 16

I awoke at dismal first light to a cold rain blowing in my face. It took a while before I realized where I was. Rolled up in a sail on the fore-deck. It all came back to me, and I groaned softly and went below to check the damage. Danny had been replaced in the salon berth and was snoring softly. A blond pigtail peeked out from the gathered sheets beside him.

The galley had been cleaned up, and Joseph sat at the chart table drinking coffee. Everybody else had left. He rose up, poured another cup, and handed it silently across to me.

"Morning, Joseph."

He nodded.

"Not a bad party, was it?" I asked tentatively.

Joseph stared at me, his face impassive.

"You get any sleep?"

He nodded again.

"You're coming to Port Townsend with us?"

A final nod.

"I thought we would leave around eleven, catch the tides in Porlier Pass, tie up at Montague Harbour tonight."

I had half-heartedly tried to talk Danny out of the Port Townsend run, worried about whether he was up to it, but he was adamant, and I hadn't the heart to insist. Most of the trip was inside at any rate, and if the weather held for another two or three days it would be comfortable enough. It could well be Danny's last trip in *Arrow*.

Bob Sproule showed up at ten, packing a long sail bag, and laid it down on the deck. It contained a brand new mainsail with the good Harken slides installed.

"I used to handle the emergency parts and repairs for Bill and Meg when they were off sailing," he said. "I still have all the lists and specs, including a full sail plan for *Arrow*. I phoned up Hasse Sails last week and they did up a rush job for me. Eight-ounce cloth, three reefs. She should make a big difference."

I tried to thank him for this magnificent gift, but he waved me off.

"My firm has been handling Bill and Meg's affairs for nearly thirty years now. We have made our share of money during that time, now I can do a little something in memory of Bill by way of *Arrow*. It's my pleasure."

I opened the mast and boom track gates and pulled off the old main, then slotted in the new. It glided up the mast and filled in the slight breeze. *Arrow* heeled and tugged at the dock lines, anxious to slip her leash.

"I'll put on some lazy jacks," I said. "With those battens she should drop and stack beautifully."

We admired the sail for a while, then dropped it down and flaked it on the boom. I invited Bob to come with us to Friday Harbor, but he couldn't spare the time. He was flying to England to visit Meg the following week, and had to catch up on office work before he left.

❁

We were under way by noon. We decided to leave the mizzen-mast down until we were out of sight of land, although after the previous night and all the loud, drunken toasts to *Arrow*, it was doubtful if there was anyone in Vancouver who was unaware of her presence. Joseph took the tiller while I ran up the main and set the big light-air genoa. The sails filled, the sheets hardened up, and we were doing a respectable five and a half knots in the light airs. I played with the new sail for a while, slipping the sheet and adjusting the traveller until I had the feel of it, and then I went below and slept.

Joseph woke me at Porlier Pass, and we ghosted through on the last of the ebb, rounding Virago Point and heading down Trincomali Channel with the wind just off our stern. Two hours later we were securely anchored in Montague Harbour. I was still a bit wasted from the send-off and turned in early. Danny and Joseph were in the salon, playing cards, and I fell asleep to the soft cadence of their voices and the pungent smell of Joseph's pipe.

We had an early breakfast the next morning and by seven thirty were under way again with the same light breeze, the dinghy trailing on its painter in our wake. It was a magnificent day for early November, almost balmy. I couldn't remember a year when the weather had held so late; it was unnatural, and I knew we would pay dearly for it at some point. In the meantime we might as well enjoy our blessings.

I sheeted the mainsail in hard and centred the boom over the companionway, then fastened a block to the track underneath. I clipped another block beneath the first and passed through a four-part purchase, then tied on to the end of Danny's bunk. Joseph stood in the cockpit and slowly pulled the line in while I lifted from below. The cot rose smoothly, and when we had cleared the steps, Joseph pulled it aft and into the cockpit. Another minute and Danny was stowed against the aft bulwarks, gazing around with hungry eyes.

"This is better than a month of treatment in hospital," he said.

I handed him the tiller, and he sat there steering all the way down Swanson Channel right through to Spieden Island, where we anchored and had lunch alongside the deer and goats browsing on the steep slopes. The wind died as we ate, and we motored the rest of the way to Friday Harbor.

The Customs officer took down our registration and crew list and gave me a clearance number. He was bored, and we talked about the unusual spell of good weather. The big high was still parked off the coast and should hold for another four or five days, according to the forecast. When it collapsed, he said, watch out. On the way back to the boat I stopped at the little tavern and bought a case of Henry Weinhard's at half the Canadian price.

We spent two days in Friday Harbor, just relaxing and lying around. We put the boat covers over the cockpit and attached the lee cloths. It made it almost a tent, impervious to all but a driving horizontal rain, and Danny stayed topsides the whole time. At night we wrapped him in a sleeping bag with a couple of bright Mexican blankets from the lounge thrown over top.

He was looking better: his colour was back and he had regained some of his lost weight. He exercised his upper body constantly, using a single weight from the dive belt at first, then slowly adding others as he recovered a portion of his lost strength.

From the waist down it was a different story. Danny worked the pulleys diligently, raising and lowering his legs for hours at a time, but they rose and fell like slabs of meat. He never looked at them, his eyes always raised, gazing into the distance.

I knew what he was seeing; a wheelchair, or maybe, if he was lucky, crutches; his powerful upper body swaying from side to side on the metal posts, the thin strapped legs below dragging after. Perhaps a half century of servitude, dependency, the always present care and attention of others. And this to the proudest, most independent man I knew.

In the evenings, Joseph rolled him over onto his stomach and massaged his back and lower spine with a reddish grease redolent of eulachon oil and native herbs. The powerful old hands dug and gouged, the thumbs sometimes disappearing entirely into the slack back muscles.

Danny never moved or flinched, seemingly unaware. I watched Joseph as he worked, his eyes focused inwards, sometimes mumbling in a low rhythmic cadence that seemed an incantation. He looked up and met my gaze and slowly shook his head, his eyes grave. He resumed his slow circular rubbing motion, and I turned quickly away.

❀

On the third day we left Friday Harbor early, just at high slack. We swung south at Turn Island and caught the ebb as we headed towards the Strait of Juan de Fuca. An hour later we shot through the slot between Cattle Point and Deadman at nine knots, coming through into the straits to a long, low westerly swell and a breeze just aft of the beam. It was *Arrow*'s best point of sail, and I stepped the mizzen-mast and hoisted the staysail and we began to fly. The swells were just long enough that we weren't coming off them, and *Arrow* corkscrewed elegantly along their lazy shifting slopes at a steady eight knots. We were around Point Wilson lighthouse by late afternoon, and it was just five o'clock when we glided past the trailer court and tied up in Point Hudson Marina. Joseph brought out the last of the Henry's, and we drank them in the cockpit, overlooked by the old false-fronted buildings to the west.

At one time Port Townsend had been slated to be the capital of Washington State, and her architecture was unique among the towns of the Pacific Northwest. She had more the look of the east coast, something you would expect to find along the Massachusetts coastline perhaps, or Maine. The air of old money made and spent hung about the brick edifices and merchant buildings like a dimly recollected memory. Nowadays Port Townsend was a bustling tourist town in the summer months, filled with milling pedestrians by day and the sounds of jazz and blues festivals by night. The hills above the town were studded with fine old merchants' and captains' residences, many with turrets and widow's walks, nearly all of them now converted to the bed and breakfast trade.

I walked up to the restaurant on the landing and picked up some takeout and a dozen Coronas and packed them back to the boat. Afterwards we played cribbage for a nickel a point. Joseph had an amazing run of luck against me.

"You have to watch him, he cheats," Danny said.

"He cheats?"

"Yes. His clan is Raven, the trickster."

Joseph regarded me impassively with those black argillite eyes. After that I did a little better, but not much. I never did catch him cheating.

I rose early the following morning, took some thousand-dollar bills out of storage, and headed for the ship chandleries to spend some serious money. I was betting the bills wouldn't attract too much attention in a town that still had a big commercial fishing fleet. It wasn't all that long since the cash buyers were flying out to the fishing grounds in chartered float planes with a million dollars plus in hand, to buy salmon roe for the Japanese market. There were still some fishermen working for the big companies who were so indebted they would sell to independents on the side for ready cash. A few thousand-dollar bills should be right at home in Port Townsend.

When the salesperson heard that I was heading to the South Pacific for a few years, the receipt wouldn't be any use to me, and I was paying in cash, he smiled and the price dropped accordingly. Nobody likes the taxman. I settled on a sixteen-mile Raytheon with the enclosed radome, paid him, and packed it back down to the boat.

Refrigeration was straightforward; there was a large, well-insulated icebox in place, and we decided to bolt a cold plate onto the back wall, then run the copper supply lines out to the compressor, which would fit into the back of a locker. I spent another happy morning in the chandlery looking at the various units before choosing a small twelve-volt model from Sweden. It was an easy decision, given the ancient

Perkins diesel engine on *Arrow*. Bolting an engine drive compressor on her would be the ultimate insult, one she was unlikely to forgive. She was hard enough to start now; the thought of having to fire her up twice a day just to freeze the cold plate was terrifying.

The bargain was struck, we shook hands, and I packed another large carton down to *Arrow*. This was fun. I began to understand how people spent years outfitting their boats for the big trip, never quite getting away. "Just one more update, matey, and then I'll be ready."

For the next three days, I installed equipment. Much of that time was spent lying on my back or stomach, peering into black inaccessible holes and cursing. Every time I thought I had found an easy way to hide the radar cable or compressor lines, I ran into a steel floor, or one of the hand-grown oak knees. It was a toss-up which would have been harder to drill. In the end I went up and through the backs of the cupboards, and finally it was done. I ran the fridge and we drank cold beer in celebration.

The weather had finally turned. The glass dropped steadily and the first big southeaster of the season was forecast. It was preceded by a steady soaking drizzle as the low moved into the coastal zone. The occasional gust of wind whistled through the rigging, causing *Arrow* to stir restlessly at her moorings. If the storm lasted very long, a surge would be coming into the marina.

I was fastening extra bumpers on *Arrow* when a fifty-foot Hatteras came in and attempted to tie up across the way. The two men on deck were having a hard time of it. They looked to be wearing street shoes, and it was a wonder they could even stand on the wet fibreglass.

The skipper brought her in nicely against the wind, then throttled back to lay her alongside, but his crew were slow and lost the bow. I could hear the curses coming from the bridge as the stern swung in and slammed the floats. He gunned the engines hard and went out and around then brought her in again. This time he jumped off himself and tied her amidships while the crew struggled with the bow and stern lines.

The old boy on the wooden Folkboat thirty feet down from *Arrow* watched the misadventures with a big, approving smile on his face, as if it were all a special entertainment staged just for him.

"Do you think we should applaud?" he called over.

"Better not. Two of those guys are pretty big."

He grinned and went below. Charterers, I thought, although it was late in the season for that. The wind was picking up now, the intervals between the gusts growing shorter. I went forward and tightened the halyards, then bungied them out from the mast to stop the slap. One end of the cockpit cover had come adrift with the wind, and I retied it. The rain was driving down hard, and the visibility was closing in. I pulled on a pair of oilskins and went up to the restaurant to call Annie on the pay phone. Although it seemed overly cautious, we had followed Clarke's advice and left our cellphones in Vancouver. She answered on the first ring.

"Hi, Jared. I was just thinking about you guys."

"We're all fine, Annie. Tied up alongside in Port Townsend. We had a good trip, Danny enjoyed it. He's looking much better, all the fresh air agrees with him. Weather has finally turned now, though. I figure on waiting out the storm, leaving right after. Might get a few good days out there, maybe even something with a little north in it."

"Yeah. Maybe. I wouldn't count on it, though. I talked to Sarah today, she's booked off next week. Arthur is going to lend us his camper. We thought we'd leave early Sunday afternoon, get there around six. Maybe we could all go out to dinner."

Her voice caught at the end as she realized we couldn't all go out.

"No problem. We'll eat on the boat. Lots of good restaurants nearby, we'll get them to make up something to take out."

"Yes, we can do that, all right," she sighed. "Jesus, he has to get better. Can he feel anything yet?"

"No. But it's still early days, Annie. Don't lose hope."

"I know that. But I worry."

"We all do. Take care, Annie. Give my regards to the boys. See you Sunday night."

When I returned to the boat, it was pitch black. Joseph had cooked up a pot of chowder, and as we ate I told them about the conversation with Annie.

"Sunday night," Danny said. "God, I hate to leave *Arrow*. It's been a great few days."

"Well, it will likely go downhill from here," I said. "Until southern California, anyway. I may stop off in Monterey for a couple of days if the weather allows."

"How long will it take, you figure?"

"Around ten days. I'll head offshore a hundred and fifty miles or so, get some sea room. Most of the Washington and Oregon ports you can't get into anyway if it's blowing. The rollers break right across the entrances."

"I remember three years ago, Jimmy Johnson was fishing tuna down there," Danny said. "Tried to get into Crescent City in a blow, the boat came down off a breaker and broke her back right in the goddam entrance."

We were still talking about the Pacific Northwest coast when there was a rap on the side of the hull.

"U.S. Customs. Permission to come aboard."

Arrow heeled slightly as someone stepped onto the deck. I went to the companionway and stuck my head out. A cold, wet revolver jammed into the base of my throat.

"Just back up slow and easy," the pleasant voice behind the gun said.

CHAPTER 17

There were three of them. The two big men from the Hatteras I recognized at once. The smaller man with the gun would be the skipper. They were all wearing oilskins and gumboots now.

"Sit down nice and easy."

I moved over beside Danny. Joseph was sitting at the chart table, watching the three men, his eyes narrowed in puzzlement.

"Start the engine," the small man said.

The third man went out on deck and turned the ignition key. Nothing happened.

"What's wrong?" the skipper inquired. He had taken off his slicker and was wearing a white wool turtleneck with a navy jacket and pressed slacks. He looked cool and expensive.

I stared at him in silence.

He leaned forward with a slight smile and raked my face with the gun barrel. I felt the blood run down my cheek.

"Why won't it turn over?" he asked again.

Then he shook his head and drew back the pistol once more.

"It's the starter," Danny said. "You have to press the starter button after you turn on the key."

"Thank you, Danny," the gunman said.

The man in the cockpit tried it again, and the old Perkins slowly turned over and then fired briefly. There was a moment when he should have gunned the throttle and then pulled it back, but of course he didn't know. He kept pressing the starter button and grinding away until the battery died and all you could hear was the clicking of the solenoid.

"It's a very old engine," I said. The leader looked at me thoughtfully. He wasn't smiling now.

"Okay, then. We'll have to tow the fucker out. Go get that big rope in the locker in the bow of our boat."

It's a line, not a rope, I thought, but remained silent. It didn't seem the time for a lecture on nautical protocol.

The man in the cockpit jumped down onto the dock, leaving only the two of them. It would take him a few minutes to fetch the line, and there would never be a better time. I gathered my legs slowly under me and took some long, deep breaths. I lowered my head and let the blood run down my face and tried to look abject. The two men were standing close together at the foot of the companionway stairs. If I could chop the skipper's gun hand on the way by, I could disable him for a few seconds while I went after the other one. He was huge, running to fat, with the crushed nose and scar tissue under the eyes that marked an old pro. I took a last, deep breath and launched on the exhalation.

If *Arrow* hadn't lurched from a sudden gust at just that moment, it might have worked. My timing was off just that little bit, and I chopped down on the gun barrel rather than the wrist. With luck I would have knocked it loose from his grip, but it wasn't my day. I focused on the big man. My right hand was extended straight in front of me in the Unsu spear thrust, and I found his neck. I hit the heavy muscles rather than the killing spot in the larynx that would have dropped him like a stone, but even so his face turned purple and he stumbled sideways against

Joseph, knocking him down. I brought my knee up into his groin and elbow-smashed his face, then spun, but I was far too slow.

The skipper had Danny by the hair, the gun jammed into his throat.

"You have two seconds," he said softly.

I raised my hands slowly over my shoulders.

"Turn around."

I turned and faced the companionway. The big man was slowly straightening himself, moaning softly.

"Tie him up, Eddie. Hands behind the back." He pulled a small coil of nylon rope out of his jacket and threw it across.

Eddie forced my wrists up high behind my back and pulled the cord so it cut deeply into my skin. When he was done he clubbed me in the kidneys, knocking me to the cabin sole. He kicked me viciously in the ribs, and I curled into a ball to try and protect myself.

"That's enough," the leader said. "Now turn the cripple onto his face and tie his hands behind his back. Be careful," he added mockingly. "You know what he did to Bruce at the lodge."

Eddie flipped Danny over and tied his wrists behind his back. The thin cord disappeared into the flesh.

"Very good. Now roll him onto the side couch and move the table out of the way. That's it. Now tie this one onto the post."

Eddie picked me up and slammed my head against the mast support, then kicked my feet out from under me. He spun me as I fell and lashed my hands behind me to the base of the post. The blood was flowing freely again, and I could scarcely see.

"That's excellent. Now tie up the old guy's wrists."

Joseph had his pipe out and was trying to light it. His hands were shaking so much he couldn't hold the match. Eddie grabbed his wrists and started to twist them behind him. Joseph uttered a loud cry of pain.

"In front," the leader said. "The old bugger is ancient, for Christ's sake. He's as stiff as a fucking board. Tie his hands in front and let him have his pipe."

He leaned across and flicked his cigarette lighter over the bowl. Joseph sat there shaking, his head bowed and shoulders trembling. He brought his bound hands slowly up to the pipe bowl, clutching it as if for warmth.

"Poor old bastard," the skipper said, "too bad you had to get involved."

"Why?" I asked. "Is it Desjardins's money?"

He looked perplexed for a brief moment. "Desjardins? You certainly don't have to worry about him anymore, that's the least of your problems. You owe him, huh? Well, he won't be collecting. Not in this life, anyway." He laughed. "Nor any of his west coast chums either, for that matter."

"Why, then?" I asked again.

He looked at me for a long moment before replying. "Just the wrong place at the wrong time, sport. First your friend, now you and the old man. Just plain bad luck."

He shook his head ruefully, a pleasant, soft-spoken man in his early forties. He could have been your local insurance guy gravely discussing life expectancy statistics. He might have said more but for the sudden sound of footsteps on the deck.

"Ah. Chuck has returned."

A dripping head thrust into the cabin. "Geez, Mr. Delaney, it's blowing like shit out here."

"I told you no last names, you idiot," the leader snapped. "Not that these boys are going to be talking to anyone," he added with a cold smile. "Don't bother yourself about the weather, Chuck, we're just going out a few miles. Soon as we're in two hundred feet of water, we'll cut some hoses, open up the seacocks. We will be done and gone within a couple of hours. Now, Eddie," he continued, "Chuck and I are going to go out and fasten the rope to the bow. Then I'll bring our boat over, and we will tie the rope onto our stern. Chuck will untie *Arrow* and we'll tow you out. All you have to do is sit here and watch these three. One is a cripple, one is a hundred fucking years old, and the other is beaten up to ratshit and tied. Do you think you can handle that, Eddie?" His voice dripped with sarcasm.

Eddie snarled what might have been a yes. He was crouched by the companionway steps, one hand holding a pistol, the other delicately cradling his testicles.

"Good," Delaney said. He reached over and switched the radio to low power, then punched up channel twenty-two.

"I'll talk to you on here. No names. Press the button to talk, release it to receive. Got that? When we're far enough out, I'll call you and tell you when to cut the tow rope. Then we'll come alongside, and Chuck will come aboard and assist you. The two of you will cold-cock the three of them and sink her." His voice was as dispassionate and pleasant as always. "Okay. See you in a while, then."

He went up the companionway steps with Chuck following close behind. A few minutes later, *Arrow* started bumping along the dock. There was so much noise in the rigging now you couldn't hear the big Jimmies coming down from the Hatteras. We sat rolling for a minute, then there was a sharp jerk; *Arrow* shuddered and started to track. We had maybe an hour to live.

At least it wasn't the money. I hadn't done this to the family. Sixty minutes from now it wouldn't matter a damn, but that made it easier. Joseph was mumbling and half chanting, rolling his shoulders back and forth, his head sagging onto his bound hands. He looked pitiful.

"What's he singing, his death chant?" Eddie snickered at his own wit.

We were outside the marina now, beginning to rock up and down in the swell. It sounded like around thirty knots of wind, not too bad at the moment, but once we cleared the point the seas would start to build. I tried to remember the charts. It seemed to me that two hundred feet of water was not very far out at all.

I tried to move my hands, but the cords were so tight I couldn't even feel them. I leaned back against Danny's bunk and closed my eyes. Soon it would all be over. I had done nothing with my life, and now it was being taken from me. Perhaps a meaningless life warranted a meaningless death. Danny's head was just beside me.

"I can't move," he whispered bitterly, "not even to save my goddam useless life."

There were tears of rage and frustration in his eyes. I couldn't think of a single thing to say. Suddenly he lifted his head, his eyes narrowing in concentration as Joseph's low keening filled the cabin.

"Joseph," Danny murmured softly. "He's going to kill Eddie."

"Sounds like a hell of an idea to me," I mumbled back. Eddie had turned his back to us and was staring out the companionway into the rain.

"He wants you to tell him when."

"Yes. Not yet. It has to get rougher. Maybe another twenty minutes."

Danny began to sing in a low voice. Eddie listened for a minute then stepped forward and chopped him on the back of the neck with the pistol barrel. "Shut the fuck up, cripple. You guys are starting to get on my nerves."

I watched him and wished my hands were free.

"You don't like that, huh," he chuckled. "Couple of fucking Indians, what you doing with them anyway? Don't you have any pride at all?"

I didn't bother answering. If Joseph succeeded, we would have to move quickly, and I couldn't handle much more damage. I dropped my head on my chest, concentrating on the motion of the boat. We were moving quicker now, *Arrow* bucking against the tow with none of the free motion of sailing. She was tracking well, though; Delaney must have lashed the tiller amidships.

Arrow took a quick, lurching roll, and Eddie cursed and gripped the handrails tightly. He was standing with his back against the companionway stairs, his head thrown back into the fresh air. His face looked oily, and I thought maybe he had a touch of seasickness. Good.

"How you doing back there?" came over the radio.

"Fine, no problems," Eddie replied.

"Okay. Another fifteen minutes and we're there."

I nodded to Joseph. His eyes had never left me. Eddie hung up the phone and as he turned, I said, "God, my fucking legs are cramping, I've got to move them."

I began stretching them slowly back and forth. Eddie was watching me and didn't see Joseph's hands creeping slowly down the inside of his shirt. Joseph began working the leather thong upwards, stiff and slow with his bound hands. Eddie turned back towards him.

"Feeling a little green are we, Eddie?" I asked.

"Fuck you," he snarled, glowering at me.

I could see the shaft of the knife now. Joseph would have to lift it clear and reverse it. It would be about a six-foot throw.

"If you'd come a bit closer I could kick you in the nuts again, maybe take your mind off puking your guts out."

I started laughing. Joseph had the knife out now.

"You cocksucker, I'll show you who's . . ." Eddie took a half step forward, and then a puzzled look came over his face. He tried to reach the knife, but it was buried right under his left armpit, and just as he got his hand close, blood gushed out of his mouth and he fell down in a heap.

Joseph stepped forward and pulled out the knife, his face impassive. He wiped it clean on Eddie's shirt, then severed the tie that bound his wrists together. He suddenly crouched, lifted Eddie's head up by the hair, and laid his knife against the edge of the scalp.

"Joseph!" I screamed.

He glared fiercely at me for a moment, then grinned and shambled forward and cut our bonds.

"I think he was only joking," Danny said.

We had just a few minutes to get ready now, and I switched on the radar and told them what had to be done.

CHAPTER 18

It was hell getting the big man out onto the foredeck. We tied a bow-line around his chest just beneath his shoulders, and I hauled from the cockpit while Joseph shoved from below. Finally we had him out on deck and it got a little easier. I crawled forward, dragging Eddie behind me, stopping every few feet to free the inert bulk when it snagged on the blocks and stanchions.

Arrow was pitching and rolling heavily now, water coming steadily over the bow and slamming against me as I moved slowly forward. The Hatteras was running without lights, and there wasn't a sign of her in the black and heavy rain, only the deep roar of the engines coming down to us on the wind.

I jammed Eddie on the starboard edge of the bow, his head and arms hanging over the side, then tied the line securing him to the tow line forward of where it fastened to the big wooden bitt. I ran back and got the heavy working jib and hanked it on, then tied it off with light twine. I clipped on the halyard and passed the line down through the exercise blocks and into Danny's hands.

"Are you sure you can manage it?" I yelled down.

"I'm sure," he replied.

I moved back to the cockpit and took the cover off the main and threw it aside. The main sat securely in the lazy jacks, held only by a pair of sail ties, the wind moving it up and down as it came across the decks fifteen degrees off the port side. I eased the mainsheet over to starboard and lined it up with the wind. Joseph sat at the back of the cockpit, cradling the Purdey between his legs, intent on cutting crosses into the .22 slugs. The knife went through the lead like butter.

"Chuck should be on the stern, hauling in the line, when we go by," I said, "maybe with a spotlight. I'll come as close as I dare. You take him out with the .22 or shotgun, then see if you can knock off the radar when we pass. I'll try for the wheelhouse windows with Eddie's gun, maybe get lucky, touch up Delaney as well."

Not much chance of that, but I could hit those big windows, get some glass flying around. Cut up the son of a bitch maybe. Joseph nodded then lifted the Purdey and sighted along the barrel. His hands were rock-steady.

I thought it through again. Delaney would turn to port into the wind when he stopped and brought in the tow rope. Eddie might slow things down a little there, add some confusion. If we timed it just right and got the sails up as he stopped, and fell off hard to port, we should still be doing four knots and going into a near beam reach. Maybe doing close to seven when we blew by. I heard the radio.

"Okay, we're just going over the edge now. Another couple of minutes."

I turned up the gain, clicked the button on and off, mumbled something. Danny was propped against the pillows, his face greasy with sweat, staring at the radar screen.

"As soon as his bow swings," I said. I ran on deck and hauled up the main. It glided up effortlessly and luffed noisily in the wind. I silently blessed Bob Sproule. Joseph sat with the tiller between his legs. I brought out the flare gun and set it on the seat alongside Eddie's pistol.

"He's turning to port," Danny yelled, "three hundred feet."

I scrambled forward and cut the tow line. There was a moment as the slack shot out, then Eddie suddenly jerked alive and soared forty feet through the air before he hit the water with a loud splash and planed off into the blackness.

"Ten," I screamed and raised my fingers high as the adrenaline pumped and I felt the craziness.

Joseph swung the tiller hard across and the jib shot up. *Arrow* heeled, and the pure motion of sailing swept through her decks as she put her shoulder down and moved cleanly through the water. I raced back to the cockpit and Joseph passed me the tiller. I knelt on the cushions, bracing myself against the cabin bulkhead, and picked up the big spotlight.

"A hundred feet," Danny yelled. "Bear off ten degrees."

I laid the tiller over some more, counted slowly to ten, then switched on the spotlight. We were forty feet behind her, coming up fast and just to port. The Hatteras looked huge in the glaring light. A figure was crouched in the stern, heaving on the line, and I just saw the whiteness of his face and the long blond hair as he looked up, and then there was the crack of the .22 followed by the louder report of the shotgun, and he fell back and disappeared.

We were twenty feet away now, the wheelhouse windows reflecting in the glare of the spotlight. I fired until the pistol was empty. Through the sounds of shattering glass I heard Joseph's shotgun firing again, and then once more. We were abeam now, so close I could almost touch her. I picked up the flare gun. The windows were out, and no one was visible. I fired up as we went past and the flare hit the cabin roof inside and caromed down. The interior lit up with a bright red glow, and I heard a yell.

"Chew on that, motherfucker!" I screamed as we passed. I jammed in the spare clip and pumped another couple of shots below the windows, and then we were clear and bearing away fast, and she was gone. There were some answering shots, and then the engines roared and I knew I had missed Delaney. I concentrated on sailing *Arrow*, getting the most from her as we raced away into the blackness. Behind me, Joseph set the mizzen, and we picked up another half knot. The red glow faded and we were alone in the night.

It was blowing a steady thirty, water coming over the decks as we reached across the inlet. I set the wind vane and went below.

Danny and Joseph were watching the radar.

"It looks like he started after us, then stopped after a couple of hundred yards," Danny said. "Maybe the line got caught up in one of the props."

Joseph murmured something and smiled.

"Or Eddie," Danny added.

I looked at Joseph and slowly shook my head. He watched me for a moment then put his hands behind his back and clapped them sharply together.

"It wasn't me who said you were old and stiff," I protested.

Danny rolled his eyes. "We are a proud and savage race," he declaimed.

We watched the radar screen until we were sure we were clear. Delaney was heading slowly south, away from us. Probably into Everett, just across the Canadian border, or maybe Seattle. I went back out on deck and dropped the main. With just the mizzen and jib, the motion eased and we were still doing six knots. I clicked off the wind vane another couple of points and we started running northwest, out past Point Hudson and back into the straits. Joseph came up and passed me a hot rum.

"I think we have to go for it, Joseph," I said, "make our run now. Next time they won't care if it looks like an accident, they will just come for us. You heard them. They are not going to stop."

He nodded sombrely, then winked and clapped me on the back. The old devil was actually looking forward to it.

In another hour we would be around the point and heading west to Cape Flattery and the open North Pacific. There weren't going to be any more easy opportunities for them, I vowed. From this moment on we would be a moving target. There was not the slightest doubt in my mind that they would be up in a spotter plane at first light, checking the coastline and anchorages. We would be at Cape Flattery before dawn, then the long slanting turn to the south and refuge. The Hatteras was damaged, and we would have a hundred-and-fifty-mile jump on anything else they could send after us. In this kind of weather, no boat was going to catch us in the open sea with that lead.

We would keep running west until we were a hundred and fifty miles out. I was gambling that with the weather deteriorating Delaney would assume we'd hole up until it got better. With an old man and an invalid for crew, only a fool would head out into a storm. Of course, he didn't really know Joseph yet; I prayed someday he would. I waited on deck until I was sure *Arrow* was comfortable with the conditions and then went below.

"So we're underway on the big trip after all, eh, Jared?" Danny said. "Not quite the way we planned it."

"We'll get by. We've got loads of provisions, a full case of rum, lots of good drugs. If it gets bad, you can take pills or get shit-faced, your choice."

Arrow was running smoothly now, but we were still not getting the full fetch. Once we cleared the cape we would start to slam in the heavy seas. I didn't even want to think what that might do to Danny's back.

"Don't worry about me, I'll be fine. This should blow out in a couple of days, and then it will be a milk run." Danny's natural optimism was back, even if his health was not. "By the time the next storm comes, we'll be in Monterey. After that it's just a few coastal hops to San Diego."

I hoped he was right, but somehow I didn't think it was going to be that easy. The glass was still dropping.

Joseph had Eddie's wallet out on the chart table and was going through it. He took out all the money, a couple of hundred American and fifty Canadian, stowed it carefully into his pocket, and slid everything else across to me.

There were a couple of credit cards, a Canadian driver's licence in the name of Edward Sellit, two condoms, a membership in a West End club, and some old gas receipts. According to the driver's licence, he lived in a bedroom community just south of Vancouver. On the back of one of the gas receipts was a phone number and a woman's name.

"Not much here. I'll send it all along to Clarke when we make the next port, along with a description of the other two. Maybe he can make some connections, find out who Delaney is, if he's working for somebody. Until that happens we're just targets. If we can find out what this is all about, we might have a chance to get back at them. Maybe take somebody out, end it."

Danny nodded in agreement. "It's not the money, it's me. Maybe not even connected with the actual robbery. But something to do with the Lebels for sure, something I must have seen. I have no idea what."

I passed him a notebook and pen from the chart table. "Write down everything that happened from the time you first met the Brothers or even heard about them; everything they said, anyone else that was around, anything. Somewhere in there is the reason for all of this, and we have to find it if we're going to stay alive. Somebody wants to kill you, and they're going to a lot of trouble and expense to do just that. We would all be dead now save for Joseph."

Our saviour sat wedged in his favourite spot, the quarter berth by the chart table, pulling a cleaning patch slowly through the barrels of the Purdey, sighting along them from time to time to check for dirt. Outside the wind rose and fell in long, keening wails punctuated by the sound of the seas sliding off *Arrow*'s hull. I took some pillows and wedged Danny into a salon berth on the lee side so tightly that he couldn't move. I dropped a thermos of water and some codeine tablets beside him.

"Take the pills if it gets too tough. A few of those and you'll float all the way to California without even knowing it."

He nodded and began to make notes. I left him to it, pulled on my oilskins, and went on deck to stand the first watch.

CHAPTER 19

Dawn broke cold and grey, the visibility increasing so slowly the difference was scarcely noticeable. There was no brightening of the sky; rather, by slow degrees, the boat emerged out of the darkness, as if the light originated in *Arrow* and expanded outwards in a gradually broadening circle. The sky was overcast with layers of dark cloud, the nearest so low they seemed almost to touch the masts as they scudded by. The wind had picked up another five knots at daybreak and was hovering around thirty-five.

I clipped on the Lirakis harness and went to the bow to fight down the jib. It took a quarter of an hour to get the sail packed and the little storm jib set on the inner forestay. *Arrow* had picked up some weather helm, and I pulled down the mizzen, then set the main with the third reef tied in. She liked that better, and we were still doing six knots with the wind just forward of the beam. The seas had a heavy, greasy look, with a long cross-swell running through every few minutes that slammed us aback.

We were twenty miles out now, the continental shelf falling gradually away beneath us. It would be a full two miles down before it levelled out for the three-thousand-mile run across to Japan at the top, and down to meet the wild Southern Ocean.

Joseph had made a pot of coffee and left it on the stove, and I drank cup after cup of the scalding black brew, staring out into the bleak sky. I ran over everything Delaney had said, how he had sounded, then went right back to the beginning, from my first contact with Clarke at the boatyard. I played it all through, like a slow-speed tape, but came up with nothing new.

Maybe I should have tried to get Delaney. It would have been tricky, but not impossible — go right alongside and over in the first confusion; I had seen Errol Flynn and Tyrone Power do it a dozen times. Once aboard, he would have been mine. Tie him up in tandem with Eddie, drag them astern for a while — he would have told us everything he knew. Now we had nothing. But if I had misjudged it, we might all have been killed. I sat there replaying it, going through all the might-have-beens. Finally I gave it up and called Joseph for his watch.

He awoke instantly, the black eyes snapping open at the first touch. Five minutes later he was in the cockpit with his pipe and coffee, wedged up under the dodger with the old Chilkat blanket tucked around him for warmth. I crawled into the sea berth, which was redolent of tobacco and the faint intangible smell of cedar that always defined Joseph. In minutes, I fell asleep, curled over on my side with my back braced against *Arrow*'s hull, my knees tucked up hard against the lee cloths.

⚙

I dreamed of sinking red-limned ships, of monstrous fish and the bloated body of Eddie swimming among them. I was in the dinghy, frantically cranking the engine, and finally it snarled into life just as something massive rose from the limitless depths and seized me.

I started up in a cold sweat, my hair plastered against my head, to find Joseph shaking me. In the seconds it took to wake, I heard the outboard's high scream turn into the deep, throaty roar of an airplane engine. Joseph had the Purdey out and was filling his pockets with shells. I grabbed the pistol, jacked one into the chamber, and followed him out on deck. The roar of the plane was louder now, flying low and maybe a mile upwind.

"Have they seen us?"

Joseph shook his head and moved his hand back and forth in a sweeping motion. The rain had slackened, but the wind was still blowing a steady thirty-five knots. The cloud ceiling seemed higher now. The noise faded, and twenty-five minutes later it came back again. They were sweeping in long forty-mile legs, running into the coast and then back out again. I tightened my grip on the pistol and crouched. If they spotted us, we didn't have a snowball's chance in hell. The noise got louder, and I stared up into the grey skies.

Too late I thought of dropping the mizzen-mast and clapping the false name back on the stern. There wasn't time now. The engine grew so loud I thought they must break out above us at any second, but then it diminished and they were past, and we hadn't been seen. I realized I had been holding my breath. I sagged back against the coaming, faint with relief. Joseph went below and poured us two fresh cups of coffee, then topped them with an inch of rum. A short time later, we heard the plane again, miles to the south.

We were definitely clear now, I thought, then reminded myself not to underestimate the opposition. This was the second time we had been lucky. It wouldn't last forever. If they were prepared to spend the time and money, they would eventually find us. Delaney knew we had his name now, and he would be relentless. He had the self-assured, monied air of a man who always got things done. He was a long way from Eddie and Chuck. They were just hired hands.

Delaney belonged to a different world, a realm of money and power where nothing was impossible, the price just became higher. And stacked above him was another tier, dark and impenetrable, where a shadowed figure nodded his head and consigned us to death. For what? It was connected with drugs. That was the only arena where they played for stakes this high. The Lebels, Desjardins, his troops — all apparently gone now. There had been a shift in power: a new alliance had formed and declared us enemies.

The conclusion was bleak and inescapable. For as Clarke had warned us, the drug chain runs from north to south, link to link along the entire Pacific Coast from Vancouver to Panama, Columbia and Peru and beyond. Contacts, mules, dealers, planes, choppers, cigarette boats, freighters, victims and abusers, all meshed in the cocaine net and all working for a common purpose, the quick and facile distribution of the drug.

Somebody somewhere thought that we could interfere with that process. Somebody with the infinite profits of the drug trade and the power that great wealth brings. For that kind of money, even the Pacific Ocean shrinks into an organized search pattern. Each country has its Customs and Immigration checkpoints, maybe two or three ports where you can clear your boat in. There was no question of a fake identity; the boat registration was required and validated each time; the numbers often checked with those graven in the ship's main beam. Most boats now had fax, single-sideband, even cellular phones and email. The infinite Pacific, greatest of all the oceans, covering an area of sixty-four million square miles, was subject in the final analysis to the same pattern of search-and-grid as the smallest lake. Our course was defined by wind, current, and the great bellows of the trade winds.

We could run for a time, maybe even for a long time, but we couldn't run forever. Sooner or later we would be found, and the killing teams would go out again. I had no illusions about the final inevitable result. We could not survive against that kind of power. Our only hope was to identify the prime mover, and move against him.

Danny was sitting up in the berth, jammed comfortably into the corner with his pillows.

"I'm hard at it, Jared." He waved the notebook. "I've covered the first few days. I never realized there were so many women around at the time. Now whenever I write down another one's name, I start daydreaming."

He flashed me the old Danny grin. "I was a wild and gusty gale of a fellow, and roared and squalled in many a port."

"Robert Service?"

"No. Fred Helene, a Kwakiutl from Bella Coola. He could go on for hours." He shook his head. "I can't see anything here that helps us, though."

"Try and put down dates where you can. It must be something you've seen or heard that connects to whoever is behind all of this. Somebody who met with the Brothers, maybe."

"Yeah, I know. Well, I still have a ways to go. Off the top I can't think of anything, but writing it down helps to bring it back. I've got the time," he added wryly. "What is the weather doing?"

"Glass is steady now at one thousand and three millibars. I caught the Coast Guard weather at six, doesn't sound too bad. They're forecasting force eight; we're close to that now. The seas are still building a little, the edges of the crests just starting to blow off. Probably thirty knots in the lulls, gusting to forty."

"How far out are we?"

"Sixty miles. There was a plane running a grid this morning. They didn't see us."

"I thought I heard something. They're not going to quit, are they?"

"No."

"It all seemed so easy at the time. A quick smash-and-grab, nobody hurt, then a couple of weeks and I'd have my twenty or thirty grand." He shook his head. "Now look where we are. Stupid, stupid!" He banged his fist against the bulkhead in frustration.

"Look on the bright side. We've still got a hundred grand plus, we've got a good boat, and we're heading south. Another seven hundred miles and we're into better weather. We will keep moving, never more than a couple of days in one place. First port we make I'm going to a gun shop and pick up some serious weapons. If these bastards want to come after us, let's make them pay. A twelve-gauge automatic shotgun with the plug out, and a good rifle. Something with a scope so we can do some damage at long range. Then one of those stainless steel flare pistols that take the shotgun shells and slugs as well. They're legal, we can leave that out, hide the ammo."

"Christ. We're in a fucking war."

"Yep. Now what we have to do is identify the opposing general."

Danny raised the pad in mock salute. "Aye aye, Captain. Back to work."

I went to the chart table and switched on the GPS. Sixty seconds later it flashed up our position. I punched in the Monterey waypoint lat and long and pressed Enter. Immediately the course and distance came up on the screen. Seven hundred and fifty-one point two nautical miles, at a magnetic heading of two hundred and fifty degrees. Another button, and up came our true speed over the bottom. Five and a half knots. When we were within a hundred hours of our waypoint, it would start displaying an estimated time of arrival based on speed, course, and leeway. There was a hundred-page book that came with the GPS outlining all sorts of other clever tricks, but I hadn't tackled it yet.

I picked up the dividers and plotted our position on the big international chart. We were in five thousand feet of water now, and it was still growing deeper. By the time we started our swing south in another twelve hours, it would be down to a mile and a half. We would be a hundred and thirty miles out by then and well beyond the range of any coastal traffic. The chances of being spotted by a plane were almost nil in this overcast, and with any luck the weather would moderate by the time we had to change course and buck into it.

We would stay well clear of the great capes that jut out along the Oregon and California coasts; even their names sounded like shipwrecks. Cape Disappointment, off the dangerous Columbia River; the rocky and barren Cape Blanco; Cape Mendocino, where a treacherous underwater ridge rises from the depths and extends the coastline in a seventy-mile tongue of toothed and serrated submarine mountains before it turns back in and runs down to the east.

Mariners believe that there is a sea change at Point Conception, a hundred and fifty miles south of Monterey. It is there that the waters begin their transmutation from the cold North Pacific green to the lighter, bluer shades of the South Pacific, and the temperatures rise in conjunction. From there to San Diego and the Mexican border is a hundred and fifty miles of the finest day sailing, with beautiful anchorages and full-service marinas everywhere.

The further south you go, the more melodious the names become, changing from the harsh, powerful consonants of the First Nation peoples to the lilting cadences of the old Spanish empire: San Luis Obispo, Santa Cruz, Juan Cadenza, Cortes Bank; I studied the charts, the names ringing like struck bell chords in my mind, and hungered for the safety they would bring.

All that day we ran to the southwest. The rain had finally stopped, but it was bitterly cold on deck. I tried on Bill's big offshore suit, stuffed and swollen like a Day-Glo Michelin Man, but it was too bulky for comfort, and I went back to the layered wool of the commercial fisherman: the good grey Stanfield's underwear, with a heavy flannel shirt and knitted wool fisherman pants overtop, and a wool jacket covering that, with oil skins as a final layer giving protection against rain and wind chill. It was the same outfit we wore on the halibut boats, whether it was freezing cold on the first trip to the Aleutians in February, or ninety degrees in the broiling sun in Hecate Straits in July. Only the jacket came off in hot weather. You were often damp but never cold, and the wool soaked up the perspiration.

Joseph and I stood three-hour watches, sheltering under the dodger or sitting in the galley, with regular visits up on deck to sweep the horizon for traffic. The batteries were still low, and we couldn't use the radar. As soon as the seas settled I would charge them with the little Honda generator.

Once we saw a tanker running north on the horizon at a speed of sixteen knots, with the wind and seas behind it. If we had happened to be on the reciprocal course, the combined speed of approach would have been in the neighbourhood of twenty-five knots. Given that your horizon is maybe eight miles under good conditions from the deck of a sailboat, we would have had a bit less than twenty minutes from the time the tanker appeared until we collided. Which was why we did the fifteen-minute checks.

Sailboats are notorious for giving a poor radar image, assuming of course that anyone is watching. I had drunk enough beer with enough big-ship skippers at the old Drake Hotel to know about their watch-keeping at sea and the logistics of emergency course-changes in a vessel that might be well over a thousand feet long. Meg and Bill told me once that they knew personally of nine sailboats that had disappeared without a trace in fine weather during their years of cruising.

I suspended these cheery thoughts and took another position that put us a hundred and forty miles off the coast. Good enough. The wind was still blowing from the southeast, and we were just making our course on the port tack. I sheeted everything in hard, the boat heeling over at thirty degrees and water coming over the port gunwales. Nobody ever said *Arrow* was a dry boat. She was wallowing, and I shook out a reef and she picked up half a knot and steadied down. The sky was brighter now, and the wind had eased to thirty knots in the gusts. *Arrow* could have handled a bigger headsail, but I wasn't sure about Danny.

I hand-steered for a while, assimilating the feel of the boat shouldering through the seas, the whole working, shuddering drive of her travelling up the tiller like the pulse of a living creature. Suddenly the sun broke free, slanting through the lowering sky in rays so sharp and separate they lit up a patch of sea ahead of me no larger than half a city block. *Arrow* powered out of the shadows. The sunlight seemed a harbinger of hope and promise, warming me out of all proportion to its heat.

The sea curled and broke ahead of us, the foam gleaming whitely in the light, and *Arrow* went at it like a dog for a bone, bounding up the trough and through the spray as quick and agile as a terrier. I laughed out loud for the pure joy of it. This being the Pacific Northwest, though, five minutes later the sun disappeared for good, and it began to rain.

For the next day, and the following, and the day after, we headed south without touching a line or handling a sail, the wind constant at twenty-five knots and *Arrow* close-hauled at a steady five, rolling up hundred-and-twenty-mile days regular as a chronometer. The boat was always wet now, the water sluicing constantly over the decks and finding its way in through unseen cracks and strains where the shrouds pulled at the chain plates. We kept the Dickinson stove lit twenty-four hours a day, and the interior grew increasingly damp and humid, the roof beams sweating with condensation that dripped below. I tied a tarp over the salon skylight and battened it tightly under the cleats around the edges. It made the skylight watertight, but the interior of the boat became even more dark and gloomy. It was hard to find comfortable bedding now, the salt crystals omnipresent, tiny sponges that soaked up the first traces of humidity, soon rendering wet and clammy what had initially seemed warm and comfortable.

It was hardest on Danny; confined to his berth, jammed in with pillows and unable to exercise or even move very much, he became quieter and quieter. He never complained, but I knew how gloomy and depressing this must be for him. The warmth and light of the tropics seemed an eternity away. I spent hours trying to cheer him up, sitting at his feet, talking about the old days, mutual friends, fishing stories, anything to break down the wall of hopeless stoicism that was building by the hour. It combined with a dour, sour Scottish streak inherited from his father, and I saw the effects increasing daily. By the third day out, he was taking the codeine tablets more and more frequently, and I took to counting them while he slept.

Joseph still worked on Danny's back every day, massaging, rubbing, and probing with an increasingly grim face as Danny lay there, inert and unknowing as a side of beef. When Joseph was finished, we rolled Danny over like a log and wedged him back into his berth again. He had stopped writing in the notebook and was withdrawing into himself, fading back behind the blank and haunted eyes, the pupils constantly dilated now from all the drugs. He was starting to scare me.

On the fifth morning, the wind shifted to the east and we were able to free up a point. By noon the sun had burned away the cloud cover, and we were down to three knots in a dying breeze. The motion of the boat was much easier, and we moved Danny back into the saloon. Joseph took the slings and ran them around Danny's feet and passed him the lines. Danny just stared at him with a slight mocking smile on his face, then dropped the lines and closed his eyes. Joseph spoke sharply to him, but there was no reply. I left them and went out on deck.

A few minutes later Joseph stamped out and joined me, his eyes snapping with rage, the smoke from his pipe sucked in and out in erratic, jerking puffs. He was muttering to himself and shooting angry glances below. Finally he quietened and lay back against the coaming, his forehead knotted tightly and eyes closed. I went up to the fore-deck and checked the sheets and sail for chafe, wanting to be anywhere but here.

Joseph uttered a low exclamation and went below. Five minutes later the shouting began. It was Danny, raging at Joseph and screaming curses. Then he began yelling my name. I ran to the companionway and halted there in shock.

Joseph had fastened a rough halter out of a blanket and slung it under Danny's arms. He had tied the ends to the block and tackle, and hauled him up so that he dangled just below the grab rails, his neck bent forward, his feet just touching the ground as he tried to flex. The lines were tied off out of his reach.

"Jesus Christ," I said.

"Jared. Get me the fuck out of here," he screamed. "Put me down, goddammit. Jared, do you fucking hear me?" He was facing sideways and couldn't pivot his body around to see me. His head twisted towards me over his shoulder, the eyes wide and staring.

"Jared. He's fucking crazy. Get me down!" His eyes were glazing, and he looked half-mad. "You cocksucking bastards! Put me down!"

He lifted his head and screamed, a wild harrowing shriek that sent shivers down my spine. He broke off, panting, and then began cursing in a steady, relentless stream of obscenity. Joseph took my arm and led me out to the cockpit. I didn't know what to do. Joseph sat staring aft to *Arrow*'s wake, his face grim and unreadable, his teeth clenched tightly around the stem of his pipe.

Danny howled and raged in anger and humiliation for a long time. Finally he was silent. Joseph left him suspended for two hours, then went below and lowered him back into his berth. Neither of them spoke. When I went below, much later, Danny was sleeping, or pretending to. I cooked a bleak supper for Joseph and myself. Danny refused to eat.

❀

The following day we were practically becalmed, ghosting along at two knots under the big genoa in a mirror-flat sea with only a slight southerly swell. I took the cover off the salon hatch and the sun poured through, illuminating Danny where he hung from the sling. He was silent, not moving a muscle. Joseph had raised him up right after breakfast. He was talking softly, but Danny never replied; he was totally absent now, the big gold body transfixed in the sun, eerily reminiscent of a crucifixion scene that had hung on the wall of my grandfather's house. As the boat rose and fell silently on the swell, he swayed back and forth, inanimate and insensitive as the lamp that swung alongside to the same slow rhythm.

I couldn't watch, and spent my time on deck as Joseph raised and lowered Danny. Two hours up, two hours down, all through the daylight hours. Danny had stopped eating altogether now, and he never spoke. I filled thermoses of juice and laid them beside him in the bunk, and he must have drunk them during the night, for they were empty in the morning. Joseph worked on his back as he swayed, rubbing in the pungent salve, working in long, circular motions from the base of the coccyx up to the neck. Danny never gave any sign or acknowledgement of his presence. I took all the daylight watches now, leaving Joseph and Danny to their grim, silent conflict.

The breeze became fluky and the wind vane unreliable. I hand-steered, grateful for the diversion. Joseph appeared on deck just long enough to smoke a pipe, then disappeared below again to massage Danny, or just sit and watch him for hour after hour.

We were getting constant sun now, filtering down through the high clouds of cirrostratus. The sea remained glassy and the wind fickle. We glided along between one and two knots in near-silence, not a fish or bird disturbing the sky or water; the only sound was the faint sigh of our wake as it spread out behind us in an ever-increasing V. The weather was unheard of for this time of year, and it only added to the unreality that surrounded us. As I sat in the cockpit hour after hour, going below only to cook or eat, the stretched, tense atmosphere played increasingly on my nerves.

I began to have trouble sleeping, and my dreams were strange and unsettled. I saw forests of totem poles stretched out as far as the eye could see in even, ordered rows like the massive war cemeteries of Europe, their images graven in strange and horrible parody of Danny and Joseph: Ravens, Bears, Frogs, Killer Whales, and Thunderbirds, twisted and misshapen on the poles, Danny always at the crossed centre, his wings and claws outstretched in supplication, while Joseph crouched and brooded in animal guise below. I awoke from my nightmares sweating and breathless, and by the pallid light of the moon I could see Danny hanging, and feel his eyes upon me, filled with hate.

I lay there in the dark, praying for a fresh breeze to weather us into Monterey. Then for the phone call to Annie to come as quickly as possible to get Danny to a clinic while there was still time. She must take all the money and use it for his care. Even in the best of facilities, it should last for a couple of years. I knew now that Danny would not need bed care for even half that long. If he did not heal soon he would die. You couldn't blame him. I might have wanted the same thing for myself.

Joseph was the son of a shaman and a powerful medicine man in his own right, but this was cruel and barbaric. I took away the pills when Danny was sleeping, but it didn't make any difference. He hung as intransigently as before, the slight rise and fall of his chest the only sign of life.

The wind died altogether, and I brought out the little generator and charged the batteries until there was enough kick to crank over the diesel. *Arrow* could easily average six knots under power in this calm; fifty hours and we would be in Monterey. When this unnatural weather broke, I wanted to be safe in harbour. I put away the Honda and turned on the ignition to start the engine. Joseph caught my hand before I could punch the starter button and shook his head.

"For Christ's sake, Joseph," I exploded, "we can't just lie here. Let's motor in, we've only got three hundred miles to go. Danny needs professional care. He's not eating. Another few days of this could kill him."

Joseph reached down, switched off the ignition, and pocketed the key.

I threw up my hands. "All right, then, have it your way! You always fucking do," I added under my breath. I exhaled to calm myself. "And just how long do you suppose this weather will last, then?"

Joseph held up his fingers. Another three days.

Yeah, right. A seven-day dead calm off the coast of northern California in early December. That would be one for the record books all right.

❖

We lay there all that day and the next, motionless save for the slight rocking in the swell, our only progress half a knot south with the California current. The moon was filling, and the nights were bright enough to read by. Joseph continued his regimen around the clock; Danny spent two hours up and then two down, with massages in between. The silence was overwhelming; even the sails had stopped their slatting and hung motionless like giant broken wings.

I tapped the glass constantly, praying for any sort of change, but it remained rock steady. A huge high had gathered and enfolded us in its centre, stationary and attendant as nature hung suspended. I no longer slept for any length of time, dozing fitfully in the cockpit for a few minutes, waking to the muted sound of the blocks as Danny rose and fell, or the unanswered whispered chants of Joseph.

By the third day I had stopped cooking meals. Neither Joseph nor I had any appetite under the translucent stare of Danny. The flesh was falling off him now, and you could see the musculature and bones beneath. Joseph's prodding fingers disappeared as he worked on the flaccid, lifeless body. It would not be long now, I thought; it seemed as if his spirit had already departed. I tried to talk to him, but it was futile. Nobody was there. The glass had started to rise, and the high was finally moving. We would have some wind by nightfall. Perhaps there was still a chance that Annie and the family could make it down in time to say goodbye.

I was dozing in the cockpit when I heard the strangled sobbing rising up from below. It was Danny. He hung in the sling, staring downward. Tears were pouring down his face.

"My legs," he whispered brokenly. "Oh Jesus. They hurt. They hurt like hell. Look."

He pointed down and I saw his feet move clearly forward a few inches against the swing of the boat.

"Oh Christ, it hurts like hell," he said again, and now he was smiling and then laughing through his tears, and I could barely see for mine.

"I never thought I would feel them again," he whispered.

I grabbed Joseph around his waist and lifted him up and hugged him. He tolerated it for a few moments, and then the vise-like pinch on my waist told me that was sufficient. When I put him down his eyelid drooped in a solemn wink. We laid Danny down on the berth, and while Joseph massaged him I cooked an enormous meal. Afterwards we sat around drinking rum and coffee until the wind came up. It rose out of the west, a fair wind for Monterey. I set everything, main, mizzen, genoa, and mizzen staysail, and we were broad reaching at eight knots under a full and shining moon.

Late that evening we picked up a school of porpoises and they stayed with *Arrow* the entire night, crossing and recrossing the bow wave in an intricate ballet of dives and pirouettes. I didn't wake Joseph for his watch but sat the whole night through, studying the porpoises as if they were the irrevocable signs of a divine providence. I leaned over the leeward rail, down close to the roiled water, and occasionally one approached, slowed its mad careen, and, half rolling, gazed inquiringly up at me. I looked down into those wise, friendly, animate eyes and felt like an electric current the benevolence emanating from them.

I woke Joseph at dawn to stand watch, and went below and fell into a deep, untroubled sleep.

CHAPTER 20

Thirty-six hours later we sailed into Monterey. The harbourmaster assigned us a berth among the commercial fishing fleet, and we slipped gratefully in between two of the big squid boats. The crew were mending nets, talking rapidly in a rich patois of English, Spanish, and Portuguese as they worked. They greeted us with the amused tolerance fishermen reserve for the dilettantes of the marine world, and one of them jumped down onto the floats and took our lines.

I thanked him and introduced myself, saying that we too were commercial fishermen, on a holiday for my partner's convalescence. This of course changed everything, and Alfonse accepted my offer of a drink, and called over his friends. There were four of them, small, dark men quick and agile as cats, with wrists as big as my ankles. They helped me move Danny into the cockpit, where he sat looking greedily around, a contented grin on his face. The change in him was astonishing. He was eating enough for two, and already the grim, wasted man of recent days was a distant memory.

The harbour was small and tight, split up democratically between the fishing fleet and the tourists. Fisherman's Wharf was just a stone's throw off the port bow, a confused jumble of cafés and shops roosting on the old pilings that once supported the bustling canneries. When the sardines vanished in the late forties, the area foundered for a period of time, then slowly transformed into the present-day tourist attraction, aided immeasurably by the stories of Steinbeck.

Not the least of the attractions were the California sea lions showboating in the harbour, diving, pursuing fish, and panhandling tourists with equal aplomb. They regularly encroached on the outside limits of the floats, hauling their glistening bulks ponderously up out of the water for a quick sunlit snooze, then sliding gracefully back in when the marina attendants came trudging dutifully down the docks to shoo them off. It was a friendly confrontation, without rancour on either side.

We lazed in the cockpit, relaxing and visiting with our neighbours. Danny was in his old form, teasing, cracking jokes, and telling outrageous halibut stories that nobody took seriously. As evening approached, phone calls were made, incoming boats were hailed, and a guitar, harmonica, and accordion appeared as if by magic, along with gallons of homemade wine and lashings of food. I set out some of Annie's hard smoked salmon for our guests while Joseph went into the bilges and retrieved one of his specialties, a fermented mix of salmon roe, berries, and eulachon oil, pressed tight and stored in a seal bladder. He passed it solemnly around, and while some blanched at the prospect, others stuck gallantly in, and one brave soul even had seconds. We filled up on calamari, salmon, and the clam chowder and sourdough bread the Row was famous for.

Late in the evening I told two of the more concerned Portuguese fishermen about Danny's paralysis, how Joseph had finally hung him and massaged his back daily, and finally the feeling, and slowly now the strength, were coming back. Jean and Charlie were impressed, and nodded gravely and exchanged meaningful looks, and made the sign of the cross, and fingered the little silver medals that hung from their necks as I described how nearly miraculous it was, and in spite of all the doctors.

At the end they rose and shook my hand and left. Later in the evening they returned, shepherding a pair of giggling girls in tight minis and teetering heels unsteadily down the dock.

"These are our masseurs," Charlie said proudly.

"Masseuses," the one with the giant breasts corrected. Three of the men grabbed Danny, who hardly protested at all, and carried him below with the girls.

"They will find muscles he never knew he had," Jean promised with a satisfied smile.

I shook my head and looked across at Joseph. He smiled and nodded his head in approval, then turned his attention back to the elderly Italian widow who lived on the tugboat four berths across and had come over to greet us with the others. She was talking rapidly, and he paid close attention, then spoke in turn. I wondered what language they were using. A short time later they left together, and around midnight the party broke up. I sat in the cockpit by myself for a while, sipping a last Scotch and making plans for the next day, and then the girls came out and I went down to my bunk. Danny was sprawled on his back, his arms thrown out by his sides, snoring loudly. I lay there for a long time before I fell asleep.

I awoke at first light, slipped on sweats and Nikes, and went for a run up into the hills that fringed the bay. I was labouring badly for the first twenty minutes, then began to find my rhythm and almost started to enjoy it. I concentrated on my form, trying to visualize as I ran, and put the separate parts in harmony.

I was just starting to feel good about myself when a tall girl with a long blond ponytail blew by me, halfway down the long slope back to the water. She was wearing an L.A. marathon T-shirt and ran with long, fluid strides, her shoulders and back dead square, her arms pumping like a metronome. If we stayed here for six months, and I ran every day, I might just be able to stay with her for a mile or so. "Probably on steroids," I muttered as she vanished in the distance.

The marina showers were cheap, hot, and lasting. I bowed thankfully under the nozzle and washed away the wine and sweat and salt of the voyage and its aftermath. I finished with an icy cold blast for penance, towelled off, and walked back to the boat. I'd had my party and my relaxation and my run, now it was time to be smart, and stay alive. The squeaking sound of Danny's blocks rising from the cabin was music to my ears.

"Ninety-nine, one hundred." He grinned up at me, his chest glistening with sweat. "Good morning, my friend. It's good to be alive."

"How's the back this morning?" I asked.

"The back is great. Sore as a bitch. And the front! Well, the front is even better. All the stiffness gone. A little sore as well from lack of exercise, but Shannon is going to work on that. They loved the blocks. I think we may have invented a new position. But enough of that. Listen, I've figured out how I can haul myself out into the cockpit. We'll run a line between the two masts, reeve a fall down the companionway hatch, say three to one. I'll buckle on a Lirakis harness, clip on . . ."

He was off and running, his face flushed and excited as he laid out his scheme.

There is nothing you cannot move fore and aft, up, down, or sideways on a sailboat. The boom will run through a hundred and eighty degrees horizontally and ninety degrees vertically, acting like a small moveable crane. Lines coming down from the masts give you forty- and fifty-foot lifting stations; the big three-speed winches and the leads and blocks running to them are stressed for thousands of pounds. It's all just a big grown-up version of the jungle gyms of our boyhood. *No wonder us guys love sailing so much*, I thought wryly.

"I'll rig it up as soon as you want, Danny."

On my run I had decided to do whatever he wanted at whatever speed he wished; I knew he would be pushing hard. It wasn't according to the book, but if we had gone by the book he would be dead by now, or paralysed for life. If he wanted to get laid six times a day and do two hundred push-ups in between times, that was okay too. He and Joseph could sort out all of that business between them. My job was going to be to set up some security.

"I'm taking off for a while."

There was no sign of Joseph. I took out the Purdey and some shells and laid them beside Danny on the berth.

"Keep these handy. We should be safe here for a couple of days, but from now on we're not taking any chances."

The animation faded from Danny's face. "Yeah," he said, "there is still that, isn't there?"

I gripped his shoulder hard. "Look, Danny. You just concentrate on getting well. There is nothing you and I and Joseph can't do between the three of us. When you are fit, we will find these guys and we will rip their fucking livers out. In the meantime we are going to enjoy life and stay safe. And you are going to heal. That's your only job now."

He put his hand over mine and squeezed. "I know. I'll do it. You won't see me down again." He smiled. "I owe you a lot, my friend. More than I can ever repay."

"I asked Charlie to have the fleet keep an eye out for strangers. I said you were fooling around with some made man's girl back home and there might be a contract out on you. After last night I'm sure he believes it."

"Thanks a lot."

"My pleasure."

Charlie was sitting on the stern of the big squid boat, drinking coffee while he adjusted one of the powerful light banks that attracts the fish. He listened gravely and gave me the addresses of a couple of gun shops.

"I can likely get you the names of some other people who deal direct if you don't want to bother with the formalities," he said.

"Thanks. I'll see how I make out at the shops first. It's pretty standard stuff."

"Don't worry about your friend, or your boat. I put the word out, we'll keep our eyes open. There's always some of us about. We fish the squid at night, but the draggers will be in then."

I thanked him again and went up the dock to phone Clarke. There was the usual runaround before they connected me, my refusal to give my name to the desk sergeant compounding the problem.

"Hi, Clarke. It's Jared."

"Jared. I was beginning to wonder. How are you? What's with the secret identity?"

"We're fine, just playing it safe. We had some unexpected company in Port Townsend."

"Did you, now?"

"There were three of them. They were very serious, and we were very lucky to get away with our lives. They underestimated Joseph."

"Never a wise thing to do. How is the old bugger, anyway?" There was real affection in his voice.

"Fine. We got in at three o'clock yesterday afternoon. He met a widow at a party last night, and I haven't seen either of them since."

"Maybe there's hope for me yet," Clarke laughed. "Did you get a good look at your visitors?"

"Yes. Full descriptions, one name and address, and the last name of the one in charge. They came into Port Townsend on a fifty-foot Hatteras on December second. The boat was damaged when we last saw it, all the glass out of the pilot house, some bullet holes, probably some fire damage as well. It looked like they were heading towards Everett or thereabouts. The man in charge was called Delaney. Probably correct — he got very annoyed when the help let it slip out. Not that he intended us to be around to pass the information on. He implied that they had done the Lebel Brothers and Desjardins as well. Maybe some others."

"Delaney. I don't recognise that name offhand. I'll run it through the computer. Where are you, Jared?"

"Monterey. I'd appreciate it if you kept that piece of news to yourself."

"You're getting paranoid, Jared." He paused. "Well, perhaps not. Listen, I think I'll come down there, take some statements. Shouldn't be a problem, the case is still open. I haven't heard anything recent about Desjardins. I'll check around, talk to Montreal. Probably be down there in a couple of days. Where will I find you?"

"We're in the harbour, right off Fisherman's Wharf. Berthed in with the fishing fleet on B dock."

"Take care. Give my regards to Danny and Joseph."

I hung up and dialled again. I could hear the happiness in Annie's voice at her first words. "Joseph phoned. He says Danny is going to be all right."

"Well," I said cautiously, "he has feeling in his back and legs, but he has a long way to go."

"But he's going to recover fully?"

"Yes, he is." I knew it was true as I spoke. "The locals have already arranged some special therapy for him."

"It's a miracle," Annie said. "Well, it's that and Joseph, anyway.

"Joseph says the three of you have decided to stay together for a while, at least until Mexico."

This was news to me.

"Well, yes, it seems like a good idea now. Danny can exercise on the boat just as well as he can on land, and he will be happier. Joseph is better than any doctor."

"Maybe that other thing is over now. Joseph said you weren't really sure if the guys in Townsend were looking for you. You just wanted to play it safe."

Her voice was slightly accusing. I had spoiled her junket to Port Townsend.

"Yes. Well, I thought they looked a bit suspicious," I said. "People tell me I'm getting paranoid."

"I know you did what you thought was best."

I was forgiven.

"Erin and Jaimie send their regards. Take care, Jared. Maybe we can all get together in Mexico. Give my love to Danny."

We talked awhile longer, and then I rang off and caught a taxi downtown to the gun shop. Harold, who ran it, was middle-aged, with the short, bristling haircut and tattoos of a vet who was still proud of his service.

"Now this one here, this one was always one of the favourites in Nam. Some guys could bring Charlie down at over a thousand yards with one of these. I was nowhere near that good. Not that you very often saw the little bastards until they were right on top of you anyway," he added ruefully. "For a boat, is it?"

"Yes. Probably something more in the sporting line would be better. There might be some chance of explaining that away. Maybe a .308? Something that is reasonably accurate up to five hundred yards, with a flat trajectory, not too delicate. Maybe a night scope too."

He regarded me thoughtfully. "You're talking some serious money now, my friend. The Starlite doesn't come cheap."

"Let's throw it all into a pile and we'll deal on it."

While he rummaged in the back room, I picked out a used Ithaca shotgun and a new stainless flare pistol. I added four boxes of shot and slugs for the shotgun and flare pistol, as well as extra cartridges for the over-and-under.

Harold came out of the back with a Winchester .308 and one of the converted military Springfield .30-06s from the late fifties, and I tried the feel of them both, finally settling on the Winchester. I threw a shooting sling, some extra clips, and four boxes of .308 cartridges into the pile. He mounted the scope and we went into the back room, where he clamped it into a vise and sighted it in.

"I won't need cases for these two, they'll be hidden away on board. The problem is, in countries where you might really need them, they confiscate them. You have to declare them when you arrive; you don't get them back until you leave. I'll wrap them in oiled flannel, find a place to stow them."

"I know a guy who builds custom cases. Sometimes he has clients who want something hidden in their house or car. He's a little weird, but discreet, and very good. I'll send him down to your boat to have a look."

"Thanks."

We dickered for a while, both of us enjoying it, and finally settled on three thousand for the lot. He pulled a couple of beers out of the fridge in the little workshop, and we sealed the bargain while he broke the rifles down and oiled them, barely glancing down as he reassembled them with quick precise motions.

"The Winchester is a good weapon, it's been range tested already. You should be able to get a six-inch grouping at five hundred yards with practice. I can get you onto a range near here if you like."

"Thanks. Maybe later."

We packed and stowed it all in a cardboard box, wrapped it up in brown paper and string, and a short time later I was pushing it down the dock in a second-hand wheelchair I'd bought at the local hospital supply outlet.

"Jesus. Any more and we'll have to raise the waterline." Danny was hooked up in his sling, his feet carrying a fraction of the weight. He moved his foot forward slowly, and then rose up slightly on it. He was sweating heavily.

"Don't overdo it, amigo."

"No problem. There's pain, but it isn't deep. More like muscles stretching."

He dropped back down and picked up the stainless flare pistol from the table. "That is a mean-looking little mother."

"Known as a machete stopper among the more paranoid Third World cruisers. Lots of boats carry them for protection. I'll mount that old binocular case by the companionway, put some shells and slugs on the bottom, flares on top. Somebody's coming down to see about storing the shotgun; the Winchester can go in the tubes alongside the .410. It will take a minute to get it out, but that's not a problem. The shotgun we want loaded and handy. Maybe put a dummy post in by the chart table, set in at the corner and carried up to the beam. Clip the gun inside with some spring-loaded latches, a hidden quick-release for the cover panel. We'll keep the .410 in plain sight from now on, declare it when we clear."

"Maybe we'll never have to use any of them." Danny didn't like the guns any more than I did.

"Did you talk to Annie?"

"Yes. Joseph had already spoken to her. She thinks you will be sprinting up and down the docks in a couple of days."

"Therapy, lots and lots of therapy," Danny said piously, "that's the key. Are they coming down?"

"Maybe in Mexico. Joseph told her you would do better on the boat. He didn't tell her about the trouble, just that we got nervous and pulled out."

"Good. No sense her worrying too. Joseph came down and gave me a rubdown. He and Maria are going out for dinner."

"I wonder how they communicate?"

Danny smiled. "Maybe he speaks Italian."

"Why won't he speak English?" I had often wondered but never asked.

He shook his head. "I don't think anybody knows for sure. It happened a long time ago; an honour thing, an insult, probably something like that. Maybe something to do with the language of the conquerors. When I was a kid l, he wouldn't even listen to it, just closed himself off. He still will, of course, whenever it suits him."

"Do you know how old he is?"

Danny looked uncomfortable. "Not really."

"But you know where he was born."

"Yeah. Masset. Haida, one of the ranking families. Erin looked up the records once when he was fishing up in Haida Gwaii. The parents' names were right, according to Annie."

"So how old is he, then?"

"Well," Danny said, "there was obviously some mistake. The missions kept most of the records, they weren't always accurate."

"So how old, then?"

"Well, according to them he'd be ninety-five years old now."

"Ninety-five?"

"Yes." Danny laughed. "Crazy, isn't it?"

"So how old do you think he is, then?" I asked.

"Well, he's pretty old," Danny muttered.

"How old?" I pressed.

"Well, he's getting up there, that's for sure."

I waited silently.

"All right, goddammit," Danny exploded, "I think the fucking records are probably right." He glared at me belligerently.

"No sweat," I said, "so do I. Let's eat. Afterwards we'll work on your transportation."

We spent the next two hours rigging up lines and blocks. I took off the main and hauled the boom up to a sixty-degree angle and brought the mainsheet down and attached it to his harness, and by the time we finished Danny could move himself from the salon to the cockpit without assistance. It was the first time in three months that he'd had any real control over his movements.

It only took another few minutes to rig up a line controlling the boom so that he could swing outboard over the docks and drop into the wheelchair. Nothing would do but we try it out at once. Danny hauled himself slowly up above the lifelines, then swung out and lowered down over the dock. I positioned the wheelchair and he dropped down into it.

"Mark where the wheels are supposed to line up," he said. "I don't want to be dangling in the air with the fucking chair four feet away."

X marked the spot and he trundled speedily away, the big arms flexing effortlessly as he spun the wheels. Five minutes later he was parked by Charlie's boat, a piece of net spread out in his lap and a fid in his hand, laughing and talking as he worked. There would be no holding him back now.

Just behind him a Catalina 27 was going out for a sail. The girl at the tiller waved to me, and I recognized her as the runner from that morning. There was a man with her, sitting in the cockpit, handling the sheets. I waved back and watched her tack down the narrow channel, the little boat spinning expertly in the confined space. The name *Moonbeam* was written across the transom in bold script. I gazed after the bright fall of her hair until she was out of sight. Unaccountably, I felt depressed, and went below to do some maintenance on the engine. No use wasting the mood.

It was six o'clock before I finished, sweaty, greasy, and irritable. Nobody else was aboard. I went for a shower and then, on a sudden impulse, caught a taxi and headed downtown.

I didn't have a destination until I saw the rundown gym with the old pugs standing around in front. There were only a few people inside, and none of them could be mistaken for yuppies. No juice bar here; a few mats scattered around, some speed and weight bags, two sets of rusted weights, and a beat-up old ring in the corner, where a couple of beefy warriors with no helmets were pounding on each other. The air reeked of disinfectant, despair, and old sweat. It could have been the prison gym. My kind of place.

I changed into sweats, handed twenty bucks over to a bored old black man leaning on a broom, and started to work on the big bag in the corner. I began with a series of katas, going through the exercises slowly, letting the fluidity build, and by the time the sweat came I could feel the anger starting to release. I moved into my kicks then — mae geri, mawashi geri, yoko geri — spinning and wheeling in different combinations, trying for maximum height and speed, my mind slowly blanking as my body gained ascendance. I brought the images gradually up out of the filmy red haze and gave them their names: the Lebels, Eddie, Chuck and Delaney, and then, beyond them and not quite visible, the secret one I lusted for.

I concentrated on his aura and moved into the killing strokes, circling and thrusting at the vague images limned in sweat on the bag. There was no sense of time or space as I worked, only the fierce concentration and the savage joy of the contact, and finally I was finished, my hands hanging numb at my sides, my chest a fiery ball as I struggled for air.

I crouched on the floor, dripping sweat, trying in vain to control my breathing. When I raised my head, no one was left in the gym except the black janitor, staring at me with a wry smile.

"Jesus, man, when you work out you really work out, don't you? We closed at nine o'clock."

I slipped him another twenty, showered, and headed out the door.

It was the kind of neighbourhood where no strangers walked alone. I ambled along with a hopeful searching, but my stroll was uneventful. The first bar I found was dark and gloomy, with a broken sign hanging crookedly outside and dirty sawdust scattered haphazardly over the spills on the floor.

Finest kind.

I ordered a double vodka, tossed it back, and ordered another, swinging around and surveying the room with my elbows leaned back against the bar. I recognized a couple of men from the gym and two hookers were working a noisy table down near the back. Their pimp gave me a hard stare, and I smiled at him and drank down the vodka and ordered another.

"You want to take it easy on that stuff, mister," the bartender said.

I gave him a big smile. "I beg your pardon? You don't like my drinking habits?"

He shook his head and moved away, a big, scarred man with a life-time of trouble in his eyes. "You do what you fucking want, mister."

"What I fucking want," I said, "is a bottle of vodka." I laid down a pair of twenties. "Buy those two fellows at that table a drink, and keep the change."

I picked up the bottle and went over to a table in the corner and poured a drink, then leaned back and let the fierce melancholia sweep out from the fiery centre of the vodka and rise up through me. Sometimes just before the blackness comes, I begin to see a sort of pattern, the beginning of an understanding, the possibility of change. But then it disappears just as I reach out for it, and I know nothing until I awake the next day in a quick, slimy sweat, my heart pounding and my head heavy with guilt and remorse.

It seemed now that the blackout came sooner each time, and the drinking became more blinding. The experience was frightening and desperate, and each time I vowed to stop, but then a month or two later the pressure built, the compulsion was loosed, and once again I started down the road that released me into pain and guilt.

A chair pulled back, and one of the men from the gym sat down across from me. He was in his thirties, balding and overweight, with heavy wrists and scarred knuckles.

"Have a drink," I said. "My name is Jared."

He poured himself a shot. "John. That was a decent workout you had there. You from around here?"

"Canada. The west coast. I'm on a boat down at the harbour."

"That was good advice Sam gave you, my friend." He motioned to the table with the hookers. Two of the men were staring at me now. "This stuff makes you lose your timing." He extended his fists in a fighter's stance and bobbed his head with a grin. "Believe me, I know. You can get into some serious shit here."

"I guess." I was trying not to slur. "Don't you ever feel out of phase with everyone else? Sort of isolated?"

John downed his drink and stood up. "Shit, boy, I got a wife and six kids waiting at home for me. Isolated? Count your blessings, my man." He grinned and slapped my back. "Gotta go. Take care, Jared. Thanks for the drinks."

"Hold on," I said. "I'll walk with you."

When we got to his place, I shoved the half-empty bottle into his pocket and told him to have a drink with his wife. I flagged a cab and went home to *Arrow*.

CHAPTER 21

Every muscle in my body screamed in protest as I dragged myself out of the bunk. It was still dark and the rain was falling steadily, but I couldn't get back to sleep. Danny opened one eye, questioned my sanity, and went back to sleep. There was no sign of Joseph.

The little coffee shop at the end of the docks was crowded with fishermen in bulky checked woollens laughing and talking over huge helpings of cholesterol and coffee. I moved past and jogged out to the road that followed the curve of the bay. The rain was warm and thick and covered me like a mantle. Cars passed taking workers into the city, their headlights outlining the slicks and puddles as I ran. I swung across the highway and headed up into the hills, feeling the strain on my thighs immediately.

I breathed deep, shortening my stride against the slope, concentrating on the rise and pumping my arms. The roads were deserted here, and I ran in a black vacuum, the only sounds the soft fall of rain and the slap of wet soles on the pavement. The hills were terraced out, and I moved in slow parallel curves against the face. Half a mile and I powered up to the next level and continued running, then up again and again until I reached the top. I crouched down low, gasping for breath, my heart pounding.

It was becoming light now, but the clouds were so low and heavy with rain that Monterey was invisible. The little knoll where I knelt was like a deserted island, rising serene and peaceful from the depths. My malaise vanished, and a sense of promise surrounded me. I waited, sweating in the warm rain, until my pulse returned to normal and the black dots swam out of my vision, and then I went back down the hill, slowly at first, then gradually speeding up as the incline pulled at me. On the final terrace I began to sprint, near the edge of control, until finally I was running as fast as ever I had, my body leaned back against the downgrade, my arms windmilling for balance. I couldn't slow it down now, so I turned it up another notch and rocketed down the final slope and out along the highway. I picked a gap in the traffic and blew across and over the beach and into the water for a dozen furious threshing strides before I fell forward and rolled over, choking and laughing, spitting out the salty iodine taste.

"Now that was impressive."

The tone seemed a little sarcastic. I shook the water out of my eyes and saw the blond runner from the day before. She was standing at the water's edge, shaking her head in slow amusement, steam rising from her shoulders. "Come on in. The water's fine."

"No thanks. I think I'll stick to showers."

I got up out of the water and walked over to her.

"My name is Jane," she said, extending her hand, "Jane Warner."

"Jared Kane." I shook the firm brown hand.

"You always run like that?"

"No, no. I was in kind of a funny mood this morning. Just felt like going flat out for a bit, you know, turn it all loose. I was a little out of control at the end," I finished lamely.

She nodded thoughtfully but didn't reply.

"Can I buy you a cup of coffee?" I asked.

She gave me a long, level look. Her face had the smooth, chiselled aspect of the serious athlete, with wide-spaced grey eyes over a thin nose and full lips.

"After our showers."

I was waiting when she came out of the marina showers, still towelling her hair. She shook it free then rolled it up into a bun and pinned it with a skewer. "Come on down to the boat. I'll make some breakfast."

"Sounds great."

She was berthed in front of the little yacht club in the corner of the marina, tied up outside of an Islander 36. There was a FOR SALE sign in the rigging of the Catalina.

"Don't feel you have to say *nice boat*," she threw over her shoulder as we climbed aboard.

"You sail her well."

She shrugged. "I've been doing it for a long time. I bought her when I was sixteen with the money from my first real job and a loan from my parents. Have a seat."

She opened a cupboard door and pulled out a Tupperware container, then filled two small bowls with what looked like the chop I had fed to the cows on the farm in Abbotsford, with raisins added. She opened another container of white powder, dumped it on top, poured in water and sprinkled some dried fruit, stirred, and it all turned milky. She began eating and I followed suit, trying to look as if I ate like this all the time. It was raw. We sat there, crunching.

"Do I have to say nice breakfast?" I asked finally.

She frowned briefly then giggled. She had a nice overbite.

"Don't tell me. You always have steak and eggs, right?"

"Well, maybe eggs sometimes."

"This is just the first course. It's very good for you. I'm going to make omelettes afterwards. Don't finish it if you don't want to."

"No. It's fine. Very Californian," I said.

She looked at me and giggled again. I loved her giggle.

"Your boat is up for sale?"

"I think it might be sold. The guy I took out yesterday said he is going to make an offer. I'm taking it over to the marina to have it hauled out and a survey done."

"Then what?"

"I don't know. Maybe use the money to travel for a year or so. I'm just through university; don't feel much like working yet." For the next two hours we sat drinking coffee and talking. Jane had taken classes at the Scripps Institute in San Diego for the previous four years, and graduated in September with a degree in oceanography. She was twenty-five, still living with her parents while she was in Monterey. Her father was a lawyer, her mother a doctor of medicine.

"He wanted me to be a lawyer, and Mom was hoping for a doctor, but I wasn't interested," she said. "I've been in and around the ocean since I could walk. I've always loved it, and it seemed sensible to try and make a living from something involving it." She shrugged. "I don't think either of my parents like what they do very much, although they would probably deny that. How about you?"

I told her that Danny and I were commercial fishermen, he'd had a bad accident last season, and we were heading down to Mexico and maybe further to rest and recuperate in the sun. His grandfather had come along to help look after him.

"They are an interesting pair. You'd like them. Come over sometime and meet them."

"I'd like that. I want to look at your boat too. She's beautiful."

She had said the right thing, and I told her about Meg and Bill and their travels aboard *Arrow*, and how reading their journals had first led me to think about one day visiting the South Seas.

"They must have thought a lot of you to leave you such a magnificent gift."

"I don't know. I think it was more that they wanted *Arrow* to travel again and thought I was the best chance. And they knew it could make a huge difference for me. Maybe change things." I stopped suddenly, embarrassed at my slip. "I have to leave now. A man's coming down to the boat to do some cabinetry and I need to be there. Thanks for the breakfast."

"You're welcome. See you later."

You can count on that, lady, I thought as I walked back to *Arrow*. Danny was sitting in the cockpit, talking to a little rat-faced bald man of indeterminate age dressed in a pair of filthy blue jeans and a ripped Stones T-shirt. A beautiful dove-tailed wooden chest lay at the man's feet. He glared at me.

"It's about fuckin' time," he snarled. "Fuckin' yotties."

"Jared, meet Wally. He's here to do the cabinetry."

"I'm here to hide the fuckin' gun," Wally said.

I passed around cold beer. Wally took his, drained it in a single hoist, belched, and threw the bottle at the garbage can. It missed.

"Where do you want the fuckin' gun?" he inquired.

Danny was trying hard to keep a straight face. This guy must be very good, I reassured myself — he wasn't getting work because of his personality.

"It has to be handy. I thought maybe we could put a dummy post here at the corner, run it up to the beam. Stow the shotgun inside with a quick release. But it has to look as if it was all original."

Wally gave me a pitying glance. "No kidding, Einstein. Just pass me the fuckin' gun."

He bent down and opened the tool chest and pulled out a wooden folding rule. I handed him the shotgun and he took the measurements, writing them down on a scrap of dirty paper. Then he took out a pair of callipers and measured the beam, using the rule to calculate angles and mumbling to himself the whole time. Only once did he speak to us: "Gimme a fuckin' beer," he growled. Five minutes later he packed his tool chest and left without a word.

"I kind of liked him," Danny said. "He has a certain laid-back charm once you get to know him. You want some lunch?"

"No. I had a late breakfast."

Danny slipped the sling under his shoulders, reached up and grabbed the boom, and pulled himself to his feet. Then he swung down into the galley and took up and fastened the slack. He hung there, suspended under the armpits, while he made grilled cheese and jalapeno sandwiches. It was a slow and awkward struggle as he lowered himself down to pull a pan from the cupboard, then back up to work at the stove and cutting board. I wouldn't have dreamed of offering to help.

"That smells good. Maybe just a couple."

He cooked up a big plateful, then handed it out to the cockpit before swinging up beside me.

"You're getting pretty slick," I said.

"Coming along. Shannon and Alana are picking me up in an hour, taking me down to their place. There's a hot tub and pool, we're going to do a little swimming and soaking. You're invited."

"Thanks. I think I'll pass this time. Clarke might be along this afternoon. I want to be here when he arrives."

"Clarke." Danny smiled. "A good man. I wonder if he'll have any news for us."

"I hope so, but don't count on it. These guys are pretty careful."

"They'll make a mistake. Or they've made one already, and we just don't realize it yet. I've been thinking about it, going back over it all, making some notes again. There is one thing in there that might have something to do with it. You want to take a look?"

"I'll wait for Clarke. Maybe the three of us can spot something."

The sun was breaking through the overcast, and the cockpit was bathed in its rays. I leaned back and soaked in their warmth. It looked like being a fine afternoon. The gulls were screaming and diving over by Cannery Row, where a group of tourists was throwing bread in the water. A few sea lions were cruising lazily in that direction, more out of boredom than hunger; they knew the pickings were more substantial at the commercial berths. I put my feet up on the cushions and closed my eyes. Danny was saying something, but I couldn't quite make out the words. There was the creak of the blocks as he swung down into the cabin, and then nothing.

We were sailing in the Tuamotus. The water was a brilliant, transparent blue, and the spray was warm on my face as we headed for a narrow pass with all sails set. Danny was handling the sheets, and there was a dogleg right in the middle where we would have to be smart with our jibe. The surf was breaking on the rocks on both sides, and Danny was laughing and yelling something above the roar of the breakers; I couldn't hear the words and leaned towards him then lost my balance and fell.

I awoke with a start on the cockpit floor, my elbow crashing against the gear shift lever. I swore softly and rubbed the sleep from my eyes. I could still hear the shouting from a tangled knot of fishermen swaying along the docks in the distance. Suddenly one of them went flying out of the centre, tripped on a cleat, and splashed heavily into the water. There was loud cursing, and other fishermen ran along the docks towards the melee. I caught a brief glimpse of something large and white threshing in the centre, and then it disappeared again. A man fell to the ground, holding his jaw, and another flew suddenly backwards as if propelled by a giant spring. The seething mass surged to and fro then crashed heavily to the dock. It writhed for a few moments and was still. One of the fishermen beckoned me.

As I approached I saw a large man spread-eagled on the dock with men holding his arms and legs, and two more sitting on his chest. He was dressed completely in white from head to foot: white shirt, white shorts, white ankle socks, white shoes, white legs. A white Tilley hat floated in the water nearby. Everything stark white except his face. That was a bulged and flaming scarlet.

Clarke. The crazed red eyeballs glared at me.

"This man, he was looking for you," Alfonse said. "He try to say he is police." He laughed. "You ever see policeman dressed like this cabrón?" He gestured contemptuously at Clarke's raiment.

"Not often," I said.

Clarke's mouth opened, but only a croak came out.

"What you want to do with him?" Jean asked. "Maybe we take him out fishing tonight, let him swim back, eh?"

Everyone nodded approvingly.

"Well," I said, "he does look a bit like a policeman I knew once."

I wasn't sure I wanted them to let Clarke free; he might kill someone. He lay there like a beached great white, his chest heaving, his jaws opening and shutting on his rage.

Someone pinched my back gently and moved me aside. It was Joseph. He went to the men astride Clarke and motioned them away. He extended his hand and Clarke rose ponderously to his knees and then lurched to his feet, glaring hideously around him. Nobody met his eyes. I retrieved his hat and held it towards him. He snatched it from me and wrung it out. A blue carryall with flight tags on it lay nearby. I picked it up and moved through the silent, apprehensive crowd. Alfonse looked at me with wide eyes.

"Thanks anyway," I whispered. Joseph pulled at Clarke's sleeve, and he turned and followed us back to *Arrow*.

By the time Clarke levered himself aboard, I had the Glenfiddich and a water glass waiting. He took them without a word, poured three fingers and downed them. He refilled the glass with another three inches of Scotch and looked at me for the first time.

"Welcome to Monterey," I said.

He stared at me. "What does cabrón mean ?"

"It means bear. A powerful man," I said.

"Yeah, I'll fucking bet. Where's Danny?"

"He's gone ashore with some friends."

Clarke's eyebrows rose.

"He's getting better, Clarke. He has feeling back, he can move his legs. He's going to recover."

"No kidding. I'll be damned. You know the doctors only gave him a slim chance at the end there. That was the main reason the department agreed to let him leave. They figured he had enough problems, they would look bad prosecuting."

"It was Joseph who did it."

Joseph was sitting right alongside the big man, puffing contentedly on his pipe. He beamed at Clarke and patted his shoulder.

"How are you doing, you old bugger?" Clarke queried. "What's this I hear about you and the widow?" Joseph's face went blank.

"She got any friends?"

Clarke nudged him with his elbow. Joseph stared straight ahead, his face impassive.

"I guess not," Clarke said. He rummaged in his bag and pulled a tape recorder out from among the bottles.

"Might as well get this over with, Jared. Then we can get down to some serious drinking. What have you got for me?"

I went through it from the beginning, from when I first saw the Hatteras docking in Port Townsend until the final glimpse of it rolling in the swells, the glass shattered, lit in a crimson glow by the flare. He questioned me repeatedly about Delaney, getting me to go over and over his description. Joseph leaned over once and drew a small pattern on his left wrist in the shape of a jagged crescent.

"On Delaney's wrist?" Clarke asked.

Joseph nodded. I hadn't seen the scar.

"We have a sheet on Eddie. Small-time stuff, mainly, although there was one armed robbery. He's known to have worked with a Charles Connor. Sounds like it might be Chucky. I've got a picture here somewhere."

He pulled it out of his files. It had been taken a few years earlier, and the hair was shorter, but it was Chuck.

"That's him, all right."

Joseph nodded in confirmation.

"Good. I'll haul him in when I go back, see if I can get a lead on Delaney. I've got squat so far." He spread his hands in an empty gesture.

"I have a feeling he doesn't usually do the heavy stuff," I said. "I think maybe he was just along because he knew something about boats. I don't think he was accustomed to it. He struck me as being a professional, maybe an accountant or lawyer. It's hard to explain, something about his manner."

"They found the boat, it turned up in Everett on December twelfth. It went missing from Seattle a few days earlier. Hell of a mess. Glass everywhere, pilot house all scorched and blistered, instruments blown out, blood all over. A fair bit on the aft deck, looks like you hit Chucky pretty hard. The locals took samples, two different blood types — so Delaney was tagged too, either by glass or a bullet. Their medical examiner looked at the boat, no arterial blood, he figures, probably nobody died if they got medical help fairly soon. They can't be certain."

I handed Clarke the gun and wallet.

"I'll take these back to Vancouver with me, run some ballistics. You never know when you might get lucky."

"Will we have to come back and testify?"

He shook his head. "No point in that at the present time. I'll change the story a little, maybe forget about Eddie altogether for the moment. You did say he returned to the Hatteras, right? He won't be missed. We probably can't charge Connor anyway — the incident took place in American waters, they couldn't come up with his prints on the boat, no real evidence. I'll try and scare him into giving us Delaney. Attempted murder, deportation to the States to stand trial. Tell him we'll arrange for him to do his time in Rikers, he'll be real popular with the black inmates, they love big blonds. None of those guys are real smart, it might work."

"Any word on Desjardins?"

"Nothing on the west coast. I called Montreal, he hasn't been seen down there for a few weeks. They had him as still being in Vancouver. He's disappeared."

"He's dead," I said.

"Probably. The question is, whose toes did he step on in Vancouver?"

"Who controls the west coast drug action?"

"Three dealers have everything pretty well divided up among them.

They each stick to their own territory. It could be one of them, but I don't think so. Not really their form. And we'd have heard something."

He paused and took a long swallow.

"No, this smells like something new, a higher level, a different style. We've heard rumours. Narcotics had someone inside the Hogue crowd for a year and a half, and she couldn't find out anything. But we will eventually. We always do."

"I hope it's soon enough to do us some good," I said.

"Hell, what are you guys complaining about? You should all be dead already." He grinned and put a massive arm around Joseph. "And you, you old bugger, how about you? You should be home rocking by the fire at your age, not knifing villains and shacking up with widows. Christ, how old are you, anyway? Seventy-five or eighty?"

Joseph smiled.

"He's all of that," I said. "How long can you stay?"

"Oh, maybe three or four days. I'm booked in at the Sheraton, just around the corner."

"There's a spare berth on the boat," I said. The idea of Clarke for twenty-four hours a day terrified me.

"No thanks. The department is paying, I might as well take full advantage of it. There's some other business with the locals I have to take care of as well, but that can wait. Aren't you joining me?"

He picked up the bottle and poured another drink.

"I think I'll stick to beer," I said. "I know when I'm out of my league."

Jean was sitting on the stern of his boat, shooting worried glances across, and I waved him over.

"Jean, this is Clarke, a friend of mine from Canada. He's a police detective."

"We've met," Clarke growled.

"I'm very sorry. We were watching out for our friends. You didn't look like a policeman. Then when Luis asked you for a badge . . ." His voice trailed off.

"I told him to fuck off," Clarke finished. He grinned and held out a ham-like hand. "No hard feelings." He began pulling bottles out of his bag. "What are you drinking? We've got Scotch, vodka, and rum here for starters, maybe some Irish whisky too, I'm not sure."

"I'll bring some wine."

Two minutes later Jean was back, bearing a gallon each of wine and pickled calamari. Three more combatants bearing their own peace offerings followed behind. Among them they had two black eyes, a cut lip, and a grossly swollen nose.

"Gee, I'm sure sorry about that," Clarke said with a big smile and an innocent look. They came sheepishly aboard and sat quietly down, but within minutes they were laughing and talking about the fight like old friends. Joseph got up and slipped quietly away. A wise man indeed.

I took the skiff and rowed over to the shops, where I bought an armload of hot sourdough bread and roasted garlic and peppers and spread it around the cockpit along with some smoked salmon from the freezer. There were already a dozen people sitting around drinking and eating. To my surprise, Joseph returned with Maria an hour later, along with jars of antipasto, a platter of mixed cheeses, and yet more wine. Maria wore a black silk blouse and dark denim slacks, perhaps a dock-side version of the widow's weeds of her people. Joseph sat perched on the cabin top, feet dangling in the cockpit while Maria passed out food. Her presence had a brief calming effect on the group, and even Clarke toned down his language and volume.

I was wondering if I dared invite Jane over, when her head suddenly popped up alongside. She had paddled over in her old, heavily patched West Marine dinghy.

"Permission to come aboard?" She smiled up at me.

"I was just coming over to invite you. We didn't plan this, it just happened."

"The best parties usually do," Jane said as she climbed over the lifelines and accepted a glass of wine from Maria.

"It's only eight o'clock," I replied. "You won't believe your eyes by midnight."

The party broke up by ten o'clock, and Jane and I were alone in the cockpit. The girls had decided they wanted Chinese food, and left with Danny and Clarke. Danny was in the wheelchair with Shannon on his lap, while Alana sat on Clarke's shoulders. They disappeared down the floats in a mad race, Danny in the lead and throwing the wheelchair from side to side in an effort to keep Clarke from overtaking. With the circus gone, the fishermen finished up their drinks and returned to their boats. Maria helped Jane and me with the cleaning up, and then she and Joseph left as well.

"Alone at last," I said.

Jane reached into her bag and pulled out a large joint. She lit it, inhaled deeply, and passed it to me.

"Here, this will loosen you up."

I took a long drag.

"You don't want to believe everything those clowns tell you," I said. We were both talking in the high, squeaky tones of people holding their breath.

"I saw you. The whole time we sat in the cockpit you were watching. Every boat that came in or out, every car in the parking lot, every person that walked along the piers. You checked them all."

"Would you believe a healthy curiosity?" I asked.

She didn't respond, just watched me with those level grey eyes.

"It's a long story," I said at last.

"Does it have anything to do with the knife wounds in Danny's chest and stomach?" she asked.

I looked up in surprise.

"I saw them when he swung aboard. My mother is a doctor, remember. I used to play with blocks in her office when she couldn't get a sitter sometimes. I grew up with that kind of stuff."

I took a deep draft of the joint, sucking it down and holding my breath until spots started to dance in front of my eyes. Neither of us spoke. We were leaning back, gazing up at the new moon. I felt the distance growing between us.

"There is an old theory about the origins of the moon that I've always loved." Jane spoke in almost a whisper. "It holds that the moon was born of a huge tidal wave of molten matter, ripped off the surface of the earth, and hurled into space two billion years ago as the planet was cooling. The sun's tides had been increasing for centuries, pulling on the thickening liquids in an accelerating rhythm until at last their motion grew too great for stability. When the mass separated, it left a giant fissure on the earth's surface. As the cooling continued the rains began and gradually filled that great depression, now known as the Pacific Ocean."

She paused for a moment.

"And now that portion of earth that became the moon precipitates the tides on the oceans of the world. What do you think of that?"

"I was in England one winter after the fishing season. In London, a few years back. Danny and I had a flat in Chelsea, we had been partying for a couple of months, practically non-stop. We decided we needed a break, something wholesome, with exercise. We heard about some canoes for rent on the Thames. It was perfect: Canadian, traditional, a good workout, and we didn't take along any booze. Of course, as we soon discovered, being the original channel of travel in the country, the Thames has many of the oldest and most beautiful public houses scattered along its banks. We paddled vigorously for a good twenty minutes before we came upon the first one. We tied up to it, had a couple of pints and carried on. In a matter of minutes we came to another pub and halted again. And so on. At nine o'clock that evening we were arrested for being drunk and disorderly in a public place, the River Thames.

"We appeared before the magistrate the following morning. He read the charge, looked at us sternly from under his wig, and asked if we had anything to say for ourselves. Danny looked up at him and said, 'In the words of the great bard, your honour: there is a tide in the affairs of men, and it must be taken at the flood.'"

Jane laughed. "What happened?"

"The judge said the usual fine for the charge was twenty-five pounds, but in our case he was prepared to make an exception and assess fifty."

"Maybe he wasn't a Shakespeare fan."

She lit another joint, and we smoked a long time in silence.

"It all began with *Arrow*," I said at last.

During the next couple of hours, I went over it all for her, omitting nothing. I told her of my attack on the Lebels, and how I had wanted to kill them so badly I could taste it. I told her about the stolen money and how we would use it to stay alive. I said that several people were dead already in this, and Delaney and the others wouldn't quit, and I was going to have to find them and kill them too. I said that at some point in this process I would become the same as the people who pursued us; I had taken the first, irrevocable step with the money. When I had finally done with killing them, it would be complete; we would be identical.

She listened to it all and never said a word. At one point she went below and fetched a blanket and sat beside me with her head on my shoulder, the blanket wrapping us both. It was midnight when I finished speaking, my throat burning from smoke and gall.

Jane stood up at the end. "It's time I was leaving. Walk me back."

I took her hand and we walked slowly back to the Catalina. It was quiet now, the only sounds the low creaking of the dock lines and the lonely splash of a fish. In the soft moonlight, her hair was spun gold. Too soon, we arrived back at her boat. She turned and looked at me as if considering. She was only a scant inch shorter.

"Going for a run in the morning?" I asked.

"No. I am going to stay in bed."

"Ah. Goodnight, then." I turned to leave.

She clung to my hand. "And so are you," she said, and led me aboard and below.

CHAPTER 22

The following morning we took the Catalina and headed south, towards Point Sur. It was overcast, with a hint of rain, but it would not have mattered to me if it was blowing a gale. We had twelve knots of wind, and *Moonbeam* beat into it like a champion. Jane tied the tiller off with bungee cord, then fiddled with the main and jib sheets until we held our course. She came and sat beside me, opening the cooler of beer we had stopped to pick up at *Arrow*.

"About last night."

"What part? The first, second, or third?"

She smiled. "Not that. That was okay."

"'Okay'?" I asked.

"Okay, it was good."

"It was good for me too," I said.

"Be serious. What you talked about on *Arrow*, Delaney and all the rest of it, I've been thinking about that. I don't agree that you have no choice but to go after them. You can turn them over to the police when you find them."

"There's nothing to charge them with."

"The attack on you in Port Townsend. You said they found the damaged Hatteras. And there is your testimony."

"Assuming we could find Delaney and bring him to trial, it would be his word against ours. He will have a three-piece suit, expensive lawyers, a perfect alibi, and an air of complete respectability. We'd have two First Nation witnesses, one a convicted felon and the other so old they'd destroy his credibility. I won't subject them to that. And then there's me. I spent two years in jail when I was a kid, Jane. Aggravated assault, and there's been other things since: drunk driving, some brawls, another assault charge. They would take us apart. But it would never come to trial."

I leaned across and touched her shoulder.

"These people don't want the publicity, regardless of the outcome. They will simply kill us, like you would swat a fly, with no compunction and no remorse. They have tried twice already, and they won't stop until somebody is dead. If we're lucky, it will be them. There is no other outcome possible. It's a war."

"It's crazy. You haven't done anything."

"It's happening all the time, everywhere. There are killings in every decent-sized city. Something like twenty people a year in Vancouver's mainland, many of them drug-related. The thing is that they don't affect most people. It is like living in a small South American republic where two opposing armies are fighting and killing each other in a remote area of jungle. If you are a civilian, and you stay away from the area, you won't be harmed. Life for the vast majority of people goes on as normal. Well, Danny went into the jungle, and he saw or heard something he shouldn't have, and now he is not a civilian anymore. When Joseph and I helped him, we became the enemy too. We don't have choices anymore. There won't be any ceasefires."

"What about Clarke?"

"Clarke is a good cop. Don't be fooled by his party animal act, he works as hard at his trade as he does at having fun. But he doesn't have much to go on. He might get lucky, nail them for something else, but it doesn't seem likely at the moment."

"So you'll keep running until they catch up with you."

"It's not so bad. We're more prepared now, Danny is getting better. Once we're away from the States, we'll be on a more equal footing. They won't have as many resources to call on. It's a big ocean; maybe we can dictate the time and place." I smiled. "We were going to travel the world anyway. This will make sure we keep moving, don't get too settled."

"Don't joke about it."

"I'm not joking." I grabbed her and squeezed. "I've picked up a fatalistic streak from my First Nation friends. Qué pasa, pasa."

"That's Spanish."

"Whatever. Let's not talk about it anymore. It's a beautiful day."

She looked up at the sky. "Actually, Jared, for southern California, it's kind of a shitty day."

We steered into a small cove, rounded up and dropped the anchor in twenty feet of water. Jane dug around the lazarette and pulled out a pair of wetsuits, assorted weights, and some masks, flippers, and snorkels.

"This suit should fit you, it belongs to my father."

I held it up against me. It looked about right. "Obviously a fine figure of a man."

"No, actually he's kind of a skinny little runt like you," Jane replied. "Have you done much snorkelling?"

"Not really. In Mexico, a few years ago."

"Okay. Use this snorkel, it has the two valves, easier to clear. You don't have much fat, try four pounds of weight, that should balance the neoprene flotation. Clear your nose every six feet or so, start shallow, go progressively deeper." She handed me a speargun. "Your range is a maximum of eight feet beyond the end of your gun. Everything looks a third bigger and closer down there. If it looks six feet out from the tip, it's probably too far away."

"What are we after?"

"Some cod, maybe a grouper, a lobster if we're really lucky. Any fish that looks good to eat usually is. As soon as you get something, hold it clear of the water on the end of your spear and bring it straight back to the boat. We don't want to encourage any sharks."

She turned away and fell backwards into the water, one hand holding her spear, the other over her mask.

"Sharks?"

Jane looked up from where she was treading water and waved me in.

"What's about sharks?" I yelled.

Her shoulders shook and she beckoned again. She might have been laughing.

"Nobody said anything about sharks," I muttered. I turned around and fell backwards into the water. It was shockingly cold at first, but then the water trickling into the suit started to warm up, and it became tolerable. Jane was ahead of me, moving slowly towards the beach, her face peering downwards. She did a quick flip and submerged in a stream of bubbles, the long, blond ponytail flowing out behind. A reef extended out from the shore, and we moved along its face, checking the caves and crevices for signs of life. A school of triggerfish swam by, their loud neon colours flashing as they arced and wheeled in bright formation. A moray eel had taken up residence fifty feet along and favoured us with an evil stare as we swam by, the long, sinuous neck twisting to follow us until we disappeared from sight.

The waters teemed with life: tiny, pulsing shrimp drifting across the bottom in translucent pink; eelpouts darting among the rocks in a never-ending search for food; schools of small fish feeding on the shrimp, and themselves subject to the predations of larger fish; little skeletal crabs darting among the rock and weed; the quicksilver flash of a school of juvenile tuna, gone before you could focus on them or even begin to aim your speargun.

Layer upon layer, life upon life, everything feeding or being fed upon in the eternal cycle; and at the very top of the food chain, Jane and me. At least, I hoped we were at the top.

I saw a quick scuttling motion out of the corner of my eye and swam over to check. Backed into a deep crack, its antenna waving belligerently out in front of it, was a lobster. We stared at each other. I wasn't wearing gloves, and its spines looked sharp. Jane swam past me and put the butt of her spear gun behind the lobster and twisted, and it came out six inches. She went in over the top and seized its midsection, then surfaced with her prize.

"I was just going to do that," I said when we had spat out our mouthpieces.

"Yes, I could see that. I thought you were a fisherman."

"I am. From a boat. We never did this mano a mano combat in the water."

"Here, take him back. There's a cave up ahead I want to check out."

By the time I had the lobster stowed in a bucket of water with the lid secured, she was back with a twenty-inch grouper wriggling on the end of her spear. I killed it and threw it in the bucket with the lobster, and then we rowed the little dinghy ashore and collected some oysters. When we returned to the boat, Jane picked up the little solar shower and hung it over the boom.

"Come on, get the salt off." She stripped down. "We'll save water."

"I have always been a conservationist," I said as I threw my trunks on the deck.

Half an hour later we were lying on the foredeck, our breath slowly returning to normal.

"I need another shower," I said.

"What's this scar?"

"A hook caught me when I was working the roller on the halibut."

"It looks ugly."

"Not too bad, really. I was lucky. I was on my knees and the hook pulled up and out, missed the bone. I was into a big string of fish and so excited I didn't even know it until after. The cook poured Neosporin into it and sewed it up. It was sore for a while, but no muscle damage."

"You really like the fishing that much?"

"I used to. No bullshit. You know in a hot flash if a man is good at his job or not. No misunderstandings. Every trip is a business venture between the captain, the crew, and the boat; you go out after the fish and sometimes you get them, and sometimes not. You can make a thousand dollars a man before breakfast, and everybody is laughing and joking and you're working twenty-two hours a day and everything is great; and then you fish for three days and catch nothing, and you're still putting in the same hours and almost the same effort, only now everything is sour, and the weather is bad too, and you want to punch out the guy across the table because you don't like the way he chews his food. Then suddenly you hit the fish and you're back on top again."

"Is that what you want to keep doing?"

"No. Maybe for another few years. It gets to you after a while, the cold and the damp. You're on deck, dressing a big string, two or three thousand pounds, sweating rivers, then you jump down in the hold and ice them, maybe half an hour, probably kneeling on the ice the whole time. Most of the older men have arthritis, swollen hands, and sore joints. You see it all the time."

Her hands were moving slowly over my back, rubbing out the stiffness. I felt her light fingers stop, then run in long vertical patterns, up and down. I knew the next question before she even asked.

"What are these, Jared?"

"Old scar tissue," I said.

She didn't reply, just wrapped her arms more tightly around me, her grey eyes looking steadily into mine.

I closed my eyes and lay my head on her shoulder. "It was my grandfather."

❀

I had been staying at my friend Billy's house after my mother and sister died in the car crash. I can remember the first time I saw my grandfather as clearly as if it happened yesterday. He stood in the doorway in his black suit, with his hat twisting in his big hands. Mrs. Arden was expecting him, and I was all packed.

Grandfather picked up my suitcase, and I grabbed my box of toys and followed him outside. He turned around and spoke to me for the first time.

"You won't be needing those, boy."

He picked them up and carried them back to the house. When he set the box down, I grabbed the little car my father had given me for Christmas and put it in my pocket. Grandfather watched me with a small smile.

"Let's go, then," he said, and took me by the wrist.

Mrs. Arden came out and hugged me. "God bless you, Jared," she whispered.

He started the truck and we drove away. I sat tight up beside the passenger window, looking back at Marsden as it disappeared in the distance.

"Show me the car," he said.

I pulled it out of my pocket and handed it to him, and he rolled down the cab window and threw it out into the ditch that ran alongside the road. He didn't speak again until we reached the farm late that night and he showed me my room.

I ran away for the first time three weeks later. I hid until the school bus had left the grounds and all the teachers had gone home, then started walking along the highway. An old couple stopped and picked me up, then turned around and dropped me off at the police station. An hour later I was back at the farm. I had packed some clothes in my school bag and taken some preserves from the fruit cellar. Grandfather looked into my bag and pulled them out.

"A thief too," he said.

He took me up to my room and threshed me with the razor strap. He said he would drive the wickedness out of me. He let me sob on the bed for a while, and then he spoke.

"Look at me, Jared."

He put his hands around my neck and pulled me close.

"We are your family, your sole brethren under God. Your father and his harlot are gone off this earth. Gone to their eternal judgement and damnation. It is my Christian duty to raise you and keep you, and instruct you in the ways of the Lord. I will do my duty."

He went to the cupboard and opened it and took out a thin malacca cane with knurls every couple of inches. He came back towards me and brought the cane down beside me with a sharp blow. I could hear the high whistle before it struck the sheet.

"This was your father's room, Jared, and this his rod. Had I used it more, he would still be here with me, at my side, doing God's work. I will not make that mistake again."

I waited six months before I left again. It was summer, and the nights were warm. I climbed out of my window at nine o'clock, and by midnight I was at the train station. It took me longer because I hid in the ditches every time a car or truck went by. I knew the freights left at three, and by dawn I was a hundred miles away, heading back to Marsden. The train stopped at Burnside, and it was only another ten miles. I got to Billy's house just after dark and went up the drainpipe and knocked at his window. He hid me for two days before his mother found out. When Grandfather picked me up, she was crying openly.

This time he used the rod, and I don't remember the end of it, only my grandmother crying, and then screaming. She put creams on my back and bandaged me, but the cuts got infected and I became feverish. Three days later, while Grandfather was out in the fields, she called the doctor. He came and treated me, and a while later a lady came with a policeman, and they all looked at my back. They asked me some questions, but I wouldn't talk to them. I heard them talking to Grandfather in the kitchen, and his high-pitched voice screaming about God.

He didn't use the cane for a long time after that, and I never ran away again. The last beating was when I was fourteen. I can't remember what it was about. He picked up the rod and started to swing it.

I turned and caught it and broke it over my knee. I had been doing a man's work for three years, and I wasn't afraid of him anymore. He glared at me, then turned and left the room without a word. After that it was like I was the hired hand. That same night I went down and told my grandmother I wanted my parents' pictures. She went and took them out of a box in the basement, and I put them up all over my room. He never came in there again.

⚜

"That's an awful story," Jane said. "In California they would have put him in a psychiatric ward, and you in counselling."

"Therapy," I said. I grabbed her around the waist and rolled her over on top of me. "I need lots and lots of therapy."

"Maybe you do," Jane said, "but I need food." She pulled free and went below.

By the time we had finished eating and cleaned up, it was time to go. We sat together hardly speaking the whole way back, just enjoying the little boat as she flew over the water, heeling sharply to the occasional puff. It was dark when we slipped into harbour and said goodnight. Jane was going home to spend a couple of days with her parents. I walked back to *Arrow* in the balmy night air, filled with a quiet contentment I had never known before.

⚜

It was another two days before Clarke finally slowed down and sobered up enough to sit with us and go over Danny's notes. He was not in the best of humours.

"Well, I can't see very goddam much in here." He threw the notebook down on the seat beside him. "It has to be that meeting, and there's little enough there." His beet red face and the top of his head were covered in calamine lotion, his manner as irritated as his skin.

"Let's go through it again, Danny. When you went to visit the apartment that day, the Brothers were in front of you, they opened the door and started to go inside, and then somebody yelled at them and they turned around and left."

"That's right. I was behind them, I glanced over their shoulders, there were three men sitting at a table. I didn't get that much of a look."

"What did the boys say after?"

"They just said something about private business. I didn't pay any attention. They were always dealing with people in private, lots of secrets."

"Did you sense any change in the Lebels' attitude towards you after that?"

Danny shook his head. "Not that you'd notice. What, you think I saw somebody I shouldn't have, and that's when they decided to kill me?"

"Maybe." Clarke reached into his folder and pulled out a photograph. "Could this have been one of them?"

Danny studied the photograph for a long minute. "Yeah, maybe. One of them had a trimmed beard, like a goatee, swarthy, wearing a light-coloured suit. Black, curly hair. I remember thinking that he looked foreign. Who's this?"

"Desjardins."

"He was sitting with his back to me, and I only got a half glimpse when he turned, but yes, for what it's worth, it could have been him."

"How about the third man? Can you describe him at all?"

"He was sitting in profile, turned and looked for a moment, then turned his head away. An older man, probably in his sixties. Grey hair, well dressed, looked like a hundred other guys his age. I remember he reminded me of someone, but I can't for the life of me think who."

"Maybe somebody you've seen a picture of in the papers or on tv. Maybe a politician, somebody like that," Clarke said hopefully.

"I don't know. Just a vague feeling I should know him. And the cars out front. That's all I've got."

211

Clarke sighed. "Yeah. Parked right in front of the building. One was a limo with smoked glass, and the other a new black Imperial. That right?"

"Yes. Parked one behind the other. Seemed unusual, a couple of expensive cars like that out on the street with the big underground parking space. Thinking about it later, could have belonged to them. They were the type who would have fine cars. Rich-looking, good clothes. Cigars. All smoking cigars around the table."

"But you're not sure it was the same day."

"No. But I think it might have been." Danny spread his hands. "That's it. You've got it all."

I looked at Clarke.

"Well," he said, "it's something. Not much, but something. I'll go back, check through the patrol reports around that time. Maybe one of them wrote something down, maybe even a licence number, if we're real lucky. Some of the patrolmen are sharp, make a note of anything at all unusual. Trying to jump up to detective grade. More fools them."

He put away his folder, opened three beers, and passed them around. He took a long, smacking swallow. "A few more of these and I might just survive until evening. God, what a time. You know, I never really believed we evolved from the ocean until last night. The things we did in that hot tub I wouldn't have believed possible. No wonder the porpoises have those big grins on their faces all the time. We should never have left the water." He turned to Danny. "Did we make any plans for tonight? The last few hours are a little hazy."

"The girls are dropping by the boat after work. I thought we'd order in some pizza, have a few beers. Maybe go out later on."

"Sounds good to me. We've only got two flats of beer left. You think that will be enough?"

"You fucking guys all asleep, or are you going to give me a hand?" It was Wally, the cabinetmaker, wearing the same clothes as before, but dirtier. He passed his lumber and tools aboard and scrambled after them, pausing to stare at Clarke from beady yellow eyes.

"What the fuck is he doing here?" he asked.

They glared at each other in mutual antagonism, each recognizing the other instinctively, as fundamentally hostile as a rat and a terrier.

"I know we talked about going fishing," Clarke said, "but surely we can do better than this for bait."

"You should pay these guys off on shore," Wally retaliated, "they'll stink up your fuckin' boat."

Clarke leaned across and stretched a ponderous hand towards Wally's skinny shoulders. I stepped quickly between them and shoved Wally below.

"Here's a fuckin' beer," I said. "There's more in the fuckin' fridge."

"I knew you lot were bent," Wally muttered. He opened his tool box. "You gonna get outta my fuckin way or what?"

I went back topsides, where Danny was explaining Wally's presence.

"That little scumbag is a cabinetmaker?"

"Supposed to be the best," Danny replied.

"Huh. That reminds me. I brought you a little present."

He reached down and picked up a small canvas bag and pulled out a pistol wrapped in a greasy cloth.

"Here we go." He held it up proudly. "A Heckler & Koch vp70. Holds twelve cartridges, very light — a sweetheart, believe me."

He handed it across to Danny. Most of the frame was plastic, with metal bonded into the outer surfaces. The company name was engraved on the firing mechanism.

"Nice." Danny raised it and sighted along the barrel.

"Ah, but here's the killer."

Clarke pulled out a piece of plastic about twenty inches long that looked a little like an art nouveau towel rack.

"When you clip on this shoulder stock, the little stud on the end engages the body of the pistol and gives you rapid-fire capability. Every time you pull the trigger you get a three-round burst. You get true automatic fire, with no runaway blast upsetting the aim."

He clipped on the stock and beamed like a proud parent. "It fires the nine-millimetre Parabellum slug. Good range, lots of stopping power. I brought some boxes of ammunition, maybe we could go out later, throw Wally over the side, I could show you."

"I heard that." Wally stuck his head out the companionway. "Lemme see the fuckin' gun."

Clarke handed it reluctantly over. Wally put it up to his shoulder.

"Nice. Course, the fuckin' Colombians will all have Uzis."

"Colombians?" Danny said.

"It's obvious, ain't it. A fuckin' boat, guns, a bent cop, what else but drugs?" He expertly unclipped the stock. "You want me to hide this too? I've got a locking clip for a Luger that I can make fit. Where the fuck you want it?"

"How about the head of your bunk, Danny?"

It was getting hard to find places for them all.

"Why not. We better draw up a diagram to help us remember where they all are."

I went below, and Wally and I settled on a location at the foot of the berth where it butted up against the forward bulkhead. He could cut through into the head and build a box to hold it out of sight under the sink. We would hang a picture over the access hole and fasten it with spring clips. Not perfect, but it would defeat a casual inspection.

"Hang the stock on the wall over the stove for a drying rack," Danny suggested. "Might as well get some extra use out of it."

"Okay," Wally said. "Clear the fuck out and let me get to work then."

Three hours later he had finished. The new post at the corner of the chart table was radiused and slotted in perfectly, running up to support the deck beam as if it had always been there. There were two slight indentations at the rear of the post where you pressed in with thumb and forefinger to remove the panel and access the gun. It was a superb piece of work. Even Clarke was impressed.

I paid Wally his money and hustled him off the boat while he was still in one piece. He rambled down the dock, the curses gradually fading behind him.

"I should run a check on that little rat while I'm down at the station tomorrow," Clarke grumbled. "I don't know what they're doing down here, a little weasel like that lipping off to a cop."

"Forget him," Danny said. "Have another beer."

"Maybe we should switch to Scotch for a while," Clarke said. "Clear the palate for this evening."

CHAPTER 23

I awoke late, with a slight headache from the evening's revels. Danny hadn't returned, and I had the boat to myself. I went for a shower and stopped off at *Moonbeam* afterwards. The seagulls had been feeding, and she was covered with shells and droppings. I hooked up the dock water and cleaned her decks.

One of the sheet winches had been a bit noisy, and I popped the circlip and disassembled it, then washed the gears in hot fresh water, greased it all, and put it back together. The truth was I was doing this so the little boat would sell. After all, Jane had said she might want to travel around for a while.

"Mind if I come aboard?"

The man was in his fifties, slender, with styled grey hair fashionably long and horn-rimmed glasses. He was dressed in pale cream slacks with a white turtleneck and navy club jacket. I couldn't see any bulges. Without waiting for a reply, he climbed aboard.

I stepped up close. "It's not my boat, it belongs to a friend. I was just leaving." I took him by the elbow.

"Bert Warner," he said, extending his hand with a pleasant smile. "Jane's father."

"Jared Kane. She's not here."

He nodded and sat down. "What do you think of the boat?"

"It goes well," I answered politely.

He grinned. "I love the name. Did Jane tell you? We bought her from an old hippie up in Big Sur. Jane thought it was romantic. Afterwards he told me she was named after the character in Li'l Abner. Moonbeam McSwine. And sure enough, that's the name on the registration. But it's served Jane well."

"Do you have a boat?"

"No. Used to, but I wasn't spending enough time on her. My buddy has an old Concordia yawl, though. Sometimes we go out for a sail. Mostly we sit around polishing her up and keeping her in trim. Once we took her down to San Diego for a wooden-boat show. But there's never enough time. Jane tells me you have a beautiful old boat."

I hadn't thought it was a casual visit.

"Yes. She's lying over there. The ketch with the white hull. Built in 1965 to a Laurent Giles design."

"I understand you are a fisherman," Bert said.

So much for pretty old boats.

"Yes."

"What do you fish for?"

"Halibut."

"I don't know much about them."

"Large flatfish. Hippoglossus stenolepis." I smiled pleasantly.

He pulled out a cigarette and lit it. This was heavy going.

"I guess it's a pretty good life?"

"Great. Hell on the women, though. We're usually gone for five months, drinking and whoring the whole time we aren't fishing, of course. Mind you, we usually breed the little woman up before we go, give 'em a little sucker to keep them out of trouble while we're away." I stood up. "Nice talking to you."

He grabbed my arm. "Please. Sit down. I apologize. I'm not very good at this."

"You don't have to worry. We're just friends. We've only known each other for a week."

"Did Jane tell you anything about me?"

"She said you were a lawyer."

"Yes. Private practice. My friend with the Concordia works for the Department of Justice. We were talking about boats, Jane had mentioned *Arrow* to me. He got this funny look on his face, said it might be a good idea if Jane stayed away from it. He wouldn't say anything else."

"We've had some trouble," I said. "I told Jane about it. I guess she will tell you if she wants you to know."

He sighed. "I suppose that will have to do. She's an only child, you know."

He seemed decent enough.

"We will be leaving soon," I said.

"What are your plans?"

"San Diego for a few days. Mexico. Then south and west. No real itinerary."

"Sounds nice and decadent. I wish I was going with you."

"Would you like to come over for a drink sometime and talk about it?" I asked politely. "Shoot up a few drugs maybe?"

He held up his hands.

"Okay, okay. Enough. I apologized once. Nice meeting you, Jared. Good luck."

I shook his outstretched hand. "Nice meeting you, Mr. Warner. Give my regards to Jane's mother."

We walked down the docks together until he turned off towards the parking lot and drove away in a black Mercedes. Another bosom buddy. From whom, I wondered, did I inherit this inborn facility for making lifelong friends out of casual acquaintances?

I spent the next two days helping Jane clean up the boat and ready it for survey. In the evenings, we went for long, slow runs, working our way up into the hills or just following the coastline towards Carmel. Jane had the flat, economical motion of the marathoner and never tired, her long, tanned legs scissoring smoothly, her chest rising and falling in easy rhythm as she glided along. After a few miles my thighs tightened and my motion became hacked and choppy. I felt like a Volkswagen alongside a Ferrari. When it became too much, I would sprint ahead till my wind failed and I collapsed in a heap by the side of the road, Jane just jogging in place beside me with a bland look on her face, perhaps inquiring if the pace was too slow. When we returned to the marina we would shower, eat, and make love in no particular sequence.

If it had not been for the threat hanging over us, it would have been perfect. But the dark cloud was there, and it would not go away. I became increasingly nervous as the days passed, and no longer slept the nights through. I took to waking in the early hours, slipping quietly out of the bunk so as not to disturb Jane, prowling around the docks until daylight, staring up at the sky and listening to the sounds of the night before I went below again.

Clarke had left, happy and sated, the skin peeling off his head in sheets. He and Danny had been inseparable the whole visit — only partly because of the girls, I thought. His final words were a threat to visit us in San Diego.

"Maybe those guys will catch up with you again, blow a few holes in one of you," he said. "Give me an excuse to get back down here again."

Joseph presented him with a carved raven amulet and Danny gave him the names of some of his Vancouver girlfriends.

"Phone me when you get to San Diego. I'll run everything you gave me through the computer, maybe I'll have something for you by then." Clarke handed me a small piece of paper. "Here's the name of an old buddy of mine. Got shot up, took early retirement. Lives in a little bungalow just north of the city. Get in touch with him if you need anything down there. Name is Len Corbin, good guy. Drinks a little too much, maybe." He winked at me. "Adios."

He turned and walked away, a big burly ridiculous man with the shambling gait of an overweight bear. I was going to miss him.

Jane came over to tell me that *Moonbeam* had sold, and the buyer wanted to take delivery in San Diego. She had agreed, providing he paid full asking price, and they were both happy with the bargain. It meant that we could buddy-boat down and spend a week together. Jane introduced me to her friend Ingrid, a Swedish phys ed instructor doing a sabbatical in Monterey who was coming along to help with the sailing. She was blond and muscled, a couple of inches taller than me and probably weighing more. She had a friendly smile, a strong grip and accent, and the biggest chest I had ever seen outside of a Hooters bar. Danny would love her.

The night before we left, we went over to the tugboat for dinner. We sat around drinking wine and talking while Maria kneaded and cut the fresh pasta on the big galley table and Joseph sat watching over us all like a benevolent don. Danny was on his best behaviour, drinking slowly and paying particular attention to Ingrid.

"Why don't you tell her about your therapy, Danny?" I said during a lull in the conversation. "Phys ed is a closely related discipline."

"I'm sure she doesn't want to talk shop," Danny said, trying to smile at Ingrid and glare at me simultaneously.

"I think it's pretty revolutionary," I told Ingrid. "He's made remarkable progress in a short time."

"A short time?" Jane giggled. "Danny, I never would have guessed."

"Dinner is ready," Maria announced with impeccable timing. When we had eaten, we spread out the charts and planned the trip. It was just over three hundred miles to San Diego, and the girls had a week to spend. The first good anchorage was at San Luis Obispo, close to one hundred and twenty miles, and we decided to overnight it. We could do the rest in leisurely day hops, anchoring early each afternoon. Jane had spent her summers sailing these waters and knew them well, and she picked the spots. It was midnight when we finally said our goodbyes. Danny and I returned to *Arrow*, and a short time later Joseph slipped quietly back on board.

We left at noon the following day in light winds, a six-knot westerly just off the starboard quarter. Jane and Ingrid had full sail up before they left the harbour, and popped the spinnaker immediately upon rounding the point. Any thoughts we had about sailing away from them were quickly dispelled, and by five o'clock they were out of sight, the only sign of their presence the jeers and insults issuing sporadically from the VHF. At twilight the wind freshened and *Arrow* began to reel them in. By ten we were abeam and shortened sail to stay even for the rest of the night.

We reached San Luis Obispo at midafternoon the following day, tying up to a mooring buoy after a radio check with the harbour patrol. They came out in their launch to collect the mooring fees, stereotypical bronzed young Californios, polite and amicable. They asked about firearms, and I brought out the little Purdey in its case; they admired the workmanship, wished us a good evening, and left. They spent a lot more time aboard *Moonbeam*.

The girls came over at five for drinks, and we played cards to see who would make dinner. Joseph sat with them, and it was no surprise when Danny and I lost. I went below and put a roast in the oven and prepared some vegetables. An hour later, *Jeopardy* showed up with Maria at the wheel. She brought the fifty-foot vessel in at a couple of knots, then hit reverse and then neutral, and laid alongside the buoy as smooth as silk, hooking on with a clip pole as it bobbed just off the bow.

"She has done that before," I said.

"Joseph said she ran the tug herself the last few years," Danny explained. "After her husband had his stroke, he still went along, but Maria did most of the work. She only retired three years ago, after his death."

Later on, she rowed over with some leftovers to go with the roast pork, and we all ate supper in *Arrow*'s cockpit, balancing the plates on our knees. It was crowded, but nobody minded. After dinner Joseph rowed back to the tug with Maria.

"He's an amazing old man, your grandfather," Ingrid said, watching him as he sat ramrod straight, propelling the skiff with short, strong strokes. "Is your grandmother alive?"

"No. She died a long time ago. Actually, they all did. He's had several wives."

"Several?"

"Four, I think. That he was actually married to."

"Four. What happened to them all?"

"He just outlived them, I guess. Indigenous people aren't known for their longevity. Joseph is the exception." I could hear the bitterness in Danny's voice.

"How old is he?" Jane asked.

Danny looked at me. "He's pretty old," he said.

"Where are we tying up tomorrow night?" Ingrid asked.

"I thought San Miguel Island," Jane said. "It's about sixty miles. There's a little cove on the east side, good holding, good snorkelling. We'll be in the lee if the wind stays in the same direction, could pick up some nice fish off the reef."

"Gee, I don't think I have the chart," I said.

"Gosh, then you had better come over with me and take a copy," Jane replied.

"That's a good idea," I said.

We climbed down into the skiff and started rowing back to *Moonbeam*.

Danny started clapping.

"Not bad," he called after us, "but it could have used a little more rehearsal."

I could hear Ingrid giggling.

"Was it that obvious?"

Jane reached across and patted my knee. "Don't worry, dear, Ingrid

222

and I had already decided you were going to spend the night on *Moonbeam.*"

"Oh. And Ingrid?"

"Her bag is packed and stored in the rubber dinghy. If it's all right with you, she'd like to sail *Arrow* tomorrow. Ingrid can handle it. She is very competent."

"Are Danny and I being manipulated?"

"Yes."

"I love it when you're bossy," I said.

We departed before dawn, slipping the mooring just as the first trace of light showed behind the hills to the east. I hanked on the genoa, a pale rose colour in the diffused light, and we left the harbour in a trail of phosphorescence. The day held the promise of warmth, but the air was still cool, and we shrouded ourselves in blankets and drank mugs of black coffee laced with rum. Jane hooked up the little Autohelm tiller pilot and we huddled together, watching the light as it gradually opened the skies. *Arrow* and *Jeopardy* still rocked in the harbour, their profiles faintly outlined against the false dawn, the low hills beyond occasionally illuminated by the flash of car lights moving along the highway. The only sound was the hissing of the water as *Moonbeam* cleaved her passage. The stars sparkled and then dimmed in the accelerating light, fainter and fainter until at last they disappeared entirely in dawn's loom. The azure sky unfolded like a bright blanket, woven through here and there with thin filaments of cirrus.

"I never get tired of it," Jane said. "It's my favourite show."

"I don't know about that. We could be in Vegas, watching Wayne Newton. He probably has more glitter."

"Always the smartass," Jane said. "You have to learn not to denigrate your feelings, be more open."

"You'll have to give me time. I've only been in California a couple of weeks. In Canada we don't even shake hands until we've known somebody for a month."

"You did more than shake hands last night," Jane said softly.

"Tactile communication. I am a firm believer in it. Any sign of *Arrow* yet?"

I stood up and turned to look.

"Sit down. I haven't finished this particular conversation yet." Her hand clamped onto a sensitive spot and pulled me down beside her. "Is that tactile enough for you?"

"Yes," I wheezed.

"What did you and my father talk about?" she asked.

"Well, I am not sure we actually had what you could call a conversation," I said. She tightened her grip. "He was worried about you and said you were an only child and asked me some questions about fishing and I was rude," I blurted.

"Daddy said you were quite prickly."

"Prickly, huh?" I leered. "Bit of a Freudian slip there, don't you think?"

She ignored me. "He isn't usually like that."

"I think it was his friend with the Concordia. Said you should stay away from *Arrow*."

"Phil? I wouldn't have thought he would know anything. He's a top lawyer in the Justice Department. Handles a lot of the case preparation for the high-profile prosecutions."

I wondered if he ever handled any drug cases.

"Clarke made a few calls, talked to some of the local detectives," I said. "Maybe Phil was briefed."

"Phil's a good guy, we've known him forever. You should see his boat. It's immaculate, belongs in a museum. He and Daddy spend most of their time polishing it and drinking Chivas. He buys it by the case."

"He sounds well off."

"Oh yes. He's a widower. His wife died in a boating accident a few years ago. Propane leak, they figure, absolutely tragic. He was very devoted to her. Children all gone now, he lives alone in this huge house. Kind of creepy, I think. Speaking of which." She gazed in mock horror at her hand, which still held me firmly. "My God. It yet lives."

"Slow to awaken, but its wrath is all-powerful. It can only be appeased by a complex and arcane rite."

"How about some good, raunchy sex?"

"Well, that too," I said.

❈

We arrived at San Miguel Island at four, just a few minutes ahead of *Arrow* and *Jeopardy*. The bottom rose steeply, and we set the anchor twice before it caught and held against full reverse. The little Danforth was a bit light for the boat, and I made a note to hook up one of the spare anchors from *Arrow*. Jane put on a mask and snorkel and dove over the side to check the set. The water was very clear, and she was visible all the way down to the bottom. I baited the crab trap with left-over roast and lowered it over the side. Jane climbed back aboard and we had a drink while I checked the rubbers on the spearguns.

"You won't need those," a voice said. It was Danny, treading water with a slow arm stroke, his feet hanging straight down. "We caught a nice yellowfin tuna just after sun-up. Probably thirty pounds. I filleted part, Ingrid's going to do some steaks on the barbecue for supper. Joseph and Maria aren't coming, I'll drop a couple off for them. Come on over anytime."

He rolled over and swam off with a steady side stroke, his head slanted and looking back over his shoulder. His fins were moving slowly up and down as he pulled away.

"He's really doing well, isn't he," Jane said.

"Yes. Considering he was paralyzed for life by most counts a few weeks ago."

He was already back to the boat and slipping into the sling. The muscles in his back flexed as he swung himself up and over the side.

His arm reached down and caught Ingrid by the waist where she sat reading in the cockpit, lifted, and they swung out again and dropped into the water. They came up with their arms around each other and stayed that way for a long time.

"Aha! If we hadn't left last night, they would likely have thrown us overboard," I said.

"Come on. Race you to the beach."

Jane went over the side in a flat racing dive and struck out for the shore in a powerful overhand crawl. We were two hundred yards off the tiny beach, resting in five fathoms of water. The cove was deeply indented and offered good protection from anything but an easterly. On each side of the beach, a low cliff rose steeply upwards before it levelled off into a shallow gravelled slope dotted with an occasional pine tree. The beach formed a crescent; at each end, a reef extended out a quarter of a mile before disappearing beneath the surf. I took a last look around and plunged over the side.

The water this far south was clearer and more temperate, but beyond that, it had undergone other, more subtle chemistries. It was somehow less dense, as if the change in colour was the result of a more integral permutation; when we swam we did so more easily, with less effort. Seeing the bottom so clearly gave the impression of being suspended between the mediums of air, earth, and water, and the distinctions between them blurred. It was as if we moved in a new element derived of a mingling of the other three and less subject to their individual laws.

In the Pacific Northwest the ocean was never this clear or friendly. I found its opacity dark and brooding, as if it contained some deep and malignant presence. On the few occasions that I dove into that dark, fathomless green, it was because of necessity, and it was a relief to be out of it.

When Jane reached the beach, I was fifty yards back, and she watched my slow progress with a critical eye.

"You need a little work on your stroke."

"We can start to practise as soon as we get back to the boat," I gasped.

"You had better take it easy. You're ten years into your sexual decline, you realize. I, on the other hand, am a decade away from my peak."

"It must be California. In Canada I was practically celibate."

"Did you have a steady relationship?"

"No. A few girls, but never anything serious. When you spend most of your time drinking in waterfront bars, you don't run across that many women. Apart from the party girls, nothing steady there. There was a girl in high school I was crazy about, but she was a year older than me. Seemed like ages at the time. We were good friends, but she insisted on treating me like her little brother. Haven't seen her for years. She married a lawyer, I think."

"I almost got married two years ago. A terrific guy. He was a marine biologist, a few years older than me. He lectured at Scripps, and I think at least half the girls in the class were in love with him. An old surfer, used to bring his board to the institute. You'd see him out there riding the waves all the time, six feet plus, blond, he was adorable."

"What happened?"

"I don't really know. We had it all planned. We would get married as soon as I graduated, have three kids, I would work for a few years first. My parents loved him. Finally it just became too much for me. Everything was figured out, it was all set. I just chickened out."

"Any regrets?"

"Oh yes, sometimes at first. But it would likely have been a mistake. I wasn't ready for anything that preplanned. It seemed like I could see my entire life stretching out in front of me, all neatly organized."

Stick with me, kid, I thought, *you won't have that problem.*

We walked hand in hand down to the water and swam leisurely back to the boat for a relaxing evening of cards and music.

When I went out on deck the next morning, a forty-foot dive charter boat had anchored off the end of the reef, and a half dozen people were sitting on deck putting on wet suits and flippers. The skipper, an older, well-built man with close-cropped grey hair, came back from setting the anchor and helped them with their tanks. He saw me watching and waved as he moved among them, adjusting straps, apportioning weights, lifting and checking the regulators and tanks. After he was satisfied, they all went over the side, splashing down one after the other like neoprene dominoes. They bobbed along in the water for a while, then disappeared below the waves.

"Company?"

Jane appeared on deck with the mugs of coffee. She was wearing a white terry cloth robe and looked about fifteen years old with her sleepy eyes and ponytail.

"Some divers. Out of Santa Barbara. Looks like they're working the outside edge of the reef."

"I don't feel like going anywhere today," she said with a yawn. "Let's just lie around, hit the beaches, be lazy. We can go to Santa Rosa tomorrow. Maybe spend a day there or at Santa Cruz, then head in to Santa Barbara. Good restaurant right on the pier, we can go there for dinner."

"Sounds fine. I'll go over to *Arrow*, talk to Danny and Ingrid."

By mutual consent we had shut off the radios. We were getting a lot of local chatter on them and couldn't find a clear channel and found it was easier and less annoying to just holler, or row across.

When I got there, Danny was sitting up in the cockpit with his back braced against the coamings, his legs stretched out in front of them. He was raising them a good twelve inches, one after the other, up and down. I watched him for a while.

"Looks like we can heave the wheelchair pretty soon."

"Yep. Next time we hit dry land I'm using the crutches. And not for very damned long either. I can take all my weight now."

He reached up and grabbed the boom, pulling himself to his feet, then released his grip took a small step forward and tripped over before grabbing the boom again and sitting down.

"Balance needs a little work yet, though," he said.

"Where's Ingrid?"

"God knows. Up at six a.m. doing push-ups, then off for a swim. Now she's taken the dinghy ashore. Probably running up and down hills. The woman is a raving jock."

"Do I detect a small note of complaint?"

"Hell, no. Did I say? When she was doing those push-ups, I was underneath."

He wiggled his eyebrows and rolled his eyes. The First Nation answer to Groucho Marx.

"Uh oh. Sun's over the stanchions. Time for a beer."

He swung down into the galley and passed up some cold ones.

"It's the yardarm. When the sun is over the yardarm."

"We don't have a yardarm. But the stanchions are nearly three feet high. Thirty inches, a yard, what's the big difference?" He raised the bottle and drank.

"Jane wants to stay for another day."

"Why not? One place is as good as another." He looked up at the sky. "Might get a little wind tonight."

"How long is Maria staying?"

"I don't know. Joseph mentioned something about one of her grandchildren. Having a first communion, I think. She wants to be back for it."

We sat in the cockpit, drinking beer and talking, until Ingrid came back. She was dripping sweat. She made a few disparaging remarks about layabouts and drinking problems, then poured herself a pint of orange juice, added some powders, and chugged it down. She wiped her lips with the back of her hand and smiled at us.

"What is that stuff?" I asked respectfully.

"Brewer's yeast, some iron. Very good for you. You done your exercises yet?"

"Yes, I have," Danny replied obediently.

"Good. Time for a swim, then."

She peeled off her T-shirt and shorts and strode to the rail. There was a brief glimpse of huge, chiselled breasts, a concave, muscled stomach. Then the powerful thighs flexed and she was over the side, twin moons rippling in the sun for a split second before she hit the water and disappeared.

"Wow." I raised my bottle in salute. "You're a better man than I am, Daniel MacLean."

Danny hauled up and swung himself out over the water. Ingrid rose up in a powerful surge, stripped down his shorts, and threw them into the dinghy in a single motion. Danny gave a martyred sigh and dropped down beside her.

"Don't embarrass the fishes," I muttered, but they were already diving down towards the bottom in a long, bubbling plane.

Jane and I spent the rest of the day ashore, climbing and exploring the island. We packed a lunch and took shelter in among a pile of rocks, drinking wine and reading, enjoying the peace and solitude. We stayed there until the sun started to fall, then went back to *Arrow* to prepare dinner.

It was too windy to barbecue, so we stir-fried the remainder of the yellowfin with some vegetables on the stove and served it with rice and some of Maria's fresh-baked bread. Afterwards we sat around and drank coffee and fought over cards. It was one of those warm, mellow evenings at the end of a long, lazy sunny day, when everyone is slightly burned and wasted and silly. The food and drink taste better and the laughter comes easier. It was one of the best nights Jane and I had.

It was Joseph who first noticed that *Moonbeam* was gone. He had gone out on deck for a pipe, and called us. The wind had risen in the course of the evening, but it was an offshore breeze and we hadn't worried. *Arrow* was swaying and rocking a little more than normal, but it had been relatively minor. I realized now that the little Catalina was more exposed, and the wind had acted more directly upon her hull. There was a slight swell coming in, and the wind against it must have created enough chop to get *Moonbeam*'s bow lifting and pulling back until she raised the little anchor and drifted back and out into deeper water. I mentally kicked myself for not hooking up the spare CQR as I had intended. I thought perhaps I could just make out her anchor light to the east.

"I've got her on the radar," Danny called. "She's out a mile and a half."

Moonbeam carried one of the better radar reflectors, and there was a clear return on the screen. It had to be her, it was stationary and just about where I thought I had seen the light, close to the edge of the drop-off.

"Right. I'll fire up the Perkins and we'll go out and get her. It's a little choppy for a dinghy run."

I went out on deck and turned on the ignition.

"Shit! She's disappeared," Danny yelled.

Sound travels at close to eleven hundred feet a second. It was another eight seconds before we heard the explosion.

CHAPTER 24

The fireball filled the sky, a blinding white-hot sun with satellites shooting off in blazing incandescent arcs. It lasted for brief seconds, and then the night closed in again with only the sound of soft hissing as pieces of *Moonbeam* fell into the water around us and extinguished.

There was an acrid smell in the air, of burnt fibreglass, and something else, reminiscent of cordite, but different.

"Oh my God," Jane whispered.

I put my arm around her and stared into the night. There was just a small fire now, at the centre of the explosion, and very soon it flickered and died, and there was nothing. Only a sudden, dark suspicion, and the beginnings of a cold killing rage in my belly. *Moonbeam* had blown up right over the drop-off.

"Haul the anchor," Ingrid said. "If we get out there quickly, we may be able to save something."

"We will."

Jane pulled away from me and sat beside Ingrid, her head down, sobbing. I motioned to Danny and we took our masks and snorkels and dive lights and slipped over the side.

It only took a couple of minutes to find it. It was fastened to the hull, just forward of the prop, with one of the underwater quick-set putty epoxies. A little black plastic box about ten inches square and four deep. There was a nervous minute as I pried it off and swam carefully back to the dinghy. Danny held the light as I gently released the screws. The seam was siliconed, and he took his knife and ran it carefully around the edges and pried off the lid. The word Horizon was printed on the little plastic unit connected to the lumpy dough and wired in series to the two six-volt dry cell batteries.

"Is that what I think it is?" Danny said in a choked voice.

"Depth sounder and plastique. Set for a thousand feet. That's why the other one went off when *Moonbeam* drifted over the edge. In that much water, no one would ever find what was left of us."

I pulled the wires out of the explosive and disconnected the batteries.

"One of the divers," Danny said.

"For sure." I remembered the shape they had made that morning in their black wetsuits, dropping down into the water like spiders.

"We'll find him."

"Oh yes. We will."

I felt the chill sweep over me. We would all have been killed if not for a bit of wind and an undersized anchor that had not held. While I had been lying around and playing carelessly at love in the sun, they had been busy. How long would it take to learn the lesson, how many more people would be put at risk before they finally killed us, and anyone close to us?

My life was not my own, and never had been. Not when I was a child, not when I left the prison, and never since. It seemed there was a special vengeance reserved for me and those I loved. My family taken as a child, and everything since a cruel irony. A second chance with Annie and Joseph and the family, and then the gift of *Arrow*, which should have changed my life but had led instead to tragedy and death for those around me. And Jane. What in Christ's name was I doing with a girl like that? I was a poor bargain for her at the best of times, now I was just an invitation to die.

No more.

Joseph was standing at the rail, staring out to where *Moonbeam* had flamed and died, his face as cold and blank as slate, his fingers toying with the thong around his neck.

"We'll sweep *Jeopardy* when we get back," I told him.

We ran to the site of the explosion and circled the area in long sweeps. We didn't find much. There was an undamaged horseshoe buoy near where she had been and some small pieces of the balsa-cored deck floating further out. She had been almost totally incinerated by the blast. At the end of two hours, we had recovered a piece of teak grating and a couple of pillows to add to the pathetic heap. Jane had stopped crying and stood beside me, her face bleak.

When we finished searching, she took the small pile of recovered gear and hurled it over the side without a word. Maria had fixed hot rums, and Jane's sat untouched beside her. I drank mine down and then switched to straight rum, filling my cup and draining it as if it were water, but the chill in my belly only grew.

I stared around me as if searching the waters with the others, but all I could see was the dive boat, and the deadly black form gliding across to us. Jane spoke to me, but I didn't answer and she fell silent.

It was after midnight when we returned. I ran *Arrow* alongside *Jeopardy* and tied off to her. We wouldn't be staying long. Danny and I went back in the water, and we each took a side and searched *Jeopardy*'s hull, then crossed over and checked each other's work. It took half an hour, and we were shivering from nerves and cold by the time we were done, but nothing was there. When we went back aboard, I packed Jane's gear and took it over to the tugboat.

"You stay aboard *Jeopardy*, we will be leaving right away. Phone the Coast Guard now, and explain to them that you were visiting on *Jeopardy* when *Moonbeam* blew. You must have left the propane on, there was an oil lamp in the salon for a night light. Don't mention *Arrow* at all."

"But we should tell the police," Jane said. "It must have been someone on the dive boat. You have the other bomb to show them. They'll investigate. They can find them."

"No. They will detain us, keep us for questioning. They'll go through the whole thing, check our records, rip *Arrow* apart in searches, we will never get away. And even if they do find them, they won't talk. And while all this is going on, we will be virtual prisoners, stuck in one place for far too long. So phone the Coast Guard. Do it now. Are you insured?"

I could hear my voice, clipped and cold. She nodded dumbly.

"Good. They will believe someone like you. Particularly when you tell them the boat was already sold. You should come out of this just fine. Go back home to your parents."

She was crying again. Ingrid and Danny glared at me.

"Jared, why are you talking to me like this?" Jane stood up and came over to me and I turned my back and walked away.

"We're leaving now," I said to Joseph, and went over the side back to *Arrow*. Jane didn't follow. I started the engine and waited for the others. A minute later Joseph climbed down with his little bag, and then Danny, swinging down the shrouds.

"I don't think you had to be quite such a fucking asshole," he growled.

"Take the fucking tiller," I said. "I'll raise the anchor. We can be in Santa Barbara by daylight."

❀

We sailed all night under spinnaker in twenty-five knots of wind. We could have done a comfortable seven and a half knots with the genoa, but I wanted the extra speed. After the last few idle weeks, *Arrow* seemed equally impatient, and she put her shoulder down like the thoroughbred she was and thundered through the night like a runaway horse.

She surfed almost continuously, riding low in the trough, then gradually rising until at last she found her wave and her haunches settled and her bow lifted and she took off, the knot meter touching ten and twelve as she accelerated, the spray alongside rising halfway to her spreaders. I kept the tiller the whole time, sitting braced against the coaming, bringing her up as she fell into the quartering seas, then falling off as we broke away over the next rise and caught our pace again.

She rocked and bucked on her passage, and twice we dipped the pole in the water, but the gear held and we sighted the Santa Barbara breakwater at daylight. Joseph was beside me, where he had spent the whole night, bringing up coffee and whisky and smoking his pipe. Danny was cooking breakfast, hanging from the sling and cursing as we crashed along, and then we rounded the corner and the seas calmed.

Joseph took the tiller and I raised the jib as we made the turn into the harbour. He released the spinnaker halyard and we glided through the anchorage while I stuffed the big sail through the forepeak hatch. There was an empty berth marked for visitors, and Joseph had the spring lines ready and passed them to me as I went over the side onto the docks.

Two minutes later we were tied up and I was prying Clarke's pistol from its clips. I stuffed it under my waistband, picked up the little box with the bomb, and started for the companionway steps. Danny's big hand caught me as I went by.

"First, breakfast."

"Those places open early. The dive boat could have left by now."

"Eat."

I cursed and sat down and wolfed some pancakes and sausages under his watchful eye.

"I am coming with you, Jared."

"I don't think you can keep up," I said.

"I'll fucking keep up," he snarled.

"Okay, let's go, then."

I jumped up and went on deck and over the side. There was cursing behind me, but I didn't look back, only started to jog. A minute later I heard the rumbling of wheels on the dock, and Danny shot by in his wheelchair. He was carrying his crutches, and as he went by he thrust them between my legs and I went crashing down.

"Race you to the ramp," he chortled.

The big hands blurred and he thundered down the docks like a crazed Ben-Hur.

"You treacherous son of a bitch," I howled.

I arose in a blind rage and started after him. I was gaining a bit until I started laughing, and then it was no contest. He was waiting at the bottom of the ramp, and I grabbed the back of the chair and helped him to the top.

"Good to have you along, friend," I said.

"He's no good to us dead, Jared."

"I know that. I just brought along the gun for show."

"I wasn't talking about the gun," he replied.

An old curmudgeon wearing a faded Lakers cap stuck full of lures was fishing off the dock in clear defiance of the regulations posted along-side. He told us that Smokey's Dive Charters was a hundred feet down the bloody dock, that the bloody boat was tied up right in front of it, and that if we weren't so bloody blind we'd have seen that for ourselves.

"So bloody there," Danny said as we went across.

The building was locked and there was no one aboard the boat, so we went into the little café to wait. There had been a football game the previous day and the 49ers had lost. There were various reasons for this aberration of nature, ranging from sheer ill fortune to an act of God. After twenty minutes, it felt as if we had been there forever. It seemed nobody was paying us the slightest bit of attention. After our second refill, Danny gave me a nudge.

A white Ford truck was going by the window, the box half-filled with dive tanks. Danny paid the bill and we went down to the shop. The man I had seen on the boat before was unloading the tanks and carrying them in through the back door of the shop.

"Morning. What can I do for you?"

He was older than I had judged him earlier, probably in his late fifties. He had the clear-eyed boyish look that some men keep all their lives. Barefoot in cut-off jeans and tank top, he had arms corded with muscle, and on his wrist was visible the faded tattoo of the elite Navy SEALs. Just the chap to know all about bombs and pressure switches, I thought, and felt the gun pressing into my belly under my shirt.

"We'd like to talk about some diving."

"Sure. Just let me finish this."

I gave him a hand, and in a few minutes we finished unloading the bottles and joined Danny in the cramped corner that served as an office.

"I'm Gerry Robinson. Everybody calls me Smokey."

"What does it cost for a full day, you and the boat and the two of us? And some lessons."

"Are you licensed?"

"No."

"Well, you wouldn't want the boat, then. We'd start you in the pool first, then go out. Three days and you'd have your certification. We charge three hundred and twenty-five dollars for that."

"Right. But then if we wanted to rent the boat and the gear. How much?"

"Four hundred dollars."

I pulled out four one-hundred-dollar bills and laid them on the desk.

"But I won't take you without certification. I could lose my ticket." He smiled at me.

"What we really want is information. I'll pay you a day's wages just to answer a few questions about yesterday's charter."

He leaned back in his chair, placed his feet on the planks that served as his desk, and spread his arms wide.

"You boys come in here, you look around, and you probably think, Geez, what a hole in the wall operation. A twelve-by-twenty-foot lease in a grubby shack, and a boat that sucks up money like a sponge. Hardly any business seven months of the year, and then a lineup of assholes all wanting you to hold their hands for them the other five. The taxman comes in and he doesn't like my records. Says if they were right, I'd be doing something else that actually makes me some money. Doesn't even pay my alimony. That's one of the pluses, by the way." He smiled.

"But it's what I want to do. I open when I want, I close when I want, and I answer questions when I want. Now you tell me what this is all about and I will tell you if I'm interested. The money comes later."

I glared at him and reached under my T-shirt to pull the pistol out and stick it in his ear to see if that would help him make up his mind. Danny caught my hand halfway.

"We were at San Miguel Island yesterday," Danny said. "The wood ketch and the little Catalina."

"I remember. I saw you swinging over the side. I thought you were just fooling around." He motioned to the crutches.

"The Catalina blew up around ten o'clock last night," Danny continued in the same even voice. "Luckily no one was on board. We were all on *Arrow*."

"I heard on the news this morning. Propane leak, they figure."

"No, it was a bomb," I said.

"A bomb?" His surprise seemed genuine. "How can you be sure of that?"

"Because this is the other one that was supposed to blow our fucking boat up," I replied as I dropped the box on the table before him. He slid back the lid and whistled softly through his teeth.

"Pressure switch. Clever."

"Maybe about what you would expect from an old SEAL," I said.

He stared at me. "I will forget you said that, friend."

"Then give us somebody else, friend," I snarled.

He regarded us for a long moment. "So why aren't the cops here, then?"

"It's still not too late for that. We can take them the bomb, and then they will be all over you, friend, like flies on a dung heap."

He turned to Danny. "Your partner always like this in the morning?" he asked.

"There were a couple of girls on the boats," Danny said. "Just innocent parties. They were supposed to be blown away too."

"And you guys," Smokey said, "I guess you aren't so innocent, huh?"

Danny pulled up his shirt. The scars glowed scarlet against the golden skin.

"I was involved in a robbery. I paid for it. Ever since, somebody has been trying to kill me and my friends. This is the third attempt, and we have no idea who or why." He handed Clarke's card across to him. "This is a detective in Vancouver. Phone him up, he will tell you all about it, anything you want to know about us."

Smokey read the card and handed it back. "No, that's not necessary, I believe you. Keep your money, I'll tell you what you need for nothing. Those assholes were screwing me around too. We'll go to the boat, I keep all my records there."

He took the OPEN sign, reversed it, and hung it on the pane of glass in the door, and we walked down to *Trident*. She was steel, a one-off design that Smokey had drawn up and welded together himself. With her long, narrow bow and high superstructure, she resembled one of the old PT boats. A big compressor was mounted just aft of the wheelhouse. When we went inside, it was easy to see where Smokey's money went. The interior was finished in solid teak and holly, and the steering station had all the latest toys, right up to a seventeen-inch chart plotter with the whole west coast of North America plugged in. The galley was all teak and stainless, and the accommodation luxurious.

"I make most of my money on the longer charters — couples, usually. My girlfriend and I take them out for a week or two, everything included except booze. Gourmet food, the best wine, all first class. It's a nice way to learn the sport, or see some marine life. Yesterday was just a day trip. Beer and sandwiches. I run them twice a week, it helps to pay the rent between the big charters. It's on a drop-in basis, fifty dollars for the day if you bring your own gear, a hundred if you have to rent everything."

He paused and poured coffee all around.

"There were eight people aboard yesterday, four of them regulars. Local people, I've known them for years, you can write them off. Also a young couple from Los Angeles, honeymooners, just dropped in on impulse, they were never out of my sight for more than a minute. And then there were two guys who drove up in a rental car, late twenties or early thirties. One about six-two, well built, a lifter maybe. Short red hair, balding. The other guy was heavy, maybe two-forty, long black hair, big moustache. Had their own gear, all first class. Didn't say much to the others. It had to be them.

"Usually the group stays together — I put them in pairs, buddy system, and I like to keep track of them all. These two said they wanted to go further out along the reef, take some pictures. They had a bag with all their camera gear in it." He shrugged. "They said. I talked to them, they knew what they were doing, the one guy had an instructor's certification. It wouldn't have taken them long, maybe fifteen minutes to get out to your boats. They headed off by themselves. When we went in for lunch they were back waiting for us."

"What names were they using?"

He rummaged around his desk and came up with a form.

"Billy Tanner and Fred Linder. Billy's the lifter. Same names on their dive cards and driver's licences. I have to check, people are always trying to use somebody else's papers."

"Do you have an address?"

"Not local. But that shouldn't be too hard to find."

He picked up the phone and dialled.

"Dave? Smokey here." He listened for a while, then grinned. "My heart bleeds. Listen. I took a couple of guys out yesterday, they were driving one of your cars. They left some gear on board but I don't have their local address. Billy Tanner and Fred Linder. Okay."

He waited, drumming his fingers and humming a tune under his breath. "Yes? It's still out. Great. And what's the room number? Thanks, Dave. You too."

He wrote on a slip of paper and passed it across with a flourish.

"Astor Hotel, room thirty. Car isn't due back until tomorrow. An airport pickup."

I stood to go. "Thanks. My apologies."

"No worries, mate."

He watched Danny lever himself to his feet, then stuck out his hand.

"I might drop in later on, get your thoughts on the plastic explosive," Danny said. "We may have a use for that sometime. Maybe you could show me how to rig up a timer, that sort of thing."

"Glad to. You've got pretty well everything you need right here. A cheap digital clock, some lengths of underwater fuse, and you're in business. Come by anytime."

We thanked him, and Danny swung out ahead of me, awkward on the metal crutches. He dropped back down into the wheelchair and we returned to *Arrow*.

"Where's Joseph?"

"He was going shopping."

"What for?" I asked.

"Didn't say. So how do you want to do this? We have to pick them up tonight."

"I don't know. Maybe they will come for us."

"I don't think so. They'll assume we ran again," Danny said. "Got scared and took off. I think what we should do is go out for a few drinks and try and come up with a plan."

"I see. And just where exactly would you like to go for these few drinks, old buddy?"

"Well, I've heard that the Astor Hotel is an interesting spot," Danny replied.

CHAPTER 25

It was noon by the time we'd rented the panel van and finished our shopping. I pulled into the staff parking lot around the back of the hotel, and we went in by a side entrance. I wanted to go in first and check it out, but Danny was having none of that.

"Screw them. Let it happen. I want them to see me."

Before I could argue, he was out the door and swinging away on his crutches.

The Astor Hotel was older, built in the forties for the carriage trade and now gone slightly to seed in a distinguished fashion. They still had the staff and the prices, but the furniture was worn and the place in need of a facelift. They had disdained the faxes, modems, and online hookups in every room, their clientele was more the middle-aged tourist. In our shorts and flowered shirts, we fitted right in.

A bellboy dressed like a town crier was on us before we had gone ten feet into the cavernous lobby. Enormous potted palms were every-where, towering up to the mezzanine above, and the walls were studded with pictures of old movie stars and media celebrities, most of whom would be dead or in private rest homes by now.

Danny slipped the boy a fiver, and he escorted us to the bar. It was old English Colonial with faded Axminster carpets covering the floors, palmetto fans revolving slowly overhead, and a shabby Bengal tiger crouched in the corner. The bartender was dressed in whites of an almost military cut and sported a waxed handlebar moustache and British accent.

"They probably only serve gin and tonic," Danny muttered.

We climbed onto the stools and rested our elbows on the polished mahogany bar. The barman served us, then retreated a diplomatic ten feet, far enough to allow us privacy, close enough to be included in our conversation should we choose.

"Pretty quiet in here today," Danny offered.

"Yes. Well, it is early yet." The bartender didn't add "for most people"; he was too polite for that. "It will start to get busy around four. After supper we have a pianist in and get a nice crowd. He is very good, does a lot of blues, takes some requests. Quite a few locals drop in, lots of singles. It gets quite lively."

I put a twenty on the bar in front of me. "We are looking for a couple of men. I wonder if you could help."

He moved slowly down the bar towards us, polishing the gleaming wood with a clean white cloth. The twenty disappeared into the circular motions like a fish swallowed up by a shark. I gave him their descriptions and he nodded his head.

"Yes, they were in here last night for several hours. Drinking quite heavily, actually. They were with a couple of ladies, left around midnight."

I laid another twenty down. In the flick of an eye it joined its predecessor.

"Do you know the ladies?"

"Dot and Sally. Part-time secretaries, they say. They are in here with different guests a lot. Freelance, I believe, although they may be in danger of losing their amateur status. If you know what I mean."

I knew. I had spent the last ten years of my life with girls like that. You bought the drinks and the food, and then one morning they were a little short on the rent, or the phone bill. They were nice kids for the most part, and you gave freely if you had it, but the terms had changed, and you both knew it.

"Management wants me to draw a line. Ten years ago it was easy, but now?" He shrugged his shoulders. "Check the outdoor pool. There's a bar there, they serve lunch. That's where a lot of the girls get lined up."

I dropped another twenty on the bar and we rose to leave.

"I would appreciate it if you forgot this conversation."

He frowned and drew himself up ramrod straight. "You forget, sir, I'm British."

"My apologies."

"No sweat, sport," he replied in a pure Bronx accent. He winked and resumed polishing the bar.

The pool was in the centre of the hotel complex, sheltered on all sides from the wind. They had paved it in black flagstone to hold the heat, and even in January it was hot. A few couples sat around tables with drinks, and some women were sunbathing on chaise lounges in front of adjustable mirrors set back from the pool. We gingerly seated ourselves at a white wrought-iron table with cute little filigree chairs. Danny gave the waiter a pair of twenties and ordered drinks.

"Buy a drink for Dot and Sally too. Tell them it's from a secret admirer. Keep the change."

The waiter nodded impassively and left. He had seen this ploy before.

"You clever rascal," I said.

The waiter filled his order and served two oiled bodies basting themselves in the corner. They took their drinks, glanced half-heartedly around behind their wraparound sun glasses, and lay back.

"I think we really excited them," Danny said.

We sat and waited, drinking our beer slowly and then ordering another. Most of the tables were filled now, the lunchtime office crowd having a quick bite and catching some rays.

"Bingo."

Two men stood by the lobby entrance, looking around. They spotted the girls and started over to their table. The tall one walked with the stiff, robotic gait of the dedicated weight man, his heavy, muscled arms hanging down at his sides. Fred moved easily on the balls of his feet, his head swivelling slightly as he checked out the crowd. He would be the dangerous one.

They were both wearing shorts and T-shirts. The waiter reached their table a scant minute after them and set down a round of Bloody Marys. The boys must have been big tippers. They drained their drinks and a second round appeared.

"I wonder why they're still here."

"Waiting for new instructions. They know they missed us by now, likely figure we're running south to L.A. or San Diego. They'll wait for word, then try again." I took a long drink. "Any ideas yet?"

"I don't know. They're drinking at a pretty good clip, let's leave them to it for a while. How about some lunch?"

We ordered steak sandwiches, and they arrived with home-cut fries and side salads. The office workers had left, and only a dozen of us remained around the pool now. The boys had settled in at a steady pace and were on their fourth drink, with no food in sight.

"Time to do a little trolling," Danny said.

He swung to his feet and headed off to the restrooms, passing right beside their table. I watched closely from behind my sunglasses, but they didn't register him. They weren't expecting to see us here and didn't make the connection. They probably had only vague descriptions, and it wasn't unusual to see men on crutches in the U.S., what with all the wounded veterans returned from their wars.

"No strikes," I said when Danny returned.

"Ah well, maybe we're being too subtle. Waiter!" he yelled suddenly. "More drinks!"

Heads swivelled at the over-loud voice.

"I hate these racial stereotypes," I said.

"Ah, but I do the drunken thing so well," Danny murmured.

An hour later, everyone in the place was watching us out of the corners of their eyes. Danny was drinking double vodkas and called me a fucking wimp in a loud voice when I declined to join him. He was throwing them back as they arrived, and had managed to smash one of the beers he was chasing them down with.

"Here you are, sir."

The waiter, round eyed and wary as a deer, set down another double and beer. Danny threw him a crumpled twenty.

"Keep the change," he slurred as he downed the vodka. He lurched to his feet, staggered onto his crutches and headed towards the restrooms again. As he passed their table, he stumbled and sprawled over it, bringing it down as he fell. I saw his elbow rise and take the redhead in the face as he went by. They both disappeared from sight to shrieks from the women and the sounds of wholesale breaking glass.

"You son of a bitch, you tripped me," Danny howled.

He was struggling and thrashing on top of the redhead. I rushed across and grabbed him. As I lifted him off, the redhead jumped to his feet, blood streaming from his nose and a broken glass in his hand.

"Billy," the dark one said in a hard voice. He sat frozen in his chair, a rigid smile on his lips, his hands grasping his knees. I could see the stretched tendons. Billy righted the table and set the glass carefully down on it. He was trembling with rage.

"Danny," I said. "Oh Jesus, Danny. I'm so sorry, he's had a hard time lately. Come on Danny, we're going back to the boat. Come on, we're leaving."

I grabbed him by the shirt and gave nervous little tugs. He shook me off.

"Fuck you, Jared," he yelled. "Fuck *Arrow*. I'm going for another drink. Too many assholes in here."

He lurched off towards the lobby.

"I am so sorry," I said again.

I dropped a bill on the waiter's tray as I hurried after Danny. "Give those nice people another round."

Danny was waiting for me beside a palm tree.

"Do you think that was too subtle?" he asked.

"No, I think that probably did the trick, all right. We'll give them a few minutes, though. They likely want to change out of their wet clothes, pick up some blowtorches and skinning knives."

When we reached the lounge, the bartender was already hanging up the phone.

"Bad news travels fast," Danny said with a slow smile.

"I'm sorry, sir, I'm afraid I can't serve you."

"One drink." Danny leaned across and laid down a fifty. "Then we will leave. I promise. No trouble. Ten minutes, and then you come over and ask us to leave, and escort us to the door."

The bartender had a puzzled look on his face. Danny's voice was low, clear, and perfectly sober.

"One drink," said the bartender, and mopped up the bill.

We seated ourselves in the far corner, partially screened by one of the palms.

"All this intrigue is giving me the hell of a thirst," Danny said after a while. "You think the bartender would go for two drinks and twenty minutes?"

"Here, have mine." I shoved it across. I saw Fred glance in the lounge door and then move past. He had changed into a sport jacket and slacks.

"Looks like they are waiting for us," I said.

"Which one do you want?"

"I think Billy likely feels he has earned the right to first dance with you. That leaves me with Fred."

"Be careful. He looks like a knife man to me," Danny said in a low voice as the bartender marched ostentatiously over.

"I am sorry, gentlemen, you will have to leave now," he uttered in his precise English accent.

"We're on our way. Give me a hand with him, will you?"

We each took an arm and lifted Danny to his feet. He had his head down and was mumbling incoherently.

"Your friend has mixed reactions to alcohol," the bartender said.

"It comes and goes. The fresh air will do him a world of good. I can handle him now. Come on, Danny," I said loudly, "the car is just out back."

I couldn't see Fred or Billy, but there were so fucking many palm trees scattered around the lobby that twenty Bedouins and their camels could have been hiding among them. I wasn't overly concerned. They'd be along. I helped Danny outside into the parking lot, shut the door behind me, and spun to the wall. Danny moved a few feet out and stood facing the door, his head slightly lowered, legs spread wide, the crutches tucked firmly under his armpits. The door suddenly burst open, slamming against the wall beside me as Billy came charging through like a maddened bull. Danny leaned even further forward and brought the tip of his right crutch up into Billy's solar plexus. I watched it disappear into his midriff, and his face turn a stark white. As he bent forward choking, Danny pulled the first crutch back and brought the other one up under Billy's chin, so quickly that it was just a shining blur. With a meaty thud, Billy dropped to the ground.

"Olé," I said.

Fred turned towards me and saw the gun before his hand was halfway to his jacket.

"Okay," he said. "Okay, no problem."

He slowly raised his hands above his shoulders.

"Easy for you to say," Danny said. He half pivoted and brought the crutch whistling around just above Fred's ear. He dropped like a stone.

"Goddam," Danny said happily. "Goddam, I really needed that. I love these fucking crutches. I may never get rid of them."

CHAPTER 26

I dragged the two of them out of sight behind the big Dumpster and backed the van up. Danny scooted through the rear door on his haunches, and between us we lifted the two men into the van. Sweat was dripping off us both by the time we had them loaded. They hadn't even twitched. I went forward to the driver's seat and started the engine.

"I hope you didn't kill them."

Danny leaned over and put his ear to the chest of each in turn.

"Nope. Fraid not."

He took the roll of duct tape and strapped their hands behind their backs, then lashed their ankles together and bent them back at the knees and tied them to their wrists. When he was finished he emptied out their pockets and threw everything in a pile on the floor of the van; wallets, room keys, loose change, and a pair of plane tickets. Vancouver to Santa Barbara, return. They had arrived four days previously. Billy was carrying a small Spyder with the serrated blade, Fred had an Italian flick-knife and a stubby .38 with a silencer screwed onto the barrel.

I headed out of town and turned down the first side road that ran towards the hills. Ten minutes along there was a gravel road marked on the map as service access for the power lines that paralleled it along the ridge above. I put the van into four-wheel drive and we started climbing. We ground along in first gear without speaking. From time to time Danny glanced in the rear-view mirror. Finally he nodded. They were awake and listening.

The first line was mine.

"Which one you figure?" I began.

"I don't think it makes much difference. Flip a coin, we'll start with either one."

"The dark one, he's in charge, looks like. Why don't we just kill the other one outright and work on him?"

"Don't be in such a rush," Danny said. "We've got lots of time, we can go slow with both of them."

"You and your bloody knives. You give me the fucking creeps. You shouldn't have hit them so hard, they're probably concussed."

"Don't worry. I'll wake them up."

"We're far enough now. Nobody will hear them."

I pulled the van off the track and bounced across a little clearing towards a dry gully that cut down the slope. I backed up until the rear doors were a short van-length away from the edge. It was a ten-foot drop to the bottom, with steep, eroded sides. I set the brake and walked around and opened the rear doors.

"Eeny meeny miny moe." Danny inserted the tip of the Spyder gently into the buttocks of the redhead, who let out a strangled scream of pain and fear. Danny lifted his head up by the hair and grinned at me.

"See? I told you they'd wake up."

"For Christ's sake, get him out of the van first. It's a rental, we can't get blood all over it."

Danny slid Billy to the edge and rolled him out. He let out another squeal as he fell.

"Sorry. Now, Billy. Who are you working for? Who sent you? What is the name of your local contact? Don't feel you have to answer right away. I've got all day."

He reached down and slit Billy's belt with a quick stroke. The Spyder cut through it like paper. He smiled approvingly. "I do admire a man who keeps his tools in good working order."

"Don't tell the fuckers anything," Fred growled.

"You're right, Jared. We only need one. Take Mr. Tough Guy down the gully and do him. We'll put Billy's prints on the gun afterwards. Not that there will be much left after the coyotes get done with them."

I dragged Fred over to the edge of the gully and gave him a shove. He rolled down to the bottom in a cloud of dust. Billy gave a little moan of terror.

"Geez. I think that might have done it."

"Go down and make sure. Hurry up. I need a hand with this one. The way he's wriggling around, I might cut too deep before I'm ready."

I picked up the silenced pistol and broke it open to check the loads. Billy was watching me with eyes like saucers. I threw him a jaunty wink and went over the edge and out of sight. Fred was lying on his back among the weeds at the bottom of the gully. His eyes were closed and a cut on his forehead was bleeding heavily. I ran a strip of duct tape around it, pressing it tightly into the thick black hair, and then continued on, running a couple of turns around his mouth. He breathed raggedly through his nose, and then his eyes opened and he looked around dazedly. I waited until he recognized me, and then I unscrewed the silencer from the barrel.

"Goodbye, Fred."

I jammed the barrel in his ear. The click of the cocking mechanism seemed unnaturally loud in the stillness. He closed his eyes. I could hear a fly buzzing nearby. I tilted the barrel and pulled the trigger. There was a sharp crack and dust flew up beside his head. He quivered and a dark stain spread out from the crotch of his slacks.

"Not so tough after all, hey, Freddy boy?" I whispered, and then I left him there and went back up the slope. From the top I could see the dust settling down on his face, and the two shining rivulets running through it.

"One down, one to go."

Billy was trying to crawl under the van, but with his hands tied behind his back and his feet bound, it was slow work. His pants had worked down to his knees. He was wearing black silk bikini-cut shorts.

"I haven't even touched him yet," Danny said in disgust. "I think maybe he's a cross-dresser. Look at those shorts, for God's sake." He opened the paper sack and brought out the propane torch and laid it carefully beside Billy, then frowned and began patting his pockets.

"Shit. No matches. You a smoker by any chance, Billy?"

"Oh God," Billy moaned softly.

I grabbed him and leaned him back against the bumper. He was literally shaking with fear.

"I'll tell you everything. Please. Keep him away. Don't kill me."

"Oh, for God's sake. Don't be such a fucking wimp, Billy. Hold out for a while. I haven't had any fun at all yet." Danny reached forward and pricked the black shorts with the tip of his knife. Billy closed his eyes and shrank back in terror. Saliva was leaking from the corner of his mouth.

"Start from the very beginning," I said.

He worked for a Vancouver tugboat company that ran between Seattle and Prince Rupert, hauling everything from chips and log booms to limestone barges. Every so often he received some packets to deliver, usually for the Seattle runs, but sometimes to the smaller communities as well. He received these packets from a man named Darnell. He was paid a thousand dollars a time, and made around fifteen deliveries a year.

Darnell told him that a friend of his needed a diver for a week's work, five thousand dollars and all expenses. Billy had picked up his dive ticket when he'd been hired on the tugboats five years earlier. He had never seen Fred before they met at Vancouver airport. They had flown into Santa Barbara and somebody had delivered the bombs to Fred at the hotel. He didn't know his name. They had told him that we were at San Miguel, and they had gone out to find us.

"How did you connect with the dive boat?"

"Just luck. We went down the docks to rent a boat and saw the sign. Day trip to San Miguel. So we went aboard."

That was it. We went back over it, tried to get some more names, but he didn't know anything else. If he had, he would have told us. His pale green eyes watched us anxiously as he talked in a rapid monotone, the words tumbling over each other in his hurry to please.

Danny looked at me and spread his hands. "I guess that's it." He leaned across to Billy, who watched him with the paralyzed stare of the rabbit for the fox.

"We're not going to kill you."

Billy closed his eyes and slumped back without a word.

Danny took the pack of cigarettes from the redhead's jacket, lit one, and stuffed it between his lips. Billy took long, deep drags and held them as if somehow the narcotic would still his inner trembling and give him back a part of what he had lost.

We went to the edge of the gully and stared down at Fred.

"That one is going to be tougher," Danny said.

"He has had a near-death experience. I think it may have altered his outlook somewhat."

"You want me to crawl down there and wave my knife around a bit? Drool, slaver, that sort of thing?"

"No. That might give him a chance to get some self-respect back. Let me try it alone first."

"Okay, Sigmund. Go ahead. Call me if you need a second opinion."

Fred lay as I had left him, not moving, his eyes closed. You could smell the stink of urine in the sunlight, and flies were buzzing and settling. I ripped the tape off his mouth with a sudden jerk, removing some moustache as well. He gave a little grunt. I crouched beside him, silent and waiting.

"What do you want?" he mumbled at last, not looking at me.

"We have most of it. Just a couple more things. Do you work for Darnell?"

"Yes. In the car lot. I do some selling, odd jobs."

That Darnell. I knew the name. A big dealership out along Broadway. Did a lot of television ads. One of the old Detroit franchises.

"How about this job?"

"Not for him. A friend of his needed a couple of divers. Jack Delaney. I used to instruct part time a few years back."

I kept my voice low and emotionless. "Did you meet with him?"

"No. It was all over the phone. He gave Darnell the money for me."

"How did you find out where we were?"

"I had a contact number."

"What is it?"

"It's in the book," he said. He frowned and shook his head.

"The phone book?"

He took a deep, shuddering breath and looked at me for the first time. "Fuck you."

I stared back at him until he dropped his eyes, then I stripped off his shoes and carried them back to the van. I removed Billy's as well, then dropped his knife down beside him. It might take a while, but he should be able to cut himself loose eventually. We climbed into the van and drove away. When we were nearly back to the blacktop, Danny threw the shoes out the window. If Billy and Fred were lucky, they would see the shoes when they went by. Or not.

"It will take them at least a couple of hours to get this far," I said. "With those faces, I can't see anybody giving them a lift. We should have plenty of time."

❀

We parked in the same spot and went back inside the Astor. There was a service elevator by the door, and we made it to the third floor without being spotted. A minute later we were in the room.

"Check the desk, I'll take the closets. It shouldn't be hard to find."

"First things first." Danny opened the freezer door and pulled out a bottle of frosted Stolichnaya. "The boys had good taste," he said.

255

"Billy did mention that they were on expenses."

I handed him the wrapped glasses and started to look through the closet. It only took a minute. The address book was in the cover of a black leather carryall. I went over and sat at the little desk and started copying.

"Why don't we just take it?"

Danny handed me the glass, the liquor giving off a frosty haze, and I threw it back and let it burn its way down, but it didn't take away any of the dirty taste in my mouth.

"I think Fred and Billy may decide not to mention today's little adventure to anybody, and we don't want to do anything to make that more difficult for them. They might need some of these numbers."

I finished writing down the last of them and replaced the book.

"Let's go."

My head was aching from the lack of sleep and the drinking. I could feel a bone-weary depression centring deep in my gut and starting to rise. I knew the symptoms.

"I need a shower and some sleep."

"One for the road," Danny said.

We had another drink, replaced the bottle in the fridge, and left. By the time we were back at *Arrow*, my head was pounding from the pain.

"We should really leave tonight."

"We'll be all right for another day, Jared. You turn in, Joseph and I will stand watch."

"Call me at midnight then and I'll take my turn."

I went below and had a long shower, hot as I could stand, then crawled into my berth like a dog to his manger. I fell asleep to a blur of burning boats, the stench of fear and urine, and the accusing pain in Jane's eyes.

They let me sleep, and the sun was well up when I finally opened my eyes. My body was stiff and cramped, as if I hadn't moved the whole night through. There were voices in the cockpit and the smell of coffee in the galley. I did some stretches, slow and languid, then took my runners and coffee and went up on deck.

Smokey and Danny were bent over the black box, talking in low, earnest voices. They looked up and greeted me, then carried on, Smokey doing most of the talking, Danny nodding his head in rapt complicity. He was learning about plastique, how to wire it, how much you needed to blow different-sized holes, time-delay fuses, all that sort of thing.

Just the sort of normal, relaxed early-morning conversation you would expect to find on a boat getting ready to leave for the carefree, fun-filled South Seas.

"Learning a new trade?" I asked.

"Well, seeing as we have the stuff, we might as well learn a little something about it," Danny said. "Might come in handy someday. Like the little scouts say, be prepared."

"Shit happens." Smokey nodded in agreement. "I'll get you a few more fuses. You've got about four times as much as you need there for a good bang. Your boat would have vaporized."

"I guess that was the general idea."

"Yeah. Danny says you met up with those guys."

"They should be leaving right about now. With sore feet and head-aches, I would imagine."

"I was hoping you would invite me," Smokey said. "I don't get much excitement these days."

"Danny and his crutches were all we needed. You should have seen him. Like Bonds or Papi in their prime. Timing, power, follow-through. Great stroke. Where is Joseph?"

"Still out looking."

"What the hell for?"

"He says he will know it when he finds it."

"Sounds very Indigenous."

"Well, sun's over the cap rail." Danny started below.

"No! No! I'm going for a run."

I pulled on my runners and vaulted over the rail.

"Don't mind if I do, partner," floated in the air behind me.

CHAPTER 27

I laid down a slow warm-up lap beside the breakwater, then headed out along the path that followed the lazy crescent of the bay. The harbour sparkled in the dappled sunlight, the water changing from blue to black to azure as the clouds crossed, the boats all shining in reflection so that even the most rust-streaked derelict achieved a certain romantic glamour from the glory of the day. *Arrow*'s varnished mainmast reached high over all but the biggest racers, the tiny figures in the cockpit visible even from this distance.

Along the boulevard, people ate early lunches under the parasols of fashionable restaurants, couples strolled hand in hand, lovers embraced on blankets spread out over the close-cut grass; everything peaceful, serene, normal. I didn't trust it for a second.

A jogger approached in the distance, a tall girl with a long blond ponytail, running in even, flowing strides. For a transfixed moment it was Jane, but then she glided by with a slight and distant smile, and it was just another of the bounteous golden girls of California.

I set the wish aside and concentrated on my pace, building up my speed, bellowing the air through my lungs, losing myself in the deep and hidden rhythms of muscle, sweat, and endorphins. I pushed it for the distance, sprinting by an elderly couple, vaulting a playful boxer on its twisted tether, taking the challenge of the boys in their UCLA sweat-shirts and staying with them until they moved away, then picking the next swaying back and pacing and accelerating till it moved towards me and then past, and seeking again, searching and overtaking until my lungs filled with fire and my vision blurred and I could no longer see the smooth stride of that slim and elegant form moving just away and out of reach.

I crouched beside the path until my breathing slowed, then walked back to the little sidewalk café and ordered their luncheon omelette with juice and coffee. While I waited, I pulled out the notes I had copied, and leafed through them.

There were thirty-three numbers in the book, most of them business-related: car dealers, auto-parts suppliers, a couple of body shops, a wrecking yard. Fred worked for Darnell as a car salesman; these would be his everyday contacts. Ernie Starrett's Chrysler deal-ership and home number were listed among them. It seemed a life-time ago that I had sailed with him and Jennie in the Sunday races. I remembered how she had tried to come visit me when I was in prison, all those years ago. Her father's picture had been in the *Sun* a couple of years back, standing on the deck of an enormous black motor yacht he had just refitted abroad. The car business must still have been doing very well.

The other phone numbers were all first names or initials. Billy, Eddie, and Chuck were all there, Eddie's number with a line crossed through it. I was disappointed to see that Chuck's remained intact — looked like we hadn't got him after all. Several women were listed, and the numbers of a couple of clubs. And then the initials, four sets of them, and only one made any sense to me: J.D. Jack Delaney. There were three numbers for him, work, home, and a cellular.

I had a sudden urge to call him. "Yo, Jack. This is Jared. How's it going, old buddy? Keeping busy?"

I wondered what it would take to get under that smooth hide, ruffle that affable composure. One day soon I hoped to find out.

I stopped at a pay phone on the walk back to the boat, but Clarke was out. He was expected in around three, and I said I would call again. The airport was next. The departures clerk was reluctant at first but finally condescended to tell me that Linder and Tanner had departed on their scheduled flight. So either we were safe for a while, or the opposition had decided to go with the local help. I really didn't much give a damn either way.

I debated whether to call Jane, but nothing had changed. I could tell her we had caught up to the men who had destroyed her boat, beat them up a bit, terrorized them, maybe located another person we could bully into giving us someone else. Just the kind of sweet talk a girl likes to hear.

Maybe later.

When I arrived back at *Arrow*, Smokey had left and Joseph and Danny were bent over in the cockpit. The old man was talking rapidly, Danny shaking his head in puzzlement. There was something on the cockpit sole in front of them, and Joseph was running his hands over it as he spoke. I had a quick glimpse of a mottled, moth-eaten rug as I stepped on the rail of the boat and grabbed the lifelines to climb over.

In a split second the rug exploded into life and rose from the deck in a snarling blur. The impression of black and brown vanished, and there was just a huge red maw filled with bright shining teeth impending on my groin. I screamed and fell backwards as the gaping jaws snapped shut inches short of their target. The beast's momentum had been arrested by a chain attached to its neck, running back into the cockpit. It landed heavily on the lifelines and leaned its head towards me where I lay spread-eagled on the dock, gazing up in horror. It was whining with a terrifying eagerness, saliva shaking from its lips and floating through the air like whipped cream as it struggled to reach me. The eyes were staring down, amber and goatish above the fangs.

"Jesus, oh Jesus," I gasped.

"It's okay, you can come aboard now, I've got him," Danny said.

I rose to my feet, heart pounding, and slowly approached the rail. The thing was lying in front of Joseph, its eyes fixed upon me in a baleful yellow glare. I had never seen eyes like that outside of a horror movie.

The creature must have weighed a hundred and seventy pounds, but its head was outsized and belonged on something much bigger. The visage was wide and brutal, flat-faced — not like a bulldog, but as if a wolf had somehow run full speed into a brick wall and had its features flattened and compressed. The neck was massive, the skin rumpled in layers over the back of it as if the impact had foreshortened the body as well, and there was now an excess of skin. It appeared humped as it crouched on the grates, the powerful shoulders running down to a narrow, skinny rump and short, muscular hind legs, with broad, thickly furred feet. The tail was thin and furless, like a rat's, and appeared to have been bitten off two-thirds of the way down. Beneath this bizarre appendage, its scrotum hung down like a sack of marbles. Its coat was a spotted blackish-brown, very short and so thin in spots you could see the liverish purple skin beneath.

It raised its head and growled, revealing a network of scars starting under the chin and running back through the chest and neck. Its left ear was half-gone, the edge serrated in little steps.

"Jesus. That's the ugliest thing I have ever seen. It must have escaped from a fucking zoo." My voice was still pitched an octave too high.

"C'mon, Jared." Danny smiled. "It's just a dog. Look, it's friendly."

He reached down and patted it, and the thing arched its head back against the caress. Its eyes never left me.

"Yeah, real friendly. I guess that's why it has a collar and leash of quarter-inch anchor chain, huh? Who does he belong to — Smokey?"

"It's just an ordinary choke collar and leash, Jared. Large size. He's very obedient. Look. Roll over."

It rolled slowly over, its slitted yellow eyes locked on mine, its balls bouncing obscenely as it revolved. Mine were still retracted somewhere deep inside my body.

"Yeah. So who does he belong to?" I asked again.

Danny looked across at Joseph. He was sitting cross-legged on the sole, smoking his pipe and stroking the animal's back. He smiled at me.

"Joseph bought it," Danny said. "For protection."

"Protection!" I gaped at Joseph. "The fucking thing is a monster. Look at the fucker. He wants to eat me so bad it's killing him."

The dog was growling low in its throat, a thick, primeval hunting sound. Danny had two wraps of chain around his wrist.

"Hey, you ugly motherfucker," I taunted. "You want me, don't you?"

I could see the claws gripping the grating, the eyes distended as it quivered with rage. Danny's arm was bar-rigid on the leash.

"Keep your voice down. You're upsetting him."

"Oh, I'm upsetting him, am I? You bring a wild beast on the fucking boat, and I'm fucking upsetting him. Pardon me!"

"Stop screaming, Jared. Once he knows you're a friend, he'll be fine."

"I'm not a friend. I don't want to be friends with a fucking cross between a Brahma bull and a rabid goat. I can't believe this." I lowered my voice. "Hell, we'll be leaving Santa Barbara in a day or so. Look, I'll stand all the watches till we leave. I don't mind. Honest."

"Joseph says he should stay with us."

"Stay with us? On the boat?"

Joseph nodded.

I started laughing. "You're both crazy. Look at the size of that fucker. What's he eat — ten, fifteen pounds of meat a day?"

"C'mon, Jared. He's not all that big. Besides, he eats fish."

"Fish? He eats fish? What does he do, go over the side and catch them?" I laughed again.

"Sort of," Danny said.

He spoke to Joseph, then reached down to unclip the chain.

"Danny!" I yelled. "No, don't!"

I sprang for the ratlines and raced to the spreaders. He waved at me in a shushing motion and slipped the leash.

"Go fish," he said.

263

The thing went over the side in a blur, landed scrabbling on the dock and raced down the pier. He launched himself into the air and soared fifteen feet before landing with a loud splash. He paddled rapidly to the beach, then turned and re-entered the water until it was chest high. He moved parallel to the shore in a series of leaps, his head swivelling rapidly at the apex, then landing stiff-legged. Two surf casters watched in amazement. After a couple of minutes he sprang sideways and ducked his head beneath the water, emerging with a ten-inch fish. He pointed his muzzle skyward and devoured it in two large bites.

"I don't believe it," I said.

"He belonged to a cruiser. A single-hander who spent three years in the South Pacific. He picked the dog up in the Tuamotus. It was a village dog, didn't belong to anyone in particular. The guy made friends with it, and when he left the dog went with him. Stayed on the boat, travelled with him for a couple of years. His name is Sinbad. He's had all his shots, everything. We've got the papers."

"Sinbad," I said.

He'd caught another fish now and wolfed it down as quickly as the first.

"Yeah. Joseph has been looking for a dog. Found Sinbad at the SPCA. He's been there for three months. The guy sold his boat, went abroad. He left some money to look after the dog for a while, give him a chance to find a home."

"Good-looking, friendly animal like that, I'm surprised he didn't go to a nice family the first day," I said.

"He'll grow on you."

"But at sea, Danny. Christ, if he gets hungry enough he's liable to eat one of us."

"We'll trail a couple of fishing lines. We'll usually catch something. Pack a couple of cases of canned mackerel for backup. It's really cheap. That's what the cruiser did."

"But the shit, Danny."

I was excited now. This was something they would have a hard time explaining away.

"Can you imagine a beast like that, Danny? How much shit he'll create? God, there will be mounds of it everywhere. I lived on a farm, Danny, I know." I tried to keep the smugness out of my voice.

"He's trained. The girl at the SPCA said the cruiser told her the dog never fouled the deck once. Goes in the water in harbour. Hangs over the lee rail at sea, or the stern."

"Hangs over the lee rail?" I said. "Come on, Danny. This is total bullshit. Dogshit," I amended.

"Would you have believed the fishing?" Danny asked.

Joseph nodded and smiled. I sensed I was losing.

"His claws. He'll scar the decks, scratch everything."

"You keep them cut short," Danny said. "You saw those thick pads, they come right down over. Not a mark."

I got down on my hands and knees and examined the cockpit grating, then studied the cap rail where he had tried to emasculate me. Nothing. Danny and Joseph were both smiling now. They thought they had me.

"Lots of countries don't allow pets," I said. "New Zealand. We might want to go to New Zealand. I have read a lot about it, sounds like a great place. I've always wanted to visit New Zealand. They hate animals on boats. Quarantines, you can't ever dock. They come out to inspect them two or three times a week. Costs a fortune. Some harbours are even closed to you. I've read about it."

"Don't worry about it. If we go there, we'll just dump him off at some deserted little island on the way in, pick him up on the way back out. Be just like old times for him."

I tried to think. There had to be other compelling reasons, I just couldn't come up with them on the spur of the moment. I needed time. The boat heeled slightly, and Sinbad came over the rail. He had a nice twenty-inch fish in his mouth. He paused to shake himself vigorously alongside me, then went up to the foredeck and curled up in the sun, chewing lazily on his prize. He looked right at home.

"He'll grow on you," Danny repeated.

Joseph stood up and patted me on the shoulder, then went below.

I gazed down the dock in contemplation. "He is your dog. I have nothing to do with him."

"Absolutely."

"You look after him, feed him, take care of any hassles."

"You bet."

"Okay. You can start now."

I pointed down the dock, where one of the surf fishermen was pounding towards us, his face as red as the cap on his head.

"There's a man wants to talk to you about a fish."

✾

"You should have called the police, Jared, this cowboy bullshit has got to stop."

It was the second time Clarke had said that.

"It wouldn't have done any good," I said into the phone. "They would have hauled us in for questioning, Jane and Ingrid as well. I doubt they could have made anything stick on Linden and Tanner, there was no proof, and in the meantime we would have been immobilized, targets. It's the same old story, Clarke. I think Danny and I got as much as anyone could have. I'll fax all the names and numbers to you." Except for one.

"Do that right away."

"As soon as I hang up."

"Their plane will be in by now, so I won't even be able to pick them up," he grumbled.

"I phoned earlier, but you were out."

"They shouldn't be too hard to find, I suppose," he said, slightly mollified.

"Any luck on your end with Chuck or the gun?"

"No. Chuck has disappeared. Nobody has seen him since the Port Townsend affair. He is either holed up recovering, or gone for good. As for the gun, nothing that ties in anywhere. So we are no further ahead than before. But some of the numbers might lead to Delaney. Too bad his wasn't there. We'll run the others down, maybe get lucky, make some connections. Don't do anything about that Santa Barbara number. You hear me, Jared? I'll give it to the locals, see what they can do, so stay out of it. Understand?"

"Yes. We're leaving anyway."

I had no stomach for any more of it in any case, but I didn't tell him that.

"Good. I'll talk to Narcotics about Darnell, see what they've got on him. Maybe pay a visit, lean on him a little, if only for the fun of it. How are Joseph and Danny, anyway?"

"They're fine. Joseph decided we needed some extra protection. Picked up a watchdog."

"Good idea," Clarke said. "What did he get, a Lab, something like that?"

"Something like that. I think we'll leave tomorrow. Stop off at one of the little islands, maybe head into Newport for a day or two, then on to San Diego."

"Take care. Say hi to Jane for me."

I stopped off at the port office and faxed him the numbers. All except Delaney's. We had a different use for that.

❈

We left the next morning at sunrise, slipping out of the harbour with the resident fleet of sport fishermen. Danny rigged up a couple of lines with hundred-pound test and shock cord, baited them with a white feathered lure and a pink imitation squid, and set them out at fifty and seventy-five feet. Just inside and between them, he tied a Coke bottle by the neck on a separate line, where it surfed and bounced gaily along in our wake.

"Acts like a big flasher. Fish comes over to check it out, then the lures go by, and *bang*. You've got one."

"I guess we don't have to hook up a bell," I said.

Sinbad was lying on his front paws in the stern, his head snaked out before him, his eyes fastened unwaveringly on the lines, his stubby tail switching slowly back and forth. I suspected he was still in a foul mood from this morning. Joseph had thrown a loaf of mouldy bread over the rail, and the seagulls had attacked it with their usual voracity, diving and fighting over the slices. Sinbad was sleeping on the bow, and at the first squawk rose up and crept along by the gunwales, crouched and stalking like a cat. As he came abreast of the feeding birds he took a quick stride and launched himself among them, head swivelling, jaws snapping, like a lawnmower run amok.

He surfaced, snarling, with nothing but a mouthful of feathers for his efforts, and I howled at the look on his face. He glared at me and swam back to the dock. The floats were a good two feet out of the water, and he just put his front paws up, humped the mass of muscle on his shoulders, and rose up as smoothly as an Olympic swimmer, then put his head down and came for *Arrow* at the gallop. I stopped laughing and retreated below.

It was a beautiful morning, and as the sun climbed and burned away the early mist, so too our worries dissolved in the beneficent rays, and we relaxed and began to enjoy the sea and sail. There was scant wind, and we loafed along under main and genoa, taking advantage of the opportunity to lie back and read or sunbathe as the fancy took us. Even Sinbad had abandoned his sharp vigil and was lying on his back, feet splayed, as Danny rubbed and tickled his belly. Joseph had the watch, steering with one casual leg thrown over the tiller, looking up from his carving occasionally to check for traffic, or chase an elusive zephyr.

We passed among the oil rigs, the high, thrusting derricks spaced out at intervals of two or three miles as far as the eye could see. They were incongruous in this marine playground of the rich, their sharp, utilitarian angles as out of place as barbed wire at a wedding. We drifted along in the shifting winds, heading in to pick up an offshore breeze, then swinging back out to drag the lures through a group of feeding seabirds. There were few boats around, and none that seemed interested in us. We ran a radar check each hour, searching for any images that maintained a constant distance relative to us. There were none.

By dark we had only covered forty miles and decided to continue straight through to Newport. The wind swung to the east, and we began to get the first traces of the L.A. smog. The refracted lights of the metropolis lit up the sky in a dim, ghostly loom, and just at midnight we ran into an inversion. There was a biting acrid smell in the air as the temperature suddenly dropped and the visibility decreased to a quarter mile. We kept to the outside limits of the sea lane, calling up the ships as we picked them up on the radar and relaying our position to them.

An hour past midnight the air turned smoky, and when we tried to wipe the condensation off the compass, it smeared in greasy yellow streaks. Even Sinbad was affected and lay in the cockpit with his head resting on the cabin stoop, growling low in his throat each time I stepped over him to go below.

By first light we were clear of L.A., and the last trace of the yellow fog burned off with the sun. The breeze backed and filled from the west, we changed down to the working jib and raised the mizzen, and after a brisk three-hour sail we checked in at the Newport police dock. They assigned us mooring buoys, and we tied up and went below for a late breakfast. A muted splash alongside was Sinbad, off in search of his own sustenance.

Afterwards Danny and I rigged up the little skiff and set out for a leisurely tour of the harbour. We didn't bother with the motor, just set up the tiny main and handkerchief jib, threw in a six-pack, and tacked off. Danny was at the tiller, and we dodged in and out among the anchored boats, some of which had been on their moorings for decades. Old wooden sloops and yawls, high-masted schooners and stubby gaff-rigged ketches with their paint all vanished years before, their topsides gaped and cracking from the sun, decks buried in inches of bird droppings, every piece of iron a brown streak of rust. Beautiful, once-proud vessels, moored and abandoned these many years, God alone knew why.

And then right alongside, a state-of-the-art racer, seventy feet long with a mast so thin and tapered it seemed to merge into the sky, every inch of her aglow with love and care, the big coffee grinders reflecting light like diamonds, her name emblazoned across her transom in letters of gold. The scene was strange and affecting, like a crosscut slice of sailing history selected and spread out before us for our sampling.

As we sailed slowly along, rubbernecking like the most gauche and amiable of tourists, I noticed a shifting pocket of activity paralleling our course along the shore. The files of walkers strolling the beach suddenly parted in agitation, falling back in stumbling steps as some immutable force swept by. The action proceeded along the shoreline like a giant undulating wave, slow, curving, and inevitable. In its wake, men stooped to pick up and throw rocks, and little children screamed in fear.

Through a sudden gap in the crowd, I caught a glimpse of a low, powerful form racing along, the head stretched out before it like a bludgeon, never altering course except to dodge the blows that rained down upon it.

"Sinbad," I whispered in horror.

"I wonder where he's going?" Danny asked.

"You imbecile," I hissed, "he's coming for us."

His plan was apparent. He was almost abeam now, and the beach curved sharply in towards us fifty feet ahead. The passage narrowed and we would approach within thirty feet of the fuelling station that abutted the channel. He would be waiting.

"What should I do?" Danny asked. "I don't think we can make headway if I turn around, the current is against us."

"Keep going. People might think we're just another victim."

Sinbad hit the fuel dock at full stride. A pretty little tourist boat was tied up alongside it, the kind that's everywhere in Newport — about twenty feet long and narrow of beam, with cute little seats and a canvas roof stretched over the top for protection from the sun. A few elderly tourists were seated inside as the guide went down the aisle, distributing coffee and sodas.

Sinbad timed it perfectly. His front legs landed directly on the canopy atop the white yachting cap a split second before his hind legs arrived on the shoulders and thrust powerfully off. The bounce carried him twenty feet out into the channel. The guide fell over the side of the boat amid exploding cans of pop and shrill cries of outrage. Sinbad had his yellow eyes fixed directly upon the skiff now, a white bow wave foaming before him as he moved towards us, inevitable as death.

My nerve broke.

"He's your dog," I yelled, and leaped over the side.

My last glimpse was of Danny sailing away down the channel, Sinbad trailing contentedly behind, his teeth clamped on the rudder, his body turned on its side and streaming in the wake.

It was after dark when they arrived back at the boat. Sinbad was crouched below the gunwales, with Danny's shirt thrown over him for cover.

"Get on the boat, you son of a bitch," Danny hissed. Sinbad slunk through the lifelines. Danny swung up behind him.

"Lie down."

Sinbad crouched flat on his belly on the cockpit grating, his eyes looking pleadingly upward.

"If you move, I'll kill you, you cocksucker. Do you understand that?"

Sinbad gave a low whine. Danny leaned back, closed his eyes, and uttered a long, drawn-out sigh. I brought up a couple of Coronas and placed one in his hand.

"Did you have a nice sail?" I inquired.

"I'm not speaking to you either," he replied.

We sat in the cockpit silently for a few minutes, then I started to giggle. I turned away from Danny, but I still couldn't control it. My jaws ached from the effort. There was a choking sound from Danny, and then

271

he broke down and sputtered and issued a braying roar, and the two of us howled until the tears ran down our faces. Sinbad sensed an amnesty in the general levity and lost his craven look. When he thought no one was watching, he slyly tipped my beer and lapped the foaming suds.

Joseph emerged from the cabin, nodded approvingly at the happy family, and handed out another round. He set down a stainless bowl for Sinbad's share, and the four of us sat drinking in silent companionship, the only sounds the slap of water against the hull and the occasional belch from the dog.

"Do you think it's safe to stay another day, or will we be lynched? I'd like to visit Minney's chandlery tomorrow, check out their used gear."

"I don't think anybody will connect Sinbad with *Arrow*. I was well away from everybody when I put him in the skiff. Joseph can stay aboard and look after him."

Sinbad raised his head at the mention of his name, then subsided again. In the moonlight his scars shone like silver wires.

"What are those scars, anyway?"

"Most of them are sharks. From the Tuamotus. They come right through the reef entrances up into the shallows. I guess he was fishing and they went for him."

"Sharks."

"Yeah, look. You can see the marks where they took part of his ear. See how it's saw-toothed? That's sharks. They got his tail too. The girl at the SPCA told Joseph that Sinbad hates sharks, goes crazy when they come around the boat. The cruiser used to do a lot of spear fishing in the Tuamotus, Sinbad would hang out with him. Soon as he heard him growling, he knew there was a shark around."

"Sort of a shark early-warning system, eh?"

I regarded Sinbad thoughtfully. Perhaps he wasn't such a bad dog, really. Ugly as sin, of course. I bent down to pet him. He uttered a low growl and his teeth snapped shut a fraction from my fingers.

"You'll be friends soon," Danny said. "You just got off on the wrong foot."

CHAPTER 28

Danny and I set off early the following morning, rowing the dinghy on a clear, windless day. The channel was busy with traffic and we held to the inside edge, succumbing occasionally to the urge to explore one of the meandering canals that branched off at regular intervals. Rows of stately homes encroached their banks, each with its own private landing and yacht alongside.

It was a showplace of marine wealth and privilege, the owners as trim and spanking neat as their possessions, moving around the perfect lawns or gleaming decks like models in an advertisement for the good life. They had the facility of looking at you but not seeing you, as if you were merely a part of the general view, with no individual identity.

"I'm getting this overpowering urge to stand up and tug my forelock," Danny said as we passed one particularly staggering estate.

"Incredible, isn't it? I've never seen this much money in one place before. It is really starting to depress me."

"Let's get out of here."

We stopped at a fuel dock along the channel, and I called Jane. Her mother answered and informed me in a clipped, chilly voice that she had gone away for a few days. She didn't say where, and I didn't waste our time by asking, just filed the news away in a hidden spot and buried it. There would be plenty of time for regrets and might-have-beens later.

We tied up at the floats and walked slowly up to Minney's, the maritime equivalent of an auto wrecking yard. Huge anchor winches, old wooden spars, shrouds and chain plates, masts and rigging enough to fit out a fleet were scattered randomly along the path, and even the roof of the rambling building was littered with stainless rails, pulpits, and bow fittings. We worked our way through and then went inside and wandered through the chaos for the rest of the morning.

I bought some extra charts and the new Sailing Directions for French Polynesia and the Cook Islands, and a guide for Tonga. From the barrels of brass fittings I found some drawer pulls that matched exactly those aboard *Arrow* and put them in a pile on the counter. Danny located a rebuilt set of injectors for the Perkins, and we put those in the heap as well. The store also had some used solar panels and a Hamilton Ferris wind generator with a set of double blades, and I dickered with the salesman for a quarter hour over the price. We kept adding items to the stack: coils of rope, spare winch handles, some extra Nicropress fittings, and a brass Whale galley pump; then we dickered again.

When we finally quit, we had the skiff filled with gear and had spent fourteen hundred dollars. It would have been five thousand anywhere else. The wind had come up on the beam and we scudded back to *Arrow*, replete with the tired satisfaction that comes to all sailors after yet another buying frenzy for their beloved boats.

The rest of the day was spent stowing and installing equipment. Danny went up the mizzenmast and bolted on a bracket for the wind generator while I ran the cables, taking them through decks with waterproof compression fittings, then putting in a Schottky diode before connecting them to the batteries. I laid the solar panels on deck until we could have adjustable fittings welded up for them.

"Starting to look like a cruiser, Jared."

"Damn it, I think we're almost ready to go. A few minor details, a couple of days to top up our provisions in San Diego, and we're gone."

"Looks like we are actually going to make it."

"Yep. Shouldn't be any problem staying here for another night. Too crowded to try anything. When we go to San Diego we'll tie up at the police dock. You get ten days there, right under the noses of the Harbor Police. Two or three nights, then we're gone. Head south and disappear."

"Joseph wants to eat out tonight. Says he is tired of everybody's cooking, especially his own. Leave in a couple of hours."

"Suits me."

I felt like getting drunk, and one place was as good as another for filling the ache with blankness. I went below and had a large Scotch while I changed.

It was just before eight when we left. Sinbad stood at the rail, watching us, an expression of sad importance on his face. Both Danny and Joseph had spoken to him, and he seemed to understand he was in charge. He sprang onto the cabin top and lay with his front legs outstretched, his head resting upon them. You could see the hump outlined in the sinking sun behind him. From this angle, he looked a bit like a dwarf Brahma bull.

Danny had overhauled the British Antichrist once again, and the little Seagull motor started on the second pull, moving us down the harbour at a stoic three knots. After a few minutes, Joseph shut off the motor and we bumped up against a dark hull. I looked up in surprise.

Jeopardy.

And there at the rail, Maria, Ingrid, and Jane smiling down on us. Joseph gave my waist a gentle pinch as his eyelid dropped in a slow wink.

❦

"Were you ever going to call?" Jane asked.

We had finished dinner and were sitting out on the deck chairs behind the cabin. The others were inside, playing cards. I reached down and poured us each another brandy.

"I finally got up the nerve to phone you today, actually. Your mother said you were away for a few days. She didn't elaborate."

She laughed. "I'll bet. They were pretty upset."

"What did you tell them?"

"I said a propane explosion. I don't think Daddy believed me, but he wouldn't have told Mother in any case."

"So she just dislikes me on general principles."

"Well, I'm an only child, you know. Nothing is too good for the Princess. You really don't measure up all that well alongside my marine biologist. I don't think they have ruled him out completely yet — he was still single, last I heard."

"I missed you. But it's dangerous."

I hadn't told her about our encounter in Santa Barbara.

"Do you think those men are still around?"

"No. We checked. They left. But there could be others. We should be all right for a few days, though." I put my arm around her again. "What are the sleeping arrangements?"

"Ingrid and Danny have a cabin on *Jeopardy*. We get *Arrow*."

"How soon can we decently leave?"

"Anytime." Her smile in the starlight transfixed me.

We rowed back to *Arrow*, taking our time, weaving in and out among the anchored boats. There was a history and spell to the watercraft of Newport that was as strong and tangible as the rays of the moon that outlined them, abandoned and looming along our path. It was as if those restless hulks contained the echoes of every step that ever trod them, the lives and loves all present still, only waiting for some secret sign to stir to life, and raise again their tattered sails and move away in ghostly procession.

I stared at them, trying to surprise some glimpse of movement, some small secret clue to their true nature, but they stood as silent as the grave, only a slight creaking of the hulls as they rocked, or the sound of a slapping halyard releasing and tightening with the motion of our passage. Jane rowed while I lay back, lost in time, caught up in the forest of masts, spreaders, and crosstrees that surrounded us.

We bumped alongside *Arrow*, and Jane made fast and climbed quickly aboard.

"Jane!" I yelled. "Wait. Sinbad!"

But she was up and over the lifelines in a flash of tanned thighs. I heard a low, keening whine and the thump of a heavy body falling in the cockpit. I threw myself between the lifelines in a desperate, lunging dive. My shoulder grazed the sheet winch and I lost my balance and sprawled into the cockpit, my head cracking the shift lever, my knees slamming against the stayed tiller. I lay there in a daze.

"Oh, you're so sweet," Jane trilled in the voice women reserve for small babies and miniature poodles. "You're just adorable, aren't you?"

I squinted upwards through the pain. Jane was crouched on her knees on the starboard seat, Sinbad splayed out in front of her, his grotesque mouth panting open, his rat tail busily thumping against the bulkhead.

"Why didn't you tell me you had a dog?"

She reached down and scratched behind his half ear. He gazed up adoringly.

"I forgot," I muttered. I rose shakily to my feet. My knee was bleeding along the graze, not that anybody gave a rat's ass. I went below and poured myself a couple of fingers of Scotch. When I returned, the love-in was still happening. I sat down beside Jane and put my arm around her. Sinbad turned his head towards me and uttered a long, low growl.

"He thinks you're threatening me." She laughed delightedly. "Isn't that cute?"

The three of us sat there in the moonlight. It was very romantic.

Finally I inveigled Jane below. The great head thrust through the companionway and watched mournfully as we disappeared into the forward cabin. I bolted the door behind us.

Jane slipped out of her shorts and blouse and stretched out on the bunk. The moon shining through the skylight laid soft bars of shadow across her smooth and golden body. I kissed her, my lips slowly traversing the long, shadowed length of her. One of the shadows moved.

Sinbad!

Her fingers became more urgent, kneading my shoulder, pulling me up beside her.

"Love me, Jared," she whispered, her eyes closed, the languorous legs slowly parting.

"But he's watching," I whispered back. "Wait. I can't when he's watching."

Her eyes opened wide in disbelief as I got up and pinned a towel across the skylight. Then she started giggling, and it was another half an hour before she took me seriously again.

❀

"Are you coming to San Diego with us?"

We sat in the cockpit, drinking morning coffee. Sinbad was gone. I had heard a splash earlier and assumed he was out hunting.

"That would be nice. I have a few days before I have to make any big decisions. There's a three-month course on ocean currents coming up at Scripps. I'm thinking of taking it."

"If circumstances were different, I'd ask you to come sailing with me. If you said no, I'd shanghai you. Keep you tied up in my cabin until we were far out to sea."

"I might like that. Being tied up, I mean."

"When it's over I'll call you. With a plane ticket, no matter where I am."

The level grey eyes studied me. "Do you think it will ever end?"

"Yes. In three months it will be finished." One way or another, I thought. "I'm not going to live my life like this."

"What are you going to do?"

"I have just the beginnings of an idea. Will you come when it's over?"

"Perhaps." She smiled enigmatically.

"Who is teaching the course?"

"An Englishman. Dr. Haldane. He's world famous, spent his whole life in ocean research. He is quite old now, probably in his early seventies."

"Does he surf?"

She smiled again.

We leaned back in the cockpit, sipping our coffee and enjoying the early-morning quiet. With a loud squawk, a cloud of brown pelicans rose from the derelict trawler moored fifty feet off our beam. The boat was inches deep in guano, and a window was out in the pilot house, where the birds nested. A tarp had been stretched over the top of the cabin in a doomed attempt to keep it clean. There was a large protuberance under the centre of it. I smiled.

The flight of pelicans circled, protesting loudly, then began to drop down and land again in twos and threes. The bump flattened slightly and moved imperceptibly aft, where the flock perched on the handrails leading up to the pilot house. My smile grew.

"What are you smiling at?"

"Sinbad. He's organizing breakfast."

"Where?"

She jumped to her feet. I had told her about how he caught fish.

"He's on the cabin top. There, under the tarp."

"How is he going to catch any fish from there?" she asked in a puzzled voice.

"He is going to eat the pelicans," I said. "Isn't that just too cute?"

"I don't believe you."

"He's under the tarp. Watch."

We watched for five minutes. Nothing moved.

"You are being ridiculous again, Jared," Jane said.

"It's him," I insisted. "Wait."

279

We waited for another five minutes. All was quiet. More and more pelicans were landing on the railing every minute. Further and further up the slope, closer all the time.

"Any second now," I said.

Jane snorted. "You are very childish sometimes, Jared."

She took her cup and went below. A minute later, the tarp exploded in a cloud of birdshit, feathers, and squawks. A mottled shape hurtled through the air and landed heavily on the decks. Something large and brown struggled in its jaws.

"There!" I yelled. "Look! He's got one."

Her acid voice rose through the companionway. "I have never heard of anyone being jealous of a dog before. I am having breakfast. Do you want some or not?"

❀

The four of us sailed out of Newport the following evening, Joseph and Maria following behind in *Jeopardy*. We knew it might be our last sail together, and the passage had the bittersweet sadness of something shared a final time.

We split the watches six and six by couples, Jane and I taking the first shift, sitting in the cockpit with a blanket over us, sometimes talking in low whispers, but more often just leaning back and looking up at the night sky.

When I was a child on the farm, I sometimes played the game of withdrawal at night, lying in the big double bed. I started by imagining myself suspended above the house, so close that all I could see was my room, and me lying there in it. Then I pulled back, and now I could see the whole farm, and my grandparents and all of the animals, everything quiet and resting. And then another giant leap back and I saw the neighbours' farms, the city a few miles distant, and the beginning curve of the earth, and everybody in their beds and me just a small part of the whole, insignificant.

And then falling back again through the clear endless night, the planets and then the stars moving slowly past until at last the earth was nothing but a pinpoint of light among them, and the life of one small boy less than nothing. Sometimes I would lie there fashioning tier upon tier until at last I reached that cold and distant plane where only God existed, and it was his blank, unfeeling eyes I looked through.

"A penny for your thoughts."

"I was thinking how puny and unimportant this all is in the grand scheme of things, and if there is anything up there, how ridiculous we must all seem."

She put her hand on mine. "You don't believe there is anything else, do you?"

"No. And you?"

"I'd like to think so."

Wouldn't we all.

We sat until Ingrid and Danny relieved us, then went below.

We awoke to the blast of sirens, so close that the noise and the wash of powerful screws arrived together. The navy was running early-morning exercises around Point Loma, the ships crossing and recrossing in intricate manoeuvres while the crew dashed from side to side. *Arrow* seemed to be at the centre of their formations.

"They snuck up on me," Danny said. "Came up from behind, blew by at twenty knots. Almost gave me a heart attack. I think they're just having fun, probably wanted something mobile to run their patterns on."

We sat and watched them surging and heeling for another hour, until they sounded three quick blasts on their sirens, wheeled in tight formation, and headed south.

"Mexico." Danny lifted his arm and pointed in their wake. "Islas Los Coronados."

The islands were caught in the first light of morning, the rocks shining white and brilliant. To the east the Mexican mainland showed a pale green above the thin crescents of the coast.

"We're damn near there," Danny said with a grin. "Another week

281

and we'll be in some little cantina, throwing back cervezas. I'll have to brush up on some of the local customs. Is it salt, lime, tequila; or salt, tequila, lime? I can never remember."

"Whatever."

But there would be no Mexico this time around. During the long, quiet night I had pondered our options, weighed the balances, summoned my final resolve, and come to the inevitable conclusion: Mexico would not do. It was too small, too placid and settled, the coast too hospitable and the waters too benign. The sun always shone and the wind was too timid, the bays all accessible and the hazards all posted.

We needed a harder school to teach our lessons.

We needed the steady bellows of the trade winds to drive us and the sudden, blinding squalls to conceal us. We needed hidden reefs, narrow unmarked passes, small armoured lagoons where a boat could hide for days or weeks, or remain forever undiscovered on the bottom.

We needed a place where cyclones spawned and grew, where charts were mere approximations, markers nonexistent, and the reefs rose sharply upwards in steep and jagged teeth for ten thousand square miles. We needed the ancient maritime killing ground that had claimed a thousand ships, and would claim a thousand more, the graveyard of the Pacific, where the only headstones were the bleached and broken bodies of the wrecks that marked her shores.

We needed the archipelago of the Tuamotus; it was there that we would write the last chapter in the clear, translucent waters of the South Pacific, and achieve a permanent peace or final resting place. A cold anticipation gripped me.

We approached the main channel, working for every mile in the slack San Diego breeze. Jane took the tiller and Ingrid ran the sheets, the two of them quick and expert, hugging the side of the channel as the freighters passed, then running a sharp tack out when the way was clear. An old Cal 36 was heading in behind us with three young men aboard, and we engaged them in an impromptu race, Jane luffing them unmercifully as they tried to pass, swinging *Arrow* across with an air of splendid innocence while Sinbad crouched at the stern, growling savagely each time they approached. The issue was in doubt until Ingrid, overheated by the contest, stripped off her top and the Cal missed a tack completely, ending up in irons. We sailed away from them, the loud cries of "Foul" and "Protest" fading gradually in our wake.

❀

We made the last tack across, dropped our sails, and motored into the arrival slip in front of the police docks. The Harbor Police were friendly and welcoming, and I paid them for the full ten days; we would leave earlier, but it might buy us a little time if anyone was checking. We ran *Arrow* across to a spare berth beside a little Columbia from Oregon that was rerigging, and tied her in.

The docks were a mass of confusion, filled with bustling cruisers under half a dozen flags of origin, all of them preparing for Mexico or the South Pacific. French, German, Dutch, Americans, Canadians, and a Spaniard, all busily installing equipment, overhauling gear, or stocking up. A steady procession of people moved up and down the ramp, carrying parcels of electronics, coils of rope, boxes of food, and the never-ending collection of spares both needed and imagined.

A battered old Chevy sedan with the legend Butchmobile spray-painted on its hood backed down the ramp and collected some rusty anchors and a pile of chain for re-galvanizing, then inched painfully back up the slope, black, oily clouds of smoke pouring from its exhaust. Above our heads three men and a woman hung from their separate masts, their shouted instructions to their partners on the winches adding to the general confusion.

And over it all, the deck speakers, all loudly tuned to the cruising net and its daily broadcasts of boats buying and selling their accumulated treasures of the bilge. People interrupted their labours and ran back aboard as a sought-after item was offered, their transmissions crossing and recrossing as they bartered, with the sponsoring chandlery desperately trying to referee. Through all the chaos ran a spirit of care-free camaraderie as alien to *Arrow* as the Arctic Sea.

Danny was talking to the couple aboard the little Columbia next to us. They looked about fifteen, the two of them chattering excitedly about Mexico, Cabo, and the fabled Sea of Cortez.

"Were we ever that young?" I said to Danny when they had returned to their work.

He grinned and thumped me in the ribs. "Come on, Jared. Lighten up. None of that moody shit. Let's load up the old girl and get out there." He threw back his head and gave a loud whoop.

"Sun's over the taffrail. Time for a beer."

We spent the next two days provisioning, and finishing the last few boat chores. We rented a car and Jane and Ingrid did all the stocking, disappearing each morning after breakfast and arriving back in late afternoon with the car laden with boxes. Danny worked on the engine, cleaning and refitting electrical connections, adjusting the valves and swapping the injectors for the rebuilds from Minney's. The gear shift had been sticking, and he installed a new set of Morse cables, the air blue for half a day as he routed and adjusted them. I finished rebedding the deck fittings and replaced the last of the old mizzen shrouds with new galvanized. If we ever became rich, we'd redo them in stainless.

In the evenings we sat around and stowed the day's purchases. By the second night I had estimated we could live profligately for three years, five if we scrimped.

"Laugh, you fools, you'll be glad of this when you're sitting off some little village and the stores have nothing but red beans and rice." Jane carefully zip-locked yet another four portions of an esoteric freeze-dried pasta and sauce and placed them in a locker.

"You'll have to come out and help us eat all of this. Or find it," Danny added.

"It's all listed," Ingrid responded. She went into a long explanation of the revised numbering sequences, complete with the lettering and shelf life of the different combinations.

"Put the alcohol under A," Danny suggested. "I don't want to get confused."

"A for asshole," Ingrid said. She picked up a case of canned soup and threw it into Danny's lap as easily as if it were empty. "Here, label these."

"Yes, dear." He bent over the cans with a grease pencil.

"That's it. I'm done." Jane stood up and stretched. "I need a run. You coming?"

We changed and left. Danny and Ingrid were sprawled on the berth by then, and he was attempting to draw a moustache on her face with the grease pen. I could see where that was going.

The road out from the harbour was quiet at this time of night, the only sound the slap of our shoes on the pavement as we moved out. As we passed the little memorial pool, a shadow ghosted out from it and merged with us. Sinbad. He tucked himself between us, running with his head at our legs as if he had been doing this every day of his life. Jane reached down and patted the scarred head without breaking her stride. He gave a low, contented growl, his muzzle turning up to grin at her, the teeth gleaming yellow in the thin amber light of the street lamps. A brilliant green feather was stuck in there, and I remembered that there were mallards in the memorial pool in the little park adjacent to the marina.

Jane increased the pace, and soon we were running freely along the sidewalk that bordered the channel. A light, cleansing rain had begun to fall, and the air felt cool on my skin. The endorphins started to release, and the slow beginnings of a sense of well-being emanated outward and gradually enfolded me in the warm rhythm of blood and pace.

Ahead the road divided, and we took the inner fork and cut away, then crossed the little park, the three of us in smooth harmony, our cadence perfectly matched as we swung again and moved away from the water; intersections, divisions, every block presenting options, changes, alternatives, a minuscule difference in the total experience that would be our lives.

A chance encounter, a careless shift, a sudden swing, and the whole outcome changed into something else, everything linked in a long causal chain that stretched back to birth, and then before, and your parents' parents, and beyond. Everything contributing to my being here at this infinitesimal tick of time, running beside this woman I cared about; prison, the fighting, the drinking and the blackness that surrounded it, all a part of it. I embraced it all for its final result, and with that acceptance came a small release, the beginnings of a fugitive forgiving, and perhaps, eventually, a final loss of guilt.

We ran on and on, side by side, mile after mile in perfect unison, never speaking. We ran in silent communion, harmonic and joined by our separate thoughts, Sinbad loping between us, his head lolling with every panting breath, a monstrous nodding metronome to our rhythm. We ran like it was the last run of the last day of our lives, on and on and on. We ran until we couldn't run anymore, and then we joined hands and walked, the sweat pouring off us in the light rain, our bodies glistening with an oiled sheen. We walked, and after a while we began to talk, hesitantly at first, then in a torrent. When we arrived back at *Arrow*, it was three in the morning. We showered and fell into a deep sleep, our arms around each other, nothing planned but everything settled.

Jane left in the morning. I said I would call when the police made their arrests and the danger was over. There were still some things she was better off not knowing. She disappeared from sight, and I wondered if I would ever see her again.

Ingrid said her goodbyes and left with Maria at noon. When they were gone, I phoned Clarke's friend to see if there were any messages for us. Nothing. So it was all up to us. I walked back to *Arrow* and broke the news to Danny and Joseph.

"No cervezas?" Danny's voice was plaintive. "Somebody is going to pay for this."

We were sitting in the galley with the charts spread out in front of us. I had been talking for the best part of an hour.

"They'll pay. If they come," I said.

"Oh, they'll come, I'm not worried about that part of it. It's what happens after they get there that has me worried."

"It's our best chance to end it."

"We won't know who they are, how to recognize them."

"They won't look like cruisers. In a charter maybe, something big."

"It's close to five hundred miles from Hiva Oa to the Tuamotus. How are we going to stay away from them for that distance? That's near on four days, any way you look at it."

That was one of the hard parts, no doubt about it.

"We'll pick our spot, wait for bad weather, slip out at night. Once we've got far enough clear, we can make sure they follow us by getting on one of the skeds with the other boats. They will be listening for us."

Joseph bent forward and studied the chart, running his hands slowly over it, his eyes half-closed.

"I don't know," Danny grumbled. "I really had my heart set on Mexico."

"The South Seas. Swaying hips and sighing palms. Romance, mystery, adventure. They say the women of Papeete are the most beautiful in the world."

"And maybe we get a chance to set the agenda for once. Okay. Let's do it, then. But I should make the call. He will be more likely to believe it if I do it."

Joseph raised his eyes and nodded in agreement. His fingers absently caressed the Tuamotus. He whispered a low word, the sibilance echoing in the cabin. Danny looked at me, his face grave.

"Death," he said simply.

❈

We squeezed into the phone booth, Danny braced against the shelf, his crutches leaning against the open door. I passed him a stack of change.

"No, let's make it collect. It's the kind of dumb shit he'll expect from me, and it will make the call that much easier to trace. Yes, operator. Good evening to you too. I would like to make a collect call to Jack Delaney in Vancouver, Canada. My name is Danny MacLean; 604-179-3800. Yes, I'll hold."

He winked at me and we waited.

"Hello there, asshole." His voice became low and slurred. "This is your old pal Danny. I just wanted to say goodbye. Adios, motherfucker." He laughed, then listened. "Why, Jack, we know all about you. We had a little conversation with Eddie before he went trolling, remember that?"

He took the phone away from his ear and banged it against the wall.

"Whoops. Sorry, Jack. Bad connection. As I was saying, won't be long now before the cops are knocking on your door." He listened for a while, his face pursed in a mime of disapproval. "No, I don't think so, Jack, you dumb fuck. You're the one that's history. I look forward to coming back and testifying at your trial. Vaya con Diablo, you motherfucker."

He slammed the phone down.

"Vaya con Diablo?"

"I wanted to make sure he got the Mexican connection. It's my low Native cunning."

"What if he figures we have actually gone there?"

"He knows the call was from San Diego. Five minutes after Customs opens here tomorrow, he'll have somebody checking where we cleared to."

"How did he sound?"

"Pretty cool at first, then heated up. Heard him slap the very drunk lady who took the call from the operator. Called me a dumb fucking Indian who got lucky. Said next time he would make sure."

"Well, just so he took it personally."

❈

When we arrived back at *Arrow*, another in the endless series of farewell parties had started, this one a send-off for five boats that had checked out with us and were leaving for Cabo San Lucas in the morning. We joined in for an hour, but our hearts weren't in it and we turned in early.

I awoke in the still pre-dawn and shared coffee with Joseph as the first cracks of light shivered the eastern sky. There was just enough of a breeze to sail with, and Joseph took the tiller while I slipped the moorings. A large pile of soggy clothes and some leather suitcases were jumbled alongside a big Canadian sailboat. The acrimonious yells had started just as I drifted off to sleep. It sounded like a woman was throwing the baggage, but it wasn't clear whether she or her partner was leaving.

Something was lying on the heap, snoring loudly. It looked familiar. I walked over and gave it a nudge.

"Hey. Watchdog."

Sinbad uttered a muted sound halfway between a moan and a growl and shifted slightly away from me. I knew he had stayed up late cadging drinks.

"We're leaving now. Are you coming?"

The ears twitched. I knew he was awake and listening.

"Goodbye, then."

Just another dockside drunk who would never make the big trip. The California marinas were full of them.

I slipped the lines and walked *Arrow* backwards out of the berth. At the last moment, Sinbad slunk by me and crept on board, moving up to the bow, where he flopped down onto the hanked on Genoa. My mean little heart pattered in anticipation.

I gave the bow a push and jumped aboard and went to the mast. Joseph tightened the mainsheet and *Arrow* stopped, swung, and slowly inched forward past the docks. As the wind came abeam, I reached high up the mast and gathered the genoa halyard and heaved with all my strength. It shot up eight feet, the quick lurch rolling Sinbad to the rail. He scrabbled desperately to stay aboard, uttering low, pitiful whines.

"Suffer, you son of a bitch," I said.

CHAPTER 29

We moved slowly out into the main channel, easing the sheets as we swung round the entrance markers, then hardening up in the light southerly breeze. Even at this early hour there was traffic about: fishing charters heading south in convoy, a cruiser coming up the channel with the crew smart in deck whites, a battle-grey navy ship warping into dry dock, a work boat crossing the channel in urgent transit.

As they passed, I wrote down the times and names and descriptions and entered them in the ship's log; from now on we would track everything, searching for anything out of the normal, from chance second encounters to an interest that seemed too keen.

The channel opened out past Point Loma, and I went below and sorted through the guides and charts we would use for the crossing. The navigation was straightforward; leave Guadalupe Island and its neighbours close on the starboard side, then bear off five degrees and head for the equator. Cross at one hundred twenty-six degrees west at a right angle to minimize the time spent in the doldrums, and then head west again when the southeast trades filled in.

It was nineteen hundred miles to the equator, a further nine hundred to the Marquesas and Hiva Oa. Perhaps twenty-five days for *Arrow*, depending on our luck in the doldrums, or Inter-Tropical Convergence Zone, as the modern-day sailors call it. We were leaving a little early, but that was to our advantage; we would arrive in the Marquesas with a month remaining in the cyclone season. The great revolving gyres that bring the seventy-mile-an-hour winds are rare by then, but there would be enough smaller depressions moving through to ensure unsettled weather, blinding rainstorms, and the swift and sudden gales that teem and breed among the islands.

There would be few cruisers present, nothing like the multitudes that would arrive with the more temperate winter climate; some French, of course, staying over with sunken moorings in safe harbours, the occasional Germans in their heavy steel boats, an American or two, and the ubiquitous English.

And somewhere among them, Delaney, urbane and smiling and deadly as a shark.

A hot impatience rose within me. I hungered for the test. I yearned for the winds and the calms, the splendid satisfaction of a two-hundred-mile sailing day and the fierce exaltation of an ocean storm. Somewhere out there was trial and resolution, the final contest, and peace at the end.

We were entering the true Pacific, the birthplace and first origins of the human race; born of sea, our bodies' blood holding the same salinity as the ocean, salt in blood, salt in sweat, salt in tears; conceived in salt and sperm and held in saline amniotic for the first nine months of our life's voyage on earth, we were going back from whence we came.

And if I perished there, if we lost and my body was sunk and ravaged, ground up through the endless chains of predators to be reduced at last to the size of the smallest diatom, my entire being gorged and disgorged, fed and fed upon in the ocean's vast teeming mill of life — why, that was all right too: infinite at last in a million motes, my being would catch the deep ocean currents, fetch up in the great revolving gyres and circle forever the farthest reaches of the globe. There were worse fates for a sailor.

But I didn't intend to lose.

"Breakfast's up."

Danny, cheerful as always now, no trace of a hangover, passing up a heaped plate of bacon and eggs.

"How is Sinbad this morning?"

"Not well."

The beast was scrunched up against the dinghy, his paws over his eyes, trying to shut out the light.

"Give him this. Raw eggs mixed with some Tabasco sauce and beer."

I carried the bowl forward and laid it down beside Sinbad. He lapped it greedily, his stub thumping gently in acknowledgement.

"If he had stuck to margaritas and beer, he would probably have been all right, but he started drinking box wine there at the end. That will do it to you every time." Danny spoke in the authoritative voice of the expert, Joseph nodding in agreement. Three supposed adults in serious discussion about the drinking habits of a dog. It didn't even seem bizarre to me.

"We'll stand three-hour watches, see how that goes," I said. "Danny follows Joseph. Three on, six off. If you need a hand on deck, call the next man up first; last man below is last man called. We'll plot a position twice a day until we get close to land, 0600 and 1800 hours. Take a bearing on all traffic, enter the description and name into the log. We'll monitor channel sixteen and maintain radio silence. If you have to transmit to a hailing boat, switch to low power; we don't want our signal getting out too far just yet. We'll keep the radar on the fifteen-minute search cycle with an eight-mile zone alarm. If anybody shows any interest in us, any course changes towards us, we get everybody up, break out the arsenal. Anything else?"

"Sounds fine to me." Danny yawned and stretched. "What's the weather forecast?"

"Ten knots variable from the west for the next three or four days, then a mixed bag for the next four hundred or so miles before we fetch the northeast trades."

"Trade winds." Danny smiled. "I do like the sound of that phrase. Brings back all the old history the Brothers were forever trying to pound into my head. Spice-laden galleons, blue skies and balmy air, pirates, all the good old stuff."

"We've got the pirates, anyway."

"Too true. Well, bring them on, I'm ready."

He pulled himself to his feet and went below, leaning heavily on the companionway rails. He had ditched the crutches and wheelchair in San Diego and was walking now. Slow, halting steps, but improving daily. If anything, his upper body strength had improved with all the exercise and the constant use of the crutches over the past weeks. By the time we reached the Marquesas, he would be as good as new.

❋

Ship's Log February 6 Day 1 1800 hours

30 miles out of San Diego in 11 knots of wind out of the north-west. Course 255. Making 5 knots under full sail. Barometer steady at 1020 millibars. 2-foot seas with low northerly swell. Skies mainly clear with some high cirrus filaments. U.S. Coast Guard vessel passed within half a mile at 1345 hours, no contact made. Coronado off port beam, numerous small vessels fishing in vicinity.

❋

None of the boats looked suspicious, and none of them left the banks they were working to approach us. Danny ran in three miles to pick up an edge and landed a couple of small tuna on the white feather. The flesh was dark and oily but not too bad grilled on the Force 10 with hot sauce. I expected to get the true ocean swell within another day.

※

Ship's log February 8 Day 3 0600 hours
Position 23 40 N 120 15 W. Winds variable 0 to 25 knots usually from north or west. Boat speed anywhere from 0 to 8 knots as
squalls go through. Steering 255. Barometer 1012 and fluctuating.
One moment we are sitting with slatting sails, and the next *Arrow*
heels and we're off at hull speed. Caught a 45-pound yellow fin on
the squid. Not boring.

※

I was sitting at the galley table, reading a book, when the rain squall hit. Although it was midday, there was barely enough light to read by. The systems were so intense their centres were visible on the radar screen, dark concentric masses moving past. We didn't bother trying to steer away from them; we wanted the wind they brought. We had changed down to the working jib so as not to be overpowered when they went through, and Danny was hand-steering, falling off when the gusts peaked, then letting them come back on the beam as they slacked.

This one seemed the same as all the others, first the quick hard beat of the rain and then, seconds later, the sudden heel as the wind came into the sails and *Arrow* paused a moment, as if considering, then tracked away, gathering momentum in her climb to hull speed. We must have been doing a good eight knots when Danny started yelling and cursing.

When I arrived up on deck, he was struggling to set up the Aries, balancing with the tiller between his knees, one hand trying to clip on the steering lines, the other wrapped in Sinbad's collar. The rain was so heavy you could scarcely make out the bow. I hadn't put a slicker on and was soaked through before I could even see what the problem was. Sinbad had the shock cord of the trolling line and was trying desperately to pull it on board. He was whining and moaning with eagerness, his feet powerfully braced, his body rigid against Danny's grip.

"Big fish," Danny gasped. "Take Sinbad."

I looked aft and saw the sleek, bullet-shaped tuna surfing in our wake as we roared along.

"I'll take the tiller," I said. "You and your dog can land the fish."

He snorted in disgust and went to the rail, where a six-foot steel gaff hung in readiness. He reached outside the lifelines and began to pull in the fishing line. As soon as the bungee slacked, Sinbad dropped it and moved up between Danny's legs, his neck stretched out, his eyes focused on the prey, his entire body vibrating in anticipation. Danny two handed the tuna up to the stern, coiled the line in his left hand, seized the gaff with his right, hauled back, and sunk it into the fish.

I was standing on the cockpit seats, steering with my foot, and could see he had placed it perfectly, just under the gills and curving up into the head. He began to haul the fish up. As it rose into view over the stern, Sinbad's head lunged under the lifeline like a striking snake and he buried his teeth into the yellowfin just above the tail, jerking backwards in a mighty heave in that same instant.

Danny was caught off balance and fell forward on his knees as the gaff and fish went under his crotch and the extended handle levered him outwards. He sprawled over the lifelines, half-dazed as two hundred pounds of dog and fish fought on the end of his gaff. His shoulders rolled with the struggle.

It was apparent that the only way he could win was to pull dog and fish outboard and lift them together over the lifelines and in. It didn't seem likely.

"Twenty bucks on the dog," I said.

He turned his head and glared at me, the veins standing out on his neck and forehead like cords.

"If you'd stop fucking laughing and help me, maybe we'd get this fucking fish on board!"

"Let go of the gaff. I'll grab it when it goes by."

"Why don't you just grab Sinbad?" he wheezed.

"Up yours."

He released the gaff, and Sinbad gained a quick five feet before I could seize it and brace myself against him. His mad yellow eyes glared at me over the tuna's threshing body. Danny's big hand came down on his neck.

"C'mon, Sinbad, you'll get your share. Drop it."

The dog growled and released the fish.

"Good boy."

Danny pulled out the gaff and used it to lever out the lure. The fish dropped onto the cockpit sole and lay there, threshing.

"All right, now. Pass me the club."

Sinbad leaped suddenly into the cockpit and with a quick, scissoring movement of his jaws took off the tuna's head and bolted forward with it.

"Hold the club," Danny said.

❀

Ship's Log February 13 Day 8 1800 hours
Position 16 51 N 122 06 W. Winds out of northeast at 18 knots. Steering 255. *Arrow* broad reaching at 6.5 to 7 knots. Barometer steady at 1020. Some scattered cumulous clouds. Northerly 6-foot swell, 5-foot waves, whitecaps, occasional spray on deck. I think we've reached the trades – Hallelujah. Saw the lights of another sailboat last night, heading in the same direction, slower. No contact made, we lost him before dawn.

❀

We were in perfect harmony now, our bodies melding into the age-old cadence of the sea. We no longer resented the ship's quick motion, our balance attuned to the sudden drops, the sideways spiralling corkscrew as *Arrow* quartered through the swells. We ate and slept and read and stood our watches in quiet succession, our bodies' clocks gradually slowing, the nerves subsiding, a sense of peace and serenity emanating from the illimitable space that surrounded us.

It was as if, suspended on that thin conjunction of water and air ten thousand feet above the earth, we underwent some subtle sea change, lost an essential part of our landlocked nature, and became more open to the secret rhythms that surrounded us. The air was clearer and the seas more transparent; when the squalls came they were darker than before, the rain warmer and the wind more cutting. We ate less and enjoyed it more. We no longer needed the instruments to gauge boat or wind speed — some inner reckoning had birthed, and it was accurate to a fraction.

Day after day we headed south, the winds constant and favourable, *Arrow* running free before them as she clocked her hundred-and-fifty-mile averages. At the start we had listened to the cruising shortwave nets, tuning in to the weather and gossip each morning, but as we moved away from the coast, we began to resent the intrusion and shut the radio off: the sharp, worried voices, the interminable apprehensions of lows and troughs and depressions, the calculations of compressing isobars and the northern proximity of the Convergence Zone; all of this science seemed foreign and out of place on our journey.

We wanted to sail the track as all the nameless thousands before us, reading the glass and sky for their messages, taking the weather as it came, and making our countermoves with the skill, knowledge, and experience that was unique to ourselves alone.

Of course we would still use the GPS for our positions; only a complete idiot would ignore such a miraculous instrument of navigation. The sextant and tables were deep stowed in a dry locker; God grant they would remain there for the duration.

✺

Ship's Log February 16 Day 11 0600 hours
Position 10 05 N 123 15 W. Wind speed gusting up to 25 knots,
boat speed 7–8 knots. Course 255. Barometer 1019 and steady.
Wave height approx. 12 feet and building, whitecaps and lots of
spray, swell from the northwest. Sky dark, some serious clouds

around, cumulonimbus with anvil on horizon. Going well under double-reefed main and mizzen with working jib, lots of water on decks, so far no leaking below. Maybe edge of Zone? Seems too far north. Hopefully get another two days before we hit it.

❋

Ship's Log February 18 Day 13 1800 hours
Position 07 23 N 123 41 W. Wind from the south at 6 knots, boat speed 2-3 knots. Steering 225, not making course. Just 75 miles made good last 24 hours. Definitely in ITC Zone, glass 1009 dropping slowly. Clouds spectacular, constantly changing.

❋

The heat from the sun's rays shining straight down at the equator causes the tremendous evaporation that forms the clouds that rise upward and spiral away due to the earth's rotation. The low-pressure areas this creates are filled by the trade winds, which sweep in from a northeast direction in the northern hemisphere and southeast in the southern due to the rotation of the earth — the Coriolis effect.

I had read about the doldrums since I was a child, and understood the simple physics involved, but nothing had prepared me for the splendid unreality that enveloped us. It is one thing to comprehend the abstract principles, quite another to be in the pulsing heart of the great solar machine that powers the trades.

As far as the eye could see, extending in all directions to the horizons, were giant palisades of cloud. They rose vertically in jagged blocks on one side, row upon angular row moving skywards until the jet stream whisked off their tops and carried them away; on another quadrant they bubbled upwards like a great simmering broth, changing aspect every second, the clouds extending and shifting shape as you watched, roiling inwards upon themselves then suddenly exploding outwards and up in a foaming mass. Turn away for seconds, and when you looked back everything had changed, and a patch of brilliant blue sky appeared where previously there had been black-and-grey confusion.

The portent of latent energy was overwhelming. The air filled with electricity and every hair on your body stirred in restless concert, the hot pressure building in the ominous silence. The wind died completely and the sky darkened, and then a blinding flash of lightning, the roar of thunder almost simultaneous, the boat heeling to a hot gust of air. Moments later, in pouring rain, *Arrow* rocketed along as the pressure filled, splitting the tranquil water with such force that the spray rose up from her bow and rainbowed in reflected light. We took our clothes off and bathed ourselves quickly, for in another moment the rain might stop and we'd be caught foolish, foamed and lathered. The wind died as at the flick of a fan switch, *Arrow* slowed and straightened, and once again we lay and waited for wind, rocking slightly in the swell.

❀

Ship's Log February 21 Day 16 1800 hours
Position 02 35 N 124 49 W. No wind. Glass steady at 1018.
Becalmed 120 miles from equator. Extremely hot and humid. Ran
at 5 knots for 4 hours to charge batteries and break monotony.
Ocean Passages says "Weather for South Pacific Equatorial
Trough is typically that in which calms and light variable winds and
fine weather alternate with squalls, heavy rain (most often in the
form of showers) and thunderstorms." So far it's bang on.

❀

The silence was unnatural, no birds feeding, no feed in the water, not a ripple to show that we were not just imbedded in some painted blue medium. The lures hung straight down in the water off the stern, visible seventy feet below, with only a slight twisting motion at the ends of their cords. The light was extraordinary, constantly changing as it filtered through the clouds or reflected off the water. It descended in shafts through the chinks between the shifting clouds, so that we were continually moving in and out of intricate patterns, giving the illusion of progress where there was none.

Danny and I dove over the side and went for a swim with Sinbad, but we quickly returned on board; there was something oppressive and unsettling about three miles of water extending beneath our naked bodies. The thought of those abysmal pressured depths, the terrifying creatures that might exist there, and the hungry focus of a giant telescopic eye gazing upwards completely unnerved me, and I scrambled back on board, followed almost immediately by Danny and Sinbad. I now understood what is meant by unfathomable.

❈

Ship's Log February 23 Day 18 1800 hours
Position: the lousy doldrums. Everything as before, except now we have a dirty swell which slats the sails continuously and is driving everyone nuts. Except Joseph, of course. Nothing seems to affect him.

❈

For another thirty hours we lay in the doldrums, the only sound the slatting of the sails, the only movement the rolling of the boat as she lay in the trough. The seas were thick and viscous, rolling in long, greasy undulations. The water had a dark, oiled sheen, as if the atmosphere's weight had somehow compressed and changed its properties like some great subterranean body of petroleum. We lay in our bunks, stifled in the cramped heat; when we sought relief in the cockpit, there was none. The air was heavy and oppressive, but it wouldn't rain. The sun had vanished behind thick grey cloud cover. It was so dark that dawn came in midmorning, twilight short hours later, the change so gradual it was imperceptible. At night the heat became even more oppressive, and it weighed more heavily upon us. Our shoulders sank beneath the burden and we moved slowly and talked little. We trailed the dinghy, and Sinbad spent most of his time lying in it, occasionally going in for a brief, lethargic swim.

❀

Ship's Log February 24 Day 19 1330 hours
Position. Latitude 00 00 Longitude – who cares? We have
made the equator at last. Drinks all around. And one for Neptune.

❀

"Well, here's to us." Danny poured three glasses of rum and we clinked them and drank. He poured a fourth shot, slightly smaller, and dumped it over the side.

"Give him a double," I said. "Maybe he will give us some wind. We're not doing very well so far. Our daily average has dropped like a stone."

"Another nine hundred to go," Danny said. "We should make it in a week. I hope I get to see the islands first. I've always wanted to shout, 'Land ho!' It's not quite the same when the land is always Vancouver Island."

We were doing three and a half knots under a fickle north wind and a clear sky. The glass was showing a slow rise, and we appeared to be leaving the doldrums. If we could get another twenty-four hours of this, we should pick up the southeast trades.

"Isn't somebody supposed to dress up like King Neptune and frolic about?" Danny asked.

"Yes. You volunteering?"

"No. I just wondered."

It was a pleasant day, the best we'd had for a while, and we had reached a milestone. It was a cause for mild celebration, and we had a few drinks, but the atmosphere was poisoned by the thought of what lay ahead, waiting somewhere among the beautiful postcard islands. The taste of things to come was bitter as gall.

"They will be waiting for us," Danny said at last. "I can feel it."

"It's what we want."

"Yes. I'm not complaining."

He sat quiet for a while, then went below and brought up the VP70 and clipped on the little plastic stock, then broke it down, cleaning and oiling it with quick, mechanical motions. It had become a ritual with him on the passage. As we drank our beers, he threw the cans over the stern and sank them with short, precise bursts from the machine pistol, his face impassive. The flat staccato bark sounded obscenely loud in that time and place, and brought something dark and ominous into the cockpit with us. Even Sinbad seemed to feel it. He left his customary place by Joseph's feet and went up to the bow, where he lay and whined. I finished my drink and went below.

❀

Ship's Log February 26 Day 21 0600 hours
Position 03 10 S 129 51 W. Wind from southeast 18 knots. Boat speed 7 knots. Barometer steady 1022. Seas 6-feet confused swell. Back in the trades. All sails up on a beam reach, 660 miles to Hiva Oa. Sunny with occasional high bands of cirrus. Sinbad got another albatross. I was dozing and didn't see it in time to warn it off. I never was a Coleridge fan in any case.

❀

Ship's Log February 28 Day 23 1800 hours
Position 05 50 S 133 35 W. Wind from southeast 20 knots, gusting to 25. Boat speed 8 knots. Barometer 1025. Seas around

10 feet, larger waves forming, long southerly swell. 360 miles last
48 hours. Rolling around a bit, but *Arrow* going well, staying dry.
Caught another bonito, fish number 11. Sinbad putting on weight.

❁

Ship's Log March 2 Day 25 1230 hours. Land Ho!
Position 09 31 S 138 35 W. Land on the horizon. Fabulous
24-hour run – 209 miles.

❁

We were all in the cockpit, but it was Joseph who spotted it first. Just a small smudge on the line of the horizon that slowly assumed aspect and colour as we made our approach, the initial faint suggestions of green changing and strengthening into the brilliant tropical hues of "the land of men."

Hiva Oa is the largest and most populous of the Marquesas. Four thousand feet high at the peaks, twenty-three miles long and ten miles wide, it rose out of the sea like a present-day Garden of Eden, lush, green, and full of promise. After twenty-five days, the smell of land was overwhelming, and we inhaled the bouquet as if it was the rarest of wine.

The island lies east–west, curving at the furthest extremity into the arc that contains Traitors Bay, and at the northern corner, Baie Taahuku and the village of Atuona, our landfall. We ran in tight against the steep cliffs of the southern coast and made our westing a mile outside the breakers, which smashed against the foot of the cliffs in huge rainbow clouds of spray. The wind was holding twenty knots, and we were doing hull speed on port tack, with the wind just aft of the beam.

We passed a fishing boat full of Marquesans coming out of the bay, a dozen of them crowded into a little sixteen-footer with a Yamaha grinding away at the stern, the children perched overhead on the plywood canopy, all of them waving, and the women bright as birds in their pareus.

Danny went forward and flaked down the jib, a slight trace of stiffness as he knelt on the foredeck the sole remaining sign of his troubles. We turned the corner around the point and headed up as we came into the lee. There was ample room in the small bay, six boats anchored out, two of them cruisers, the other four local fishermen. Some smaller boats were tied up against the jetty that came out into the entrance, none of them over twenty-five feet and all of them local. We ran out five to one on the Danforth and backed down hard. She dragged for half a length then grabbed and held in full reverse. We laid out another sixty feet and shut the engine down. Danny rigged up the half-inch nylon springs on the chain back to the Samson post while I took bearings on the jetty and an isolated palm tree in the other quadrant and entered them into the log book. Danny brushed by me and went below. He returned bearing gifts.

"Haere mai. Welcome."

He passed Joseph and me the frosted bottles. "Pia is beer. What else is there to know?"

We settled back and looked around.

CHAPTER 30

After the weeks of sailing and constant slap of waves and sails, the quiet was eerie. *Arrow* rocked gently in the swell, but the wind had died and the rigging was silent. Thin tendrils of mist drifted along the shores, and across the bay the hills rose in gentle, curving terraces, fragrant with the scent of blossom and promise of fruit.

Beyond the jetty, the road to Atuona stretched out in a long curve around the bay before rising up and disappearing into the hills. Apart from two trucks on the pier and a few children playing in the surf, there were no signs of life. A dog barked from a clearing beyond the beach and another joined in, the two of them prancing stiff-legged around a third, who stood with tail erect. Sinbad finished his beer and hurdled over the lifelines in a direct line towards them, hitting the water with legs splayed and churning landwards.

"That's a sailor's landfall for you," Danny said. "First you have a drink, then you get laid, with maybe a fight or two in between. Looks like we've got company."

A battered plywood dinghy was rowing towards us from one of

the anchored boats. A young couple sat in it, the girl pretty and dark-haired, the man tall and stick-thin, with a scant blond beard.

"Welcome to the Marquesas." They smiled and handed up a woven palm-frond basket filled with fruit.

"Thanks. Come aboard."

They were Will and Penny, Americans who had spent the previous six months in French Polynesia. In another four months they would leave and head home by way of Hawaii, then make the big curve into the northern latitudes until they reached the westerlies and could make their course to San Francisco.

"Clearing in is no problem," Will informed us, "just go into town, the gendarmes handle it all. Very low key, very friendly. Only a couple of them for the whole island, though, and they're often away, so best to go in early. If you're in and out of Polynesia in under thirty days, you don't even need the thousand-dollar bond. Better to get it in Papeete in any case. The bank here converts your currency into French francs and then back again, it can cost you fifteen percent. Use an Aussie or New Zealand bank in Papeete, you save the exchange."

They chattered away, friendly and innocent as puppies, full of good information and kind intentions. We had a chunk of dorado left in the fridge and invited them for supper.

"Sounds great," Penny said. "I'll bring a salad, you're probably starved for fresh vegetables. Atlantis gave me some fresh lettuce this morning."

"Many boats around this time of year?" Danny asked.

"Too early yet. They'll start to arrive in numbers in another seven or eight weeks. Still the stormy season here. You're one of the first."

He motioned across to the big hard-chined sloop carrying the German flag. "Atlantis came in last week from Puerto Vallarta, a young couple aboard with a little girl. The rest of us have stayed in Polynesia for the season. There are half a dozen boats up in Nuku Hiva as well, last I heard."

"There was that huge motor yacht last week," Penny said.

"Oh well, they don't count. I was talking about real boats. Sailboats."
Will smiled and took a sip from his beer.

"Where was she from?"

"I don't know, it anchored way outside. Big black mother, probably over a hundred feet. They came into the harbour in an eighteen-foot launch with two eighty-horse Mercs on it. Can you imagine? They carry that on deck, for God's sake. Plus ski jets, windsurfers, and an inflatable, no doubt. Maybe a helicopter too, for all I know." He shook his head in disgust at such decadence.

"Sounds like a boat we met in San Diego," I said. "Couple of old guys on board with their wives and some New Zealand crew."

"No. There was a younger couple came ashore in the launch. I can't remember the name on the hull. Some animal, maybe."

"I guess it wasn't them. Who's for another round?"

We drank beer and chatted until the sun went down, and then we lit the barbecue and broiled fish steaks. We ate them with the French wine our guests had brought, and finished with coffee and brandy.

"One of the few things that is reasonable here." Penny held out the bottle for our inspection. "Wine, cheese, butter, and baguettes. All subsidized. Pretty well everything else is expensive. But the fruit is free, they don't even carry it in the shops, you can't buy it. Nearly everyone has their own trees, or their friends do, you only have to ask."

"How about beer?"

"Good, but not cheap. Around four-fifty American a litre."

Danny looked at me reproachfully. "I knew we should have gone to Mexico."

They left at eleven, slightly tipsy, calling out promises to take us snorkelling in the near future. Joseph took the first watch and we turned in.

❧

I rose early and rowed ashore with the ship's papers in a waterproof bag. Around the corner from the stone jetty was a dinghy landing with limited swell, and I arrived on shore only slightly wet. I rinsed myself off under the freshwater shower set up for the fishermen and started walking to Atuona.

The sun was out, and within five minutes I was dry and sweating from the heat. I had covered less than a mile when a truck stopped and picked me up. They put me in the back with an eight-foot shark and two giggling kids whose only word of English was Canada. I tried some of my French on them, and they giggled even more. They let me off in front of the tiny police station, where one of the biggest men I had ever seen in my life was behind the counter. When I handed him the Canadian passports he beamed and chattered away to me in French. I wished I had paid more attention in school. We managed to carry on a conversation of sorts, though, and I think maybe he had a cousin who'd emigrated to Quebec.

Taking our neighbours' advice, I told him we would be leaving French Polynesia in less than a month. He shook his head sadly at my lack of judgement, and stamped our passports with the visas. He filled out the carte du voyage and wrote down *Arrow*'s description and the electronics and radios aboard. No pets and no firearms. Bien, bon voyage, monsieur. Merci, monsieur, au revoir.

The little bank cashed a thousand dollars for me, and I walked away carrying a thick wad of exotic bank notes, all of which ended in multiple zeros. The wealthy feeling lasted until I went into one of the little general stores that fringed the road and paid a hundred thousand francs for a few provisions. When I asked for a taxi, the storekeeper called his wife and she drove me back to the dock in the family pickup.

Nobody seemed to have cars here; new trucks with four-wheel drive were everywhere. They were strangely at odds with the barefoot populace, the modest dwellings, and the evident minimal incomes. Some aberration of the French colonial presence, no doubt.

"What's the town like?" Danny inquired around a bite of cheese and baguette.

"Pretty, flowers and fruit everywhere. Not very big. People are all very friendly."

"Joseph and I are thinking of going in later. You want to come?"

"No thanks. I'm going to write some letters, maybe do a little varnishing."

"Jesus, you guilt-tripping already? We've only just got here. Take it easy."

"No, no. Nothing like that. I just feel a little wasted from the trip, don't want to leave the boat. You go ahead."

"I went on the Nuku Hiva net again this morning," Danny said. "Checked in, identified ourselves, chatted for a while with a boat from Seattle. Said we'd be here for a week or so."

"That should do it if they are around."

"Yeah. There's a small depression forming at the edge of the Zone. Travelling at twenty knots and carrying a fair bit of wind. Some boats out there getting hammered. They figure the main track should pass south of Hiva Oa, but you know."

I knew. With the advent of onboard weather fax, the South Pacific was suddenly filled with amateur meteorologists who spent hours poring over the weather charts that they received several times a day. They sometimes got it right, but even the subscription weather nets were frequently mistaken.

"We should be fine here. As long as it doesn't swing to the northeast."

"Yep. That's not bad beer at all. Proper size, anyway." He finished off the litre of Hinano and stood up. "Seen Sinbad today?"

"No."

"Probably hanging out with his lady friend. Speaking of which, did you see any lonely-looking women in town?"

"I saw a lot of awfully big guys. Two-fifty is small here. Legs like tree stumps."

"Caution is my middle name. Besides, we're practically related."

Joseph appeared carrying a small pack, and the two of them climbed over the side into the dinghy and rowed away.

I wrote a letter to Jane, telling her about the trip. I told her that the Marquesas were beautiful, the people delightful, and that I missed her. I said we had changed plans at the last minute as we felt we would be safer here than in Mexico, there was no sense in taking unnecessary risks, especially as we had talked to Clarke and he had informed us that arrests were imminent. When I was finished I stuck on one of the exotic stamps I had purchased at the little post office and went on deck to do some penance for my lies.

With respect to varnish, wooden boats are akin to one of the great bridges where they finish painting at one end just in time to resume again at the other. The forward end of the cabin was already crazing where the spray and weather had worked on it; the tropical sun would be even harsher. There were those Philistines who painted the bright work with a coat of latex paint for protection and ease of maintenance in the tropics, then stripped it off on their return to the temperate zones, but I knew the ghost of Bill Calder would spin in his grave at such a travesty. I dug out some two-hundred-grit paper and set to work.

In that setting, even varnishing was almost a pleasure. All around me the island's jagged peaks were gathering clouds like magnets as the weather showed the first signs of change. The soft, billowy cumulus of the trades were elongating now, stretching and fining across the sky before piling up against the mountains in a tumbled mass. Four miles distant, Mount Feani was obscured by black sheets of rain for a short minute, then the cell passed and a bright rainbow shone across the peak that had been veiled and hidden moments earlier. The air was rich with fragrance: hibiscus, frangipane, bougainvillea, and a dozen other scents I couldn't begin to recognize or put a name to.

An old man in an outrigger moved away from the far shore and slowly paddled out into the bay. In a few minutes he came alongside and handed up a skein of green drinking coconuts and a stalk of bananas, welcoming me in a soft patois of French, English, and Polynesian. I invited him aboard, whereupon he took his machete and cracked the tops off two coconuts as quickly and easily as if they were boiled eggs. The juice was cool and slightly sweet.

"C'est meilleur avec le rhum," the old man said.

"Mais certainement."

I fetched the bottle and topped the coconuts up, and as we drank he told me about his family, and how they had been here long before first the English and then the French came, and of his life in the village as a young man, but now it was all changing, and the young people were leaving for the cities, and nothing was the same. He lapsed often into the Polynesian dialect, and I only understood a half of what he said in French. I lay back in the sun and let the words and the place wash over me. There was no trace of bitterness or complaint in the old man's voice. When he finished his drink he stood to leave. I thanked him for his gift, and he said the fruit was for everybody. He took some canned salmon in trade and paddled away, not much different from those ancestors of centuries past that he had spoken of.

I spent the rest of the afternoon working at odd jobs, cleaning and greasing a noisy winch before going up the mast to replace a trilight bulb that had failed halfway through the passage. From the masthead I could see beyond the spit across Haava channel south to Tahuatu Island. There were good anchorages there, and the snorkelling was said to be excellent. Perhaps we'd get over there in the next few days. My zeal passed, and I spent the remainder of the day reading a book and had a quiet evening.

I awoke the next morning to the sound of wind and the slap of halyards echoing through the anchorage, and lay there absorbing the feel of the boat. The swell was down, and the pale reflection of the sun through the starboard porthole told of a ninety-degree swing on the anchor. *Arrow*'s motion was easy, surging gently against the snubbers, no sound of chain stretched out and coming in over the rollers yet, the nylon shock bight still hanging loose.

I filled my cup from the coffee pot and joined Danny and Joseph in the cockpit. We had alternated watches until one o'clock, when Sinbad returned to the boat; then we retired for the night, leaving the decks to his suspicious prowling. A white luminous ring had formed around the moon, portent of the storm to come.

"About thirty knots," Danny said. "Coming from the northwest. Looks like the forecast was right. Feels like it's still building."

The air was hot and sticky, the clouds so low there was no sky and we appeared to be resting in an opulent green bowl, the curved sides of which were only a few hundred feet high, the roof an arching translucent dome.

Joseph went below and turned on the cruising net. It sounded like the low had swung and was now heading towards us. It was expected to last for another two days, with a deeper tropical depression following, this second one down under a thousand millibars and projected to drop still further.

Danny raised his eyebrows. "Well, the weather is right, anyhow."

"Yes. Let's hope they show soon."

I spoke briefly with the skipper of a New Zealand boat we had met in San Diego. They had headed further west than us, and their passage had been quicker. The net soon degenerated into bitching about the unfairness of the boat bond imposed by the French authorities, and I signed off.

"We met Will and Penny downtown yesterday," said Danny. "They're coming around this morning to take us snorkelling. They have a friend with a truck, we're going up through the mountains then back down to a little sheltered bay on the other side. Supposed to be some nice langouste there. Joseph is coming along, there's a village right up at the top that's famous for its carvings. Maybe pick one up for the boat. You should join us."

I stood up and faced into the wind and stared through it and out to sea, my every nerve alive with prescience. My eyes watered, and for a second I thought I saw the sharp outlines of a huge steel ship in the corner of the bay. I blinked and the apparition disappeared.

But Delaney was coming, I knew it, moving in with the foul weather, my senses registering his proximity as clearly as the clouds racing overhead presaged the storm.

"I think I'll hang around," I said. "Maybe scrub the bottom."

We made a breakfast of fruit, baguettes, cheese, and coffee. Will and Penny called on the VHF, and Danny and Joseph collected their gear and rowed off to meet them. They disappeared from sight around the point, and I put on my mask and snorkel and went over the side. The water was murky with runoff and mud kicked up by the swell, and I had to follow the chain down to find the anchor. It was well dug in, only a foot of the stock protruding from the thick volcanic silt.

Sinbad had followed me over the side and swam slowly behind me, his eyes half closed in concentration. With a bubbling hiss, a steaming, sulphurous mass of half-digested feathers and bone rose up behind him.

"Jesus, Sinbad, not so close, for God's sake."

I waved him away. He gave a low growl and approached even closer, his yellow eyes staring balefully into mine. I waited for the warm jet of water, but then he growled again and circled the boat in the opposite direction.

There was a scum line a foot above the boot stripe from where we had been heeled on the one tack for so long, and I gently scrubbed it off with a soft brush. The rest of the hull was clean except for a row of goose barnacles under the curve of the transom, and I took a softwood wedge and removed them. The Max-Prop had some growth on it, and I scraped it clean and folded and unfolded it to make sure it wasn't binding. The shaft zinc was still in good shape; marinas, with all the electric current in the water, are what really eat those up.

I swam back to the boat ladder and climbed aboard. Sinbad followed in his usual fashion, hauling himself over the transom of the tied-off skiff, then springing aboard *Arrow* from the seat. It took perfect timing for him to come under the lifelines without hitting them, and he never missed. I waited resignedly as he came over and stood beside me and shook himself.

I spent the next few hours hauling water in five-gallon collapsible jugs. It was easier than moving *Arrow* alongside the jetty, and I needed the exercise. If Danny and Joseph were back before dark, maybe I would go for a run.

I was just heaving the last load of water aboard when I heard the whine of high-speed outboards. A black motor launch raced into the harbour under full throttle, twin rooster tails arcing up behind it as it made the long turn around the corner. A slender, dark-haired woman stood behind the wheel, and I watched as she headed towards *Arrow*, waiting for her to swing by and turn away. She saw me and waved, then cut the throttle and brought the boat alongside, flipping fenders over as she came smartly in.

There was something familiar about her, and as she raised her head to throw me a coil of line, I realized to my amazement that it was Jennie Starrett, from so long ago.

"Hi, Jared." She grinned behind the oversized sunglasses. "Small world, huh?"

She jumped aboard and threw her arms around me. She was extremely thin — anorexic, even — and as we awkwardly embraced I was conscious of her delicate, almost bird-like bones.

"Jennie Starrett. I don't believe it."

"Daddy heard you on the cruising net last week. I didn't realize it was you until you had signed off. We were hanging out in Papeete. Daddy was getting bored and wanted to get moving. Besides, I don't have that many old boyfriends in this part of the world."

"Jennie."

I leaned back and looked at her, my arms still encircling the tiny waist.

"I know I look a wreck." She laughed nervously and pushed a hand through the thick black hair. "I've been ill. I've come out here with Daddy to convalesce."

She didn't look well. Behind the deep tan were the signs of illness. Dark, smudged bruises showed around the edge of her sunglasses, and her skin was stretched taut over her cheekbones. She wore a long-sleeved T-shirt and her wrists were bone thin, the veins pale blue lines. She still had the muscled legs of the runner showing under the cut-offs, but they were cruelly thin now, the tendons standing out like cords.

"You look good to me. It's great to see you. How long has it been, anyway?"

"Too long. Aren't you going to offer a lady a drink? Vodka and tonic, if you have it. Anything else if you don't."

She sat down in the cockpit and lit a cigarette, exhaling in short, quick puffs. She gave off an aura of nervous energy that was almost visible. There was little remaining of the girl I remembered from high school. I made the drinks and handed one to her. She closed her eyes and took a long swallow.

"That's better," she said with a smile. "Let's see, it must be all of eight years. You crewed on Daddy's boat after you came back. I remember you had a friend with you."

"Danny MacLean. He's still with me."

I had run into Ernie Starrett and his daughter at a marine chandlery a year after I left prison. Danny and I had been picking up some hooks and line for the coming fishing season. He had insisted I come out with him for a short series, said he was desperate for crew and wouldn't take no for an answer. It hadn't worked out very well. The crew were friendly enough, but they knew my history, and there was a restraint that we couldn't get past. For my part, I found them spoiled and childish, and we had nothing in common but the sailing. I think Ernie and I were both relieved when the series ended. Jennie and her new husband were aboard for one race, and she had seemed very happy. I hadn't seen any of them since.

"How is your husband?"

I couldn't remember his name. Young, good-looking, and obviously successful, they had made a pretty picture together.

"Richard is fine, I suppose." She gave a brittle laugh. "I have another one now, he's flying in on a charter sometime today. I'll introduce you to Jonathan at dinner tonight. Daddy insists you come over. He wants to know all about you, how you came to be out here, everything. He said to invite your friends as well."

"They're out just now. Should be back sometime early evening."

"Great. Then it's all settled." She held out her empty glass. "A little stronger this time, please. And then you can tell me what you're doing out here on such a beautiful boat. Is she yours?"

I poured another drink and told her about how I had inherited *Arrow* and the three of us had decided to go cruising. She didn't really pay much attention. We were very different people now, and I think we were both realizing that we might have preferred our memories.

"Show me your boat," she said, and we went below.

I gave her the standard tour and she oohed and aahed at the standard places. The only thing that really interested her were Bill and Meg's journals. She sat quietly for the first time, reading passages at random, and I caught a glimpse of the old Jennie under the brittle exterior.

"They cared for each other very much, didn't they?" she said finally, a sad smile on her face.

"Yes. They were very nice people. I'm hoping that Meg will come out and join us for a few weeks."

She jumped suddenly to her feet. "Come on, I'll show you Daddy's boat. Don't bother changing, you're fine just as you are. We can call your friends later."

She ran up the companionway stairs and over the lifelines to the launch. She slipped slightly as she stepped aboard.

"Whoops."

She giggled and bent down and started the engines while I untied us, then accelerated away with a jerk that almost knocked me over. She drove fast and well, bringing the boat out of the harbour into the chop at full throttle, then easing back until she was in synch with the waves. We dipped around the lee of Hanakee Island and pulled up to the huge black-hulled motor cruiser anchored there. There was a gangway alongside with a dock at the bottom, and Jennie threw a line to the big man in whites who was waiting there. We walked past him as if he were invisible, and ascended the steps.

"Paid crew," Jennie said. "There are four of them on board, plus the cook."

It didn't surprise me. They probably worked full-time keeping up the varnish and polishing the stainless. The boat was magnificent, an older style yacht, built in steel and beautifully faired, with teak decks and mahogany everywhere. She had the high, flared bow of the ocean cruiser, with the cabins raked low and set back in her lee for protection, the whole in proportion and the craftsmanship superb.

"Jared Kane. What a pleasure."

Ernie Starrett strode towards me, his hand outstretched in welcome, a big smile on his genial face, the trademark yachting cap perched on his styled grey hair. He hadn't changed a bit. I had always liked him — he had the successful salesman's knack of making you feel that your opinions and well-being were the most important things in the world to him.

"How have you been? Here, let me fix you a drink, you must tell me all about yourself. I couldn't believe my ears when we heard you on the net."

He went over to the big bar in the corner and mixed some drinks. Jennie took hers, then walked over and added more vodka to it. She still wore the sunglasses. He watched her impassively then turned back towards me.

"Where are your friends?"

"They're away for a bit. They'll be back later on."

"You must give them a call when they return. We'll send the launch across for them. I remember Danny well." He smiled. "You've never been aboard *Impala*, have you?"

"No. She's beautiful."

"Thank you. Oh, by the way, Jennie, I heard from Jonathan. He should be joining us in an hour or so."

Jennie nodded. She walked over to the window and stared out, cradling her drink against her breast. Her father watched her, a frown on his face, then turned back towards me, genial again.

"Come on," he said. "I'll show you around."

She had been built in a Seattle yard in 1972. Ninety-eight feet long with a twenty-four-foot beam and nine feet of draft, she carried five thousand gallons of fuel and had a range of forty-five hundred miles at a cruising speed of nine knots.

"*Impala* is a true ocean-going vessel," Ernie said. "She can carry six couples in comfort plus the crew. I had her completely refitted three years ago. Took her over to Taiwan, put her in a yard over there. They ripped out all the original panelling, completely redid her in mahogany and teak. Some of the best craftsmen in the world over there."

She was a showpiece. We went below and walked through the large double staterooms, each of which had its own bath and shower. The owner's suite was splendid, with a Jacuzzi and sauna.

"She's beautiful," I said again.

"Very comfortable." Ernie smiled. "Of course, what with business and all, I don't get to spend nearly as much time on her as I would like. But sometimes I have the chance to mix a little business and pleasure. Like now." He winked at me.

"Crew quarters is up there." He waved vaguely towards the bow, where a bulky redhead in crew whites emerged from the forward cabins and headed below. We followed him down a brief stairwell then walked along a narrow corridor past a large kitchen gleaming in stainless and copper. A man in a chef's hat was chopping vegetables on a butcher-block counter.

"This is the main galley. We have a smaller snack bar and galley topsides."

"Of course," I said.

"Here we are," Ernie said. "Look at these beauties. Twin four-hundred-and-sixty-horsepower Cat diesels."

The floor was so clean you could have eaten your dinner off it. Another crewman was running a spotless rag over one of the engines. The rag would still be spotless when he had finished.

"When we crank them up, we can do twenty-two knots. Plays hell with the fuel consumption, mind you."

A smaller engine was running quietly in the corner. "That's the generator diesel," Ernie said. "We have a pretty good power draw, but the little Perkins keeps up with it when we're at anchor."

I noted that the "little Perkins" was bigger than *Arrow*'s main engine. It came to me that if I had inherited this boat, I could have afforded to run it for maybe a month. With no crew.

We wandered about the engine room for a bit, Ernie talking about the fitted workshop with twenty thousand dollars in Snap-on tools, the five thousand dollars in battery banks, another fifty thousand dollars tied up in spares. Everything with a price, the amounts staggering. He spoke with a distracted air, and I thought perhaps he was worried about his daughter. When we left the room to go back topsides, he put an arm around my shoulders.

"You know, Jared, I've always liked you. I wish it could have turned out differently."

"Thank you, sir. It was a long time ago," I replied.

Jennie was still standing at the window, staring out. She turned when she heard us. She had a full glass in her hand. "Well, what do you think?" she asked. "Pretty impressive, isn't it?" Her voice was thick and slurred.

"I think it's time for your nap now, darling." Her father reached out and pressed a button recessed in the wall. "You know what the doctor said."

"Ask him where he got the money," Jennie said.

The salon door opened and one of the crew came in. Her father nodded towards Jennie, and the crewman walked over and took her drink from her and set it down. He put his hand on her shoulder, and she twisted angrily away.

"Don't touch me, damn you," she said. Her face was distorted and unrecognizable. Then it suddenly crumpled like a small child's, and she ran over to her father and threw her arms around his neck.

"I'm sorry, Daddy," she whispered. He looked down at her with a sad smile.

"I know, baby. Try and get some rest. We'll call you for dinner."

She turned and walked away, the crewman padding softly behind.

Mr. Starrett turned towards me and spread his hands out in a help-less gesture. "I'm sorry about that," he said. "She's been ill, you know. Let's have another drink, Jonathan should be here shortly."

We sat down, just the two of us in the big salon, and talked with the strained bonhomie of people who don't know each other very well. I wished I hadn't come. It would have been better to have remembered Jennie as she had been. I wondered what had happened. There was the sound of an outboard approaching, and Mr. Starrett got up and looked out of the cabin window.

"Good. The Zodiac is back. They're right on time."

He went and opened the cabin door and stepped aside.

"My son-in-law," he said as the man entered. "I believe you two have met."

The man came across the room with his hand outstretched as if in greeting, but there was a gun in it.

It was Jack Delaney, and Chuck right behind him.

Now I really wished I hadn't come.

CHAPTER 31

He stood in front of me, smiling.

"Don't bother getting up, Jared. Life is full of little surprises, isn't it?"

"So you're Jennie's husband. No fucking wonder she drinks."

With the same pleasant smile, he reached forward and slashed me across the face with the pistol. I felt the sights cutting, and the blood beginning to run.

"There's no need for that," Starrett said.

I looked at him. "Of course. You were the one in the apartment."

He nodded in agreement.

"Danny didn't recognize you."

"We had to be sure. There was a lot at stake."

I thought of Jennie. The sunglasses, the long-sleeved shirts, the nervous, emaciated body.

"And what about Jennie, does she get the family discount?"

Starrett's face flushed. "That was not supposed to happen," he said.

Poor little Jennie. I wondered if she had started to punish her father when she learned about the drugs, or if Delaney had been responsible.

"Where are your friends, Jared?" Delaney asked pleasantly.

"Fuck you, Jack," I replied, equally pleasant.

He smiled and struck me again.

"They're away, he told me earlier. Don't keep hitting him." Starrett was staring at us, his face twisted in revulsion.

"What's the matter, Ernie, no stomach for the wet work?" I spat at him through the blood, then Chuck stepped behind me and my world crashed down.

"Take him to the engine room," I heard dimly through the pain.

They twisted my arms up behind me and carried me below. They tied me to a chair in front of the workbench and threw a bucket of water in my face.

"Okay, you can leave now," Delaney told Chuck.

He waited until the door shut then turned towards me.

"I want you to call Danny and the old man."

"They won't come. They aren't as stupid as me."

He hit me with the pistol again, the blood running down onto the polished metal floor. Starrett wasn't going to like that. He was proud of that floor.

"Try anyway." He took a handheld ICOM off the wall and held it out in front of me.

"I don't think so."

He sighed. "You always want to do things the hard way, don't you, Jared?"

He reached behind me and cut the bindings on my left hand. I swivelled to hit him and he casually stepped back and struck me at the base of the neck. When my head cleared, he already had the four fingers of my hand in the big machinist's vise mounted at the edge of the workbench.

"Now Jared, let's make that call, shall we?"

"I think you'd do it anyway, you sick asshole. I wouldn't want to spoil your fun."

He smiled and began to twist the handle. He did it one-handed, the other holding my head up by the hair so he could see my face. I felt blood dripping down, and then the sweat sprang up and they mixed in a salty and coppery taste in my mouth. I stared into his bright blue eyes and focused on my hatred and tried to draw back into that deep and lonely space where the child I had been had always hidden. The pain rose from my hand and travelled up my arm in a fiery burning red; I watched the blue eyes, and then they turned red from the pain and I focused on the red circles and they exploded and engulfed me.

❁

I awoke alone in the darkened engine room to the low sound of the Perkins ticking over in the corner. My arms were tied behind me, and when I tried to move, a wave of pain and nausea washed over me. I breathed deeply and flexed my hands. They felt thick and distended with blood, and there was no slack at all. My feet were lashed to the chair legs. I leaned back and forth, trying to rock myself closer to the workbench — maybe I could reach a tool, cut myself loose. The chair tilted but didn't go anywhere. Even in the gloom I could see the tools were all stowed in neat little pouches up on the wall anyway. *Anal-retentive assholes,* I thought bitterly.

I looked out the port light and tried to estimate the time. It was pitch black. Maybe nine o'clock. Time passes quickly when you're having fun. Would Starrett phone *Arrow* and talk to Danny? Probably not — he might want to talk to me, and they would have a hard time explaining that away. They wouldn't take the chance. Delaney would go over later with Chuck and the boys. Well, at least with Sinbad, Danny and Joseph would have some warning, maybe some kind of a chance. My thoughts were interrupted by the sound of the door opening.

Round two.

I took a deep, shuddering breath and turned to face him.

It was Jennie. She came over and put her arms around me.

"Jared. What have they done to you? I was awake, I heard them talking."

323

She was sobbing, her head shaking in bewilderment.

"I'm all right," I said. "Just cut me loose."

She disappeared into the corridor and returned moments later with a big Sabatier carving knife from the galley. She went behind and cut the rope that bound my wrists.

"My God. Your hand."

Her voice was low and shocked. She reached across to the work-bench and passed me some clean towelling. I lifted my hand around in front of me and wrapped the cloth tightly around it. It looked like raw hamburger. I could feel the bones in the fingers grating, but it only served to focus me.

"Cut my feet loose."

She knelt down behind the chair and slashed the ropes. She was just getting up when the lights came on.

"Well, well. This is very disloyal, Jennie. I wondered where you had disappeared to." Delaney glided into the room and moved towards me, the pistol extended straight out in front of him.

"Don't even fucking twitch, Jared. I'd just as soon kill you now as later."

He looked at the coils of rope lying on the floor and shook his head.

"Well, not to worry. We have lots more."

He turned and took a step back towards the door, and in that instant Jennie went for him. She held the knife out high in front of her and had covered half the distance when she crumpled and fell. The shot was loud in the confined space.

Delaney stepped forward and crouched down beside her, the gun rock steady in his hand, the half smile still on his face. She looked like a little child lying there, all the tenseness gone forever now. Delaney turned her over. I could see the blood on her breast.

"Well, she was getting to be a bit of a problem anyway," he said.

I watched him and slowly tensed my body. I could see the spot on his throat where I would hit him. If I could push off strong enough, I might still have enough force to kill him, even with a couple of bullets in me.

He looked up and took a quick step back.

"No chance, Jared. Don't even think about it."

I was a second away when Starrett came running through the door.

"I heard a shot. What's happened?"

He looked down and saw her.

"Jennie," he whispered, "Jennie."

He dropped to his knees and picked her up and cradled her against his chest.

"It's okay, baby, it's okay. Daddy's here." He rocked her back and forth, tears pouring down his face.

"She's dead," I said. "Delaney killed her."

The words slowly penetrated. He turned towards him.

"No," he said.

Delaney shrugged. "She cut Kane loose and came at me with a knife. I had no choice."

"No."

He was still rocking Jennie back and forth. Blood ran down the front of his shirt and pooled on the floor. He stared down at it, mesmerized. Chuck came through the door and stopped suddenly, taking it all in. He looked up at Delaney.

"Help Mr. Starrett to his cabin, Chuck. Give him a couple of Jennie's pills."

"No," Starrett said dazedly.

He reached into his pocket and slowly pulled out a gun. He was bringing it up on Delaney when the bright rosette appeared on his forehead and he slumped forward over Jennie, the two of them falling together in slow red harmony.

I rose crouching from the chair, half spun, and sent it whirling at Delaney. It hit him across the shoulder as he dodged, and he slipped and sprawled in the slick of blood. Chuck was swinging towards me, and as he turned I picked up the knife and he froze. I kicked him in the groin with all the rage that was in me. He fell across Delaney and I ran.

I could hear them yelling behind me as I went up and through the salon. The cook was setting the dining table. When he saw me coming all bloody with the knife, he raised his hands in supplication. I smashed his face with my knuckles around the knife, and he fell across the table and down to the floor in a shatter of crystal and china.

Out the door and down the gangway in two long jumps and into the launch. The wind had risen, and it was rocking violently against the landing. No keys in the ignition. The Sabatier went through the fuel hoses like butter. I heard them coming and dove over the side and came up beside the Zodiac. I drove the knife into the tubes on both sides and split them open. The deck lights flashed on, and it was suddenly daylight, the water lit up for a hundred feet in all directions. I filled my lungs and dove down deep.

The water felt warm, the same temperature as the air, and more soothing. A few feet under the surface, the turbulence died and it was almost peaceful. I kicked off my shoes and moved away from the boat in a slow, easy side stroke, my left hand pulled in tight, holding the cloth against my body. I saw the dark ribbons of blood streaming out from it in the light coming down from *Impala*, and tried not to think how few parts per million would summon the sharks.

I concentrated on my stroke, willing myself through the water, trying to keep the panic down. Perhaps fifty yards to the rim of light, then another mile or more back to *Arrow*.

A long way.

Never mind. Concentrate on the first fifty yards. Delaney and his crew would be waiting when I came up. The waves would help, though. I'd exhale on the rise. Say three seconds to take in more air. Maybe a second or two for them to spot me and bring the guns to bear. It would be tight.

I swam until my lungs were bursting and bright points of light danced before my eyes. It was hard to keep a sense of direction. I exhaled and went to the surface. There was a shout and I took a long gasping breath and went back under with little geysers boiling around me.

When I came up the second time, I was clear of the light. A spotlight was playing back and forth, but it was a forlorn hope. I swam on my side, my head turned back, and went under when the light came close. From below you could see it pass over like a giant moon lighting up the water. My hand was throbbing and I pulled off my T-shirt and wrapped it tightly to slow the bleeding. I began counting the strokes, willing myself towards *Arrow*. I became light-headed, and once when I looked up I was swimming back towards *Impala*. The waves broke over me and I choked on the brine. There were lights ahead, but I couldn't pick out *Arrow*. They seemed an eternity away.

I stopped for a moment to rest, and the moon came out and outlined the dark, tapered shapes surrounding me. I tried to scream, but salt water filled my mouth and I went under. I was sinking when something bumped me and I saw the great white teeth and they sank into my shoulder. I opened my mouth but no sound came out, just a long line of bubbles streaming up towards the surface.

❄

I came to lying on my bunk in *Arrow*. I tried to rise, but something held me down.

"Take it easy, partner, we're not done yet."

Danny sat on the floor, his back towards me. My arm was stretched out in his grasp and Joseph was working on my hand. I couldn't feel a thing.

"You have more drugs in you than a Davie Street junkie. There shouldn't be too much pain for a while."

Joseph looked up and smiled, then went back to his stitching.

"How bad is it?"

"Two fingers broken, the forefinger and the index. Forefinger a clean break, the index more complicated, maybe three fractures. Joseph says it will be all right if it doesn't get infected. Going to smart for a while, though. He put twenty stitches in your face. You look like shit."

"How long have I been here?"

"A couple of hours. You can thank your buddy Sinbad. We were worried, didn't know what to do when we got back and you didn't show up. Then we saw the searchlights waving around out there, figured maybe it had something to do with you. We took the guns, headed towards the lights, Sinbad in the bow. Gone about half a mile when he jumped over, took off through the water. Dove down and got you, we never even knew you were there."

"I thought it was a shark."

"I put you over the seat, Joseph pumped some water out, we brought you back."

"It was Delaney," I said. "He's Jennie Starrett's husband. He killed her. We have to get out of here." My thoughts were disjointed from the drugs. I could hear my voice slurring. "*Impala*," I whispered, "Chuck, at least four others. Starrett's dead. It was him in the apartment that day."

The boat was rocking sharply now, the oil lamp swinging shadows back and forth across the cabin.

"We have to leave," I murmured.

Then the shadows swung and lengthened and stayed, and everything faded.

❀

When I awoke again, it was still dark. The galley clock read two thirty. The wind was moving through the rigging in long, soughing gusts, and heavy rain pounded on the decks. I felt nauseous, and my throat was parched from the drugs. It was the noise of the anchor chain coming aboard that had woken me. My hand was a dull, aching throb — I could see the bandages gleaming faintly white in the half light, and the outline of the splints underneath. It rested in a sling across my chest.

I rolled to my feet and waited for the dizziness to pass. The anchor crashed into its chocks, and a minute later Danny crouched beside me.

"I was just coming to see how you were. We're going to try and get out of here. I think we have a fair chance of slipping by them without being seen. They're swinging the spotlight around once in a while, but nothing for the last hour. The weather's picked up a bit, a few squalls going through, they'll never hear the engine. We'll hug the shore, the seas will help break our profile. If the cloud cover stays, there should be no problem." He shrugged. "Their radar is anybody's guess. If it keeps raining, no problem. If it stops they might get something."

"What's the wind doing?"

"Twenty-five knots, gusting higher occasionally. Steady now from the northeast. It will be on the beam till we get around Point Teachoe, then she'll be on the aft quarter down the channel. About as good as we can hope for."

I swallowed some painkillers, washing them down with a mouthful of rum, stuck the bottle in my pocket, and followed him out on deck. The wind was much louder out here, whistling through the palms that dotted the shoreline. The trees were bending under it, and there was the occasional crash of falling coconuts. Joseph sat under the dodger, the rifle and shotguns wrapped in oiled cloth beside him. He had an unlit pipe clenched between his teeth and was staring up at the sky with a thoughtful look. I hoped he saw good omens there.

Danny brought the bow around, and I took the tiller while he hanked on the jib and took the covers off the main and mizzen. We'd keep the sails lowered until we were clear of *Impala*. The harbour entrance was less than two hundred yards away, and then it widened out into Vipihai Bay. *Impala* was anchored in the lee of Hanakee Island on the west side. We wouldn't have to come any closer than a quarter of a mile at the nearest point. When they found us gone in the morning, they would have to start looking again — we could have headed to any one of a hundred anchorages.

We crept along, hugging the shore. The islands rise straight up out of the sea in the Marquesas, and the water along their sides is deep.

"There's a good squall showing on the radar," Danny said, "maybe enough to get us by." He went below and brought up the pistol, then mounted the stock. Joseph had the rifle out and was checking over the night scope, training it on the darkened hulls of the anchored boats we passed and nodding his head in satisfaction. He filled the rifle's magazine and shoved extra shells into his pockets.

I took the spotlight and plugged it in to the socket and threw a roll of electrician's tape down beside it. Danny loaded the pistol and passed it to me. The shotguns and pistol would be nearly useless if they decided to stand off and rake us, but it was comforting to see them there. I tried not to think about the big weapons locker Starrett had shown me on my tour of *Impala* "in case of pirates," he'd said, when they went through the straits to Singapore.

Arrow was moving along comfortably, the engine just ticking along at a thousand RPMs. The wind was blowing down from us to *Impala*, and we couldn't risk more noise. She loomed ahead, the deck lights all on, but a big enough patch of darkness between her and the island for us to slip through. They would have been better off shutting down the lights and keeping their night vision.

We didn't talk, and I found I was holding my breath. It seemed to take forever to bring *Impala* abeam. I put the binoculars on her and Joseph brought the night scope up, but we couldn't see anyone. They must have assumed I drowned, and were coming for *Arrow* later. Finally she moved slowly by, and we began to increase the distance between us.

We were just beginning to relax when we heard the unmistakable sound of twin outboards firing up, and seconds later the launch burst out from behind *Impala* and headed towards us.

"Oh, shit," Danny said.

"No point in running now."

I reached down and switched off the engine. The scream of the Mercs filled the air.

"I'll hit them with the big spot when they get nearer."

Joseph said something to Danny, who nodded and turned towards me. "We have to get them in close. Don't fire till Joseph starts." He gave a low whistle, and Sinbad dropped down into the cockpit and crouched at our feet.

"That's a fine boy." I bent down and patted him with my good hand. He lunged and his teeth snapped a fraction short as I jerked it back. He lay there growling softly as I picked up the pistol and stuck it in my belt. I lifted my arm out of the sling and taped the spotlight to my wrist.

They came down quickly, bouncing from crest to crest, the engines revving when the props came out of the water. When they were two hundred yards away, they throttled back and lay in the water, idling just off our bow. Their spotlight played over us. They weren't completely sure.

"Come on, you motherfuckers," Danny whispered.

Suddenly the engines roared and the bow lifted out of the water and she shot towards us. They passed a hundred yards away, bouncing along the tops of the waves, laying down a steady stream of fire. They were going so fast that the spotlight swung crazily, on us for an instant then skyward as they slewed down the trough. I could hear the thud of bullets smashing into *Arrow*, raking along the cabin top and kicking splinters over us where we crouched in the cockpit.

"Oh, you bastards," I whispered.

We crouched low, not moving as she swept past towards the shore then swung back in a long, looping circle and came towards us once more. They moved in from the bow, in line with *Arrow*, then veered off a short two boat lengths away. Joseph and Danny rose onto their knees and fired as I stood up and switched on the spotlight, holding it high above their heads. I heard the roar of Danny's shotguns as he triggered his mixed loads of slugs and shots, the spent shells bouncing on the deck, and then the sharp crack of Joseph's rifle firing in quick staccato, the smell of gunpowder hot and acrid and the brass cartridges flashing in the light. There was the whine of a ricochet and the tearing sound of bullets slamming into *Arrow*'s hull.

As they came abeam, I emptied the machine pistol in three shot bursts, keeping them low. There were three of them, and I saw Chuck's long blond hair streaming in the wind as he crouched beside the driver, and heard a muffled yell as they blazed by. I put the pistol under my arm and took the spare clip from between my teeth and slammed it in. The air reeked of cordite and burnt oil, and spent cartridges were rolling everywhere.

I took a hit of rum and passed the bottle to Joseph. He shook his head and Danny plucked it away.

"They're coming again," he yelled.

I watched grimly as the launch moved away from the beach in a long, lazy arc and curled towards us once more. We had missed our chance. The launch would keep us pinned down now, and *Impala*'s steel bows would ride us under.

I focused the spotlight on the speedboat as she bore towards us, going even faster than before, too fast, rising up out of the swell and going her length in the air, the noise deafening as the engine accelerated, and then the crash as she hit. She went by a hundred yards off, only the man in the stern firing now, and Chuck crawling towards the man slumped over the controls, ripping at him.

Danny and I emptied our weapons, but the launch was too far away. But then Joseph fired again and Chuck fell forward over the console and the Mercs screamed even louder as the launch swung away towards the beach, going straight in, faster and faster all the time.

The beach was narrow and steep, with boulders scattered all along the sand, and they went in deep on a high, rolling breaker and ploughed a fifty-foot furrow before they hit the first big rock. The tiny doll-like figures rose through the air a split second before we heard the crash and saw the ball of flame that was the launch. For long seconds it was bright as day, and then night fell once more. In the stunned aftermath, the sound of *Impala*'s anchor clanking aboard seemed very loud.

"Now we run," I said.

We were still inside the bay, not yet subject to the full force of the wind. Danny hauled up the main and the jib and cleated off as Joseph set the mizzen. *Arrow* heeled over, paused for a brief second as if filling her lungs, and then accelerated.

"Two miles to the point," Danny yelled, the words snatched away by the wind.

If we were lucky, we had maybe a one-mile head start on *Impala*. It might be enough. Once we rounded the corner, *Impala*'s radar wouldn't pick us up until she cleared. Delaney would assume we were heading for one of the downwind anchorages at Tahuatu. If we kept in tight to the island all the way down the canal, he might not pick us up again. There was a westerly current in there, and with the wind against it, the seas would be wild. By the time he checked out Tahuatu, we would be halfway to the Tuamotus. It was three thirty now. If we were wrong and he caught us in the open sea at daylight, we were dead.

The seas began building as we moved further out into the Bay at a steady eight knots. *Impala*'s lights were swinging as she turned onto our course. She would gain quickly for the first couple of miles. Once she rounded the point, the seas would slow her as well.

"Gusting to thirty-five," Danny yelled.

We hadn't reached the canal yet. The passage runs between Hiva Oa and Tahuatu, the peaks rising steeply on both sides creating a venturi effect as the wind compresses and accelerates down it. The seas in there would be ugly. In those conditions, *Arrow* would not be disadvantaged. She had been designed and built for the raging storms of the English Channel, the bleak and wintry rollers of the North Atlantic, and the steep and sudden storms of the North Sea — all those vast and pounding waters that had challenged the best of British boats for centuries. She would be wet and miserable, she would jar and thresh and roll until we were so tired and numb from hanging on that our bones would ache and cry for mercy. But she would endure.

"Blow you motherfucker," I screamed. "Blow!"

As if she heard me, the wind picked up yet another notch, the rise in pitch as clear and plangent as the change in scale on a guitar. *Arrow* was singing now, high, keening notes picked out on the rigging and transferred down through the decks in an age-old maritime rhythm until the furthest timbers of her hull thrummed in accompaniment.

As I stood with the tiller between my legs and braced back against the mizzen, my body swaying to the secret melodies, there was nowhere else on earth I would rather have been. The water was coming over the bow in long, sluicing sheets now, foaming down the deck and breaking against the dodger in green phosphorescent clouds.

"Do you want the mule?" Danny asked. I turned to the flash of teeth. "Hell yes," I said.

Danny hauled the mizzen staysail and the purple colours broke out between the masts and *Arrow* laid over, and for a long moment I thought she'd broach, but then the keel caught and held and she powered out, tracking down the trough in a long, surging run before shuddering back on her hindquarters as the waves broke by. She paused, bows up and waiting, then her stern rose and we surfed again, blowing down the waves in a thundering cacophony of noise and foam and exaltation. I had never been so proud of her. If we lived through the next few days, it would be because of *Arrow* and all the love and skill that had formed and built her.

Joseph started below then turned quickly and spoke to Danny, who yelled in my ear, his voice grim: "We're taking on water!"

In the din and confusion we hadn't heard the bilge pump or seen the red warning light that brightened the galley. The water was six inches over the sole, sloshing up the cabin sides as *Arrow* heeled and rose, and heeled again. I could see the water coming in from the bullet holes in the cabin top, spraying as *Arrow* submarined, then subsiding to a slow drip as she crested, then spraying again under the pressure of another sea.

"That's not the main problem," Danny yelled. "We took some bullets in the hull. The bilge pump can't keep up with them."

He dropped to his knees and began emptying out the starboard lockers. Joseph moved out and took the tiller, and I went below as he fitted the handle in the cockpit bilge pump and started the long, even

334

strokes that would move out thirty gallons a minute. It was nowhere near enough. I grabbed the handle for the other Whale mounted under the chart table and pumped with my good hand. The water had risen another four inches. Floorboards were floating where they weren't fastened down. We were running out of time.

"Not that one," Danny said.

He threw the contents back into the locker, slammed the door, and started on the next one. There was a warning yell from Joseph, and we took a slow roll and then a sea slammed us as the boat fell off a crest. I pitched forward face first into the water and lay there dazed for a moment. Danny reached down and picked me up by the collar and threw me back into place then continued his frantic searching.

"Danny. It's not salty enough," I sputtered.

"They've punctured the freshwater tanks. That's where the holes are."

He sprang up and threw the cushions off the starboard settee, then removed the panels. From where I sat I could hear the water gurgling in. Danny hunched over the tank, his neck and shoulders bulging as he strained, and there was a splintering crash and the tank was out and lying in the aisle. Water was jetting out from where it had been.

"Six holes," he said. "Broom handle for five of them, I'll need a big bung for the other. I'll use the one from the forward sink."

I threw him the broom handle and he broke off short lengths, whittled points, and jammed them into the holes. He pounded them in with the bung then shoved it in as well, hammering it tight with his foot. Then he picked up the water tank and replaced it, stuffing rags tight between it and the plugs.

"That will do for now, we'll tidy it up later."

In another ten minutes you could see the difference, and in half an hour the water was below the sole and the electric bilge pump was holding it. I went back on deck while Danny and Joseph plugged the leaks in the cabin top. The holes were fairly uniform, and it was a simple matter to cut plugs from a scrap of yellow cedar planking, coat them with caulking, and tap them in. Then they removed the hull plugs one at a time and did the same for them. Joseph found another row of holes above the waterline on the weather side, and they plugged those as well — they would have leaked when we changed tacks.

It was breaking dawn by the time they finished. The bilge pump was cycling on once every half hour, and then only for a couple of minutes.

"I think we can live with that," Danny said. "I'll shut off the electric pump, hand pump every hour, and count the strokes. If it doesn't get any worse we'll be fine."

We sat in the cockpit, drinking hot rums, the three of us squeezed forward under the dodger and Sinbad sprawled on the cabin top against the windscreen. Joseph had managed to heat some water in the heavy going, the stove swinging sixty degrees on its gimbals, the kettle lashed down with shock cords. The rum was sweet and strong, the hot bite of it cutting through my exhaustion. My hand was throbbing painfully, and my face felt as if a pattern of red-hot wires was laid on it.

We had come out of the canal and were running in open water. Danny had hooked up the vane now that the wind was true, and we surfed along, the knot meter ticking off ten and twelve on the runs, then dropping down to seven or eight when we shuddered back. We were pressing *Arrow* hard, but there was no choice now. The wind was holding steady at thirty-five knots, and we had put the second reef in the main. She had a tendency to broach as she came off her runs, but the wind vane adjusted instantly and steered her out of it.

"Anything yet?"

Danny searched behind us with the binoculars, scanning the brightening horizon for a sign of *Impala*.

"Nothing. Be a while before we can be sure. Light isn't good enough yet."

We needed three days, time to move in and hide among the reefs and atolls of the Tuamotus — that lonely, wreck-strewn area encompassing a body of water larger than Europe, but with less than fifteen hundred square miles of land mass. Eighty islands strung out across a thousand miles of ocean, less than half of them inhabited, and all, save one, low-lying coral atolls rising a mere six to twenty feet out of the water. In a storm they would be invisible in the waves until it was too late.

GPS and electronics were only rough guides there, and an automatic pilot an invitation to disaster, the reefs rising so sudden and straight from the vast underwater mountain ranges that even the depth sounder was too slow to pick up the changes. You were in a thousand feet of water one minute, aground sixty seconds later. If anything, the number of shipwrecks had increased with the new aids, people placing blind faith in the precision of their toys and neglecting to allow for the inaccuracies of the original charts.

Magellan sailed through the Northern Islands and saw but one; Bougainville saw enough of them to call it the Dangerous Archipelago; Cook went through a year earlier and warned his contemporaries of their dangers. The charts were scant, some of them still no more than hand-drawn sketches a hundred and fifty years old, the landmarks all gone now, the entire physiognomy of the atolls changed by the cyclones that swept through regularly.

It was an area as old as sailing, where the old rules still applied, navigation was by eyeball and the colour of the water, and the ghosts of a thousand drowned sailors waited on your mistakes.

❀

"You don't look well," Danny said.

I sat up with a start, conscious that I had been dozing off.

"I thought Starrett would be a better host," he added. "I would never have guessed it was him in the apartment that day. Not enough of a look. I only met him that one time. And now he and Jennie are both dead."

I told him how it had happened.

"That fucking Delaney is a madman."

"No, he's very cool and calculating. My guess is he's the driving force behind the whole thing. Starrett was just the front. A greedy fool who got caught up in it." I hoped it was true; I still found it hard to hate him. He had paid full price for his sins; the look on his face when he held Jennie would be with me until I died. Someday soon I wanted to see that same look on Delaney's face.

"How many you figure are left?"

"Three. Delaney, one crewman, and the cook."

"Well, the numbers are even now, anyway. I wonder how he'll explain the crash of his launch on the beach, guns, bodies, the whole thing?"

"You're right. The French authorities will certainly want to talk to him. They should be looking for him right now."

Danny switched on channel sixteen, but there was no radio traffic. The sky was light now, and Joseph spent a long five minutes sweeping the horizon in all directions with the Steiners. Finally he shook his head. My whole body sagged with relief.

"Bunk time, Jared."

Danny guided me down the companionway and stripped off my wet clothes. He shook some pills out into his palm, and I swallowed them obediently, then half fell onto my berth. Danny rubbed me down with a towel then pulled the blanket over me. As I drifted off I heard the squawk of the receiver but couldn't make any sense out of it.

When I awoke, Joseph was beside me, his oilskins wet and shining in the cabin lights. My mouth was so swollen I couldn't eat, and he fed me some pills and a foul-smelling broth. When I tried to get up, he shook his head and pressed me back down. I mumbled a protest, but the curtain fell and I slept again.

CHAPTER 32

I awoke to a sense of changed motion, the rolling of the boat heavier and deeper than earlier, but less quick and somehow damped. Joseph and Danny were sitting at the galley table, talking in hushed voices, Sinbad stretched out sleeping at their feet. The wind was howling even louder than before. Seen through the port lights the seas were huge and rolling, towering above us with overhanging crests and the foam blowing off them in creaming white waterfalls. As I watched, we took a deeper roll, *Arrow* staggered under the weight of water, and the world outside turned green as she buried herself. It seemed a long time before she rose again and the port light cleared.

"We're under trysail and storm jib," Danny said, "graduated from a strong gale to a full-fledged storm. Last time I looked, she was gusting upwards of fifty knots."

"How far have we come?"

"Two hundred and seventy miles." He smiled at my expression. "You've been out of it for a day and a half, Jared; we've just passed Napuka and Tepoto, the Disappointment Islands."

No wonder I felt so stiff. And hungry. I hauled myself gingerly out of the bunk and wedged in beside them. Joseph produced a cup of soup with cheese and crackers and I attacked them greedily. My face felt less swollen, and my hand was just a dull ache.

"Is it still building?"

"No. Any more wind and we'll have to heave to, and we really don't want to do that. A plane came over yesterday, right down low, had a good look; no official markings, no contact made."

"Not the authorities, then."

"No."

We sat there, considering.

"Well, we should have enough of a lead. Delaney won't do all that much better than us in this. Depends where he was when he heard."

"There's nobody in sight, we're taking a look every hour. Visibility is poor, though — a lot of spray flying around. He'll have a hard time spotting us even if he does get close. Hang on."

Arrow took a quick, hard roll, then shuddered as a wall of water banged into her. She stopped dead, then started climbing a sea larger than the others, pausing at the top before falling off as it passed under her. All the long way down, then rolling on her side at the bottom, the following sea curling over and crashing down on the decks, suddenly dark and pressured inside from the weight of water, the spray misting in over the companionway boards. A slow, laborious righting, then heeling, and the climb beginning again.

"Reminds me of the Aleutians," Danny said. "We were caught in a gale up there in a seventy-foot steel trawler. Same kind of wind, but the seas were bigger. Tore the main hatch cover right off, two men pumping steady, and we barely kept even. Icing up too. At least here it's warm."

For the next thirty hours we crabbed along, making under seventy miles. The wind was up and down around fifty knots; every time it dropped enough for us to consider putting up sail, it came up again before we could act on the notion. We tried taping the French weather broadcasts from Papeete and playing them back, but there were always some words I couldn't get. Perhaps another forty-eight hours and then slackening, I wasn't sure.

We pumped and played cards and fiddled with the single-side band radio and tried to sleep. The boat was wet, and when you put on dry clothes the salt crystals were in them, and you were damp again an hour later. We couldn't open any hatches and the humidity was overpowering, water gathering on the deck beams and dripping down on us when we tried to sleep. In this kind of weather the Dorades were useless, and Danny had screwed in the seals and duct-taped them against the water. The air became stale and feverish, and reading gave me a headache.

Every hour, one of us put on our oilskins and fought our way out on deck. In some ways it was more pleasant out there once you were used to the size of the seas. The water was deep enough and the waves far enough apart that they weren't stacking, and *Arrow* climbed up and over them with relative ease, only occasionally getting caught as she rolled too far and a rogue broke over her. Crouched under the dodger, making ourselves as small as possible, we escaped the worst of it.

There was heavy cloud cover much of the time, and the new moon threw scant light into the infrequent clearings. The seas were invisible at night, only the foaming crests at the top illuminated, the big ones first sensed by the building roar as they advanced, and the shock of pressure before they hit, like the dark rush of air from the subway tunnel that precedes the train.

❀

It was just before sunset on the third day when we finally started to relax. We were a hundred and twenty miles from the Tuamotus, and another day would see us safely among them. There would be no hiding there, but we could pick our spots, seek out the narrow passes, the shallow lagoons where the steel bow of *Impala* couldn't reach us. As long as Delaney didn't catch us in the open water, we would be on equal terms as we played our deadly game to resolution. He wouldn't leave, and he couldn't let us leave. Only one boat was coming out of the Tuamotus.

All we needed was another twenty-four hours.

"I seeeeee youuuuu."

The voice echoed over the VHF. I was buckled in at the galley, opening cans of soup, and it froze me to the spot.

"Jaaarrred. I seeeeeee yoouuuu."

The syllables were stretched out like a child's sing-song, followed by a long, low laugh. It was Delaney.

"Can you hear me, Jared? Oh, I think so. Won't be long now, Jared. Shortly after daylight, I figure." He paused. "It has been quite a chase, Jared. You have been very fortunate, you know? But it's nearly finished now. Did Ernie give you the tour, Jared? Tell you all about his beautiful boat? I'm sure he did. She's steel, but of course you know that. Weighs a hundred and twenty tons."

Danny and Joseph sat at the table, listening, Joseph's face thoughtful, Danny's grimly clenched. Joseph went over to the chart table and switched on the radar.

"Two hundred and forty thousand pounds, Jared. A hundred and twenty tons of steel coming over your pretty little boat at around twelve knots. I don't think there will be very much left, Jared. Of you, your Indian friends, or *Arrow*. What do you think, Jared?"

I looked at Danny. "Should I tell him what we think?" I asked.

"Why not. What is he going to do, get pissed off at us?"

I held the mike button down. "We think you're a raving asshole, Delaney."

He laughed in delight. "Ah, Jared, I knew you weren't drowned. I do admire your spirit. Too bad you're on the wrong side. I see why that fool Ernie liked you. He wanted to let your friend go, you know. He didn't think he had been recognized. Jesus. A forty-million-dollar-a-year business, and he's going to put it into jeopardy because of a dumb fucking Indian. But Ernie never did have much ambition. He just stumbled into it, you know? Always living beyond his means: the big house, the sailboat, the yuppie daughter and all her toys. He was stretched awfully thin. I was his accountant, so of course I knew it. I gave him a contact I knew, and all he had to do was meet them at sea and take a load in and all his troubles were over. Guy like him, it was easy, who'd suspect? And then just a couple more for gravy, and he thought he would stop."

He laughed. "What an idiot. Of course, by then I had all the records, videos, everything. Then I married the silly cunt and I was running it all."

"So you killed the Lebels too."

"Of course. Do you know what Starrett said when they came out west? 'There's plenty for everybody.' He was going to try and make a deal with them, for God's sake. Can you believe that? He was so goddam dumb. I don't know how he ever managed to make a success of the car business. Wearing that stupid fucking yachtie cap all the time. Mind you, look at the rest of them."

"Well, you're rid of him now," I said.

"Yeah. And his dumb daughter too. That was a bit of a shame, though." His voice turned low and confiding. "She was a great piece of ass, Jared. You wouldn't think that, would you, her so skinny now and high class? But when she wanted the nose candy she would do anything." He paused.

I sat and waited. I was glad we had no recorder on board.

"You know what I mean, Jared? Anything. She liked it rough and dirty. Was she like that when you knew her, Jared?" He gave a low chuckle.

I didn't say anything. I just stared at the speaker and pictured his face. Danny reached across and picked up the mike.

"Hi, asshole. Don't you ever get tired of this? What are you now, zero for four? When are you going to learn? You're out of your element here, Delaney, we're going to finish you. By this time tomorrow, you'll be in a shark's belly. Hold that thought."

"You've been awfully lucky," Delaney snarled.

"Fuck luck, Jack. We're better than you are. The guy in the hospital, and Eddie? They were taken out by my grandfather. He's near a hundred years old, for Christ's sake. What does that tell you, Jack?"

"Very funny. We'll see who is laughing tomorrow. Gotta sign off, boys. Big day coming up. By the way, we've got the storm windows screwed on this time. Inch-and-a-half Lexan, absolutely bullet proof, but don't take my word for it. Have a go when I get close."

He laughed and hung up. In the sudden silence, you could hear the wind howling in a long, rising gust. Joseph motioned to the screen. There, eleven miles back, was the blip that was *Impala*. He would wait until first light to make his run. It was 1900 hours now. We had just under eleven hours to make a hundred and fifteen miles. It was impossible. Even if we went for it, *Arrow* could never handle it. We would rip her masts out. It was still blowing a steady forty knots.

"Let's hang some canvas," I said.

I brought *Arrow*'s bow around into the wind, and Danny fought up the mainsail with the third reef tied in. There was a nervous moment when she swung back through the trough, laying over as the wind worked on her sails and hull, the rail pressed down and water pouring into the cockpit, then the wind spilled out the top of the sail and she slowly rose up and started to run. I hand-steered for a few minutes and she didn't have a tendency to broach yet, so I called for the high-cut yankee in place of the storm jib. Danny clipped onto the jackstays and crawled forward on his hands and knees, dragging the sail behind him. It took him twenty minutes to make the change, and part of the time he was out of sight as the bow plunged and green water covered the decks. The difference was noticeable at once as *Arrow* accelerated. She was pressing dangerously hard now, and at the end of the surfing runs she had a tendency to come around into the wind. I could feel the complaint in the creak of the mast and the weight of the tiller as *Arrow* strained, and I leaned my weight against it to keep her true. The seas were running near thirty feet now, with the occasional larger one coming through, and we traversed them at an angle, racing ahead of the curling tops that loomed above and behind us at one moment, and the next rising up on the crest and riding it until it too passed and we came down off the back of it and paused, waiting for the next to raise our stern again.

And all the time *Impala* crept closer.

It was exhilarating and wildly exciting, and a moment's inattention could spell disaster. Tonight would tell us what *Arrow* and her crew were made of. Tukekoto was somewhere a hundred miles ahead of us, and if we weren't within sight of her at daybreak, then we might just as well be lying dismasted and helpless somewhere in between. It had to be one or the other now.

All through the night we alternated thirty-minute shifts at the helm. At the end of our watches we were exhausted, but nobody slept. We brewed endless pots of coffee and drank them black, sitting in the cockpit, watching the waves that chased us, occasionally shouting a warning to the helmsman when a cross-breaking sea came through. One of the rogues caught Danny at the tiller, knocking him down to his knees and filling the cockpit with water before he could react. His legs floated straight out in front of him as he clung to the tiller and cursed, fighting *Arrow*'s bow back round again. Joseph was the best helmsman, his touch light and sure, seeming to know instinctively when a big one was coming, and laying *Arrow* off before it.

Every fifteen minutes we pumped the bilges and checked the gap between *Impala* and ourselves on the radar. It was slowly narrowing, and once I thought I saw her lights. If nothing changed, she would be upon us at daybreak.

"So tell me the plan, Captain," Danny said.

It was 0300 hours and *Impala* was three miles back and gaining inexorably. Katiu and Makemo were roughly fifty miles away, both with wide passes and deep water. Even in this weather there was a fair chance of getting inside one of them without damage. But once in their lee, we would be trapped with no chance of escape. *Impala* would follow us through and ride us down. We might escape with our lives by fleeing ashore, and hide out until Delaney was forced to leave, but

Arrow would be lost and he would have won, no matter the final outcome. That was unacceptable.

Fifteen miles closer was a small, uninhabited atoll that stretched three miles wide and a mile across: Tukekoto. On the DMA charts it was just a small-scale drawing in the corner. It showed a forty-foot-wide pass a scant fourteen feet deep, bordered with knife-edged reefs on either side. Inside the lagoon was twenty feet of water studded with coral heads.

"We're going in there," I said.

Danny leaned over the chart and stared at it. Then he looked up at me as if I was crazy.

"Do you know what that pass will be like in these conditions, Jared? It's on the weather side. You won't even be able to pick it out with the seas this high. The chart can easily be several hundred yards off. There will be thirty-foot breakers stacking crosswise through there, it's a goddam funnel. We'll never make it. *Arrow* will break her back when she comes off and hits the bottom, or is thrown onto the reefs alongside. And even if we were blind lucky and made it on the hundred-to-one chance, *Impala* will be right behind us. Steel, bigger, she will have a much better chance."

"Yes, I know," I said.

I pulled out Bill's journals and showed him the sketch of the atoll he had made when he was there. Then I told Danny the plan. He stared at me and opened his mouth and then closed it again. I waited while he looked at me and shook his head slowly, and then he started to speak but thought better of it. He got up and took the bottle of Bundaberg from the rack and poured a half glass and drank it down like water.

"I'm open to any other suggestions," I said.

"I'm scared to ask. What's the date on the sketch?"

"Nineteen eighty-five."

"I thought so. I suppose you know that coral grows an inch a year. That's roughly two and a half feet less water now, assuming Bill's soundings were accurate in the first place."

"But it will be approaching high tide, so I should get that back, plus maybe a little more. The depths will be for dead low tide."

At least I hoped so. They were for all commercial chart soundings, and I was gambling our lives that Bill had been seaman enough to follow that practice.

"I don't even know why we're sitting here discussing it. It's insane. I can think of a dozen reasons why it won't work. What if he just stands off and watches us go in? Waits around, and if there is anything left of *Arrow*, comes in through the pass when it moderates, runs us down. We'll just be a fucking raft by then. And that's if everything goes according to your plan. We'd be sitting ducks."

"That's why you have to make sure he follows us in."

He put the rum bottle in his pocket and went up the companionway steps. "The condemned man takes his last drink," he muttered dolefully. "I'll send in Joseph."

The moment he slid back the hatch, a sea came aboard and washed the charts off the table.

"There's a fucking omen for you," Danny said as he climbed out and shut it behind him again.

I wiped down the charts and waited for Joseph. A minute later the hatch reopened and he stepped over the boards and came down beside me. I laid it all out for him, but there was no change of expression on that ancient, weather-beaten visage. Sometimes I wondered if he understood half of what I said.

"I realize it's desperate, but it's a chance. There's nothing else for it. I don't want to put Danny on the bow, but there's no choice. I can't see well enough from the cockpit. He'll have to lash himself in."

Joseph looked at me gravely, then put his hand on my shoulder. "Don't worry, my son," he said in a whisper so low I thought for a moment I was imagining it. "I will be on the bow."

He gave me a brief pinch then turned and went out on deck.

The false dawn came with the promise of better weather. The moon was running in and out of the high cloud, and the ill-omened halo had disappeared. The wind was veering and less constant now, gusting to forty knots but dropping down to thirty in the lulls. The seas were unchanged, but the vicious cross-swell had gone; *Arrow* ran truer, without the sudden corkscrewing that had marked her passage earlier. The salt spray that had stung and blinded us when we turned to face the seas was gentler now, less horizontal and driven.

As the light slowly increased, seabirds emerged from the dark and circled us, the first harbingers of land. *Arrow* flew among them, the greatest bird of all, her white sails filled and extended, soaring high among them one moment as she crested, and plunging away the next in a foaming cloud of spray.

I looked behind me, and there, less than half a mile away now, was *Impala*, the bow wave rising up even with her decks as she careened along, and then the whole of her disappearing up to the wheelhouse windows before she rose again like a vengeful black leviathan and came inexorably on. She was pressing hard, and we were still too slow.

"We'll have to cut her loose," Danny yelled, as he sprang to the boom and took out the reefs, hauling the mainsail up with his great strength as I fought *Arrow* back and through the eye of the wind, the decks completely underwater as we heeled, the shrouds vibrating in protest. For long seconds it seemed we'd lost her, but then she rose up out of the sea, gave a quick hard roll as if shaking herself, and caught her wave. We rose up on it like a demented surfer and *Arrow*'s speed increased still more, the roar of the breakers curling under us lessened by the hiss of our bow wave as it rose up the sides to the lower spreaders.

The knot meter surged to thirteen and then fell back to zero; it was out of the water as the front half of the boat hung suspended in space. *Arrow* stayed at the curling edge of the wave, hanging there for long, heart-stopping seconds as we waited for the pitchpole. Through the spray her bow jutted out thirty feet above the trough, equal portions of her length in air and water. Then the wave passed under us, the bow rose, and we fell back in the trough until the next wave caught us and we started to rise again.

Above the noise of the spray and the waves was another distant, booming percussion. It was Danny who recognized it first.

"The atoll," he yelled.

It was just another cloud of foam and spray stretching across our path two miles ahead. I took the glasses and searched for the pass, but the surf line was even, three miles of breakers rising up and striking the reef, and the spray hanging in the air a hundred feet above them. I stared at the deadly foaming line and my heart rose into my throat: there was no way on God's earth we could find the pass.

Wordlessly Danny passed me the rum and I drank deep and the fiery liquid jolted me and rushed straight to my brain and the old madness rose up in my blood like wine.

"Showtime, Danny."

I felt my lips stretching in an insane grin.

"Wooden ships and iron men, old buddy. Go kick-start that racist motherfucker."

Danny looked at me for a long moment, then his face broke into an answering smile. "It's been fun, Jared."

We shook hands, and he slid back the hatch and went below, Joseph following him down. Ahead of me, less than a mile away now, a small grove of palm trees glimpsed occasionally through the welter of boiling foam and spray gave indication of land rising above the water. I turned and glanced over my shoulder. *Impala* was less than four hundred yards away, a small figure with a rifle crouched on the foredeck, alternately clutching the rail and then raising the rifle and firing. I gave him the finger and turned back; getting shot was the very least of my worries.

Danny's voice rose in loud protest from below, and I knew Joseph had told him that he was taking us through. The voices stopped, and a minute later Joseph came on deck, naked except for the Chilkat blanket pulled over and hanging down to his knees. He was wearing his amulet outside it and had one of the old shaman rattles in his hand.

Sinbad was at his heels. I handed Joseph the Lirakis harness, and he smiled and shook his head and walked up to the bow like a man on a Sunday stroll. He spread his feet wide and grasped the inner stay with one hand, the other holding the rattle extended straight out in front of him. He moved it to port and I brought the bow across onto the new course and he held it straight again.

Sinbad stood between the spread legs, his head thrust forward and ears pricked, his weight swinging from side to side as he balanced. The water was shoaling up now, the waves steepening and compressing as they ran up against the atoll. *Arrow* was fighting them, her rhythm off as they lost their symmetry.

She took a vicious heave, and there was a loud crack from the top of the mast, and I flinched but I didn't look. It was too late for caution now, there were no choices left.

"Good morning, asshole, puking much today?"

Danny's voice rose up from below, the Haida accent pronounced, the insolent slurring calculated. He told Delaney in abusive detail that he had missed his chance again, and in a few minutes we would run the pass and be safe inside the lagoon beyond. There was a crackling, and then Delaney came through, but I couldn't make out the words. No matter, there were other things on my mind.

The fringing reef was ninety feet across and rose to the surface in a circle around the entire perimeter of the atoll, save on the northeast corner where the treacherous main pass was located. But according to Bill's sketch there was a small false pass two hundred feet east of that where the reef dipped down to an underwater shelf that was thirty yards wide and had six feet of water over it at low tide. Twenty-odd years ago, anyway. In calm weather it would be easy to avoid the false pass, the water over it brown, and the safe channel a shade of blue, the darker the deeper. In this turmoil the whole area would be raging white water and the shelf nearly invisible. I was counting on it.

Joseph swung his arm again, and I corrected in blind faith as a cloud of spray enveloped me, cutting my vision to a scant boat length.

The noise of the surf was deafening now, the jagged teeth of the reef revealed for a moment, rising up among the maelstrom. Joseph had his head thrown back and he might have been singing; in that moment he was the reincarnation of all the shamans who guided the enormous Haida war canoes in the pictures of Edward Curtis.

I glanced behind me, *Impala* a hundred yards back now, her bow enormous and the little figure clinging there puny and insignificant. A sea broke under her, and she rose forty feet above the trough then plummeted down in a cloud of spray that obliterated her for a moment before she broke through and ploughed on again. Delaney was driving her ruthlessly.

"Going through now, asshole, you'd better heave to." The mocking words rose up from below. "Wouldn't want to scratch your pretty boat, now, would you?"

Danny hung up the mike and ran up the stairs, locking the cabin behind him.

"Jesus," he said in a shocked voice as he looked aft. He turned and faced forward. "Jesus, oh Jesus," he howled. "Where's the fucking pass?"

We were in the full break of spray now, and the visibility was down to a hundred feet. Ahead of us the reef came up between the breakers like the teeth of some long-stranded giant. I thought I saw a flash of blue to starboard in the midst of the churning foam, but it was impossible to be sure, and I kept my eyes on Joseph. Danny threw the life raft onto the deck behind us and tied the pull cord to the rail; if we failed, it was our last, slim hope. He took the last drink of rum from the bottle and hurled it aft, and I swear to God I heard it strike and shatter on *Impala*'s bow. Danny stuck the knife between his teeth and grasped the mainsheet. We were both stripped down to trunks, and he looked like a pirate from an earlier century, swarthy and crouched, his face frozen by the knife into a fierce semblance of a grin.

One last look. *Impala* fifty feet behind, nothing visible but the bow rearing above us as Delaney drove her down our transom.

"We've got her," I yelled, then Joseph's arm swung ninety degrees to port and Danny hardened the mainsheet as I threw my weight on the tiller and swung it across to starboard. I saw the flash of brown water just ahead as *Arrow* broached and laid over on her side, and I knew that Joseph had found the shelf. *Arrow's* masts slammed into the water and there was a horrendous shattering and Danny cut the sheets just before the green water thundered over the port rail above us and there was another crash, and we stopped for an eternity while I hung suspended in my harness, tangled up with Danny and both of us underwater now, and I thought we were never coming up.

And then the sound of a larger concussion as *Impala* struck, rising above the madness and the water and the roar of the surf, and the shock of her wave lifted and pushed us across the shelf, every grinding foot like iron filings on my teeth, and *Arrow* trembled like a whipped dog and then she slowly righted.

I thought my lungs would burst, but finally there was air, and Danny gasping and choking alongside. It seemed almost calm, the seas well down inside the lagoon, where *Arrow* now lay like a crippled seabird. The life raft floated on the end of its tether to leeward, just beyond the tangle of wire, wood, and cloth that had been our rig. There was nothing left on deck over a foot high. Joseph and Sinbad were gone. Danny looked to weather, his fist clenched, his face a fierce mask of exultation.

Impala lay at a forty-five-degree angle, her bow pointing into the air, a twenty-foot gash underneath extending down into the water. Black smoke poured out of her, and then there was a muffled explosion somewhere deep inside. She quivered and slowly slid back off the reef stern-to into the water and settled until only the top half of the wheelhouse was visible. I waited until I was sure nobody was coming out, and then I turned and searched the swells.

Danny was in the water, swimming hard for the top of the mast that was floating there. I saw Joseph's dark hand clenched around it, and the frantic threshing under the sail that could only be Sinbad.

Danny dove and freed him, and the three of them made their way back to the boat. I went to the bow and untangled the Bruce and threw it over and felt the shock when it grabbed and held. Then I went back to the cockpit and started pumping.

❈

"Horseshit luck," Danny said, "dumb stupid horseshit luck."

We sat in the cockpit, drinking rum and coke, listening to the intermittent whine of the bilge pump. We had stove in three planks, all in the same spot amidships, and the gummed plywood patch had slowed the leak to a mere trickle. Another plank had sprung and the rib cracked behind it, but we had forced it back and jury-rigged a Spanish windlass to hold it in place until we could get to a yard.

The rig was cinched up in the water alongside. The sails were salvageable, a few tears we could patch, but the mainmast had shattered in three places where it had laid into a bommie just inside the reef. We'd cut it loose and let it drift away when it started pounding the hull. The mizzenmast was sound; we had disconnected the triatic stay before we hit the shelf. We could move it forward, jury-rig something. We would worry about that later. Maybe tomorrow, maybe not for a few days.

"I knew if we tried to go over the shelf upright, she would break apart when the keel struck," I said. "Broaching across we would draw less, and the whole hull would absorb the impact. Wooden hull, more resilience, maybe a chance. We were lucky, all right."

The seas were coming down every hour, and the glass was rising. You could see now where the Bruce had hooked into the coral twenty feet down, and we couldn't have been sitting prettier. I planned on getting really drunk. I reached down and poured Sinbad another one. He gave a low growl of appreciation. It seemed he planned on joining me.

"Let's blow that son of a bitch off the reef tomorrow," I said to Danny. "She must be hooked. It slopes down to three hundred feet just behind her. She's caught on the edge. Think you can do it?"

"No problem. We've got the explosives. I'll set a small one to move her off, then another a few seconds later to blow her into pieces. Nobody will ever find her. Not enough to identify, anyway. Just another unsolved mystery of the sea."

Joseph suddenly stood and pointed across at *Impala*. She was three hundred yards upwind, and something was crawling across her house. It disappeared as we watched, and then the Zodiac appeared on the far side of her. It was only partially inflated, and someone was trying to row her to the atoll half a mile distant. You can't row those bastards when they are full of air. *Impala* lay directly upwind and the inflatable slowly blew down upon us. We watched as the man worked frantically, and then he saw the futility of it and slumped back in the seat. His face was black with the char of explosion, and blood ran down from it into the water. Patches of torn scalp were showing, and his leg was twisted at an odd angle. I didn't recognize him. Danny lifted the binoculars.

"Delaney," he said.

Joseph turned and went below. He returned with the twelve-gauge and filled the magazine with slugs, then sat there waiting with it lying across his knees, his face impassive. Danny reached across and took it from him and laid it carefully on the seat beside him.

"He's mine," he said.

I started to protest, but then the picture of Jennie lying on the engine room floor rose up in my mind and I just shut my mouth. We sat and waited.

When Delaney was a hundred feet away, he suddenly screamed and seized the oars again and began rowing frantically towards us. It was then that I saw the first of the fins moving around the dinghy. He scrambled up on the seat and managed to get clear of the water, but you could see now that the entire port tube of the inflatable was flat, and the water was inside. The sharks were bolder now and began bumping against the tubes. The Zodiac spun with their impact, and then the back of one came up out of the water. It was a tiger.

Delaney was fifty feet away now, his voice sobbing and frantic. He jabbed an oar at the pack, and it was jerked from his hand and disappeared, and he was hopelessly trying to paddle with just the one.

Danny picked up the shotgun and walked to the bow, his face carved in stone. Delaney screamed and pleaded, and the words were rushed and garbled. He babbled about money and cocaine and power and women as Danny raised the gun and fired, the shots sounding in quick succession, the sound all rolled into one, cutting sharp and loud over the echoing boom of the surf.

Delaney raised his hands and flinched, and the water alongside the dinghy boiled with the impact of the shot, and then there was blood everywhere and the raging swirling insanity of the sharks in a feeding frenzy, and Delaney still balanced precarious on his perch among them.

A wounded tiger rose out of the water and rolled. Its guts spilled out and it devoured them greedily. Another took the dinghy in its jaws and tore out a section, the impact flinging Delaney down into the bloody water that nearly filled the inflatable now. He scrambled back upon the little seat and turned to Danny, his face insane with terror. He saw Danny lay the gun down and raised his arms in supplication.

"Help me, in the name of God," he screamed.

Danny nodded and bent down into the tangle of ropes and rigging at the bow.

"Here, catch this," he said.

He straightened with the hundred-pound Luke anchor in his hands and raised it effortlessly high over his head then hurled it the twenty feet into Delaney's arms. There was another brief scream, higher than any of the others. I closed my eyes and turned away as Delaney vanished into the bloody maelstrom.

When I looked again, there was only the crimson-streaked Zodiac drifting towards us, then Danny fired twice more, and it was just another piece of wreckage. I raised my glass and drained it.

Joseph had to refill it for me, I was shaking too much.

CHAPTER 33

The morning broke clear and sunny, with just enough breeze to cool the cabin. It was a different world now, as if the days of storm and tempest had never been, the only signs the ravaged decks of *Arrow* and the shattered hulk that had been *Impala*. The high, puffy trade wind clouds were back, and the placid, rolling seas beckoned us on. We had a leisurely breakfast and began making *Arrow* ready for the next leg of our passage.

Danny and I brought the sails on board and cut all the rigging clear, saving anything that looked reusable. There wasn't a lot. Danny dove on the prop and checked that it wasn't foul while Joseph mended the sails. I spent my time doing a careful survey of *Arrow*. When I'd had a chance to check out all the damage, I wasn't nearly as smug.

Parts of the deck had lifted where the shrouds connected, and it would be a tricky and expensive repair. The lifelines were all torn and hanging, and several of the stanchions had cracked the bulwarks. The pulpit had somehow survived intact, but the stern pushpit was just a twisted mass of stainless tubing and the Aries cracked and bent. The dodger had vanished without a trace. The whole starboard side of the boat where we had scraped across the shelf looked like it had been rough-sanded with twenty-grit paper. We were talking serious money.

If you were to calculate the most expensive ports in the world to rerig, Papeete would make the top three. We didn't have a choice, though — anywhere else was out of the question in the shape we were in. We would be lucky to have enough funds left to get home again by the time *Arrow* was finished.

"I guess we'd better blow that mother before anyone else sees her," Danny said. "Now that the weather has changed, there could be some cruisers heading this way. Not to mention the gendarmes, who will be looking for *Impala*. If they see the two boats together like this, we will have a lot of explaining to do."

"I'm sure we could leave it for another day or two."

In spite of all the liquor I had consumed the previous night, ten-foot tiger sharks had cruised through my dreams. I had no desire to go in the water anywhere within a hundred miles of this spot, let alone right next door.

Danny read my mind. "Come on, Jared. We'll take Sinbad, he can keep watch. There's nothing to worry about if you don't get them excited with blood or bad vibrations."

"When did you become a fucking expert on shark behaviour, anyway? Is this another part of your inherited wisdom from your forefathers? I don't recall tiger sharks being a part of the Haida legends."

I knew I was being shrewish, but I couldn't help it. My hand hurt and my head ached and Danny and Joseph were both grinning at me.

"Let's go, Jared. I've got all our gear, the plastique and the timers. A few minutes' work and she'll be ready to go. Smokey told me all about it, fixed me up with fuses, the works. No sweat. We'll take the hard dinghy."

I hauled myself up and went reluctantly over the side and into the skiff. Danny took the oars and Sinbad sat in the bow, his head stretched out and snaking downwards. Now that the swell had laid down, you could see through the twenty feet of water to the bottom. It was lukewarm, and I lazily trailed my hand along in it before remembering and jerking it quickly back.

Impala lay right over on her side, and it seemed to me that she had settled down even further during the night. It shouldn't take much to jar her loose and send her backwards and down into the twenty fathoms that fell away beneath her stern. The tide was coming in and she rocked gently, rising and falling without a sound, assuming already the ghost-like aspect of a lost ship. As we watched, a small shark swam out of the rip in her hull. Sinbad gave a low growl and snaked his head even further over the edge of the skiff.

"Just a little reef shark, not to worry," Danny said.

He took us alongside the wheelhouse, and we stepped gingerly aboard. Only three feet of *Impala* was out of the water now, and thick, oily sludge lapped around our knees as we entered the tilting cabin. The nav station was still clear of the water, and all the electronics looked as good as new.

"Anything we want?" Danny asked, motioning towards them.

"Not a single damned thing," I replied fervently.

"Right, then. We'll just pick up the safe and be on our way."

"What!"

"The safe. You don't think we're leaving without that, do you? That bastard owes us. You know there will be one somewhere. There might be enough there for the refitting and repairs, maybe even a little something extra for cruising. We have to take a look. It will probably be in the salon. Shouldn't be more than fifteen feet under, not too bad."

He pulled the masks and snorkels out of the bag where he had hidden them. I gazed into the oily water and thought of all the excellent reasons for not going down inside there. Apart from pure, unadulterated fear.

"You don't have to come." Danny uncoiled the line he'd brought and tied one end around the big captain's chair bolted in front of the wheel. "Just give me the general layout."

"No, I'll come."

358

There could be something in there for Clarke as well. Nail some of those other bastards that were involved, maybe make some final good come out of all this. I sat in the chair, thinking, running the interior layout through my mind. It wouldn't have to be that well hidden, there was always crew aboard. And Starrett would want it to be convenient. Aft, in the owner's suite somewhere, most likely. Maybe behind one of the pictures.

"Okay, follow me."

I put on my mask and snorkel, walked the few feet down the slope until the water rose to my shoulders, then took a deep breath and went under. Once you were down three feet, the water was clear, with enough light filtering in from the submerged cabin windows to see by. The oily sludge over my head was filled with floating objects: chairs, a wooden box, black oil-soaked cushions, food, clothes, cardboard boxes, and a dozen other things I couldn't identify, all of them bobbing over our heads in the same ghostly rhythm.

Something blanched and flaccid rolled languidly in the corner, and the hand that hung down from it waved softly in greeting. Stifling the gorge that rose in my throat, I went to the main cabin bulkhead. Danny appeared beside me and tied the rope off to the grab rail beside the door to the suite. I went inside and ripped away the first picture, and it floated up and the safe was there behind it. Danny went by me and looked at it and nodded, and we went back and up into the air.

"No problem. Shouldn't take too long to get it out. I'll start. Give me a jerk at forty-five seconds, two at a minute if I'm still down there."

He took the tool bag and disappeared, and I timed him and signalled, and he came back out and then I went down and chiselled clumsily for as long as I could hold my breath. It only took a few trips before Danny rose up with the safe cradled in his arms. It wasn't very big, and in the water it was easy to handle.

"Just one more quick trip," Danny said and disappeared again, returning with a soggy case of Laphroaig. "Waste not, want not," he said.

We carried our booty out and loaded it into the skiff, and then Danny got to work.

"I'll set the first charge underneath the hull, just to blow her off the reef, and then a couple of others to break her up, fifteen seconds later."

I hoped he knew what the hell he was doing. I waited nervously while he went over the side with the gear. Fifteen minutes later, he climbed back aboard the dinghy.

"Piece of cake."

He gave me a thumbs-up. I rowed quickly back to *Arrow* and we waited. Danny said half an hour, and it was exactly that when she went. There was a muffled explosion, and she rocked back and her bow pointed slowly skywards and she seemed to hang there forever before she began to slide gently back and down. "Well done," I said and clapped Danny on the back a fractional second before the whole world concussed and exploded into a blinding ball of light. The remaining twenty feet of *Impala*'s bow disappeared, and a three-hundred-foot fireball rose up in its place just as the shock wave hit and knocked us all flat. For long seconds the sky was filled with glowing debris, and then the objects rained down and sizzled in the water around us. We leapt as one through the companionway into the cabin as pieces of red-hot metal fell from the sky. One landed on the cockpit grates and started to smoke. Joseph waited a moment then moved swiftly back up the stairs and doused it with a bucket of water. Another two had fallen forward, and I ran up and kicked them over the side. The sea was ablaze where *Impala* had been, and thick clouds of dense black smoke rose high overhead. An eight-foot wave appeared and swept past and left us rocking violently in its wake. In another two minutes the fire had died, and the only sign of its presence was the sooty ash drifting down upon us.

"Piece of cake," I said through blackened lips, when we could hear again.

"I guess I could have used a little less," Danny said.

"Don't worry," I said. "If anyone saw it, they'll just assume it's the French running another fucking nuclear test in the South Pacific."

❊

Four hours later we motored out through the pass. There was no trace of *Impala*: what hadn't burned had sunk or drifted off. It was as if she had never existed. The atoll spread out behind us like the tropical dream of a Madison Avenue adman — beautiful, sparkling, serene. I wanted only to forget it.

Katiu was eighteen miles downwind, an easy pass and a good anchorage just beyond. We arrived there just before dark, slipping through Pakara Pass then dropping the hook in front of the little village set back off the beach among a grove of palm trees. Danny opened a bottle of the Scotch, and we passed it around and started to relax and become acquainted with the fact that it was all over. I drank little, and that night I had no dreams.

It took us most of the following morning to open the safe. We used cold chisels and the big ball-peen hammer until we managed to get a crack started along the side of the door, and then we put in a tungsten hacksaw blade and took turns dragging it back and forth. It was all case-hardened steel and took forever.

"Maybe I should blow it open," Danny said.

Joseph and I turned and glared at him.

"Just joking," he said.

When we finally got the safe open, we found it half-filled with kilo bags of cocaine. We took the bags out and slit them open one at a time and let the fine white powder blow away on the wind. When it was ten feet away, it was already invisible. Underneath we found two hundred and eighty thousand dollars in used American bills.

"That should cover the expenses nicely," Danny said when he had finished counting it.

Joseph reached over and took five thousand and tucked it up care-fully under his shirt, then sat back again as if nothing had occurred.

The last thing in the safe was a black leather diary. It was filled with the details of transactions: dates and places, and the names of all the participants except Starrett and Delaney. It must have been their insurance policy. Clarke would love it. It might be hard to buy a new vehicle in Vancouver for a while, though, judging from the number of car dealers listed.

❁

We spent a week at Katiu, working on the boat and enjoying the com-pany of the people from the little village of Toini. We told them how we had been dismasted and driven onto the reef in the big storm, and they commiserated with us and insisted on helping with the repairs. We traded canned goods for fruits and coconuts, and Joseph presented the old headman with a case of rum. The pair of them spent their days walking together, or fishing from one of the outrigger canoes on the outside reef.

Danny and I worked on the rig in the mornings, and went spear fishing and diving for lobster with the men in the afternoon. The south end of the lagoon was crisscrossed with long strands of rope holding oysters seeded with black pearls, and sometimes we went out and helped overhaul them. It was easy, pleasant work with the best of climate and companions, and slowly the bad memories faded.

Each evening we were invited ashore and dined on the day's catch with a different family. Afterwards there was coconut wine and dancing to the carved wooden drums. When the women realized how it embar-rassed me, it became their special delight to seize upon me. Danny, of course, loved it and was soon as adept as the men at the quick, thrusting heel-drumming rituals.

We moved the mizzenmast forward and bolted it into the main tabernacle, then cut some tapered wedges and drove them in to hold her fast. It was fussy moving the mizzen shrouds forward and adapting them to the old main fittings, but we had lots of time and got it done. We cut the smallest of the main shrouds for a forestay and spliced up a pair of running backstays with bulldog grips and were finished. *Arrow* wouldn't break any speed records, but she would get there.

A feast was held the night before we left, one the whole community took part in. Joseph presented the headman with the Honda generator and twenty gallons of fuel as our farewell gift to the village. There was a lot of dancing and drinking, and a few headaches the following morning when they escorted us out through the pass in the big racing canoe with twenty men paddling and gave us the ancient blessing. We hoisted our meagre sails, and five uneventful days later we arrived in Papeete and tied up stern-to along Boulevard Pomare.

There was some concern when the authorities discovered that we didn't have an exit stamp from Hiva Oa, but I shrugged my shoulders and feigned ignorance, and they let it pass with some comments about imbecilic North Americans, which I presumed not to understand. I posted all the bonds with cash at a local bank and that was an end to our troubles. A week later, a police inspector came down and asked us about a big steel power boat called *Impala* that had gone missing, but we had never heard of her and he left shortly after.

Danny phoned Clarke and told him the news, and he and Joseph left for Vancouver on a flight. Danny intends to return in a month or so and says Clarke is talking about coming back with him. I can't decide if that is good or bad news. Joseph just smiled when I asked him if he would come back sometimes. I miss him already.

They took fifty thousand with them for the family, though I tried to give them more. There should be enough left to keep Danny and I going for a few years if we are careful.

The yard is hauling *Arrow* next week. An American shipwright from Massachusetts lives aboard here in the most beautiful wooden cutter I've ever seen. He has run low on travel funds and will be doing the hull and deck repairs for us. Danny and I made lists of all the rigging screws and turnbuckles we will need, and he's going to bring them back with him. We will do the rigging ourselves, and everything will be in stainless.

I spent two days trying to write a letter to Jane, and finally I ripped it up and sent her a telegram care of Ingrid. It just said "All-expenses-paid cruise in South Pacific with experienced captain, problems over, no strings attached. Love, Jared."

The answer came this morning and is sitting on the chart table in front of me. Maybe after another couple of drinks I will have the courage to open it.